*It is with enormous gratitude that I thank the following people for their support in not just this book, but for all the books, projects, and creative works I've produced over the years. It's rare to find someone willing to go down the rabbit hole with you during your sometimes-crazy schemes and cheer you on the whole way down. And, it seems I have an entire team.*

*Thank you to Cindy Readnower, who has been a true friend and colleague providing publishing, promotional and editorial support for all of my books, workshops, and other professional endeavors. To Jane Parker for her keen insight into human nature and beta-reading skills that helped me give more depth to my characters. To Elizabeth Von Hohen Brosha for hand-painting the cover of this book. To Graham Mack for co-producing the audio version of all my books, helping bring my characters to life. And a special thank you to my husband, John Palli, for providing technical guidance, beta reading, and loving support for this book and everything I do. I'm a lucky gal.*

# Contents

# If I Didn't Care

Danielle Palli

IF I DIDN'T CARE



ISBN: 978-1-7367982-1-8

LCCN: 2022906167

# Prologue

The year is 1997 and at the height of the Tech Boom. Startups are all the rage, and a select few have access to inventions that won't be readily available to the public for another decade or more. The Internet is still considered a passing fad, and only a small percentage of people carry cell phones. For those of us who were there to bear witness to how quickly technology has evolved over the past few decades, we might laugh. What we once considered in 1997 the "Tech Boom" might now be referred to as the "Stone Age."

# Chapter 1
# But He Didn't

A Thursday Evening in 1997: Rue's Apartment

Rue Brennan was used to him forgetting. In some ways, she blamed herself. Or at least, she blamed her parents...that was easier. You see, "Rue" meant "regret" and "Brennan" meant "sorrow." So, her parents had, by choice, given her a name that meant "regret" and "sorrow" and, by golly, she was determined to live up to it.

Rue lived in a one-bedroom walk-up apartment in the Lower East Side of Manhattan. It was one of those "open" designs where there was no door separating the bedroom from the kitchen and dining area, just a cut-out space where a door and a kitchen hatch should be, giving the illusion that the place was larger than it truly was. The bathroom was, unfortunately, just beyond the kitchen. It had a large built-in bookshelf. Rue never understood why you would want to keep books on the shelf in a room that got humid when you ran the shower.

Of course, if it were Spencer, it would be one non-fiction book at a time that he'd conveniently leave on the top of the toilet bowl so it was there the next time he needed it. He'd often disappear into her bathroom with a book, most likely about the French Revolution or some time in history that wasn't the present, and she wouldn't hear from him for a good half hour.

It should be noted here that no one else thought this was a bookshelf at all, but a place to hold towels and linens and such. But since Rue only had two towels and as many washcloths to her name, but hundreds of books that she refused to part with, she had to settle on the bathroom to house her collection—for now.

She caught a glimpse of herself in the bathroom mirror just as she'd settled on pulling her slightly worn copy of *The Alchemist* from the shelf. From what she could tell, she didn't look all that much different from yesterday. Her hair was still a murky dark brown, framing her round face in a bob. The bags under her hazel eyes didn't seem any baggier, though the crow's feet that extended from the edges did look just a little deeper and more pronounced. Rue was underweight and waif-like, not that you'd know it from her face. *No matter how much weight I lose, I still look like a chipmunk with cheeks full of nuts.* She decided to blame this on her parents as well as her unfortunate name.

There was a knock on the window. The only actual windows in her little hovel were in the bedroom. She set the book back on the shelf and made her way, barefoot, across the hardwood floor.

Peering through the window, with hair as curly and red as a Raggedy Ann doll, was her neighbor, Midge. She was standing on the fire escape, holding up a bottle of wine and what looked like a semi-wrapped block of cheese. Rue struggled to open the rather stubborn window. Finally...success.

"Happy birthday, Rue!" Midge thrust the bottle of wine through the window by way of presentation. "It's not super fancy, but eco-friendly and organic, so at least we won't be drinking pesticides and additives."

*Midge remembered my birthday,* Rue thought. *But Spencer didn't.*

"Aww, thanks Mensa. You are the sweetest," Rue smiled sadly in spite of herself. "Why don't I join you on the ledge? Give me a second to throw something on other than pajamas. I have a red dress that I had planned to wear this evening for a date I no longer appear to be going on. Let me put that on."

Midge set the bottle down on the windowsill.

"And don't worry," Rue wrenched the knit dress free from the tiny closet where hangers weren't really needed to hold the clothes up. They all supported each other as if they feared sudden abandonment. "I'll wear leggings, so I don't accidentally flash any pedestrians on the ground level." Rue darted behind the wall separating the kitchen from the bedroom to change.

"Don't forget the wine glasses," Midge called. "And a blanket if you have one. I still have ass prints from sitting on the metal rails last time." Midge hailed from the Tri-State area, having lived in New York, New Jersey and Philadelphia. Her blended accent reflected that.

Rue pulled on her thick black leggings that came down to her ankles, pulled the dress over her head, and then dutifully grabbed two stemless red wine glasses from the kitchen and a single towel from the bathroom. "Here," she handed Midge the towel, "the other one is drying over the shower bar. But don't worry, I don't mind ass prints." She laughed. "You can use this one, and I can sit on the rails."

"Want me to go back upstairs and grab one of mine?" Midge offered.

"Nah, don't bother," After offering Midge the glasses, she climbed through the window and onto the fire escape. Midge had set the cloth-wrapped cheese on a checkered red kitchen towel with the bottle of wine and glasses next to it. Rue shimmied to one corner of the fire escape, sitting carefully with her feet dangling over the ladder. Midge did the same, on the opposite side, facing her friend. "This was awfully nice of you, Mensa."

"Mensa" was Rue's pet-name for Midge, even though Midge pretended to hate it. They became friends a year ago when they both learned they had a penchant for people-watching from the fire escape, Rue on the third floor, Midge on the fifth. They didn't know who lived on the fourth. Drapes covered the windows, and no one ever seemed to go in or come out of the place.

Rue had just moved to the Big Apple from a little town in Pennsylvania. Manhattan seemed like the best place to go if you wanted to escape from your past and get swallowed up and lost in a big city. No one would think to look for her here, would they? For the first month, she didn't know anyone.

Then, one night, when Midge had gone through a nasty breakup, Rue invited her neighbor down to her apartment, and consoled her with margaritas and nachos. This is the time when they both learned that tequila was not their friend. In a semi-drunken state, Midge proclaimed, "The problem is that I'm just too smart for them." She had waved her plastic margarita cup in the air, threatening to spill it from the fifth floor of the fire escape. Her words were ever-so-slightly...slushy. "I told Darius that he was as big a troglodyte as the lot of 'em. He couldn't appreciate the fact that I have a 146 IQ and am very smart. That's why men don't like me for very long. I'm too much of a challenge. They don't like to be challenged." She blinked and swayed slowly in the breeze.

Rue had felt the need to gently call Midge out on her bull-shit. "Well, Mensa, are you sure it's not that they're put off by you calling them troglodytes?"

Midge eyed her slowly, before laughing so hard she spit a little. "Maybe," she acknowledged. "And don't call me 'Mensa' when I have a perfectly good name...Midge. I'm named after a blood-sucking fly." She laughed again. The "Philly" in her accent getting stronger the more she drank.

"Here, open the bottle. It's a twist-top." Midge brought Rue out of her daydream. Today's Midge was not drunk and after sending Darius packing, followed by Ben, and then Dave, she decided she had sworn off men for a while.

Rue dutifully opened the bottle. Midge leaned forward and carefully held the glasses out in front of her for Rue to pour them each some wine. She handed one to Rue.

A fresh breeze blew through the street and Rue shivered a little. Perhaps, this was the last official day where she could get away with wearing only a dress and leggings as the Fall weather was becoming progressively colder.

"A toast." Midge raised her glass, the sun shining on her face, making her complexion look even paler in contrast to her crayon-red wavy hair. "To the birthday gal! May the next year be full of adventure and fun surprises!"

"I'll drink to that," Rue smiled, clinking her glass against Midge's. The wine was earthier than she expected.

"It's a Rioja," Midge offered. "I figured it would go with the Manchego I bought." She broke off a chunk of the cheese with her fingers and handed it, open-palmed, to Rue. Rue took it without complaining. *What's a few germs between friends?"* she thought. *"I'm probably dying of something right now and don't even know it."*

Midge watched as Rue took a nibble of the cheese. "Take another sip of wine, quick," Midge commanded. "They go well together, right?"

Rue nodded. She wasn't really sure how to tell, but she was all about free food and beverage, and she sure as hell wouldn't be spending *her* meager savings on fancy wine and cheeses anytime soon.

"So, where's Spencer taking you this evening?" Midge wanted to know.

"Not sure he's taking me anywhere," Rue confessed. "I don't think he even remembered it was my birthday."

Midge let out a huff. "And *how* long have you been together?"

"Midge, don't start. I'm already bummed."

"Sorry," Midge offered, taking a sip of her wine and sheepishly averting her eyes.

In truth, Spencer and Rue had only been dating a little over a year. Therefore, she reasoned, he'd only been through one birthday previously. And she's pretty sure he missed that one, too.

*It never used to be like this,* Rue thought to herself. In the beginning, Spencer seemed sweet and kind and understanding. After all, she had led a rather sheltered life before moving to New York. He didn't mind her naivete and seemed excited to introduce the world to her. But lately, the more hobnobbing he did with the upper echelon of society, the less patient he became with her, as if she suddenly didn't fit in with the new world he was creating for himself.

As if he were somewhere, hearing her thoughts, Midge's cell phone rang. She set down the wine and cheese and fished it out of her back pocket.

"Hullo?" She raised her eyebrow and waved her hand in confusion. "Spencer? Why are you callin' me? Oh, yeah, she's right here." Midge thrust the phone toward Rue. "He says he's been trying to call you on the phone all afternoon."

"Hello?" Rue answered. "We're out on the fire escape," she yelled over the roar of an ambulance that went barreling down the street.

She covered her left ear and leaned into the phone as if that would make a difference. "Where are you?"

"Down here." From the street, Spencer waved his arm wildly, phone still against his ear. Rue saw him and waved back.

There, stood Spencer. Good old practical Spencer, dressed in a suit and tie with overpriced cuff links and shoes that he had professionally shined.

"C'mon up. I'll let you in," Rue answered. She could see him nod before hanging up.

"Well, that's my cue." Midge stood.

"No, you don't have to go so soon. Come inside and chat for a bit."

"No thanks. Spencer is..." she paused to find the right words, "so perfectly coiffed, I'm afraid his head might explode just being in the same room with me."

"Suit yourself, Mensa. But hey," she called as her friend started her climb back up to her apartment, "thanks for the wine and cheese. Much appreciated."

"No prob, friend," Midge saluted her. "Yuz guys enjoy." With that, a fire of red hair and bell bottoms that went out of style more than two decades ago ascended to her flat above Rue's.

Simultaneously, there was a knock at the door. Rue grabbed the leftover food and wine and struggled through the window. "Hang on!" she called. "Almost there!"

She plopped the leftovers on the kitchen counter and sprang to the door, flinging it open with all the enthusiasm of someone who was secretly hoping her boyfriend held a wonderful birthday present in his arms for her. He didn't.

"Hi, Rue, sorry I'm later than planned," he apologized, giving her a quick peck on the lips. "Work was beastly today. You have no idea. But that's all over now and I have a surprise for you." He took her by the shoulders and smiled. Midge was right, his wavy brown hair was quite perfectly placed. His skin equally radiant. Rue suspected it was an experimental age-remedy called "Botox," but Spencer never offered that info, so she never asked since she wasn't sure it was even legally on the market yet. She just noticed over in the past year that one day he had worry lines and the next, they seemed to magically disappear.

Rue's eyes grew wide with hope. "What's the surprise?"

With that, Spenser reached into his pocket and pulled out a business card, handing it to her as if it were the key to the city.

"What's this?" She wrinkled her nose at it, confused.

"A business card," he answered, eyeing the wine on the table. He tilted the bottle back with one hand, eyeing it distastefully.

"Darwin Fennec," she read. "Contract Cyber Forensic Consultant and Private Investigator." She lowered the card. "What's this about?"

"Well, you were complaining last week that you were, and I quote, 'on the fast track to middle age with nothing to show for it' and wanted a career beyond fluff journalism and posing nude."

"That last part was not at all what I said," she corrected. "And being a figure model for one of the most prestigious art universities in the country is a bit different from the way you describe it. There is some skill to it, and yet, you make me sound like a prostitute posing for a trash magazine on weekends."

Spencer cleared his throat, uncomfortably. "You know that I support all of your endeavors, darling. But you have to admit, it is a little embarrassing for the founder and CEO of an up-and-coming tech company to have to explain your particular...skill set...to investors."

"Sorry my career is so embarrassing for you, Spencer." Rue flopped into a kitchen chair.

"Oh, come on. Be reasonable." He ran his hand over the top of her head. "That's not a career, that's something you do to work your way through college. Not something an older woman does as a—" He stopped when he saw her face and took a moment to glance between his girlfriend and the wine and cheese on the table.

"What am I missing?" he finally asked.

"My birthday, Spencer," Rue answered flatly. "You're missing my birthday."

"Oh, my darling," He stroked her head again. "I'm so sorry. How unthoughtful of me." He paused a moment. "So, who left the wine?" He cringed at the label.

"My upstairs neighbor, Midge."

"Oh, is that the small unpleasant gal with the bright red hair."

"Yes, but I don't find her unpleasant at all. She's my friend and I like her...and," Rue added, "*she* remembered my birthday."

"I said I was sorry, and from the looks of the wine she bought, she's not that good of a friend. I don't know what that is, but I wouldn't qualify that dime-store swill as wine."

"Snob," Rue wrinkled her nose at him and attempted a smile. Rue rarely got to celebrate birthdays in the past, which made his forgetting sting all the more. Maybe she was making too much of it?

"Tell you what," he finally said, "get dressed, and I'll take you someplace really nice for your birthday to celebrate."

Rue looked down at her dress. "I kinda thought I already was dressed."

Spencer paused, awkwardly. "Oh, right."

"You know what, Spencer? Turns out, I'm really tired after a long day. Maybe we can take a raincheck on my birthday dinner?"

"Of course, my darling. Whatever you say." Spencer seemed somewhat relieved. "Just do me one favor?"

"What's that?"

Spencer pointed toward the business card still clenched tightly between Rue's fingers. "Call Darwin in the morning."

"Who is he?"

"He's a guy I hired to do a little contract investigative work for my company. Remember how I told you I suspect B. A. Ellis industries, SpencerTech's competitor...my competitor...is stealing proprietary info from us?"

Rue's blank expression indicated that she did not.

Spencer dismissed it. "Anyway, I got into a conversation with him waiting in line at the coffee shop and learned he's looking for an administrative assistant." He fanned his hands open in the air as if placing something in the lights over Broadway. "Administrative assistant...doesn't that sound nice? There's real potential there."

Rue bit back several expletives. "Thanks for looking out for me, Spencer." She clenched her jaw.

"Don't look at me like that," Spencer chastised. "I told him all about you and he's eager to interview you."

"I'm a figure model and journalist. Not sure if there are transferable skills there that lend themselves to administrative work."

"Come on, now," Spencer reasoned, "how hard can it be? Answer a few phone calls, schedule a few meetings..."

"While I'm sure there's more to it than that, how is this better for me than being a journalist?" Rue wanted to know.

"Because you wouldn't be scrounging for freelance work, day in and day out. It's a steady, respectable job with growth potential. You would get to work with a detective, which has to be more exciting than...what was your last gig? Covering Drag Queen Bingo at a local diner in Tribeca."

"I had no idea you thought so highly of my work," Rue pursed her lips.

Spencer took her shoulders. "Sweetheart, I just see more potential in you. And think of your career move as an investment in...us."

"How is this an investment in 'us'?" Rue wanted to know. "This sounds more like an investment in 'you,' meaning you require a girlfriend whose work and friends don't embarrass you."

"You're being overly emotional...is it that time of the month again?" Rue's face turned crimson and it appeared as if she were ready to, literally, let off steam through her nostrils and ears. "I'm sorry. I know you're still cross with me because I forgot your birthday. I promise I'll make it up to you. Just do me one teensy favor and call him in the morning? I've got a good feeling about him." Spencer pulled Rue into his chest for a hug. After a minute of her arms awkwardly hanging by her side, she relented, hugging him back and settling into his embrace for a moment.

"Fine," she conceded, breaking from his hug. "I'll be certain to reach out to this..." she read the card again, "Darwin Fennec in the morning."

# Chapter 2
# Darwin Fennec

Saturday Morning at Pier 17

"This seems a little odd to me." Midge took two small steps to each of Rue's long strides. "Why would he have you meet him by a park bench at the pier instead of his office? Doesn't he work in the financial district?"

"I don't know," Rue answered, her long ruffled skirt making swishing noises in the breeze as she walked briskly toward their destination. She tugged at the fitted black cotton blouse that was bunching up under her arms and kept moving. "But Spencer seems to trust this guy."

"Yeah, well I don't trust nobody," Midge answered, looking over her shoulder as they passed under a bridge near the East River, heading toward the South Street Seaport. "What's this joker look like, anyways?"

"He said he would wearing a white polo shirt and a blue base-ball cap."

"What team?" Midge asked.

"What are you talking about?"

"The cap...New York Yankees or somebody else?"

"He didn't specify." Rue and Midge reached Pier 17 and started walking along the edge of the water. Rue shielded her eyes from the sun with her hand.

"Excuse me," a male voice from behind her asked quietly. "Are you Rue Brennan?" Rue turned to see a tall man, his features obscured until her eyes adjusted to the light. White polo shirt, blue cap with no distinguishing marks on it. A few pieces of brown hair stuck out from the edges of the cap.

"Who wants to know?" Midge nudged Rue aside, placing herself between Rue and the man as if a shield.

"Oh, I beg your pardon," he apologized. "I'm Darwin Fennec and I have an interview today with a woman named Rue Brennan."

"No, you're not," Midge retorted.

"Sorry," the man furrowed his brow, confused. "I'm not...what?"

"You're not Darwin Fennec."

"I'm afraid I am."

Midge was persistent.

"There is no way your name can be Darwin Fennec. That's a made-up name. Who's named after two different types of foxes?"

Darwin found this amusing and reached into his back pocket to retrieve his wallet. From it, he flashed his driver's license at Midge, who eyeballed it closely as if it were a fake.

"I am," he answered simply. To Rue, he offered his hand. "I'm assuming I was correct the first time...you are Rue Brennan?"

"Yes," Rue shook his hand in return. "But how is it that you picked me out of a crowd so easily?"

"I am an investigator, after all," he answered, removing his cap and running his hands through his disheveled hair in an attempt to reset it from wearing the ball cap all morning. "Kinda my thing." The side of his mouth curled up on one side in an unbalanced grin.

The sun passed behind a cloud, enabling Rue to observe his features a little more closely. His hair was parted to one side with medium-length brown locks fringing the sides of his long face. From what she could tell, his eyes were a pale gray.

He then offered a hand to Midge who took it and leaned in to get a closer look; then her demeanor changed entirely. "Well, aren't you a tall drink of water?" (Except when she says it, it comes out "whuh-tr.)

Her head tilted to look up at him. If Midge cleared five feet tall, Rue would have been surprised. "Mr. Darwin Fennec, would you mind sitting down? I'm getting a crick in my neck just trying to look into those beautiful eyes of yours."

"That's okay," Rue intervened. "Midge isn't staying." Rue glared at her friend as she started to protest. "It was nice running into you, Midge. Perhaps when you're done with your errands, we can meet up here for lunch? Say, in an hour?" There was nothing subtle about Rue's expressive facial features. And yet, Darwin Fennec didn't seem to notice, even when Midge abruptly dropped his hand.

"Okay," Midge relented, "be back here in an hour." But she leaned over, tilting her body between Rue and Darwin, both of whom had already taken a seat on the bench. "Here if you need me," she placed a reassuring hand on Rue's arm.

"Uh, thanks, Midge." Rue didn't really see the need for Midge, but did notice that her friend was, for the second time in a row, aware of the happenings in her life, unlike some people. Case in point, Spencer had both forgotten her birthday and was absent this weekend...working on a project with a tight deadline and seemingly having no qualms about her meeting a strange man about a job on a bench at the South Street Seaport.

Once Midge had made her exit, Darwin turned to Rue and asked, "Do you often bring friends to job interviews?"

Rue bristled a little, leaning forward on the bench. "I don't know," she answered curtly, peering up at him. "Do you always conduct job interviews on a park bench?"

"Touché," he replied, pausing a moment as if considering his next move. Rue's small frame fit neatly on the bench, which sat low to the ground. But Darwin was noticeably oversized in height and his knees seemed to fold almost up into his chest as he sat. Noticing her gaze, he quickly stretched his legs casually out in front of him, crossing one ankle over the other. "Sorry about that," he answered. It was only then that she noticed he was carrying a faux leather attaché case that was strikingly out of place for a man wearing jeans and a polo shirt (now, sans blue cap). He set it on his lap and reached inside, pulling out a simple yellow legal pad, clipboard and pen. "My office is being renovated today and since I am need of a new assistant sooner, rather than later, I thought this was the best option."

"What happened to your old assistant?" Rue was curious. It should be noted that Rue had been a freelance journalist for more than a decade and she therefore had lost her ability to present well on interviews. She was, however, completely comfortable asking the questions.

"She moved on to other interests," he answered cryptically, sucking in his breath. "Now about your qualifications..."

"I have none," Rue blurted out.

"I see," Darwin tapped the edge of his pen against his yellow notepad. After an unbearably long silence, he asked, "Rue, do you even want to be here?"

Rue let out a sigh. "Honestly, no." She shook her head. "Darwin!"

Darwin cleared his throat, uncomfortably, as two young women descended on them. "It's so nice to see you!" A tall woman with black hair, a red scarf and bright plum lips leaned over the bench and gave him a kiss on the cheek before he could protest, leaving a lipstick stain in its wake. The other, a curly blonde-haired, twenty-something-year-old tousled his hair before eyeing Rue, distastefully.

"Who's she?"

"My new assistant," Darwin answered without hesitation.

"Oh," the blonde woman bit a long, lacquered nail. "What happened to Ashley?"

Darwin let out a sigh. "She moved on."

For the briefest of moments, the black-haired woman's eyes lit up. By Rue's estimation, they were nearly two decades younger than the brown-haired Darwin who had tiny wisps of gray hair creeping in. *Guess he likes 'em young,* she thought to herself.

"Aww," the woman pouted her lips, pinching Darwin's cheek while he tucked his chin as if embarrassed. "That's too bad. Who would up and leave our Darwin?"

Darwin adopted that sheepish grin again, the one that Midge seemed taken by, but to which Rue was unaffected. He even seemed to be blushing a little.

"It's all right, I suppose," he answered with a quiver in his voice. At that moment, with his head hanging down, his eyes floated up briefly to meet Rue's gaze. And that's when she saw it. The tiniest of glimmers. He was messing with her.

"Well, Darwin," the blonde answered, peering over her shoulder at Rue. "You have my number. Be sure to give me a call if this...new arrangement doesn't work out. I may not be as polished as Ashley, but I'm sure I can handle answerin' phones and such."

"Actually, I have a bit of contract work for both of you. I'll be in touch soon with your next assignment."

"We'll be waiting with bated breath." The black-haired

woman blew Darwin a kiss, clenching the red scarf against her neck.

Rue bit back a few choice words. From her estimation, Darwin Fennec, cyber forensic whatever-the-hell-that-was, was also Darwin Fennec...cad.

After they left, Darwin turned to Rue. "So, where were we?"

"I was just leaving." Rue stood. "Sorry to waste your time, but this meeting was a mistake."

"Hang on," Darwin stood, putting his hands out in front of him as if to stop her from leaving. Unfortunately, as he held them in the air, they seemed to line up perfectly with Rue's breasts. She backed away. He realized how his gesture may have been perceived and lowered his arms.

Rue let out a huff. "What?"

"It is clear to me that you don't like me very much—" he began.

"You are a very observant detective," Rue countered. Darwin was taken aback by her brutal honestly and lack of impulse control.

"Investigator," he corrected. "However, I suspect that it means a lot to you to make your boyfriend Spencer happy—"

"What do you know about it?" she challenged.

"Not much," he admitted. "But let's just say that I am in desperate need of an assistant...or at least someone to *pose* as my assistant, at least for the time being."

"What the hell does that mean?"

"I really can't say," he answered.

In truth, he *could* say. He just *didn't*.

"Then I really have to go." Rue started to leave.

"No, wait...please," Darwin requested. "What salary would your Spencer deem acceptable?"

"Excuse me?"

"C'mon, we both know you wouldn't be here if it weren't for

him. I'm asking what would get your boyfriend off your back? Enough where you could give up whatever it is you're doing that he so disapproves of and come work for me for twenty-five hours or so a week with potential for full time if it all works out."

"Why are you doing this, Mr. Fennec?" Rue demanded. "You have no idea as to my qualifications, and, as you've pointed out, we are not exactly compatible on a personality level."

"No," Darwin agreed. "But I suspect we need each other."

"Do we?"

Darwin's expression grew somber. "You have no idea what's at stake," he said.

He searched her eyes for some level of compassion.

Rue's eyes peered back, expressionless.

Finally, Darwin's face crumbled as he covered it with his palm as if covering up some level of desperation.

"Cut the bullshit, Mr. Fennec."

Darwin dropped his hand and the act, confused. "Why are you so mean?"

"I don't like fake," Rue answered. Unfortunately, as she did so, images of Spencer in his Bergdorf suits and Ivy League haircut wafted through her mind. "And you, Mr. Darwin Fennec, are as fake as they come."

"Perhaps," he smiled, knowingly. "But you have my card, yes?"

"Yes," she answered. "But I won't be calling."

"Well, if you change your mind and decide to work for me—"

"I won't."

"Very well," Darwin answered. "Thanks for meeting me, anyway." With that, Darwin pulled on the blue cap that he had tucked into his back pocket, placed it on his head and tipped it, as if sauntering off into the sunset.

Rue also stood, taking a moment to stretch out her legs before heading home. As if on cue, Midge sidled up beside Rue, hunched over as if she were going to steal Rue's purse. She grabbed Rue's arm with such force that Rue turned and nearly walloped her friend with her free fist.

"Whoa!" Midge called. "Hold the phone, sista. Just seeing if yuz was okay."

Rue let out a sigh. "Midge, don't scare the crap out of me like that." She turned and kept walking. "But yeah. I'm fine."

"So, what happened with Gumbie?"

"What? Oh, nothing."

"What do you mean, 'nothing'? Didn't the interview go well?"

"It was less of an interview and more me deciding that this was a horrible mistake."

"Wait! Why?" Midge stepped in front of Rue, nearly tripping her friend. Rue stopped abruptly.

"I get the impression that he's a womanizing lech."

"So, what does that have to do with working for him?" Midge was confused. "Do you think he'd put the moves on you, or something?"

"No, but I have standards."

"I'm failing to see the connection between his personal life and his work life. With that said, I have an important question for you."

"What's that?" Rue let out a huff.

"Since it seems you are not interested in him, personally *or* professionally, mind if I have a go?"

"A go at what? Personal was never an option. I have a boyfriend."

"Yeah," Midge twirled her finger in the air in mock awe. "Spencer."

"What's wrong with Spencer?" Rue demanded.

"I don't think we have that kind of time," Midge retorted as they resumed their brisk walk toward Delancey Street.

Spencer may have been a little overbearing lately, but Rue was certain that he was simply struggling to fit in with the big wigs in the tech world, to be swimming with the sharks.

"Yeah, I get it. You two don't exactly like each other. But he's my boyfriend, and I like him just fine." Rue kept walking. "But what, exactly, did you want to have a go at? Did you want to apply as Darwin's assistant or something?"

Midge contorted her face in a "don't be ridiculous" way. "I'm a senior level Information Security Expert. While his detective agency could benefit from my skills tremendously, I'm pretty sure he can't afford me."

"Snob," Rue stuck her tongue out at Midge. "You and Spencer may be more alike than you think."

"I resent that," Midge countered. "But no, not professionally. I mean, personally."

"Really? I'm not sure that's wise. He seems to be sort of a player." Rue replayed the encounter with the two women who surfaced during their interview.

"Just my type," Midge concluded.

"Really?" Rue was surprised.

"What? Don't judge me. I like a challenge. He'll be eating out of my hand in no time."

*Well,* Rue thought to herself. *Then perhaps Midge is in luck. Because Mr. Darwin Fennec certainly appears to be quite the challenge.*

Back in the Office of Darwin Fennec

Darwin returned from his meeting with Rue to an office in disarray. The front door was wide open with papers scattered all over the floor, some of which had already blown into the street.

One filing cabinet was overturned with a couple of chairs knocked over, in what Darwin could have sworn was "on principle." His minimalist oak desk had been ransacked, the drawers dumped on the floor with a variety of files, pens, rubber bands, paper clips, notepads, and the odd hole punch strewn everywhere.

Darwin took a moment to sift his hand through the mess...and smiled. Things were going exactly according to plan.

"Okay to come in?" a voice asked. Darwin looked up to observe a woman of medium height with mahogany hair tied back with a red ribbon. She wore a form-fitting navy top and white linen pants, appearing as if she'd stepped off the cover of a Macy's catalog. The single oddity was her plastic black gloves... and the fact that she was obviously very pregnant.

"Of course," Darwin flashed a grin. "So, what happened?"

The woman set a pair of binoculars on Darwin's desk and removed the gloves. "Took the bait just as you expected," she reported. "Oh, and the gals left thank you messages for you today, you scoundrel!" She wiggled her eyes suggestively, slapping him on the arm. The woman handed him the phone messages that she had carefully scribbled on post-it notes. "I left them on the answering machine if you wanted to listen for yourself, 'Darwin honey.'" She rolled her shoulder and pursed her lips, imitating the baby-doll sounding voice messages she'd retrieved.

"Excellent," he smiled, ignoring her gestures. "Thank you, Ashley."

"No problem. Oh," she remembered, dropping her shoulder, "how did it go with the girl today? The one Spencer is dating?"

Darwin thought a moment. "Honestly, I'm not sure."

"Really?" Ashley was surprised. "The famous Darwin Fennec unsure?"

Darwin blushed a little, but unlike the presentation he made to the women at the pier, this one was quite a bit more genuine.

"Unfortunately, yes."

"Hmm," she thought a moment before planting a kiss on his cheek. "That's okay, you'll figure it out."

"I hope so," Darwin answered, a hint of skepticism in his voice.

"Do you need help cleaning up the mess all over the street? Hope those particular papers were not terribly important."

"Not terribly, no. And I can manage, thanks." He glanced at her large belly and thought better of asking her to do any of the cleanup.

"Well," Ashley wrinkled her nose at him, "you know where I'll be if you need me. Otherwise, see you in a few months."

Darwin wrapped his arms around her in as tight a hug as he could give a very pregnant woman as she turned her belly to the side. "Thanks, Ashley," he answered. "I can always count on you. I love you, you know."

# Chapter 3
# The Gambler

Sunday Morning at Rue's Apartment

Rue awakened to a tapping at her window. She rolled over and groaned, forcing her eyes open to gaze at the clock beside her bed. It was only 7:23 am. She sat up and made her way toward the tapping and pulled back the pillowcase curtain to reveal an overly energetic Midge smiling at her. She held up a bottle of champagne and a carton of orange juice.

Rue lifted the window. "Mensa, it's Sunday. Why are you at my window so early? And furthermore, how come you never use the front door anymore?"

Midge thrust the orange juice through the window for Rue to take, which she did, walking it to the kitchen table while Midge clumsily stepped over the sill, carrying the champagne.

"For one thing," Midge smiled, "I wanted to share the news." She waited for Rue to ask 'what news' but she didn't. Instead,

Rue leaned in on the table with her hand and let out a yawn. She hadn't even changed out of her nightgown yet, a fact that made Midge's visit that much more annoying.

"Anyways," Midge continued, "it's a shorter distance to climb down the escape versus using the stairs. If you were as smart as me, you'd have realized that." She glanced back at the pillowcases over the window. "Ever think of blinds?"

Rue gazed at the makeshift drapes above the windows of her bedroom. They were, essentially, two pillowcases nailed above each window, each one tied together with a yellow ribbon that wrapped around yet another nail situated on the far ends of the windows. At night, she unraveled the ribbons for privacy. Juvenile, perhaps, but at the time, she hadn't really seen herself living there for more than a year, so practical things such as drapes and frames around pictures hanging on the wall seemed like an impractical waste of effort.

A long pause ensued. "Aren't you going to invite me to sit down?" Midge complained. "After all, I brought us mimosas. At the very least, you could offer me toast or something."

"Please," Rue clenched her jaw. "Sit down." Moving over to the counter, Rue procured one flute glass and one small juice glass. "I think we need to have a talk about boundaries, Mensa. You can't keep showing up at my window unannounced. Maybe call first to see if I'm even up for company...or even better, to see if I already *have* company?"

"Oh please, when has Spencer ever stayed over at your place? He's too pretty to hang out for more than ten minutes in a hovel like this."

"Lots of times," Rue protested, handing the flute glass to Midge.

"I counted twice over the past year."

"How would you even know that, Mensa?"

"Let's just say that the walls in this building are thin," Midge answered, followed by a well-timed pop from the champagne cork.

Rue turned red. Midge went to add champagne to Rue's glass, but she covered it with her palm. "No thanks. It's not even 8 a.m. yet. I'll just stick with juice." She poured a little orange juice into her glass.

Midge shrugged and added a healthy dose of champagne to her own glass. "Mimosas are a perfectly acceptable breakfast drink," she protested. "Sunday Fun Day and all." She held up the bottle again, in case Rue changed her mind, but Rue shook her head.

"Did you actually want some toast?" Rue asked.

"Nah," Midge answered. "It'll just ruin the flavor of the mimosa." Midge took a seat at the table. Rue sat in the other. "Come to think of it, so will the juice." With that, she topped off her glass with more champagne.

"I'm surprised you drink so much, Mensa, given how smart you are. Doesn't alcohol kill brain cells?"

"Only the weak ones," she reasoned. "The good ones will survive."

"I don't think it works that way," Rue argued. "So, what's your news?"

"I have a date with Darwin Fennec Wednesday night."

"Really?" Rue's eyebrows shot up. "That was...fast."

"If you see something you want in this world, you just gotta go after it!" Midge pounded her fists on the table, nearly spilling her drink.

"Well, if a womanizing charlatan is your thing, then congratulations."

Midge pointed a finger at Rue. "You don't know that. You just assume that based on very little information." Midge took a sip of her drink. "And besides, I really don't care."

"Just be careful."

"And while we're on the subject of Darwin, I really think you should take the job working for him...and this I say despite the fact that it was Spencer's idea."

"I'm not taking the job. Why would I?"

"Working for a cyber forensic analyst and detective..."

"Investigator," Rue corrected.

"What?" Midge lost her train of thought. "Anyways," she waved a hand in the air, "sounds intriguing to me. Maybe he'll train you. Not a bad career move, if you ask me. And Darwin is not exactly awful to look at."

"Why would you want me looking at your future boyfriend?"

"Whoa, let's not jump the gun!" Midge held her hands up. "Besides, I'm not selfish. I don't mind sharing."

"That's disgusting, Mensa."

"To yous, maybe," she defended. "What-chew got goin' on today?"

"Oh, I have an advertorial to write for a new boutique pet store and have to create an online events calendar for a holistic center."

"Sounds riveting," Midge answered flatly.

"It's bad enough I have to work on a Sunday; I don't need you and Spencer dissing my work."

"I'm sorry. You know I only have your best interest at heart. Anyhoo..." Midge stood. "I was going to invite you to take a road trip down to the shore with me, but since you're busy..."

"You know, we have closer beaches, right?" Rue asked, eyeing the now nearly empty bottle of champagne.

"Well, duh," Midge rolled her eyes. "But you can't gamble there. I wanna try my luck with the one-armed bandit in Atlantic City, and there's a bus leaving from the Port Authority in less than an hour...so, I gotta scoot." She paused, with one leg stretched over the sill in an amazing display of flexibility. "And don't think I didn't notice you eyeing the bottle. I'm not driving, nosey-pants." She climbed onto the escape before remembering something. "Oh, and can you be a dear and recycle that for me? Thanks!"

Rue let out a sigh as she picked up the bottle and set it by the door as a reminder to take it down the hall to the recycle bin later that day—which also meant that she'd probably actually have to change out of her nightgown at some point and put some clothes on.

Just then, Rue's phone rang. "Hey Rue, it's Donna over at Garnet Media. Sorry for calling early on a Sunday morning."

"Oh, hey, Donna," Rue replied, stretching the phone cord and tucking the receiver between her ear and shoulder. "No problem at all. In fact, I'm slated to work on the calendar and pet store advertorials today and the entertainment section tomorrow. I'm making good progress." Rue placed the leftover orange juice in the frig and closed the door.

"Oh," Donna sounded disappointed. "Listen, Rue, I really hate to do this to you because you're my favorite journalist but..."

The pit in Rue's stomach dropped.

Donna continued, "But my boss just called after reviewing the budget. Somehow, his team missed a huge discrepancy, and the Early Edition doesn't actually have the funding it thought it did, so..."

"What are you saying, Donna?"

"We're shutting down the print and new electronic site immediately and all journalists, editors, and graphic designers on the contract are being temporarily put on hold. I'm really sorry, Rue; I don't know how this happened, but I promise to cover you for the pieces you are currently writing—no need to finish them though. Just invoice me and I'll take care of it."

Rue's entire face felt hot. The Early Edition was, by far, her largest contract. Without it, she was left with modeling, which Spencer disapproved of, an as-needed gig writing press releases and blogs for a local optometrist, and...she hated that this had even entered the equation—becoming the administrative assistant to Cyber Forensic Analyst and Private Investigator Darwin Fennec.

Ten Minutes Later...

"Hello Ms. Brennan," Darwin greeted, picking up the phone on the second ring.

"How did you know it was me?" Rue asked, suspiciously.

"It's my job to know, Rue," he answered smugly.

Rue bit her lip. Her rent was due in two weeks and short of asking Spencer for help (which she vowed never to do), this was the quickest way to an income. "Then you know why I'm calling," she answered, not without a hint of sarcasm.

"I suspect I do, yes. You've re-thought my offer?"

"Of working for you, yes. But you didn't actually tell me what I'd be doing or how I'd be paid."

"Tell you what, meet me at my office tomorrow morning. Eight a.m. would be ideal. You know the skyscraper on the river, 200 West Street?"

"Wow," Rue was impressed. "That's your office?"

"Not even close," he continued. "But if you follow that street to the end, you'll find the only one-story triangular building on the corner with a blue door. You'll see a Cyber Security and Investigations sign on the window. That's my office."

"Oh," Rue seemed disappointed. "Well, I'm sure I can find it. But about everything else?"

"I can give you more details tomorrow, and we can talk numbers, sound good?"

"Are the renovations finished already?"

"The what?" Darwin thought a moment. "Oh, yes. Just finished this afternoon."

"Convenient," Rue muttered. "Okay," she finally answered reluctantly, "see you tomorrow morning."

"Don't sound so thrilled," Darwin teased. "Oh, gotta run. Talk tomorrow."

With that, he abruptly hung up the phone.

# Chapter 4
# Gretchen

Monday Morning in Battery Park

A tall woman, dressed in an overabundance of beige, slunk her way into Darwin Fennec's office at precisely 7:13 a.m., exactly three minutes after Darwin, himself, had arrived. He hadn't even had a chance to lock the door behind him and was still brewing a morning cup of coffee in the kitchenette area when she arrived. She wore a matching scarf, hat and dark sunglasses, shielding her face. She closed the door quietly behind her, fighting as it caught clumsily on the door frame. Eyeing the small window to the outside world, she quickly drew the blinds.

"Good morning, Mrs. Ellis," Darwin greeted, without turning around.

"Good morning, Darwin," Gretchen Ellis answered with a level of sophistication that was matched only by her love of beige. She unwrapped her scarf and removed her hat, revealing a short, cropped bleached-blonde hairdo that never once moved when she removed her hat (probably out of fear). "You are a clever boy, aren't you?"

Darwin turned around, holding a cup of freshly brewed black coffee in his hand. "Coffee?"

"No, thank you," she answered. "I shan't be long. I just wanted to talk with you for a moment, if I may." Gretchen Ellis removed her glasses, revealing somewhat striking pale blue eyes and slight crow's feet around her otherwise stretched-looking face.

Darwin offered her a chair, but she declined. Instead, she stood by the doorway, already preparing to make her exit.

"I know you've been investigating my family," she revealed.

"Yes," Darwin answered flatly. "That was made evident when you had your security guards ransack my office the other day."

"Sorry about that," she sniffed unpleasantly. "It would have been easier if you'd just told me what dirt you'd dug up for Spencer Hargrove."

"You know I can't do that, client confidentiality and all. It would be unethical."

"Hmmm," Gretchen eyed him curiously. "I didn't realize that ethics were a concern of yours." She turned dramatically toward the window, suddenly remembering that there was nothing to see as she'd closed the blinds. She pressed on, "Since Spencer sees fit to trust you, I'd like to employ your services."

"Really?" Darwin was cautious. "In what capacity?"

Gretchen turned to face him. "I want you to investigate my son."

"Astor? But why?" He suspected he already knew.

"Oh, come now, Darwin. Don't pretend to be stupid. You know as well as I do that Astor has an eye for the ladies. He's soon to be taking over as CEO for his father's company, and that's not the kind of press we need, particularly when he's about to be married."

*Ah, yes.* Darwin thought. *Portia LaMonte, socialite, yuppie, and heir to her family's line of pet products. Who knew there was so much money to be had in squeaky dog toys and ferret hammocks?*

Gretchen reached into her purse, which had up until now, blended in with the rest of her. "Here," she handed him a folded piece of paper. "The latest of my son's trysts."

Darwin accepted the note. In it, was a handwritten message, signed with a name and a physical address.

"Clarissa Sauer?" Darwin read the name.

"Let's drop the charade, Darwin. Shall we?" She waved her hands in the air. "You know who she is as you've already been investigating Astor and my husband to find evidence suggesting we're stealing company secrets from SpencerTech."

SpencerTech was Spencer Hargrove's baby, a start-up company he founded last year and a soon-to-be direct competitor for her husband, Byron Ellis's, well-established company, B. A. Ellis Industries. Spencer was on the verge of developing a new animation product that would bring computer animation into the forefront of movie making. What's more, there was not the need for pesky plug-ins to allow his graphic design program to talk seamlessly with others, no matter the operating system or version.

Spencer bragged about this regularly to both Rue, and apparently, Darwin. By his estimation, his integration would enhance cinematography and animation while cutting production time for artists and designers by a good 35%. And that, he reasoned, was very good for business.

Distracted at this moment, Darwin had only one thought. *Why are all of these men so obsessed with naming their companies after themselves?*

Darwin re-directed his attention toward the current conversation. "What is it you'd like to have me do, Mrs. Ellis?"

"Clarissa Sauer is pregnant," Gretchen Ellis answered flatly. "She's been not-so-subtly requesting money so that we could 'make the problem go away.'"

"I see," Darwin answered, folding the note.

"No, I don't think you do, Darwin," Gretchen retorted. "While my son is a playboy, he's definitely *not* the father."

"There are tests for that."

"My son is sterile, Darwin." She held up her hand. "Please don't ask me how I know."

"Don't worry," Darwin reassured her. "I won't."

"Then, just yesterday, this arrived." Back into the purse she went, digging around until she'd found what she was after. She pulled out a second piece of paper. This one was a printout from her personal email.

"Emma Post," Gretchen read the name. "I don't know how she even got my email address. I've only just recently begun using email and barely remember my own address. Look at the message."

Darwin read the text. *Dear Ms. Ellis, or should I call you Mom? Astor and I are expecting. Just thought you should know. Perhaps we can schedule a time to meet to discuss it?"*

"So not one, but two women are coming forward claiming that Astor Ellis is the father of their babies?"

"Quite," Gretchen pursed her lips, bitterly. "All happily coinciding with Astor's impending marriage, his rise in the ranks at B. A. Ellis Industries, and with Byron on the verge of launching a new invention that will put him within the top 2% of the richest men alive. Which, I might add, has nothing to do with Spencer Hargrove's meager start-up."

"How very inconvenient," Darwin acknowledged.

"I don't want Portia LaMonte to get wind of my son's infidelity. The marriage will be very good for our families."

"So, what would you have me do?"

"Find out exactly who Astor has been running around with and any dirt you can about them. It will make getting rid of them that much easier."

"Getting rid of them?" Darwin was skeptical.

"Paying them off, Darwin," Gretchen was exasperated. "Obviously, it's a scheme cooked up by these gold diggers to get money out of the Ellis family. But I don't intend to make ongoing payments for babies that don't exist...or at least aren't ours. I'm willing to offer each of these whores a one-time payout to keep their mouths shut if they did have romantic liaisons with my son. But first, I need you to confirm who they are because I'd be willing to bet that Astor has never laid eyes on either of these girls, let alone anything else."

"My rate is $300 an hour, Mrs. Ellis," Darwin explained.

"Preposterous," she answered. "I happen to know you're only charging Spencer $200 an hour and much of the investigative work overlaps." Mrs. Ellis then realized her mistake. She smiled. "You certainly are crafty, Darwin Fennec. I'll agree to your $300 per hour on one condition."

"And what's that, Mrs. Ellis?"

"That you share any information you give to Spencer Hargrove about my family with me."

"You know I can't do that, Mrs. Ellis," Darwin explained.

"Right," she nodded. "Code of ethics."

"Exactly."

"But taking a case that's a clear conflict of interest with the one you're currently on is perfectly acceptable?" Gretchen eyed him suspiciously.

"Perfectly," Darwin nodded. "My code. My rules."

"I see. Does your *code* include how much you charge your clients?" Gretchen demanded.

"Completely unrelated," he admitted.

"Then why, may I ask, are you charging me more than what you're charging Spencer Hargrove? Tell me you're not taking advantage of the fact that I have money?"

"Not at all," Darwin answered.

"Then, why?"

"It's very simple, Mrs. Ellis." He paused for a moment. "I don't like you."

"Oh, I see," Gretchen Ellis's eyes grew wide in surprise, a small smirk forming at the corner of her lips. "So, you base your fees on how much you like a client. Am I to assume you like Spencer Hargrove?"

"No," Darwin shook his head. "As it turns out, I don't like him very much either." A sad fact that he'd learned too late.

"And yet you haven't raised his rates. Why?"

At that moment the door handle fumbled. Rue had arrived early for her first day on the job. Darwin glanced up, surprised, before remembering.

"Mrs. Ellis, I'm afraid I will have to cut this meeting a bit short. I have an appointment to keep."

Rue finally managed to jar the door open, and when it finally gave, she almost smacked Gretchen Ellis, who now had her sunglasses and hat back on and was in the process of wrapping the scarf to cover her chin.

"Oh," Rue's eyes opened wide. "I'm so sorry."

Darwin stifled back a laugh.

"It's okay, Ms. Brennan," Gretchen answered, "I was just leaving." She brushed past Rue, almost knocking the much smaller young woman over in the process. Before she'd crossed the threshold, she glanced over at Darwin. "Oh, and I agree to your fees. I'll see to it that a deposit is wired to you by the end of the day. Nice working with you, Darwin."

"Oh, and Mrs. Ellis?" Darwin stopped her.

"Yes? What is it?"

Darwin walked over to the door and handed Gretchen Ellis his business card. "My email is on here. Would you please forward Emma Post's message so we can look into it?"

After one final glance at Rue, Gretchen answered, "Of course." With that, she forcefully shut the door behind her.

Rue gestured in Gretchen's direction. "Who was that and how'd she know who I was?"

"Good morning, Ms. Brennan," Darwin greeted, ignoring her question.

Rue hadn't realized they were being so formal. "Uh, morning, Mr. Fennec." Without thinking, she plopped her duffel bag filled with a wrapped peanut butter and jelly sandwich and a bottle of water on the chair in front of Darwin's desk—one of the two meant for clients—and proceeded to remove a tattered rain jacket from her shoulders (even though it was sunny that day).

"And that was?" she reminded him.

"Yes, of course," he walked over and motioned to her belongings. "Might want to throw these under the counter in the kitchen," he said, pointing. "We should leave these seats open for clients."

"Oh, right." Rue realized her mistake and moved her belongings.

"That was one of our new clients, Mrs. Gretchen Ellis," Darwin called after her.

Rue started for a moment. Why was that name familiar? She tossed her belongings under the counter, but only after she'd retrieved her lunch. Eyeing the kitchen, she spotted a mini-refrigerator located just underneath where the coffeemaker sat on the counter. "Okay if I store my sandwich in the frig?" she asked.

"Sure," he answered. "Might need to move stuff around to find room."

Rue fumbled with the door and, getting it open, spotted a jar of green powder, a half-drunk smoothie in a glass, and a deli-bought salad. She threw her sandwich on top of the salad container.

Darwin waited for Rue to finish organizing her things before continuing. "Which brings me to our first item on the agenda for today."

"Oh, what's that, Mr. Fennec?"

"Client confidentiality is our most important code. I only stay in business because my clients trust me. Therefore, while I know that Spencer Hargrove is your boyfriend, he's just one of several clients we currently have."

"Which means?"

"That anything unrelated to his case, no matter what it is, is strictly confidential and can't be shared with anyone—not even him. In fact, it might be best if all the information about the investigation comes from me, not you, just in case."

"In case what? I don't follow."

"For example, Gretchen Ellis, who just blew through here in a whirlwind of beige is Byron Ellis's wife."

"The tech mogul who runs B. A. Ellis Industries?" Rue asked. "The one Spencer has been complaining about for the last year?"

"The same," he answered. "If anything comes to light that confirms they are, in fact, pilfering information from Spencer-Tech, and you share it over dinner, there's no guarantee that Spencer won't confront them, half-cocked, and blow our entire operation."

"You must think I'm really dumb," Rue folded her arms.

"I don't think that at all, Ms. Brennan." He offered her one of the unoccupied chairs. She sat. "I do, however, question your boyfriend's reasoning behind suggesting you come and work for me, considering the delicate nature of this work."

"And yet, you hired me," Rue shook her head slightly.

"I did," he confirmed. "Sometimes, I question my own reasoning as well. Should we move on to the work you'll actually being doing for me?"

"Please," Rue agreed. "But then can we get back to why Gretchen Ellis was here in the first place?"

"Certainly, but first..." Darwin outlined Rue's weekly salary. She held a poker face after the announcement, since it was a good bit more than what her current contract work was offering. There was the usual answering the phone and responding to emails and the occasional fax, sending and tracking invoices to clients, and so forth.

"I think I can handle all that," Rue answered, confidently.

"Well, good," Darwin replied. "But there is a bit more to it."

"Such as..."

"Such as, I need to train you on basic encryption and security operations here. Data is sensitive and we do our damnedest to protect it. This won't happen overnight, but over the next three months..."

"Three months?" Rue questioned.

"Well, yes? Did you not expect the training to be that involved, or not to be working for me for that long?"

Rue wrinkled her nose and shrugged her shoulders.

"It's both, isn't it?" Darwin let out a long sigh, clasping his hands to his hips.

"I'm sorry," Rue smiled, a bit apologetically, "but I'm still trying to wrap my head around this whole scenario."

"Understood," Darwin answered. "Er, there is one more thing..."

"And that would be?"

"Everyone I work with is vital to my team. And no one is on

the sidelines. There are times where I may ask you to get in the trenches, so to speak."

"What does that mean?" Rue asked.

"It means that beyond being an assistant, I may ask you to be on the scene for some investigative work. Can you do that?"

Rue felt something in her heart do a flip-flop. The vibration traveled from her heart to her lungs and finally bubbled into her throat. She swallowed, hard. There was something exhilarating about the prospect of 'getting in the trenches.' After a moment, she answered, "Yes. I can do that." After a moment of silence, she added, "Is that all?"

"Just one more thing, Ms. Brennan," Darwin said. "A question, really."

Rue leaned in, curiously. "Yes?"

"Just how good are you at keeping secrets?"

# Chapter 5
# Training



Tuesday Morning in Battery Park

While the rest of Rue's first day on the job was very basic and somewhat bland, she was intrigued to learn that they would be investigating Astor Ellis while also gathering intelligence on B.A. Ellis Industries. Rue wasn't sure how to describe the new excitement she was feeling about the work. It was almost as if she could feel warm blood coursing through her veins for the first time in a very long time, and she liked it.

"So," Rue smiled coyly as she took her seat in front of Darwin's desk computer in preparation for her first lesson in logging sensitive data. "Are you looking forward to your date with Midge?" She hadn't forgotten that Midge and Darwin had plans Wednesday night.

"Midge?" Darwin remembered. "Oh, yes. Of course, I am. Your friend seems like..." he thought a moment, "a lot of fun."

Rue's expression darkened. "She's more than just 'a lot of fun', mister. She's probably my best friend, despite her unnatural clinginess," Rue considered. "But never mind that, just be respectful is all." If Rue were being honest with herself, she would have been more concerned with Midge's behavior around Darwin.

"I'm hurt that you think I would be anything but." Darwin's face dropped.

"Frankly, I am a little surprised."

"At?" Darwin leaned a hand on the desk. Rue could feel his energy as he stood behind her. She shuddered for a moment but then shrugged it off. She never felt odd like that when Spencer was near her. But then, she'd known him for a year, so maybe she just got used his proximity? She drew her mind back to the conversation.

"You just seem like an odd couple, is all," Rue confessed. "Forget I said anything. Let's focus." She looked at the dark screen that was Darwin's computer. "What are you going to teach me today?"

"Glad you asked." Darwin pulled up a chair and sat next to her. "See those filing cabinets over there?" He pointed to the two tan columns that sat in the corner of the room.

"Yeah?"

"They're pretty much just for show."

"What?"

"I mean," Darwin held his hands up, "not entirely. They contain take-out menus and a few office expenses. But let's just say there's nothing overly sensitive in there."

"Then, why do you keep it locked?" Rue asked. "You specifically gave me a key for it yesterday so I could grab a Rolodex with a phone number on it you were looking for."

"Well, part of that is out of an abundance of caution with

regards to people's personal information. But the other part is to create a red herring."

"A red herring?" Rue was confused.

"Yes, a misdirection," Darwin explained. "For example, the other day, the lovely Gretchen Ellis, who you had the great fortune of meeting, had some of her thugs break into this place. They got nothing...except for what I wanted them to get."

"From the locked cabinet," Rue confirmed.

"Which they had broken into," Darwin finished.

"Did they not get anything off of your computer?" She motioned with her eyes back toward the screen at her desk.

"They couldn't," Darwin answered. "And sadly for them, not sure they would have been able to even if I hadn't password-protected and encrypting everything...not the brightest bulbs in the pack, I'd say."

"So, what did they get?"

"Well, if memory serves...there were about a hundred ski ball tickets left behind from when I took my friend's son to the arcade, the newest Dim Sum menu from Chang's restaurant..." He paused for a moment, as if pretending to think. "Oh, yes. And a few working animation grids and a blueprint of SpencerTech's animation software."

"What?" Rue sat up.

"From three years ago," Darwin finished. "B. A. Ellis Industries might very well assume that Spencer's designs are outdated given the old-style programming. And, if they didn't, they will have fun spending the time working through the bugs he took years to work out."

"Clever," Rue acknowledged. "So, where do you keep the actual info about your cases—clients, clues, evidence, etc. I assume they live...somewhere?"

"Yes, of course," Darwin answered, eagerly. "That's what I

want to show you. May I?" He once again leaned over her shoulder to power up the computer. "You can go ahead and drive," he told her once the screen had awoken to reveal a blinking curser.

"Drive what?"

"Oh," Darwin hadn't realized quite how green Rue was about technology. "Take the mouse and keyboard and I'll walk you through everything. But you're in control."

"Ooh," Rue nodded, "I get it."

"Let's start with the login for information surrounding a bogus family I created for training purposes, okay?" Darwin suggested. He pointed on the screen to a little obscure icon in the lower-left-hand corner. "Click on that," he commanded. Rue clicked on it. "Now, the username is..."

Rue stopped to pull out a pen and paper from the desk in which she was sitting.

"What are you doing?" he asked, part annoyed and part surprised.

"I figure you're gonna give me a username and password for the account, right?"

"Wrong," Darwin corrected. "I'm going to give you a few back-end codes that you can use to access this information. But I don't want you writing any of it down."

"Why not?" Rue asked.

"Security. We were just talking about it, remember?"

"But then, how will I remember once I start working on several accounts?" Rue protested. "Surely you don't expect me to memorize them all. Or do you?"

"While that would be nice...no. But what I do want you to remember is *the pattern*."

"I'm afraid I don't follow."

"That's okay," Darwin answered, patiently. "I can give you an example using the mock-up file I created to train people. Go ahead and type in the letters, numbers, and symbols I give you." Darwin rambled off an odd sequence which Rue struggled to find on the keyboard and type in quickly. "That username is assigned to all the cases surrounding our fictional John Doe. Now, type this in." He went on to provide an entirely new set of codes.

Within moments, the file of a John Doe popped up, presumably with a fake photo and detailed information about the person including basics such as approximate height, weight, hair and eye color, all the way to details about where they had been and why, preferences on food and beverage choices and any interesting factoids that seemed irrelevant to the average person.

"What do you notice about this file?" Darwin asked.

"Well," Rue was hesitant. "Not entirely sure what you're after, but I notice his headshot and bio at the top, his physical features on the left, preferences on the right, and below that, you have photos, notes, and timestamps about where he's been."

"Excellent," Darwin praised. "Anything else?"

Rue looked closer. "I see that you have a hypothesis section with ideas as to what might be happening next to a confirmed list with these blue, underlined words."

"Click on one of those underlined words," he told her.

Rue was not particularly computer savvy, but she knew enough to click the mouse over the link. Nothing happened.

"Double click," he instructed patiently. Unsure, she clicked twice, and a new screen opened up connecting him to a Jane Doe. "See all those underlines?"

"What about them?" Rue asked.

"They either connect to other people or to relevant evidence."

"Oh," Rue was impressed. "That's amazing. On the few times I've been on the Internet, I seem to go in circles."

"This isn't the Internet," Darwin explained, "it's our private server." Rue's face was blank. He was using terms that she had heard Spencer use, but since Spencer got impatient when she asked questions, she simply stopped asking them. To Darwin, she merely nodded.

He motioned to the screen. "If you click on the Xs in the corners, you can close out these screens. Just one click."

She carefully clicked them and watched with amusement as they vanished.

"Now, go back to the home screen." Darwin folded his arms and waited, giving Rue a moment to figure it out. Finally, she did.

"Good. We're going to try a different client. Let's go to Jane Doe." He rambled off new codes which Rue typed in quickly. As with John, Jane popped up. "Now, let's pretend we've just learned that Jane had been in contact with John at 10:57 p.m., using the phone in her apartment. We want to note the time, phone number, and any other information that could be relevant. Click on that plus sign." He motioned to the corner of the screen, and what looked like a pad of paper popped up. "Click your cursor in the box."

Rue followed along.

"Type your note...just make something up." Rue typed in the time, a made-up phone number, and decided to add that Jane Doe sounded as if she were crunching on potato chips at the time and the sound of the rustle of the bag. "I applaud your imagination," Darwin laughed. "Now hit the save button," he pointed. "Always save after every bit of information."

Rue clicked the "save" button, turning to Darwin who was silent for a few moments as if letting the information sink in. "What now?" she asked.

"Now, I'd like you to spend the next couple of hours clicking on buttons and becoming familiar with the interface." Rue looked apprehensive. "Don't worry, it's just a sandbox," he explained.

"Sandbox?"

"Yes, a learning platform. Pretend you are adding and deleting info, looking up people, and connecting accounts. If you get stuck, write down your question and we'll go over it when I get back."

"Where are you going?" Rue wanted to know, slightly nervous.

"I need to do a little digging into the first case I am going to enlist your help on...finding out more about Astor Ellis's romantic liaisons." Darwin grabbed a jacket off the back of his chair and put it on. "I'll tell you more after you've gotten spun up on how the system works. For the time being, if anyone calls, you can jot down the message there," he pointed to the notepad and pen by the phone. "If someone comes in enquiring about anything, just get their information and tell them that I'll get back to them later today. Understood?"

Rue nodded, a lump forming in her throat. Part of the allure of being a journalist and a figure model is that in both cases, you worked alone and if you did have to interview someone for an assignment, it was on your terms because you had reached out to them. She was a little daunted by the simple task of having to answer the phone without knowing who was on the other end and what they wanted. She had the same apprehension about someone walking through the front door.

"You'll be fine," he smiled. "I won't be gone long." He started to leave but circled back. "By the way, notice anything about the username and password patterns?" he asked.

Rue thought a moment. A lightbulb went off in her head. "All the usernames had two letters, two numbers, two symbols and then one of each, in that order. All the passwords looked like phrases with numbers in place of vowels. Can't figure out the pattern for the symbols though."

"That's okay," he encouraged. "You're on the right track. Play with that pattern and see whom else might be on the server. Perhaps Jane and John Doe have little Does running around, or even a dog named Rover Doe."

With that, he closed the door and Rue went back to her studies. Truth be told, until last year, Rue didn't even have her own personal computer, relying on reserved time at the local library or in the offices of one of her freelance locations. When work finally became steady enough, it was Spencer, in an uncharacteristic show of support, who bought her an Intel computer and dial-up service that gave her access to the Internet. Frankly, she wasn't sure the whole Internet and email thing would ever take off, but the computer was a huge time saver compared to her old electric typewriter.

Spencer had made a show of it, bragging that he'd managed to get her a $1,400 computer for $750 at wholesale. Somehow, Spencer, showing how frugal he was did not impress her. Him actually showing an interest in her work, for once, however...did.

Rue returned her attention back to the task at hand. She tried a few random passwords, struggling to figure out Darwin's pattern for organizing them. She randomly glanced around the room—one small window, the front door, the small kitchen with three appliances placed neatly across the countertop. In her mind, she replaced objects with numbers and symbols, almost seeing them float up in front of her.

"Wait a minute," she smiled, excitedly. She typed in a username and password. Sure enough, the video of a wagging dog showed up with the words "congratulations" written at the top. "Now, go find the cat." Rue thought a moment, used the same username with a new password and an image of a purring cat named Rufus popped up. Rue was determined to find all the members of the Doe family before Darwin returned when she noticed something—they all had specific notes tying them together. Some were questions like, "Where is Rufus's collar?" and "Why was Jane Doe meeting a man named Jack at the bowling alley on Sundays?" And while it was all a game to get Rue actually interested in solving the puzzle, she dove into it with all the enthusiasm of someone who once had dreams of becoming an investigative reporter.

# Chapter 6
# The Theater

Wednesday Evening at the Theater

A frantic call came in from Midge at 5:30 p.m. just as Rue was returning from her third day of training at work. Today, Rue learned how to upload and move files around, send encrypted emails and the basics of preparing legal documents should a case have to go to court. Her brain was hurting, but oddly exhilarated at the same time.

"Hey," Midge responded as soon as Rue picked up the phone. "Glad you're home. I remembered to call first, instead of just stopping by...which, apparently, you hate...you're welcome."

It took a moment for Rue to respond as she'd barely gotten her jacket off and locked her front door. She stretched the phone's cord so she could deposit a small bag of groceries on the kitchen table as she talked.

"Uh, okay. What can I do for you, Midge?" Rue asked hesitantly. "Aren't you supposed to be getting ready for your date with Mr. Fennec?"

"Mr. Fennec," Midge laughed. "Listen to you, Miss Formal. Actually, my tall drink of water cancelled on me at the last minute. I don't wanna sit in a lonely private booth all by myself, so would you be a doll and be my plus one for the evening?"

"Sure," Rue answered, confused. She seemed to remember Darwin actually leaving early to beat rush hour traffic because of his plans that evening. "That's so odd. He was talking about meeting you tonight."

"Well, he called my cell phone—something I suggest you invest in, by the way. It would be way easier to get ahold of you. Anyways, he said he started feeling off when he returned home and bailed on me. But the tickets are at the box office in my name if you wanna meet me there."

"Hmm," Rue thought. "I hope he's okay."

"So, you'll come with me?"

"Uh, sure. Why don't you meet me downstairs at 6:30 and we can take a cab together?"

"No can do," Midge answered. "Still at the library researching somethin' for work. But I can meet you at the box office at 7ish. Just grab our tickets if you get there first."

"Okay, I can do that," Rue agreed.

Rue really didn't mind. She liked the theater, though she rarely had the funds to go unless Spencer took her, which wasn't very often as Broadway "wasn't his scene."

At that moment, a siren blared outside her apartment just as the phone went dead.

"Midge?" There was nothing but a dial tone. Rue hung up the phone and then went to drag a little, black cocktail dress from her closet, the one she wore when she wasn't sure what to wear, and then sifted through a pile of shoes on the floor, pushing aside sneakers, boots, and flats and settling on a pair of one-inch beige heels, the only pair of dress shoes she actually owned.

"Eat your heart out, Gretchen Ellis," she joked to herself.

Rue reached the theater at 7:15 p.m. thanks to traffic jams and a rough time hailing a cab. She assumed Midge would have already arrived, but she was nowhere to be found. Finally, she gave Midge's name at will-call.

"Oh, yes," the woman at the will-call booth answered, passing Rue a single ticket. "A woman left a message for you." She pulled it close to her nose to read it. "Hate to do this to you, but I've decided I'm not feeling theater-y after all. Not to worry, though. I sent someone else to accompany you so you wouldn't be alone. Have fun, M."

"What the heck is she talking about?"

"Hey, don't shoot the messenger." The lady at the window raised her hands up, defensively. "I got this call a half hour ago and am just passing it on."

"But she mentioned two tickets when I spoke with her earlier," Rue clarified. "Where's the other one?"

"Sorry, I only have one ticket on file under a Midge Pasternak." The woman's eyes peered over Rue's shoulder, leaving the not-so-subtle message that there was a large line forming at will-call. "Maybe the person she was sending has it already?" she suggested.

"Thanks," Rue answered, absentmindedly accepting the ticket.

Rue had just enough time to present her ticket to the usher at the entrance, find the nearest ladies' room, grab a whiskey sour and make her way to the balcony for the show.

By then, it was nearly time for curtain call. She showed the usher her ticket stub. "Oh, wonderful," the round woman smiled pleasantly, displaying a row of uneven teeth where one was distinctly missing. She was dressed in a crisp white shirt with black pants and a suit jacket with a colorful red cravat around her neck. It was one of the few distinguishing clothing choices that set her apart from the other ushers who stuck with the basic black and white ensemble. Her hair was a peppery gray and black, combed straight to her shoulders, the ends a little split and frizzy. "You've got my favorite box." She leaned in as if telling a secret. Her breath smelled of burnt cigarettes. "The famous Ellis family, you know—B. A. Ellis Industries—has Box 12 reserved exclusively for them all year long. It's just next door. But I think Box 11 is much nicer. The view is perfect. Right through here," she lifted the red curtain separating the private box from the hallway.

*Seems the Ellis family is everywhere I turn lately,* Rue thought to herself.

After adjusting to the light, Rue noticed there were four padded, upright chairs in the box, unlike general theater seats where they were locked together with fold-down bottoms. The box was rather spacious with a red carpet and the railed balcony overlooked a full view of the stage from a slightly off-center angle.

It was only then that she realized that there was another person in the box, and he was already standing when she'd arrived. His expression showed that he was just as surprised as she was, and yet in some ways—not at all. He politely pulled out a chair for her, not that it needed to be pulled anywhere, and motioned toward it.

Mr. Darwin Fennec.

Midge had set them up.

# Chapter 7
# Balcony

Wednesday Evening at the Theater

Despite the company she had inflicted on her that evening, Rue had to admit that the show was rather remarkable: the set design, costumes, musical numbers, the dancing, the singing. Honestly, she couldn't remember the last time she had enjoyed herself this much (and she thought about this really hard, but she was at a loss for coming up with a single date between her and Spencer that was this entertaining).

Her unintended escort actually surprised her as Darwin offered her his opera glasses to get a closer look at the stage, even though he only had a single pair. Instead, they took turns handing the glasses back and forth during varied performances. He also made sure that she had an unobstructed view of the stage since she was rather short, while the balcony rail was rather high. He even asked if she were comfortable. Not used to such questions, she merely nodded awkwardly, her shoulders shrugging in an "I guess so. What does that even mean?" sort of way. She was having a difficult time separating Darwin the boss vs. Darwin the cad and Darwin the...date?

At that moment, the lead singer for the evening launched into a modern performance of the 1930's classic, "If I Didn't Care." Rue leaned forward, resting her arms on the balcony rails of the lower wall and let out a blissful sigh (which was, fortunately, muted by the sounds coming from the stage). Dressed in a red, ruffled, evening dress with a long hem and a revealing open back, the singer swayed slightly in her scarlet, slip-on high-heeled shoes while delivering her final notes from the stage below. She even did a gratuitous spin for emphasis and to show off her well-toned back muscles and arms. Her hands and forearms were adorned with black, elbow-length silk gloves.

Darwin went to hand Rue the opera glasses for her turn when he noticed how transfixed she was. Rue was almost out of her seat, pitching as far as she could without actually leaping from the balcony toward the stage. He smiled to himself. *You know,* he thought, *if she weren't so determined to be disagreeable, she might actually be a pleasant person to be around.*

Darwin had seen this show before with a different lady friend just several nights prior. Therefore, he knew, even without surveying his program, that it was near the intermission. To avoid the crowds of people in the hallway vying for bathrooms, drinks, and bar snacks, he thought he'd dart out early. "Be right back," he whispered to her, who merely nodded as if he were a fly buzzing in her ear, somewhat annoyed that he'd interrupted the song she was trying to enjoy.

Darwin disappeared behind the curtain where the usher sat at the ready by the entryway between their box and the one just next door. She leapt to her feet, shining a flashlight at the floor so he could see his way to the exit. It was too dark to see her, save for a shadowed outline and a flash of white teeth as she smiled politely at him.

Fortune was with him (or so he thought) as he was quite alone in the hallway and opted to make a beeline for the men's room first. *Good thing the ladies' room is on the other side of the corridor,* he laughed to himself, *or this hallway would be considerably more crowded right now.*

Sadly, he didn't realize the gravity of this small fact.

Applause followed the final act of part one and the lights dramatically went out for what seemed like an unusually long time. Murmurs could be heard from the crowd. But then, just as the house lights went up again, Rue heard a loud wail coming from behind the box's curtain. Jarred, she instinctively jumped from her seat as a woman, none other than the one who had just been on stage singing her most popular aria of the evening, burst forward, lunging straight at her.

Up close, it was clear that the dress didn't fit the woman as well as it appeared from the far-away stage. She was too tall and thin, and her costume was too wide around the middle and short, with the exception of the train that dragged on the floor. Her Spanish-heeled shoes brought her height well above Rue's petite 5'3" frame. Unfortunately, that wasn't what Rue was concerned about at that very moment. As the woman sailed into the balcony rail, her heel got caught on the hem of her dress. She spun around in an attempt to free her heel from her dress, revealing a large knife protruding from her belly and dark blood soaking the front of her stomach and beginning to drip slightly down one leg.

The woman looked down in horror as if she had only just now realized that she had been stabbed. Somehow, she seemed oblivious to the pain and distracted by some other thought. She backed up toward the balcony wall.

Fearing the tall woman was about to pitch herself over the edge, Rue reached to grab her arms.

"The baby," the woman gasped, reaching toward her belly.

"No, that's not a good idea," Rue tried to warn her about pulling the knife out with no way to stop the blood.

By this time, the woman's lower back hit the rail and she was now falling backward over the ledge. Rue tried to grab a leg, the hem of the dress, anything really. But all she managed to secure was the knife. It slid out of the woman as she tumbled from the balcony. Rue watched in horror as the woman landed across several orchestra seats on the ground floor, some of which were still occupied, injuring a few theater-goers unlucky enough to be there at that exact moment.

Several patrons rushed to the aid of the theatergoers, while security guards fought through the crowds and forced everyone to move away from the fallen woman. The dead woman lay draped across the chairs, blood spilling over them. There was no question about her state of "deadness" as the guards refrained from moving the body. What they had on their hands was either an accident, a suicide, or a crime scene.

It was only when they peered upward that Rue realized that she was still holding the knife, which was, fortunately, obscured by the balcony wall. She dropped it on the floor, nervously, just as Darwin emerged from behind the curtain.

"I didn't..." Rue tried to explain.

"I know," Darwin replied, shaken. "Clarissa stumbled into me, almost knocking me over as I reached our box. She was facing away from me, so I didn't even realize..." He held his hand to his mouth, queasily, as he noticed a few droplets of blood on the balcony rail and wall.

From outside the box, Darwin and Rue could hear a commotion as loud steps thundered in their direction. It was then that they looked at each other with a sudden realization.

Darwin had been alone in the hallway, coming back from the restroom. Meanwhile, Rue had been alone in their theater box when the woman burst in. The usher was suspiciously absent, meaning that neither person had an alibi at the time the singer burst into the private box and fell clumsily to her death.

Darwin bolted toward Rue, all but knocking her into one of the chairs. "Hey," she protested.

He pulled out a handkerchief, knelt to pick up the knife from the floor and wiped the handle haphazardly, placing it back on the floor and tucking his handkerchief back into his pocket. He then stood and quickly pulled Rue into his chest, hugging her tightly.

"What the..." Rue mumbled, instinctively trying to push him away with her hands.

"Rue, you're trembling," he said, wrapping his arms around her a little tighter. "It's okay, there's nothing you could have done."

Peering past Darwin's tall frame, two armed security guards fumbled through the curtain, opening it wide to reveal a host of onlookers behind them, watching the scene with wide-eyed fascination.

Rue took the cue and wrapped her arms around his waist and crinkled her face up. She buried her face into his chest and sniffed a little, as if sobbing.

"Were the two of you the only ones here when it happened?"

"I'm afraid so," Darwin lied.

The guard looked to Rue for confirmation, who merely sniffed and nodded.

"We're going to need you to remain here until the police arrive."

"We understand," Darwin answered, calmly.

Just then, the pepper-haired usher returned, the smell of burnt menthol cigarettes wafting after her. She sucked on a mint, nervously. "What happened?" she demanded of the guards.

"Clarissa is dead," the oversized, bulky one answered with some annoyance.

"Clarissa?" The woman was taken aback. "*Our* Clarissa? What the hell was she doing up here?"

"Dying," the smaller-framed guard answered simply. "Fell over the balcony. Where have *you* been, Loralei?"

"Went out for a smoke break. The other guy was supposed to cover for me," she defended. "Highly unprofessional of him to not wait for me to return, even if we are just volunteers."

The two merely shrugged their shoulders. They hadn't seen the other man who was supposedly on duty.

"Well, don't go nowhere," the large guard commanded. "The police detective will be here any moment for questioning."

The woman took a seat, crossing her ankles and shrinking like a small child in her chair, wringing her hands nervously. "I only left for a few minutes," she sulked. "Why does stuff like this always happen to me?"

Darwin's brow furrowed a moment in disbelief before he regained composure.

Rue finally broke the embrace, pulled her face from Darwin's chest and rubbed her eyes a little harder than necessary. She peered up, red-eyed, as the police detective, several officers and a few crime scene detectives arrived on the scene.

"Police Detective Ortega," he announced, flashing his badge so fast that he almost smacked Rue in the face as she leaned in to look at it. "You two witnessed what happened here?"

"Yes," Darwin answered quickly before Rue had a chance to react. "I was just about to get my lady friend and I some drinks at intermission when a woman pushed past me and stumbled over the balcony. Rue tried to catch her but..." He ran his hands through his hair.

"Right," the detective eyed him suspiciously. "Lady friend, you say?"

"Yes," Darwin confirmed quietly. "We're friends, and as you can see, she's a lady."

The detective eyed Rue up and down with disinterest. To the officer next to him he ordered, "Clear the scene and separate the witnesses."

Rue looked up at Darwin fearfully as she was escorted in one direction, he in the other. "I'll call you later, Rue," Darwin said over his shoulder. Rue nodded.

And just like that, Darwin and Rue's lives became intertwined, both suspects in a murder, and both one another's fictitious alibi.

# Chapter 8
# Questioning

Late Wednesday Evening at the Theater

"Please, have a seat, Ms. Brennan." Police Detective Ortega motioned toward a very ordinary and uncomfortable-looking folding chair.

Ortega had taken over a small upstairs office in the opera house accessible for theater personnel only and this one was sparse, containing a table and a few folding chairs, along with a poster of last year's fall lineup of shows that was half falling off the wall. There were a few random cables on the floor in the corner and an abandoned computer monitor that probably belonged to someone who worked there a very long time ago. Obviously, this room wasn't used very often.

Rue sat across from Ortega, clutching the underside of her chair, uncomfortably.

"Want to explain to me what happened tonight?"

"Er," Rue was confused, "starting from which part?" Really it felt like a loaded question, from the part where she was getting dressed for the show, where Midge stood her up or...

"How about the part where Clarissa Sauer took a tumble off the balcony from the private booth where you were standing?" Detective Ortega interrupted her thoughts.

"Oh," Rue thought a moment. *Why was that name familiar?* It was then that she remembered something curious. Darwin said the woman's name. She replayed it in her mind. *Clarissa stumbled into me.* And then she had another thought that made the hairs on the back of her neck stand up. It was when Darwin asked her, *how good are you at keeping secrets?*

"Something the matter, Ms. Brennan?" Detective Ortega rubbed his eyes uncomfortably. He hadn't expected on working late on a Wednesday evening.

"No," she answered cautiously. "I was just so shocked when it happened that I'm trying to remember it accurately."

The detective cocked his head to one side with curiosity and waited.

She had no opportunity to compare stories with Darwin to make sure they lined up. So, she decided, she would stick to the truth...mostly...and keep it as simple as possible. It had to be something she would remember, and that Darwin would most likely say as well. She replayed his earlier statement in her head. *I was just about to get my lady friend and I some drinks at intermission when a woman pushed past me and stumbled over the balcony. Rue tried to catch her but...*

"It was intermission," Rue began. The detective leaned in with interest. "Mr. Fennec ...the man I was with...went to get us drinks when the woman who had been singing on stage a short time earlier stumbled into our box."

"And what did you do when that happened?"

"Her behavior was erratic," Rue remembered. This part was very true, and the memory disturbed her. "Her eyes were wide, and she moved so clumsily, I'm not even sure if she realized at first that she had a knife in her stomach."

"Because she'd been stabbed," Ortega finished.

"Yes," Rue answered. "I assume so. Not like someone would do that to themselves, right?" She chuckled awkwardly. She hadn't meant to, but somehow, she couldn't help it. At that moment, her brain couldn't seem to come up with the appropriate response.

Ortega did not laugh.

Rue cleared her throat. "Anyway, she fell onto the balcony rail. She was so tall," Rue paused as her face crumpled at the memory. She didn't like the memory. She wanted it to go away. "I don't know whether it was the shoes..."

"What about the shoes?" Ortega asked.

"Well," Rue was careful. "When she was onstage, I noticed that her dress seemed long and her heels ridiculously high. Seriously, I couldn't even walk in heels that high," Rue offered.

"Focus, Ms. Brennan," Ortega cautioned.

"Right," she continued. "What I mean to say is, she was so tall that when her back hit the railing, she immediately started to topple. I tried to grab her arms, but it was too late." Rue teared up, for real.

Detective Ortega paused for a ridiculously long time.

"What's your relationship to the man you were with this evening, this Darwin?"

"Oh," Rue knew this wasn't going to land well. "He's my friend..."

"And..." Ortega sensed more.

Rue sighed. "He's also my boss."

"Oh, really?" Ortega's eyebrows went up. "Do you often accompany your boss to the theater after work, reserving a private box for the two of you?"

Rue's face became flushed. *Should she tell him about Midge?*

*No,* she thought. *Why drag her friend into this?* Still, the question made her indignant.

"Is this relevant to your investigation?" she bristled.

"I don't know," he answered, "is it?"

Rue took a deep breath and waited a beat to calm down. "No," she finally answered. "I don't believe that it is."

"Then I just have one more question for you, Ms. Brennan... for now," he couched his comment. "The knife that stabbed Clarissa Sauer was lying on the floor of your booth and not in her belly. Wanna explain to me how that happened?"

Rue turned red. She remembered Darwin wiping the fingerprints clean from the knife before the detective arrived. It was to protect her...or was it? There was no way to realistically claim the knife had "accidentally" fallen out of a woman's stomach.

"An answer, Ms. Brennan," Detective Ortega was insistent.

"Well," she answered cautiously. "As I mentioned, it all happened so fast. I reached out to grab Clarissa...as you said her name was... but I was too late. I honestly don't know if in my attempt to grab her arms, I grabbed the knife or knocked it free...somehow."

Ortega looked down at Rue's arms. "And yet," he said, "from what we can tell so far, there were no fingerprints on the weapon. And you, Ms. Brennan, do not appear to be wearing gloves."

Rue thought a moment and suddenly it hit her. "No," she answered in a measured tone. "But now that I remember, Clarissa was wearing long black gloves." She sucked in a breath. "Is it possible that in the mayhem, she panicked and pulled the knife out herself?"

"Did you actually see that, Ms. Brennan?"

Rue thought of Darwin. She had no idea what he may or may not say. So, she didn't want to begin spinning any tales. Instead, she answered, "No, I didn't. As I mentioned before, it all happened so fast."

"Care to tell me how it is you know Clarissa Sauer...knew?" Detective Ortega corrected himself. It was Astor Ellis's turn to be interviewed by Ortega after Rue had been dismissed for the evening. After all, unbeknownst to Darwin, the entire Ellis family: Byron, Astor, Gretchen and the soon-to-be wife of Astor, Portia LaMonte, sat in a private box just next door.

Astor Ellis pulled a handkerchief from his suit jacket and coughed into it, fighting off a gag reflex. Unlike his imposing father, Byron Ellis, Astor was a thin man of average height with a soft-spoken, nasally voice and a far less commanding presence than his father. At 39-years-old, he was soon to be one of the youngest men to be placed at the helm of his father's multi-million-dollar company—something which his father, 40 years his senior, was fond of pointing out.

"Well," Astor answered, hesitantly. "I didn't really know her all that well."

"But you did know her?" Ortega persisted.

"Vaguely," he answered. "Portia, my fiancé, is a true patron of the arts and often visited the Artist Atelier school to support its fundraising efforts. Clarissa, being at art model at the school, met Portia at one such event." Astor paused for Ortega to ask a question that did not come. After a moment of awkward silence, Astor somehow felt the need to fill it. "In fact, that's why we're here tonight. Clarissa mentioned to Portia that she had a lead role in the show. And since Portia and I just announced our engagement to the world, we were simply enjoying a night out as a family to celebrate while also supporting Clarissa's debut."

"I see," Ortega tapped his fingers on the table as he thought. "So, Clarissa was a model *and* an actress?"

"Apparently," Astor answered. "As I said, I really didn't know her." Astor let out another cough into his handkerchief, sniffing uncomfortably as if he'd suddenly developed an acute case of sinusitis.

"Interesting," the detective answered.

"Why is that interesting, detective?" Astor used his handkerchief to wipe his sweaty brow.

Detective Ortega retrieved a notepad from his back pocket. "We are entering a handwritten note into evidence that was found on the body of the victim." Astor coughed, placing the handkerchief over his mouth with one hand, and placing the other on his stomach to calm the queasiness. "A note that appeared to be signed by you, Mr. Ellis."

"I don't know what you're talking about, detective. A note, you say?"

"Yes, from you." Ortega eyed him suspiciously.

"Perhaps, I should refrain from saying anything further until I talk to a lawyer."

"So," Ortega conveniently ignored him. "You didn't send Clarissa Sauer a note asking her to meet you at Box 11, the one your family has exclusively reserved for the season?"

Astor sat upright in his chair with a hopeful expression across his face. "No, I did not," he answered triumphantly. "And besides, if I had written such a note—which I didn't—I most certainly wouldn't have sent her to Box 11. The family box is Box 12."

"I see," Ortega acknowledged. "And who else was accompanying you in Box 12 this evening?"

"Portia LaMonte, my fiancé, as I mentioned, my father Byron Ellis, and my mother Gretchen."

"Any chance you know the people who were occupying Box 11 tonight, a Rue Brennan and Darwin Fennec?"

Astor thought a moment before shaking his head. "No, neither of those names mean anything to me."

"All right," Ortega answered. "You're free to go...for now. But you are a person of interest. To your earlier comment about talking with your lawyer? Well, I'd say that's a very good idea. Don't leave town until further notice, Mr. Ellis. Is that clear?"

"Crystal," he answered miserably.

Portia LaMonte was unflappable. Called in directly after Astor, her energy floated through the room like a calm breeze—counter to Astor's sweaty nervousness.

"I'm told that you knew Clarissa Sauer quite well," Ortega sought the woman's face for recognition. Portia was a good five inches taller than Astor and much thinner, too. Her features were narrow and sharp as if she'd stepped out of a Charles Addams cartoon.

"I wouldn't say well," Portia corrected. "But I did know her, yes."

"Was she the reason you were at the theater this evening?"

"What an odd question," Portia observed, eyeing Ortega curiously. After a long pause, she answered, "Indirectly, yes. I'm sure my fiancé told you that we are celebrating our engagement."

"Congratulations," Detective Ortega muttered gruffly.

"Yes, well, this isn't exactly how I had expected the evening to go. Very inconvenient."

"I'm sorry a woman being stabbed to death has been so inconvenient for you, Ms. LaMonte." Ortega tapped his notepad with the small ballpoint pen that he kept fighting with.

"No need to be rude," Portia retorted, nonplussed. "I'm sorry the girl is dead, but I can't say that we were friends."

"What was your relationship to the deceased?"

"As you probably know, my family has always contributed a great deal to the arts. It just so happened that I was hosting a gala at the Artist Ateliers several months ago when Clarissa Sauer approached me about a job."

"A job?" Ortega clarified.

"Yes," Portia confirmed. "She asked me to get her an audition for this very show even though she is not a member of any actor's union and has very little theater experience to speak of."

"And what did you say?"

"Well, naturally I was eager to help a rising star."

"Naturally," Ortega was unconvinced.

"Are you always this passive-aggressive, Detective Ortega?"

"No, usually I'm just aggressive, but I've been warned that I'm too mean to witnesses and suspects. I'm trying to be better." Ortega took out a handkerchief from his jacket pocket and wiped his moist brow. The theater felt warm to him, but maybe it was the fact that he was wearing a suit. Either that or his blood pressure was up again. "Please tell me why it is you were willing to help Clarissa Sauer even though she was unqualified?"

"Well, if you had ever heard her sing, you would understand. She was quite exquisite this evening. Once I heard her voice, I was sure to introduce her to all the right connections in the industry. She became a protégé, of sorts."

"I see." Ortega paused as if weighing the next question in his mind. "Any idea who might have been an enemy of this protégé of yours?" He eyed her suspiciously. After all, he may not have known Ms. LaMonte very well, but her fiancé's wandering eye was pretty common knowledge in the tabloids.

"No idea," she answered simply.

It didn't take long for Detective Ortega to understand how it was that Astor Ellis came to become engaged to Portia LaMonte. Money and connections aside, she was eerily like her future mother-in-law, Gretchen Ellis. The older woman may have been slightly heavier with cheeks that were unnaturally stretched through cosmetic surgery, but they each looked down their nose at the world in the exact same way.

"How long is this going to take, Detective Ortega?" Gretchen Ellis complained. "As you can see, I'm not a young woman and I am very tired this evening."

"Yes, I can see that," Ortega answered in a deadpan expression. Gretchen shot him a disapproving look. Usually, that was someone's cue to tell her how fabulous she looked, not a day over 40 (She was 67). Then she noticed Ortega biting back a smirk and realized he had set her up for a reaction. She crossed her arms over her already crossed legs and leaned forward, waiting for him to stop sniggering and ask her a question.

"Did you know the woman who fell over the balcony to her death this evening?"

"Vaguely," she pursed her lips.

"How so?" he pressed her for an answer.

"I met her briefly at my future daughter-in-law's charity event at the art school some months ago, a detail I forgot until Portia reminded me that she was performing this evening."

"So, you met her, but she wasn't very memorable," Ortega confirmed.

"I meet a lot of people, detective," Gretchen Ellis sighed. "And most are quite forgettable."

"You didn't share Ms. LaMonte's appreciation of her singing?"

"I wasn't aware of such an appreciation, nor had I ever heard the girl sing before this evening."

"And what did you think?"

"Of what?"

"Of her singing."

"Is this relevant to your investigation, detective?"

"I'll ask the questions, if you don't mind, Mrs. Ellis."

"Fine, if you must know, I didn't think all that much of her performance...not enough to kill her, if that's where you're going with this," she chuckled.

Ortega didn't laugh.

"Just one more question, Mrs. Ellis," Detective Ortega leaned in from his chair, placing his elbows on the table that sat between them. "I don't suppose you know the couple in the next box over? A Ms. Rue Brennan and a Mr. Darwin Fennec?" Gretchen Ellis sucked in her breath. "I can tell from your expression that you do."

Gretchen Ellis said nothing. Unlike Portia LaMonte, Gretchen Ellis was very flappable.

"I want my lawyer present before I answer any more of your questions, Detective Ortega," her face became flushed.

"I think that's a very good idea, Mrs. Ellis."

# Chapter 9
# Breaking the Silence

Late Wednesday Evening in a Taxi

"Want to talk about what happened?" Darwin asked as he and Rue settled into the back of a taxi off Broadway. He had planned on phoning her until he remembered the small fact that Rue didn't own a cell phone, relying on her landline at home. Therefore, he waited patiently outside the theater for her to emerge.

"Not really," Rue confessed, "but I guess we should." Rue was exhausted and her head was pounding.

"Perhaps, I could tell you what I saw and what I shared with Detective Ortega?" Darwin glanced at the driver in the front seat. He was playing what sounded like Bollywood music and clearly not paying attention to their conversation, which was just as well.

"Please do," Rue wrapped her arms around herself in a comforting hug. "Because I had no idea what to say...or not say. I felt guilty even though I don't think I did anything wrong." She thought about this for a moment. "Except for pulling the knife out of her stomach, of course."

The taxi driver glanced up, momentarily.

"D&D role-playing game," Darwin explained to the driver. "We were at a throwback party."

The driver merely nodded and turned his music up a little louder. He had no idea what a 'throwback party' was, but he was fairly confident that he didn't care.

Darwin leaned a little closer to Rue, speaking in a hushed voice. She got a momentary chill. Something about his nearness made her edgy, though she couldn't figure out exactly why. "That was an accident," he reassured her. "Besides, by the way she went over that balcony, she would have broken her neck, regardless."

The driver furrowed his eyebrows but kept his eyes on the road.

"Perhaps we should talk at my place," Rue suggested, "since you insisted on dropping me off first, anyway?" Darwin was in midtown, Rue near the Bowery. It didn't make sense for Darwin to travel all that way only to have the taxi circle back to his home, but he insisted.

He nodded, eyeing the driver. "That's probably a good idea."

Rue wasn't sure if Midge would make one of her unwelcome appearances outside her window and she wasn't up for explaining what happened to her "not really feeling like the theater" friend that evening. Rue figured she'd fill her in the morning. Once Darwin was inside the tiny studio, she quickly drew the pillowcases functioning as curtains.

Darwin raised an eyebrow, curiously.

"Midge," she explained. "She has a bad habit of always showing up via the fire escape."

"Why does that not surprise me?" Darwin commented. He glanced around the tiny apartment. From his estimation, her entire apartment could fit in his living room. His condo was about three times the size which wasn't saying much in Manhattan as rent-controlled apartments, and more inhabitants to habitats, meant that everything was overpriced and underwhelmingly small.

"I know what you're thinking," Rue sighed. "I'm such a loser for living in such a tiny hovel...at my age. This is the apartment for a college student, right? Clearly, I'm not living up to my potential."

"I wasn't thinking that at all," Darwin eyed her, quizzically. "I know little about you, Ms. Brennan, but something about you tells me you're a go-getter. There's nothing wrong with where you live, though I do sense this is a stepping-stone to something more to your liking."

Rue wasn't sure what to make of this as Spencer always had less than kind things to say about her studio.

"Want something to drink?" she asked, opening her refrigerator. "I've got filtered water and..." She glanced at the leftover wine that Midge had bought her for her birthday, but since Spencer also had a thing or two to say about that, she didn't mention it. "So, I've got water," she finished, letting out a disappointed sigh. Had she not drunk all of the juice Midge brought, she could have at least offered that.

"I'm fine," Darwin answered. "Perhaps we could just sit and talk?" He motioned to the kitchen table. Rue set her purse down, wrapping her evening jacket around the back of her chair and sat. Darwin took the chair opposite her, closest to the door.

While Rue was convinced that Darwin was a womanizer, she had to admit that his presence was somehow comforting. She felt safe around him. That only served to annoy her. *After all*, she thought momentarily to herself, *what's wrong with me that I'm not worth hitting on?* She pushed that out of her mind, clearly, not a priority this evening.

"Someone bumped into me briefly before I returned to our

box," Darwin finally shared. "A moment later, I saw Clarissa Sauer stumbling through the curtain heading toward you. By the time I got there, you were trying to stop her from going over the ledge."

"But you didn't tell the police that, did you?"

"Of course not," he admitted. "How could I? Then both of us would be suspects, or at least accomplices...one of us doing the stabbing, the other doing the pushing."

"How do I know *you* didn't stab her, Mr. Fennec?" Rue asked, candidly. She didn't really believe that, or else she wouldn't have invited him up to her apartment in the first place.

"If I did," he replied, "which I didn't, of course, why would I have gone through great pains to wipe the knife down so your fingerprints weren't on it?"

"Because if you stabbed her, your fingerprints would have been on it," she reasoned. "Maybe you were just covering up for yourself."

"Is that what you really think, Ms. Brennan?"

Rue thought a moment, "No, but if you had told the detective the truth, you would have sooner been a suspect than me."

"Would you like me to call him up and set the record straight?" Darwin offered.

After what seemed like an eternity, Rue answered, "No. At this point, it will just make matters worse. They'll still wonder how I came to pull the knife out of her and how she managed to take a topple over the ledge while I was standing right there."

"Agreed. And for the record, had I not wiped the knife clean, your prints would have been on them, possibly connecting you with the killing."

"And so would the killer's prints," Rue reasoned.

"Pardon me for saying so," Darwin offered, "but I suspect killers are better at this than we are. I'm pretty sure they would have been wearing gloves."

"Hmm," Rue thought.

"What is it?" Darwin asked.

"It just has me curious if the police stumbled upon anyone with blood-stained gloves this evening...or anywhere on their clothing, for that matter."

"If they did, I doubt they'd share it with us."

"Why not? You are an investigator, after all," Rue pointed out.

"Yes, but I'm also a person of interest. I don't think Detective Ortega has any intention of enlisting my services."

Rue nodded. For the next half hour, they clarified their stories. Fortunately, they were largely similar and equally cryptic.

"Just one more thing," Rue asked, "how did you know Clarissa Sauer?"

Darwin let out a sigh. "Well, I was planning on getting you a little further along in your training, but..." He paused for a moment. "Remember Gretchen Ellis's visit on your first day?"

"Yeah?" Rue nodded.

"She hired me...well, us...to look into her son's extracurricular activities."

"Clarissa Sauer being one of them?"

"Exactly. And a woman named Emma Post."

"Emma?" Rue was surprised.

"You know her?"

"Only in passing. She's another model at the Atelier. Don't think I've said more than three words to her over the past year."

"Well, according to Gretchen Ellis, both were pregnant with Astor's baby."

"Oh!" Rue sat upright.

"What is it?" Darwin was concerned.

"I forgot all about it under the stress of this evening. But the only thing Clarissa said to me when she came flying into the box was 'the baby.' I didn't realize it at the time, but she must have been worried about her unborn child—hence why she was trying to remove the knife right away instead of waiting for help.

"Did you happen to tell that to Ortega?" Darwin asked.

"No, it completely slipped my mind. Do you think I should have?" Rue was concerned.

"No, because I spent the better part of the evening trying to pretend I was with you at the time of the murder. Had you said that it would have made it quite evident that I wasn't in the box at the time."

Rue thought a moment. "So, Astor knocked up two women while being engaged to someone else...nice."

"Only his mother seems to think that's impossible. It seems that Astor cannot have children."

"Then who do you think the father, or fathers, are?"

"No idea," Darwin confessed. "Hmmm, Clarissa Sauer and Emma Post...one singer and one figure model. You've never crossed paths with Astor Ellis, have you?"

"Never met the man," Rue shook her head. "I've heard of his name, along with his fiancé, Portia, in art circles. And I know Spencer used to be friends with him before their falling out several years ago, but that's about all."

"Do you know what the falling out was about?" Darwin asked.

"Spencer hasn't told me much, honestly. Heck, you probably know more than I do," Rue paused to gauge Darwin's reaction... there wasn't one. "I only know it had something to do with intellectual property."

"Strange that the very people we're investigating happened to be in the next box over during a murder."

"Strange, indeed."

The next morning, the New York Times had a front-page story about the murder. It read, "Pregnant Diva Dies at Theater after Falling from Balcony." Unfortunately, not only was the Ellis family and Portia LaMonte named in the article, but so were she and Darwin. Fortunately, however, Spencer Hargrove's name wasn't linked to the event at all, which Rue thought would have been bad for SpencerTech. "Thank goodness for that," she said to herself, breathing a sigh of relief as she finished her morning tea before heading into the office.

# Chapter 10
# Searching for Clues

Thursday Morning at the Theater

Detective Ortega took each murder investigation personally, as if the perpetrator were out to get him, specifically. If he were the sort of man who did any kind of soul-searching, he would realize that he somehow blamed himself if a case went unsolved and he couldn't bring a murderer to justice. Therefore, he was thorough...very thorough.

"Detective Ortega," the lead forensic scientist on the case called as soon as he'd reached the crime scene at the theater that morning.

"Good morning, Penelope," Ortega greeted, walking over to where another officer was taking photos of what appeared to be a large footprint on a chair.

No one questioned the impropriety of him referring to Dr. Penelope Washburn by her first name. If they had a shared history, no one else knew about it. And since Detective Ortega had been happily married for more than a decade now, no one asked.

"What have you found?" Ortega asked, peering at the chair. Penelope was considerably taller than the short and round detective. She reached over his shoulder and pointed.

"You see this very large dusty footprint on the chair?"

"Clearly," he replied, staring at the soot-covered plush chair, now adorned with a very obvious boot print.

"Well, first it seemed odd that someone would be standing on a chair in the theater at all."

"Perhaps they were short and needed to reach something overhead." Penelope waited for Ortega to look up toward the ceiling and realize that there was nothing to reach for. "Moved from another location?" he offered.

"Doubtful," she answered. "This chair hasn't been touched since last night. This was the same chair the usher sat in when working."

"You'd think she would have noticed the dirty chair and brushed it off," Ortega reasoned.

"Exactly," Penelope answered. "Which makes me think it was left after she went to take her little smoke break."

"So, you think this was left by Clarissa Sauer's killer?"

"It's a stretch, but a possibility."

"Why would her killer stand on a chair to deliver a knife wound to the woman's stomach? Seems impractical?"

A couple feet from where they stood a few officers listened in on the conversation. A rookie whispered to Officer Dennis, "How'd he get to be head detective? He's as dumb as a rock."

Officer Dennis was offended on his supervisor's behalf. "He most certainly is not," he defended. "It's part of their process."

"Process?"

"Yes," he explained. "One person shares the clues they found while the other asks the most basic questions that no expert would think to ask."

"Why?" the rookie wanted to know.

"Because according to Detective Ortega, sometimes the experts get so tangled in the overcomplicated clues, that they miss the obvious."

The rookie looked at Ortega with new appreciation. "Fascinating." The two watched the continued exchange between Penelope and Detective Ortega.

"Here's the thing," she offered. "Look at the mild indentation on the chair. The weight doesn't match the shoe size. It's as if—"

Detective Ortega's eyes lit up. "The person was wearing shoes far too large for them."

"Exactly," she nodded. "Maybe a men's size nine or nine-and-a-half. And according to the coroner, the knife wound in her belly matched someone tall."

"Tall," he answered, "or, standing on a chair."

"Why would the killer want to stand on a chair to stab our victim?" Now it was Penelope's turn to play the dolt.

"To frame someone else," Ortega concluded.

"If I had to guess based on the footprint alone, the person wearing this shoe was either a woman or possibly a man with very small feet."

"Realistically?" Ortega asked.

"I would have thought a woman, except—"

"Except that the usher, Loralei, mentioned a man who stood in for her while she went for a smoke," Ortega finished. Turning to Officer Dennis, he said, "Did she give a description of the man in her statement?"

Officer Dennis tapped the rookie's shoulder who handed over the appropriate folder from the heavy stack he'd been holding for a very long time. The rookie struggled not to drop the lot of them. Officer Dennis groaned as he prevented the stacks of folders from falling to the floor. "Careful, man!" Dennis complained. Officer Dennis was annoyed by the fact that he always seemed to get saddled with the newbies. To Detective Ortega, he said, "Nah, Loralei complained that she was having a nic fit and was getting the shakes. The only thing she clearly remembers was that he was wearing a red cravat, like her, which she thought was odd. She considered it her 'signature style'," Dennis added with air quotes. "And..."

"Yes?"

"He seemed to have a loud shuffle to his feet."

Detective Ortega and Penelope looked at one another. "From someone wearing shoes at least two sizes too big," Ortega's eyes lit up at the realization. "And clearly the person who stepped in knew about Loralei's style choice."

"Assuming Loralei is telling the truth," the rookie called over Officer Dennis's shoulder.

Detective Ortega eyed the young man who seemed to shrink behind officer Dennis from drawing attention to himself.

"What's your name, son?" Ortega asked.

"Ernest," he answered, shyly.

"Ernie," Ortega replied, automatically shortening the man's name, "what makes you think she was lying?"

"Just a thought," he answered sheepishly. "It was stupid."

Officer Dennis nodded in agreement.

"No," Detective Ortega answered. "It's not. Officer Dennis, do we have confirmation that anyone saw Loralei Stephens leave for her smoke break?"

"There were at least three other actors who confirmed they snuck out for a smoke and saw her outside." Officer Dennis glared at Ernest, annoyed.

"That's okay, son," Detective Ortega eyed Ernest. "It's good to question everything and explore all possible scenarios."

Ernest lifted his chest with pride and then immediately

dropped it. He now regretted having called his boss *dumb as a rock. In fact,* he thought to himself, *perhaps that's why Officer Dennis was so impatient with him now.* It became clear that while Detective Ortega appeared a little rough around the edges, most everyone working with him held him in high regard. Ernest vowed to do better going forward.

"And what about the single witness to the crime...Ursula Gorky?" Ortega asked.

Officer Ernest shuffled through his notes. "When we interviewed her, she claimed to have only seen Rue Brennan on the balcony when Clarissa Sauer toppled over the ledge," he announced. "She was in the booth on the opposite end of the theater, waiting for her part in the show."

"She had a part from the balcony?" Ortega was confused.

"Yeah," Officer Ernest confirmed. "Kind of a kitschy thing theaters are doing these days. There was going to be a scene where she started singing from off stage. Only, Clarissa was murdered before Gorky's big number. She was so excited about her part that she always sat through the intermission just to make sure she didn't miss her grand entrance."

"So where does that leave Darwin Fennec?" Ortega wondered aloud. "Says he was in the booth the whole time, but Gorky says he wasn't."

"Could he be the killer?" Officer Dennis asked.

"Except that it seems the killer may have been short, trying to pretend they were tall," Penelope added. "Darwin Fennec has got to be almost six feet tall."

"Fennec also said he's never met the victim," Ortega offered. "But Astor Ellis, in the next booth over, had. In fact, he's the one named in the note Clarissa received."

"And," Ernest chimed in, now eager to be useful. He shifted the heavy stack he was holding to his other arm. "I read through all of these reports. There's a good chance the killer accidentally sent Clarissa to the wrong booth. Maybe Astor was the one being framed? Perhaps the note wasn't sent by him at all."

"Nah, that doesn't add up," Ortega shook his head. "Astor's too short compared to the height the imposter was obviously going for."

"But both Portia LaMonte and Gretchen Ellis, on the other hand…" Ernest offered.

"Both taller than Astor Ellis and his father, Byron," Officer Dennis confirmed, looking at the reports before giving a nod to Ernest. "Not bad, rookie," Officer Dennis admitted.

"Hypothetical wrench in the works," Penelope chimed in. "At this point, we're assuming Astor Ellis did not write the note and we're assuming that someone was trying to frame one of these two women, or at least someone tall. And we're also assuming that Clarissa ended up in the wrong booth."

"Lot of assumptions," Ortega admitted.

"Any chance it could simply be that one of the Ellis men did it and stood on a chair to throw suspicion off of them."

"No," Officer Dennis shook his head. "I don't think so. Of the fourteen ushers on duty that night, one is unaccounted for."

"Oh?" Ortega raised an eyebrow.

"Fourteen ushers reported for duty that night. But a fifteenth stood in for Loralei. No one saw that usher during the show, except for Loralei. But they all confirmed seeing Loralei out having a smoke during the break."

Detective Ortega rubbed his forehead. "This is a needle in a haystack search. There had to be more than 1800 people in the theater that night."

"Yes," Ernest confirmed, "1500 theater goers, 14 ushers, 45 staff members and 37 members of the cast and crew."

Detective Ortega noticed that Ernest was not referring to a single document that he was holding. "How is it that you remember all that, Ernie?" he wanted to know.

"Well," Ernest answered. "I did say that I read all the reports...three times, if I'm being honest. And, I guess I just have a head for numbers."

"Any chance someone on staff or the theater troupe had a chance to change out of costume and then return without being noticed?" Officer Dennis stepped in front of Ernie, upstaging him so that he was now blocked from making eye contact with Detective Ortega. *After all*, he reasoned to himself, *he's making me look bad.*

"Doubtful," Ernest answered, peering around Officer Dennis. "The lights went up at precisely 9:13 p.m. Clarissa fell over the balcony just after the lights were turned on, and by 9:17 p.m., the security guards were alerted, and the theater was on lockdown.

Penelope held her camera at her hip as she gazed out one of the long windows outside of the private theater box. She had a clear view of the street below. It was bustling with lots of small alleyways and clusters of people vying for space on the sidewalk. Several pedestrians darted between cars on the main stretch as they honked, annoyed at pedestrians not using the crosswalks. She then lifted her chin to look to her right, spotting a clearly marked "exit" door.

"What is it, Penelope?" Detective Ortega asked.

"Do we know what time the main doors would have opened to the outside for intermission?" she asked. "You'd think they would open them just beforehand in anticipation of some theater goers wanting to step outside during the break."

"Don't know," Ernest offered, "but I'll bet we could find out."

"What are you thinking?" Ortega pressed her.

"Well, there wasn't really time for someone to change out of their costume or suit, commit a crime and then change back in time, no matter how fast the transition. But..."

"Yes?" Ortega's eyes grew wider.

"During an intermission, who really cares who comes and goes? I mean, really, who's going to try and sneak into a theater halfway through a performance? What if the killer snuck in during intermission, already dressed as an usher? No one would think anything of it."

"And," Officer Dennis caught on, "they could have slipped out the exit just after the crime, before the theater was locked down."

"Exactly," Penelope nodded.

"All right," Detective Ortega announced. "Officer Dennis, see if you can find out when the doors were opened for intermission and if anyone spotted an usher coming in just before the break. In the meantime, let's pause for lunch."

"C'mon, rookie," Officer Dennis poked Ernest in the arm. "Wanna hit the deli on the corner with me? They make a mean Reuben sandwich." Officer Dennis wasn't often gracious, but he realized that Ernest might actually turn out to be useful for the team. And, if he was staying, it's best if they got along.

"Sure," Ernest agreed. "But can we lock these in the squad car first? My arms are killing me."

"Here," Officer Dennis finally intervened. "Give me those. We can drop them off for sure."

"Not that way!" Ortega stopped them at the exit. "We still need to sweep that for clues. Penelope and I will block it off before we break, but I don't need either of you accidentally mucking up the crime scene."

Dennis and Ernest rolled their eyes at one another and grinned, but they were smart enough not to say anything. They retreated toward the carpeted theater steps leading to the main entrance.

"What'll you say, Penelope? Join an old friend for lunch?"

"I suppose," she answered, packing up her camera and boxes marked for evidence. "Let's drop these off at the precinct first."

"Here, let me." Ortega picked up one box while she slung her camera bag over her shoulder and grabbed the other. Detective Ortega let out a sigh. "I'm getting too old for this shit," he muttered.

"Who are you kidding?" Dr. Penelope Washburn teased. "You *live* for this shit."

# Chapter 11
# Artful Dodging

Thursday Morning in Battery Park

The reporters were already surrounding the office of Darwin Fennec, cyber forensic consultant and private investigator, when Rue arrived Thursday morning for work.

"Rue Brennan?" A woman from the local news shoved a microphone in her face while several other competing stations surrounded her and did the same. It was only then that Rue discovered that she was highly claustrophobic and struggled to catch her breath. She could feel her heart racing.

Rue regretted wearing a very bold patchwork, multi-patterned jacket as she realized she stood out like a sore thumb.

"Yes," she answered instinctively. "I mean, no," she countered. "Please, let me through. I'll be late for work." She pushed her way past them while photographers flashed cameras in her face.

"Did you know the woman who fell to her death at the theater last night?" one reporter asked.

"If you didn't kill her, who do you think did it?" asked another.

And then the most dreaded question of all, "We heard a rumor that you're dating your boss, Darwin Fennec. Can you confirm that for us?"

"No," Rue answered, annoyed.

"No, you're not. Or, no you can't confirm it?" the reporter persisted.

"No, I'm not dating Mr. Fennec."

"Then why were you at the theater with him last night?"

"What, I—?" How was Rue to explain that she ended up on a date with Darwin by accident. She suspected the story would have gotten twisted somehow, anyway. Once again, she thought of Midge. *No sense bringing her into this,* she reasoned.

Just then, the door to Darwin's office swung open, briefly. An arm grabbed her, pulling her inside. Darwin slammed the door shut and drew the blinds on a photographer who was snapping photos of them from the outside window.

"Good morning, Mr. Fennec," Rue caught her breath. Somehow, that was the only thing she could think of to say.

Darwin smirked and furrowed his brows at her, quizzically. "Good morning, Ms. Brennan. How are you this fine morning?"

Outside, the reporters pounded on the door and screamed as if they could be understood from the other side of the wall. The desk phone began ringing incessantly. Somehow, it sounded even louder than usual, each ring followed by an odd buzzing.

Darwin just realized something and motioned for Rue to keep talking.

"Oh, fine, thank you, Mr. Fennec. And you?"

"Just lovely. I decided to take in a show."

"Really?" Rue played along. "And how was it?" He

unscrewed the receiver and transmitter on the phone and frowned...nothing.

"Absolutely delightful, until about halfway through, when the lead performer fell from the balcony."

Darwin flipped the phone over. *Sloppy work, if you ask me,* he thought, as he pulled back a small piece of black electrical tape holding a tiny microphone. He pinched the microphone between his thumb and forefinger. *Police issue,* he realized.

"Why, that sounds dreadful, Mr. Fennec."

"Believe me, it was."

Darwin removed his shoe, placed the bug on the table and smashed his heel over it so hard the table shook, and Rue jumped at the sound.

"Sorry," Darwin apologized, placing a finger over his lips.

Rue fell silent.

Darwin did a cursory search of the rest of the desk, but knew a thorough check would take more time than they had.

Outside, reporters grew restless, and the sound of voices grew louder. More people were arriving. One turned on a boom box and faced the speaker at the window. It was a heavy metal song Rue didn't recognize. They turned the volume up.

*Are they trying to force us out, with...noise?* Rue wondered.

Darwin reached in his pocket and pulled out what Rue could only assume was a portable phone as he punched the keypad on it and held it to his right ear. He pushed his forefinger in his left ear to muffle the sounds from outside.

"Yes, I'd like to order two pizzas to be delivered to the fox hole...the under fifteen minutes or it's free deal. Yes, swiftly." He held a button down on the keypad and slipped it back into his pocket.

Rue shrugged her shoulders, questioningly. Darwin didn't even try to explain. Instead, he reached into a desk drawer and pulled out two sets of ear plugs, handing Rue a pair.

*Exactly how often does this happen?* Rue wondered, accepting the foam plugs and pushing one in each of her ears. Unfortunately, they didn't help much.

Moments later, a car horn could be heard from outside, honking in a very distinct pattern...long, long, short...pause... short, short. Long, long, short...pause...short, short.

"Time to go," Darwin yelled. "Keep your head down."

As soon as he opened the door, they were flanked by two very tall, very large and intimidating men. One took Rue's arm, the other Darwin's, as they were escorted to a black stretch limousine with its emergency lights on, blocking a one-lane road in the alley between Darwin's office and an accounting firm. The guard gently, but with considerable pressure, pushed Rue's head down as she climbed into the passenger seat. Darwin jumped in the opposite side. Then, the men merely turned their backs on them, standing at the trunk-end of the limo with arms crossed as a barrier to the vehicle.

A single photographer had figured out the arrangement and stood defiantly in front of the limo, snapping photos at the driver.

The driver seemed nonplussed. Instead, he darted out of the driver's seat with the swiftness of a fox, grabbed the man's camera, holding it over his head with one long arm. With the other, he pushed into the man's chest, holding him at arm's length. "What's more important to ya," the driver asked the photographer, "the camera, or your life?"

The photographer grew wide-eyed. "You wouldn't," he dared.

The driver grinned. "Nah, I know how crappy a photo-journalist's salary is," he laughed. "But I'm gonna need the film." With that, he tugged the back of the camera open and pulled out the reel.

The photographer let out a few expletives.

The driver handed him back the camera. "You have 15 seconds to clear out so I can leave."

"I'm not going anywhere," the reporter grabbed his camera, standing disobediently a few paces in front of the limo.

"Suit yourself," the driver crinkled his lips and hopped back into the vehicle, slamming the door behind him. He revved the engine and put one foot on the break and one on the gas. The limo squealed mournfully as the now terrified photojournalist jumped to one side. The driver wasted no more time as he removed his foot from the brake and the limousine lurched forward and then sped through the alley to the street on the opposite side.

It wasn't until they were halfway through the Lincoln Tunnel that anyone spoke. "You guys okay back there?" the driver asked.

It was only then that Rue caught a glimpse of their rescuer. He had round cheeks in an otherwise long face, an olive complexion, and a five o'clock shadow around his chin and lips. He wore a plaid cabby cap with bits of a dark brown hair creeping out from underneath it.

"We're fine, Bristol, thank you." The driver nodded. "May I introduce you to my new assistant, Ms. Rue Brennan?"

"Nice to meetcha," Bristol nodded, eyeing Rue curiously through the rearview mirror. Before Rue could answer, he added, "What happened to Ashley?"

The pit of Rue's stomach gave a small, bitter lurch.

"Leave of absence," Darwin answered, simply.

Bristol merely nodded and kept driving. It wasn't until about thirty minutes later that he announced, "We'll switch cars once we reach Hoboken and circle back to the fox den."

"Excellent," Darwin answered. "Thank you, Bristol. It's nice to know that even when we lose touch for a few months, I can always count on you."

"Sure thing, Finn," Bristol answered. "You know I've always got your back."

Rue looked at Darwin, questioningly. "We need to relocate," Darwin read her expression. "I'll explain later. But don't worry, Ms. Brennan. You're in safe hands."

The "fox den," Rue would come to learn was Darwin's one-bedroom condo in midtown, while the "fox hole" was the office. By Manhattan standards, the condo was spacious with a large, three-paned window overlooking the city with a faux brick wall on one side and a pale gray wall on the other. If Rue had to guess, the entire space was likely around 900 square feet or so. There was a clearly defined office area with one desk flush against the window, providing the best view overlooking the city, and a second desk against the brick wall. When facing away from the office, Rue observed what she assumed was the living room. It had a plush, black, wrap-around couch and small glass coffee table facing the back wall where a large TV screen was mounted to the wall. It was the largest and flattest TV Rue had ever seen outside of a movie theater and Rue thought it remarkable that anyone could have a mini-movie theater in their own home.

Next to the office area was an efficiency kitchen with a small table and two chairs beside a tiny window. Adjacent to that, was the entryway to what Rue assumed was Darwin's bedroom.

"Sorry about today," Darwin apologized, "but given our perceived involvement in Clarissa Sauer's death and the uncomfortable reality that everyone is going to make lots of assumptions about a detective dating his assistant—"

"We're not dating," Rue jumped in.

"Clearly not," Darwin cleared his throat, "but that's what everyone will infer given our appearance at the theater."

Rue let out a sigh. *Damn it, Midge! Why couldn't you have just met Darwin at the show like you were supposed to?"* She brushed the thought aside. After all, that would have meant that Midge might have been in her place when all this happened instead of Rue. She felt guilty for even having had the thought as she sensed the next few weeks of investigations and interrogations were not going to be pleasant.

"So, what do we do now?" Rue asked.

"Well," Darwin sighed. "If you are amenable to it, I suggest we work from here for the time being, just until the case is solved, and the reporter intrigue dies down a bit."

"You want me to work in your apartment?"

"Condo, actually," Darwin corrected her. "But, why not? It's a little further for you to get to work, but the view is nice, and I can convince the building manager to let us use the service entrance, so it'll be easier for us to come and go undetected."

"But," Rue paused, "you *live* here."

"I am aware of that, yes."

"Won't that just feed into people's perception that a boss is dating his assistant if and when they find out?"

"We can't go back to the office, at least not right now. Between the cops bugging the place and reporters surrounding it, we have no hope of solving Spencer's security leak or the status of Astor Ellis's romantic liaisons for Gretchen. Furthermore, we won't get a moment of peace until Detective Ortega discovers who really murdered Clarissa Sauer."

Rue wasn't sure what to make of this suggestion. After all, she had her own thoughts about Darwin and none of them were particularly flattering.

"I suppose it's fine, but what do we do after hours? I mean, do you think the press will be hanging outside my apartment?"

"Probably," Darwin admitted, pointing to the ground level of the building, seven floors below. There was a small gathering of reporters, photographers, and a camera crew (not much more than action-figure sized at this distance) at the front entrance with the doorman, who was holding them at bay.

"Shit," Rue cursed under her breath. "Can I borrow your phone for a minute to call Spencer? I haven't even filled him in on what's happening yet."

"Sure," Darwin reached into his desk drawer and pulled out one of several burner phones.

"Why do you have so many cellular phones?" Rue asked.

"Security," he answered simply. "I'll explain later." Spencer handed one to her. "Just keep it short. Minutes are expensive and the longer the call, the easier it is to trace."

Rue accepted the phone, staring at it for a moment.

"Is there a problem?" Darwin asked.

"Just never used one before, is all." Rue, quite logically, found the "on" button. And, after a moment, figured out how to make a call. Meanwhile, Darwin disappeared into the bedroom and closed the door, taking another phone with him, presumably to make a call of his own.

Spencer picked up on the third ring, as usual.

"It's me, Spencer," Rue announced.

"Rue? Where have you been? I've been trying to phone you all morning. I even stopped by your place and witnessed a few reporters mulling about. Are you okay?"

"Hmmm," she answered. "Don't remember seeing anyone when I left. They probably only just now figured out where I live."

"What's going on?" Spencer demanded.

"I was at the theater last night and witnessed a murder. And," she paused a moment, "there's a good chance that I'm a suspect."

"What?"

"Listen, I can't talk for long. I just need to stay at your place for a couple days until reporters lose interest."

"Oh," Spencer answered quietly. Rue heard a shuffling sound as if he were shifting papers around.

"Don't sound so thrilled, Spencer," Rue answered flatly. "The truth is, very few people seem to be aware that I'm your girlfriend. It's the best option until this blows over."

"Well, okay," Spencer relented. "I suppose a couple of days will be okay."

"Thanks for making me feel so...welcome." And there it was, that gnawing in Rue's belly. It was the one that told her something was not quite right.

"It's not that, darling," Spencer answered quickly. "It's just that I'm so focused on work right now, that I don't want you to feel...lonely, is all."

"Don't worry, Spencer," Rue read between the lines. "I promise not to distract you from your precious work. I can feel equally lonely in your place as in mine."

"Well, now you're just being snarky."

"Whatever," Rue answered curtly. "Listen, I've got to go. See you tonight."

"Uh, okay. Just phone me when you're heading over. So, I can be prepared."

*Prepared for what?* Rue wondered. "Sure," she answered finally. "Phone you when I'm off work."

Rue hung up the phone just as Darwin re-emerged from the bedroom. He eyed Rue's expression, curiously. "Everything okay?" he asked.

"Just peachy," she forced a smile. "I'll just be staying with Spencer for a couple of days until all this blows over. I already have a few changes of clothes over there, so it shouldn't be a problem."

Darwin cleared his throat uncomfortably and nodded. Despite his keen awareness that Rue was Spencer's girlfriend, somehow hearing about the fact that she had clothes over at his place bothered him. He pushed those feelings aside.

He smiled at Rue. "Let's get back to your training, shall we?"

# Chapter 12
# The View

Saturday Evening at a Restaurant in Manhattan

"A little late, but hopefully worth the wait," Spencer held up a glass of champagne. "Here's to you, darling."

Tonight was her last evening at Spencer's place, since it seemed the press had stopped dropping by her downtown apartment. A fact that she confirmed with her at-home watch dog, Midge. Darwin's office, on the other hand, was still abuzz.

Rue blushed a little and raised her glass in return and clinked the edge of it to his before taking a sip.

"Veuve de Clicquot," he explained. "I hope you like it."

Just then, the waiter stopped by their table. "Nice to see you again, sir," he greeted Spencer.

Spencer shook his head. "You must be mistaking me for someone else," he replied carefully. "This is the first time my girlfriend and I have been here."

The waiter coughed awkwardly, embarrassed by his error. "My mistake," he smiled at Rue in a very practiced way. "Well then, welcome to The View. The rooftop revolves every hour giving you the most spectacular view of Times Square. I'm your host, Andre." Andre was very polished, wearing a crisp, white dress shirt and black pants with matching vest and a starched service towel hanging over his arm. "I see that our sommelier has already brought you champagne. For the lady," he offered Rue a menu. "And for the gentleman," he handed Spencer the other.

"Uh, thank you," Rue answered glancing at the menu that was handed to her.

"I'll give you a few moments to look it over and will be back to answer any questions you may have and take your order." With that, Andre tiptoed away with the stealth of a silent ninja.

"Spencer," Rue leaned in and whispered after glancing at the menu. "There are no prices listed. Are you sure you can afford this?"

Spencer leaned in and touched her hand. "Relax, Rue. And don't worry. I'm not exactly poor, you know. And once Spencer-Tech rolls out its latest digital animation software in a few months, we'll be eating caviar for breakfast, lobster for lunch, and bluefin tuna for dinner."

"That's a lot of seafood Spencer."

"The point is, we'll be in a much better place. And who knows? Maybe you won't even have to stay an administrative assistant for long. You could do something else like..." He paused to think of something.

"Write?"

"Write? Write what?"

"A novel, Spencer. Or, I don't know, maybe become an investigative journalist." Come to think of it, Rue realized she sort of *fell into* writing, somewhat by accident. But somehow, it suited her. She felt privileged to share people's stories, and loved the back and forth between conducting interviews and then holing up for the weekend, crafting her words in solitude. *I wonder what else I could write?* she thought to herself.

"Hmmm," Spencer answered, pulling her back into the moment. Somehow, he hadn't thought of that. "Well, whatever. You'll figure it out." He paused to look at the menu. "Grilled steak in a miso-truffle butter," he said out loud before peering over his menu at her. "What are you having?"

"It looks like I'm supposed to pick three courses so…" Rue scrunched her nose and was still deciding when the waiter showed up.

"Do you have any questions about the menu?" he asked politely.

"Nope," Rue smiled, her eyes suddenly growing bigger than her stomach. "I've got it." She shifted in her seat, excitedly. *Spencer did say not to worry about it.* "I'd like the scallops to start, then the sea bass and the sorbet for dessert."

"Excellent."

"Nope," Rue grabbed the waiter's arm as he went to take her menu. Spencer glanced around the room, slightly embarrassed by her enthusiasm. "Scratch the sorbet. Make that the cheese plate."

"Excellent selection, miss," Andre finished. She suspected he'd have said the same thing no matter what she'd picked. It's probably good for business to compliment the diners on their choices as it reassured them that they made the right food decision.

Spencer placed his order so quietly that Rue could barely hear anything other than "medium rare." She took another sip of her champagne. *Maybe I could get used to not being poor,* she decided, sliding back in her chair and peering out the window at Times Square.

"Speaking of work," Spencer returned to their previous conversation and waited for a moment while Rue caught up with the shift. "How is it going working with Darwin Fennec, particularly after the..." he lowered his head and coughed a little, nervously, "incident."

"Well," she answered hesitantly. For some reason, Spencer was reluctant to talk about Clarissa Sauer's death, even though he wasn't at the theater and as far as Rue could tell, would have no reason to know her. The best he could muster was the occasional check-in to see how Rue was handling the trauma of witnessing the event and her guilty feelings about not being able to save the woman. Aside from that, he was largely absent, coming home late for the past two nights, usually just when Rue was already curled up underneath his 1000 thread-count Egyptian cotton sheets.

"After the...incident...we were questioned by the police; that much you know."

"Yes," Spencer shook his head. "I'm still annoyed with Midge for getting you into this mess in the first place. If she liked the man, why did she back out?"

"I dunno," Rue answered, biting her lip. In her mind, she *did* know. Midge had been playing matchmaker, despite Rue reminding her that she already had a boyfriend. She did her best to dissuade Midge, but once her friend got an idea in her mind, it stuck there like Gorilla Glue. "But the next morning, the office was swarming with reporters, so we had to relocate to Darwin's home office in midtown."

"Home office?" Spencer was curious.

"Yeah," Rue answered. "I told you all this Thursday night."

"I'm sorry, my darling...just focused on work is all."

"Well," Rue was annoyed, "far be it from me to let a murder investigation get in the way of your work," she whispered angrily.

"There's no need for attitude," Spencer leaned in, giving her a warning look as he peered around the restaurant. Above all, Spencer was all about keeping up appearances. "Let's just try to enjoy the evening, shall we?"

Rue relented. After all, he was trying to make up for the fact that he had forgotten her birthday. "Anyway," she continued, "Mr. Fennec had to send in some of his buddies to relocate the computers to his condo after we clawed our way past the media. Fortunately, he has a friend in the limo business...Bristol, I think he said his name was."

"Bristol?" Spencer clarified.

"Yes," Rue confirmed, "Bristol."

"What kind of a name is that?"

"I dunno," Rue was flustered. "Maybe he's from Bristol, Pennsylvania, or New Jersey, or New York. Whatever...the point is, he's the guy who picked us up and drove us there."

"To Darwin's condo?"

"Yes, exactly." Rue thought about this. "You know, for a cad, he sure does seem to have a lot of friends."

"Bristol?"

"No, Darwin!" Rue let out a huff. Spencer just wasn't listening.

"So, you'll be working from his living quarters from now on?" Spencer clarified.

"Bristol?" Rue asked.

"No, Darwin." Spencer let out a huff.

Communication is hard.

"It looks like it, unless that bothers you and you want me to quit?"

"No, not at all. I trust him," Spencer decided, sipping his champagne.

"Really!" Rue thought about this. "Why? I got the impression he was a bit of a womanizer."

"Nah," Spencer laughed. "Frankly, I suspect he's a little light in the loafers."

"Light in the—" Rue shook her head, confused.

"Gay," Spencer whispered. "I suspect he's gay. He's a little too sensitive and charming. And, as you said, he seems to date a number of lady friends...probably a cover."

"Oh," Rue answered quietly. Somehow, the thought of him not being attracted to women bothered her. *I mean,* she considered this to herself. *I certainly don't like him and it's best if we're working together that I don't have to worry about him putting the moves on me.* But still... She brushed the thought away as their appetizers arrived.

The evening ended with Spencer presenting Rue with her belated birthday gift just as the cheese plate and a glass of a Willamette Valley pinot noir arrived.

Spencer was disappointed that she chose an Oregon wine over a more popular French Bordeaux or California cabernet. But Spencer seemed to be concerned about lots of things that didn't really matter, Rue decided.

"Here," he handed her a shoebox-sized gift.

She looked lovingly at the camembert, Roquefort and gruyere plate that was perfectly accompanied by melba toast and both red and green seedless grapes before catching a glimpse of Spencer's excited eyes as he handed her his present. She pulled her attention back toward his gift, accepting it graciously. Rue unwrapped it carefully to reveal a rectangular phone with buttons and no chord.

"Nokia cell phone," Spencer explained. "That way, I won't have to phone Midge to get ahold of you anymore. And check this out." He pulled a similar device from his jacket pocket and used his thumbs to awkwardly type at the keypad. A moment later, Rue's new phone buzzed. She looked down to read the first text message she'd ever seen in her life. "Happy birthday, darling," it read. "You are my favorite star stuff."

# Chapter 13
# Love Notes

Sunday at the Police Station

"It seems sad, really," Penelope commented to Detective Ortega as they were writing possible clues they had gathered so far on the large whiteboard they had bolted to the wall in Ortega's office.

"What does?" Detective Ortega asked, re-reading the message from the note they found tucked underneath the bra strap of Clarissa Sauer's dress after they found her dead, sprawled across several theater seats in the orchestra section following her fall.

"Well, if she and Astor Ellis *did* have a relationship, that she wouldn't recognize his handwriting," she explained.

"I'm afraid I don't follow," Ortega confessed.

"I mean, that evidence would suggest—at least so far—that the letter did not come from Astor Ellis himself, but someone just pretending to be him. Which means that in all the time that

Astor and Clarissa knew each other, she most likely had never received a love note from him...not even a card. Otherwise, I would think she'd know if it was his handwriting or not."

Detective Ortega thought about this for a moment. "Did I never write you a love note?"

Penelope was so surprised by the personal question that she gasped a little.

"Not unless you count pathology reports," she finally grinned, wryly.

"Well," Detective Ortega replied after a long and uncomfortable silence, "that was wrong of me."

"No use getting sentimental now," Penelope answered, adding a few more notes to the board with a green dry erase pen.

"What happened to us?" Ortega asked, seriously.

Penelope let out a sigh. She knew this question would come someday. Yet somehow, she thought 'someday' would have been more than a decade ago. Not now that Ortega had married and they'd both moved on. "Your work happened to us," she finally answered. "It's still happening to us," she confessed. "Only, it really doesn't matter anymore, does it?"

Detective Ortega thought of his wife. Nancy was a wonderful woman. Was he slowly pushing her away, too, in his quest for social justice? Maybe he was as bad a husband as he'd been a boyfriend when he and Penelope were together. Things at home had been strained lately.

He assumed they were normal stressors: finances, demanding relatives, Nancy's unruly teenage son who was not too keen about his mother being married to a police detective, and of course, work. Work was always stressful. There was no getting around that.

"It's so strange," Penelope drew Ortega out of his mind wandering.

"What is?" he asked.

"It's strange how there is nothing on the body or the scene—no stray hairs, no dandruff flakes, fingerprints, nothing to help connect us to the killer."

"They left the knife and the note," Ortega reasoned.

"Yes," Penelope acknowledged. "If I didn't know any better..."

"What is it?" Ortega persisted.

"It's almost as if the killer only left clues they wanted us to find." Penelope cycled through questions in her mind. *Had the killer accidentally sent Clarissa to the wrong box? Or were they trying to frame Darwin Fennec and Rue Brennan? But Darwin and Rue didn't know her. At least, that's what they said in their statements. What if they were lying?*

"Clever," Ortega acknowledged. "But if that's true, they'll make at least one critical mistake."

"What makes you say that?" Penelope wondered.

"Clever murderers are often narcissistic, at least the ones I've seen," Ortega answered. "They'll have to brag about their brilliance to someone."

Penelope paused for a moment "I know it's a long shot, but is there any chance that Clarissa was sent to that booth to discover Rue and Darwin together? Perhaps they were being outed and Clarissa Sauer and Darwin Fennec actually did know one another and quite well?"

"I suppose anything's possible. But then how does that explain how Clarissa ended up with a knife in her belly?"

Penelope pointed to the "weapons" section of the dry-erase board. "The knife was a prop from backstage. Though, I can't understand why a sharp kitchen knife was being used as a prop. Maybe Clarissa brought it with her?"

"What? To murder Astor Ellis? The note supposedly came from him and it sounded reconciliatory: 'I miss you. Can I see you? Meet me at Box 11 during the intermission. I made a mistake. Love, Astor.'" Ortega re-read the note, peering off into space. "Did I *really* never send you a love note, not a single one in three years?"

"Focus, Jose," Penelope called Detective Ortega by his first name. "Detective Ortega," she corrected as several officers passed the office door.

"Sorry," Ortega apologized. "It's just that...I'm trying to be better." He paused for a moment. "Nancy complains I don't listen to her. Did you feel that way, too?"

"Sometimes," Penelope admitted. "And only when you had your head buried in a case...which, now that I think about it, was most times."

"I'll bet your boyfriend, Garth, is a better listener."

"Gareth," she corrected.

"His name isn't Garth?"

No," she grinned. "It's always been Gareth."

"Hmmm," Ortega acknowledged, "maybe Nancy is right." Ortega scanned the dry-erase board trying to connect the dots.

How were Clarissa Sauer, Darwin Fennec, Rue Brennan, Astor Ellis, Byron Ellis, Gretchen Ellis and Portia LaMonte connected, other than being in neighboring booths during the show? An idea suddenly struck him.

Penelope recognized that look. "What is it?" She stood upright in anticipation.

"Rue Brennan is Spencer Hargrove's girlfriend," Ortega stared off into space. "I remember reading it recently in the tabloids, but she was at the theater with her boss, Darwin Fennec. Spencer Hargrove runs SpencerTech, while the Ellis family runs B. A. Ellis Industries. They hate one another."

"Do you think the murder is related?" Penelope asked. "Of course, you do, or you wouldn't have mentioned it," she shook her head at her own silliness.

"Let's just say my spidey sense is tingling," he joked, referencing the famous words of Spider Man. "Somehow, I feel this has less to do with Clarissa Sauer and more to do with Rue Brennan."

# Chapter 14
# SpencerTech

Monday at SpencerTech

"Thanks for meeting me here, Darwin." Spencer met Darwin at the back of a co-workspace ThinkLab building. "Let's take the stairs," he suggested, unlocking a door marked "members only."

It wasn't enough for Darwin to move his business to his home office, he still had to skirt the media. Fortunately, it seemed they had quickly lost interest in Rue and given up stalking her at home. She was still relatively unknown, whereas Darwin had been involved in several high-profile cases over the years.

*"Did you know Clarissa Sauer?"* they asked. *"Who was the woman you were with that evening on the balcony?" "An anonymous tip said the woman of interest is named Rue Brennan. Can you confirm that?"* It was relentless. Darwin and Rue began taking the service elevator and leaving his condo through the employee entrance and exits. The building's superintendent

wasn't too thrilled about it, but he agreed with the investigator's reasoning that the attention was causing concern from the other residents of the building. Their poor doorman faced the brunt of the onslaught and ceased to answer or acknowledge a single reporter's presence. On three occasions, security had to ask them to stop loitering or they would call the police.

SpencerTech was comprised of a large suite on the fourth floor, complete with three private offices, a common area, a room dedicated toward housing servers and equipment, a shared bathroom and a small utility closet, expensive by New York standards, but modest for a tech company trying to make itself appear bigger than it actually was.

"Hey dudes," a small, thin-framed man in his early twenties greeted the men as they passed his office. He was wearing a gray earflap beanie and a checkered flannel shirt over a plain black t-shirt and jeans.

Darwin gave a two-fingered salute, touching his forehead as if he were tipping an imaginary hat. "Hey Max," he acknowledged.

A taller, bulkier, and older man almost bumped into Darwin before catching himself. He had his nose in a pile of papers he'd just printed out. "Whoops, sorry D," the man touched Darwin's shoulder.

"No worries, Zain," Darwin responded. Zain was in his late thirties and still wore a dress shirt and tie to the office, regardless of whether they were seeing investors that day. He had dark skin and a thick accent and chronically had his head either in his books, paperwork, or behind a computer. Zain nodded and kept going. He was a busy man and the new lines of script he was formulating weren't going to code themselves.

Darwin and Spencer continued down the long hallway to Spencer's office—the largest and with a window view of the city. The room was sparse with one long chrome-colored desk and white leather chair lit by several overhead fluorescent lights.

The desktop was filled by two side-by-side full-sized computers with external speakers and a computer tower that stood between the two displays. On one corner of the desk sat a telephone with a small notepad, pen, and Rolodex. On the other was a stack of printed papers waited to be filed in one of the three file cabinets on the opposite wall.

There wasn't much in the room by way of personal memorabilia, though Darwin did note that Spencer had taken the time to put up exactly three framed pictures—one featuring a "Best in Innovation" award from B. A. Ellis industries, one with his Computer Science degree from NYU and an old photo of himself as a young boy with his arms around a long-haired Australian Shepherd. He was smiling as the dog's tongue hung out to one side, staring straight ahead with excited eyes.

*A picture of his old dog,* Darwin noted. *But not a single photo of Rue, not even a small one on his desk...interesting.*

"Well..." Spencer began.

Darwin held up a finger to his lips and Spencer fell quiet, nodding.

Darwin nimbly moved around the room, feeling under the desk and around the photo frames, taking parts of the phone receiver off and peering inside, looking for any signs of a bug.

Finally, he gave an all-clear sign and Spencer let out a sigh.

"Any new incidents?" Darwin asked.

"No," Spencer answered. "We've been shutting everything down each night after encrypting our data and backing it up to the server. The new security software, firewalls, and blockers your guy put in place seems to have our computers on lockdown."

Darwin wanted to tell him that the "guy" was actually a "gal," but kept his mouth shut.

"What about your home computer?"

"I've been really careful," Spencer explained. "I'm the only one able to remote in given your new protocol, not that I worry about Zain and Max. Zain I've known since we were kids and Max is my nephew who I practically helped raise. I trust them both completely. But..."

"But what?" Darwin pressed him.

Spencer crossed his arms. "When I was meeting with a potential investor the other evening, he very candidly told me that it was between supporting my new project, or a similar one being developed by my old employers at B. A. Ellis Industries."

"What's odd about that?"

"It's something he said." Spencer thought a moment. "While he had signed a non-disclosure agreement, he let something slip about the design software project they are ready to launch just two weeks after mine, unless I can get mine to market sooner."

"What was it?" Darwin stood upright.

"He said something about it having a stardust feature."

"Well, it is graphic design and computer animation software. Wouldn't it be likely that there would be a few built-in applications for the sun, moon and stars?"

"But he said stardust," he confirmed. "Stardust has been the name we thought about giving our product. Except, no one outside of the team knows that, and at this point, it's just an internal nickname."

Darwin let out a sigh. "Well then, I'd better get a couple of my team members to scour this place and your condo to make sure they're clean."

"Er, not the condo," Spencer hemmed and hawed.

"We have to secure your computer and make sure there's nothing compromising your outgoing or incoming messages."

"Look, I'm happy if you want to have your guy hack into my home computer, ethically of course, to see if they need to shore up any security issues, but I can assure you I don't talk business with anyone on my landline or cellular phone and the only one in my condo at present is me. And," he let out an awkward laugh, "I'm certainly not talking to myself!"

"Obviously, you're my client and I'll honor your wishes," Darwin conceded. "Though, I definitely think we should ensure that we investigate all sources that in any way send and receive info—either through your internal system or via external wires."

"Yeah, about that 'we'."

"Yes?"

"How is it going with Rue?"

"Oh, Rue...well, fine," Darwin stammered. "I'm beginning to teach her the basics of encryption and making sure confidential content is protected beyond simply usernames and passwords. She really is a quick study."

"Well," Spencer answered, "don't feel obligated to teach her too much."

"Eh, why's that?"

"I don't anticipate you needing to have her in your employ for long," he answered.

"Oh?"

"No, I just need you to...distract her, for a few more weeks, just until I secure the investments I need and beat B. A. Ellis Industries to market."

"Distract her? You mean...keep her out of your way?"

"Exactly," Spencer's smiled dropped when he saw Darwin's questioning expression. "Oh, don't get me wrong, she's a great girl. But she's not exactly the sort to make a good impression among investors, the media and future buyers...particularly not now with the recent spotlight on her."

Darwin ground his teeth but said nothing until he'd carefully framed his words. "I don't understand how she threatens to make a bad impression."

"Oh, come on. You've seen her!" he chortled. "She dresses like a bohemian, says whatever comes to her mind. Hell, she even eats green beans with her fingers...not even using a fork. Who does that?"

*I do,* Darwin had to admit to himself. *What's wrong with eating food with your fingers? Lots of countries around the world do that.*

Spencer interrupted Darwin's thoughts. "Just give her something to do to make her feel useful, as if she's helping me in some way by working for you. Understood?"

"Perfectly," Darwin answered, between clenched teeth.

That day, Darwin called Bristol from a spare Tracfone after walking down several flights of stairs, two at a time. He held his foot between the door and the frame to keep it from locking behind him.

"Hey, Finn, what's the word?" Bristol answered the phone in a huff. "Finn" was Bristol's nickname for Darwin, but it only made sense to the two men, as it came from a story from their somewhat murky past. Behind him, the sound of loud banging and a bandsaw could be heard.

"Need you to get our two trusted buddies to meet me at the dorm rooms to inspect the place for mice."

"You got it, Finn. You there now?"

"Just outside," Darwin answered.

"Great, I'm sure I can get them there in a jiffy."

"Oh, and Bristol?"

"Yeah, Finn?"

"Tell 'em to ignore the termites."

A snort could be heard on the other end of the line.

"Whatever you say, boss," he laughed.

"One more thing, just do me a favor and do your shimmy in about ten minutes? I need a distraction for Frat Boy."

"You got it, boss."

With that, Darwin hung up the phone.

He made his way back up the steps, winded this time. Darwin reminded himself that he should get more exercise. He did a fair bit of walking during the day, but he'd gotten lazy about taking the stairs instead of the elevator, a situation that had only gotten worse with the recent publicity and wanting to stay out of sight.

"Two of my team members should be here to secure the place in a few minutes. In the meantime, mind if I do a cursory search?" Darwin asked Spencer.

"Suit yourself," Spencer agreed. "Hey guys?" Spencer stood between the two rooms where Zain and Max were glued to their respective computers. "Mind if Darwin here scans your offices for bugs? He's also got a couple of his men stopping by, too."

"Nah," Max knew the drill and went to follow Zain to the common area for coffee, leaving behind their personal satchels and backpacks for inspection. Just for fun, Max turned suddenly to Darwin, contorted his face, and proceeded to pull up his black t-shirt, flashing his bare chest. "See? No wires!"

Zain flicked him on the arm. "Dweeb," he laughed.

Max dropped his shirt and beat his chest like Tarzan.

Darwin shook his head and smiled. *Inside every male web developer, programmer and cybersecurity nerd lives a 12-year-old boy just dying to get out.*

Just then, Spencer's phone rang.

"Hmm," Spencer furrowed his brow. "Excuse me," he told Darwin. On the other end, Bristol's boisterous voice could be heard. Except, it was distinctly more Jersey sounding than his usual voice. "Hey man, when you gonna come pickup your caw (car). I ain't got all day, ya know?"

"Who is this? I think you have the wrong numb—"

"Is this..." Bristol repeated the number.

"It is, but..." Spencer was flustered.

Darwin quickly made the rounds, planting a few cutting edge "termites" not available to the general public, in each of the "dorm" rooms, to include one in the bag Spencer left in his office. *For people so concerned about security, that was far too easy,* Darwin grinned as he once again, took the steps to ground level two at a time. He met his backup—the two young women Rue mistook for Darwin's paramours that day at the pier.

"Darwin, honey," the dark-haired woman cooed in her sultry voice, "we gotta stop meeting like this."

"Just lock the door behind you when you leave," he smirked, waving a finger at them. "And no funny business."

"Sure thing, Finn," the blonde answered, winking at him.

"Define 'funny business,'" the brunette demanded.

"The boys are off limits as are wallets and all things bright and shiny."

The blonde pouted. "When did you stop being fun, Finn?"

"I was never fun," Darwin countered. "Which reminds me. May I please have my wallet back, Candice?"

"What? I didn't..." the blonde appeared offended.

"C'mon, Candy," the brunette slapped her friend's arm. "Hand it over."

"You too, Monica." She was going to protest, but knew it was useless. Monica handed over Darwin's Breitling Chronograph watch.

"It's Monique now," the dark-haired woman protested. "And your watch is a knock-off, about as fake as my name...and yours."

"I am aware of that, thank you...Monique."

"You shouldn't carry this much cash on you, Finn," Candice handed him his wallet. "That's what banks are for."

"Thank you for the tip," he paused a moment, his wallet extended. "Ahem," he coughed.

Candice rolled her eyes and forked over the wad she'd already procured from his wallet.

"It was for expenses," she wrinkled her nose at him. "You think I wake up this beautiful?"

"I am very certain that you do," Darwin shot her a practiced smile.

"Glad not everyone is as much of a gentleman as you, Darwin," Monica who goes by Monique now explained, opening the employee door wide just as an older, balding man walked past, eyeing the women with interest. She purposefully shifted her hip to one side so the gawker could get a better look. "It'd be bad for business."

"As I mentioned," Darwin reiterated.

"We get it," she interrupted. "No touching the boys. C'mon Candy. We got work to do."

With that, Darwin put on a ball cap, lifted his shirt collar and did his best to slink his way through midtown unseen.

# Chapter 15
# Merriam Hall

Friday Evening at a Dance Hall

"I can't believe I let you talk me into this ridiculous dress, Midge." After a long work week, Midge insisted that she and Rue needed to 'let their hair down' and go clubbing.

"And the boots," Midge pointed a red lacquered nail toward Rue's faux leather, lace-up ankle boots with high heels. "If you're going to credit me, you gotta include the shoes."

"I wasn't crediting you, Midge," Rue replied, lining up behind a dozen other people at ten o'clock at night, waiting to get into Merriam Hall, Manhattan's premier dance club...for those just barely of legal drinking age through those who hadn't realized that they weren't in college anymore.

Midge fell into the latter of those categories but refused to be pigeon-holed by age. It seemed to work for her as her red hair, white powdered face with black lipstick, and her lime-green cocktail dress caught the admiration of a number of men a good decade her junior as they eyed the other women in the queue. "I was blaming you," Rue finished, tugging at the form-fitting leather mini-dress with a silver zipper that ran the length of it.

"Oh," Midge waved a hand at her. "Trust me. You'll thank me later. You look sexy as hell. If I went that way, I'd be all over you by now." Midge licked her forefinger and held it in the air like a barometer. "Gonna get chilly tonight on account of the winds."

"You are the weirdest person I have ever met."

"Why, thank you, Rue," Midge beamed proudly.

"That wasn't a compliment."

At that moment, a burly security guard mumbled a few words into a walkie-talkie as he surveyed the line. He eyed Rue from head-to-toe curiously. Midge smiled seductively, putting a hand on her thigh and thrusting her hip to one side. He was taken aback, but merely wrinkled his nose and moved on.

The security guard motioned to two women further down the line from where Midge and Rue waited for the doors to open. The two young ladies, falling into the "just barely legal" category, walked by proudly in their spiked heels and thigh-length dresses toward a roped-off door. The guard un-roped it as another attendant opened the door to the club and ushered them inside. The door was closed and the rope replaced.

"What the hell was that about?" Rue complained. "We've been standing here a half hour, and they got to waltz right past us!"

"Eh, don't worry about it," Midge replied. "They let the trampiest girls in first because it draws the men to the club. The more men there are, the more they spend on drinks for themselves and the ladies."

The guard walked down the line again, past a few college boys ogling the women around them, a few of these men cat-calling to several young ladies who were passing by. One of whom flicked them a finger. One particularly distasteful young man, standing just in front of them, followed the long line of Rue's zipper from top to bottom as if unzipping it with his mind. The guard took the cue.

"You can go on inside," he told Rue in a deep voice.

"Me, too!" Midge grabbed Rue's arm. "It's a package deal."

The corner of the guard's mouth started to twitch until he beat the smile down and returned to a frown. "You girls enjoy your evening."

Apparently, the two were fairly high on the trampiest looking list.

"Catch you inside," Midge told the young man who had been eyeing Rue, fingered the collar of his dress shirt and winked, never losing his gaze. He grinned back as one his friends jabbed him in the ribs as if egging him on.

"What was that about?" Rue whispered when they'd reached the door.

"Two things, really," Midge explained. "Once he realizes that one, your legs are closed and are not open for business, and two, that acne-prone face isn't gonna get him too far, he'll fall right into my web."

"That's disgusting, Midge," Rue chastised. "And I thought you had a new boyfriend." Rue vaguely remembered Midge recounting her latest trip to Atlantic City, but she tuned out the details of the man she supposedly met at the roulette table. Midge did a lot of dating...a lot of gambling...a lot of drinking... well, a lot of everything, really.

Once Rue reached the door, she pulled out cash and the attendant inside stamped her hand with a green, glow-in-the-dark logo.

Midge fished around in her purse for money and a few coins spilled out over the floor. "Sorry," she apologized to the impatient attendant, kneeling down to pick up the change she had strewn.

Rue couldn't even lean over to help her because the dress was too tight and so short, she really didn't feel like revealing her underwear to the world.

Midge finally resurfaced, handing the attendant the change and ever-so-slowing dipping into her purse and digging for a few more dollar bills.

"You know what?" the attendant forced a smile, peering at the fresh crop of women trying to get in followed by the few men that they were finally admitting. "Don't worry about it. You just go on inside and enjoy yourself." The attendant stamped her hand.

"Thank you," Midge tipped an invisible hat, grabbing Rue's arm and leading her toward the first bar they could find. "Works every time," she yelled above the pounding mix of rock and metal music.

"What does?" Rue wanted to know.

"I only paid $5.75 for admission instead of $15. That's a bargain if you ask me."

"That was a scam?"

"More like a grift," Midge explained. "C'mon, if they're gonna rob us by charging $6 for a bottle of Corona, then I think I should at least get my first beverage on the house."

"Alabama Slammer," Midge called to the bartender who nodded before turning his eyes to Rue.

"Uh," Rue fumbled.

"She'll have the same," Midge finished. The man nodded, wiping out a few glasses and then pulling a bottle of Southern Comfort off the shelf.

"What happened to the Corona?" Rue was confused.

"What?" Midge was distracted. In fact, she looked as if she were twitching and ready to jump out of her very skin. "By the way," she continued. "I think your white lace panties would have gone better with this dress, just sayin'," Midge offered helpfully.

Rue was dumbfounded until she realized that with her friend crawling on the floor gathering her change, she had gotten an intimate look at Rue's...well, intimates. "Do I even want to know how you know what's in my underwear drawer?"

"Probably not," Midge confessed. "Let's just say it was laundry day and I would have been going freestyle if I didn't."

"Midge!" Rue held up a hand. "Boundaries! No rifling through my drawers anymore, got it?"

Just then, the bartender set the drinks down with a smirk. He winked at Rue. Rue grabbed the drink and took a large gulp. "You're getting this round," she commanded of Midge. "It's the least you can do for violating my underwear drawer."

"Deal," Midge plopped a twenty-dollar bill on the counter. "Keep the change," she said to the bartender.

"There isn't any," he grumbled, swiping the bill and delivering it to the cash register.

Midge didn't seem to notice, nor was she inclined to leave a tip. "Let's dance," she finally suggested, grabbing Rue's arm and dragging her to the main dance floor. There were three others, one on the lower level, one on the second floor, and another down the hall. This room was the largest and featured a series of long stone steps leading all the way up to what one would assume was an altar if it were Aztec times. Instead, the DJ sat on his thrown on high, strobe lights flooded all around him with a movie screen behind him flashing odd abstract images.

Rue was a lightweight and within minutes on the dance floor was already beginning to feel the effects of her beverage. However, she noticed, the alcohol dulled the obnoxiously loud music and sounds from the crowd, so she kept drinking.

Two men slinked up to the ladies and Rue suddenly had a dance partner who reached out and gently touched her hips with his hands and began swaying. Instinctively, Rue, in turn, put her hands on his shoulders as the two continued to move in an awkward side-to-side motion. Occasionally, her new dance partner would take a step forward or back and Rue would follow.

At some point, he took her hand and led her through a twirl, but halfway through it, another woman grabbed the forearm of Rue's dance partner and he willingly dropped Rue's hand to go off with the new woman. Rue turned, surprised, standing alone on the dance floor, surrounded by a crowd, some couples and some dancing in a group.

She drained her drink and deposited her plastic glass in a bin near the bar. As Rue spun around, it seemed she already found herself with a new dance partner. This man was much shorter than the first and a bit grabbier. He wrapped an arm around her waist and pulled her to his chest, lifting her right hand with his and hugging it to his shoulder. This man smelled like whiskey and Marlboros and made her nose itch. He was also a little too sweaty.

Rue tried to politely back away, no easy feat with the dance floor so packed that many were shoulder-to-shoulder. She gazed around the room trying to find Midge, but despite her obvious bright red hair, Midge somehow blended in with the strobe lights and smoke machines obscuring everyone's features.

"Where ya goin', darlin'?" The man pulled her aggressively toward him.

Rue shook her head, pulling away. "I can't hear you!" she explained in vain. "But I don't want to dance anymore!"

He couldn't hear her either as he merely smiled and tugged her in a hug, planting a kiss on her cheek—a sweaty, whiskey and Marlboro one. "Where ya goin' darlin?" he said again, blinking as if in slow motion.

This time, Rue pushed her hands against his chest. "Sorry!" she yelled, pointing toward the DJ, "but I can't hear you above 'Smells Like Teen Spirit!'"

The man obviously misinterpreted her gestures, smiling and

turning toward the DJ, holding up a clear plastic cup with a lingering piece of ice melting at the bottom. "I feel stupid and contagious," he started yelling the song lyrics and smiling. He thought she just really liked the song.

Rue took it as her cue. As he gazed up the steps at the DJ stand, singing at the top of his lungs, she pushed her way through the crowd until she came to a dark hallway leading to another room. Grateful to get away from her dance partner and the noise, she followed the hallway which opened up to a smaller room that was slightly less crowded. In it, a live band played a combination of reggae and funk.

"You look like you need a drink," a well-muscled man with long dreadlocks handed her a glass filled with ice and clear liquid. He smiled. "Go ahead, I didn't take a sip yet, and can get me another."

"What is it?" she asked curiously. To be clear, Rue most certainly did *not* need another drink, and had she been right of mind, she wouldn't have accepted this one.

"Oh, just a gin and tonic," he smiled, signaling to the bartender standing behind a nearby counter for another. This dance hall seemed to have a three-to-one ratio of bars to dance floors.

"Thanks," Rue smiled, taking a sip. This man already seemed more polite than the last.

"What's your name?" he asked, flashing his pearly whites.

"Rue Brennan," another woman answered, agitated, slinking up next to the man and taking his arm, possessively—Ursula Gorky.

Ursula was a fellow figure model at the Artist Atelier. She had a slightly larger frame than Rue and her long brown hair cascaded over her shoulders. She flashed her blue eyes at Rue. "I saw you at the theater the other night," she stated coldly. "I saw what you did."

"I don't know what you're talking about," Rue answered, taking another sip of her drink. Her head was starting to feel a little fuzzy which she attributed to having two drinks, dancing, and possibly being a little dehydrated.

"You pushed my best friend over the balcony," Ursula clarified.

"Whoa, ladies," the man put one arm around each of them, detaching from Ursula's grasp. "Let's not argue. You're much prettier when you smile. Let's have a smile." Ursula was unresponsive. He tried again, "Let me get you a drink," he offered.

"No thanks," she spat, but he'd already retreated to the bar to pick up his replacement beverage.

"I didn't push her," Rue explained, "I tried to catch her."

"Then why did you lie to the police?" she challenged.

"What are you talking about?"

"You told them your date was there with you when it happened, but I saw you from the opposite balcony. You were alone with Clarissa." Her eyes grew red with anger.

"Listen, I can't say anything about the case while it's being investigated..."

"You mean while *you're* being investigated."

"And," Rue realized, "how could you possibly know what I did or did not tell the police?"

Someone bumped into Ursula from behind. "Excuse me." It was Midge. Attached to her like lichen on a tree branch, the acne-ridden boy from the line clung to her, his arms wrapped around her waist as he sniffed her hair and smiled. To Ursula, she commanded, "Just shut your pie hole. You don't know what you're talking about."

"Freaky," the muscular man returned, offering a beverage to Ursula who turned it down a second time. He was staring at Midge's hair and lime green dress with admiration.

"I'll take that," she grabbed it from him and gulped it down in under ten seconds. "Thanks, I was parched."

"No problem," he smiled at her.

Just then, an athletic-looking woman with short brown hair and blonde streaks in it bounced in.

"Ursula," she called loudly.

For a moment, Ursula put her aggression on hold. "Emma!" she squealed, giving her friend a huge hug that involved rocking from side to side for an uncomfortably long time. "You made it!"

"Let me introduce you to Jordie, my...new friend."

Jordie, the smooth-talking man who liked delivering drinks like Santa during Christmas, flashed a toothy grin at Emma.

"Nice to meet you," he almost growled, surveying the woman from top to bottom.

Emma noticed and didn't appreciate it.

"Get you a drink?" he asked, winking.

"Long Island iced tea?" she asked. He may have been lechy, but drinks at the club weren't cheap, so...

"My kind of girl," he grinned, while Ursula shot him her best, 'you're supposed to be with me look.'

The fogginess in Rue's head worsened. She grabbed Emma's arm and asked, "Sure you should be drinking...in your condition?"

Emma pulled her arm back. "What the hell are you talking about, freak? Condition? I'm not pregnant!"

"Sorry, I just..."

"Hey, listen, Rue," Midge interrupted, "can you find your own way home? Tommy here invited me back to his place."

Rue's brain fumbled to make sense of what Midge was asking as the strobe lights and loud music further confused her.

"I can see to it that your friend gets home safely," Jordie offered.

"No, you can't," Ursula jumped in. "She can find her own

damn way home." She dragged the man reluctantly to the dance floor in time for a slow song. Over her shoulder, she called, "I told the cops I saw you with that man. Even if you didn't do it, you're hiding something."

Midge flicked her middle finger at Ursula.

Rue put her hand on Midge's arm to steady herself.

"Hey, you okay?" Midge asked, concerned.

"Yeah," Rue answered. "Think I need some fresh air. I'm gonna head out. I'll catch a cab or something."

Tommy nibbled on Midge's ear. Unlike the whiskey and Marlboro man, Tommy smelled like Nag Champa and possibly weed.

"Okay, catch you later," Midge turned and planted her lips onto Tommy's and the two remained lip-locked as they headed to the dance floor.

Emma, it would seem, was left abandoned by everyone, so she approached the bar to order her own Long Island Iced Tea. She let out a sigh as she took a sip. *Sometimes, I wonder about my life choices,* she thought to herself.

Meanwhile, Rue stumbled to the nearest exit sign. The cold wind hit her in the face and she accidentally dropped her empty cup on the ground. It tumbled quickly away, but she was too dizzy to go after it. Instead, she hung onto the outside wall of the club as the door behind her slammed shut. She gazed groggily around at the back alley where she landed. It smelled of sewage and urine. Large trash bags were piled up in varied spots on either side of the narrow walkway. She jumped as a large rat darted past her in search of its next dinner. She heard a noise behind her and turned to see two men making their way toward her. It was dark and she couldn't see their faces in the shadow.

"Hey, lady," one of them called to her.

The hairs on her neck stood up. *This can't be good,* she thought to herself.

She went to tug at the club's door, but there was no handle. She was locked out.

She moved as quickly as she could toward the other end of the alley where she had a partial view of the streetlights and road.

"Don't be afraid of us, bitch," the second man yelled, picking up speed. They could have caught her easily in her state, but they seemed to enjoy watching her terrified reaction as she fled and were careful to keep just enough space so she had the lead. Like two cats cornering a mouse, they were playing with her.

It wasn't until she'd reached the street that one of them grabbed her arm. "What's your hurry?" he asked, pulling her toward him and pushing her against the wall of the club.

"Get away from me," she called, raising a knee to his groin. He doubled over in pain and let out a few expletives as she shoved him into his friend. The friend pushed him aside and lunged for Rue.

She began running, as fast as she could in clunky, high-heeled shoes and a form-fitting leather dress. She regained some of her balance, probably due to sheer adrenaline.

Despite the millions of people living in New York City, they appeared to be the only ones around on this desolate stretch of road at this time of night. There were several lanes going in each direction, divided by a small concrete island. The wind howled as the temperature dropped. Rue shivered.

The men were gaining on her, this time not intent on letting her get away.

Just then she heard a car horn blaring as a yellow cab darted across multiple lanes of traffic, navigating expertly around the island, and stopping at the curb in front of her. The passenger door clicked open.

"Get in," the driver commanded through the open window.

She obeyed, slamming the door behind her just as one man reached through the window and tugged at her hair.

He yelled a few more derogatory words at her as his friend slammed the trunk of the cab with his fist as it sped off, leaving the two of them alone in the middle of the street, one holding a tiny clump of Rue's hair.

It was only then that Rue realized who the driver was.

"Bristol?" she asked.

"Guilty as charged," he grinned. He was wearing a cabby cap and chewing on a toothpick. He eyed her dress curiously. "Eh, nice dress." He left it at that.

"How did you know I was here?"

"Well," he stammered. "Let's just say it was my turn to look after ya."

"Look after me?" She heard and felt her stomach growl. Rue was feeling a little queasy.

"GPS tracker in your phone," he explained. "Say, are you all right?" The sound of her stomach did not escape his attention.

"I feel a little funny," she cringed as her stomach cramped.

"We're only a few blocks from your place, hang tight." He hit the gas and picked up speed, strategically taking a few little-known side roads to get there faster. Fortunately, traffic was not as heavy as it usually was in the Greenwich Village area.

Rue's head was pounding. "How do you know where I live?" she wondered aloud. She'd always taken the subway to Darwin's place, walking the final few blocks in an attempt to avoid reporters who appeared to have gotten bored with *her* story after only a few days, but seemed overly curious about her interactions with Darwin Fennec. "The tracker thingy?"

"Exactly."

"I didn't know phones had them."

"Most don't," he explained. "But give it a few years and every phone will have one."

"Why would people want the ability to be tracked through their phone?" Rue doubted the logic of this invention.

"Well, tonight's a good example."

Rue moaned. "I don't feel so hot."

Bristol parked on the corner of Rue's apartment complex in a handicapped zone. He quickly hung a paper tag on the mirror.

Rue was feeling too sick to argue, but Bristol could read the judgment in her eyes.

"What?" he defended. "It's for emergencies."

He helped her out of the car, but she pushed her way passed him. She managed to climb the steps at lightning speed as Bristol was still grabbing the door at the base of her complex so he didn't get locked out. He followed her, taking the steps two at a time.

She burst into her studio apartment and ran to the bathroom, just in time to vomit into the toilet. In her kitchen, she heard Bristol opening cabinets and the refrigerator.

Embarrassed, she flushed the toilet. Fortunately, she was otherwise unsoiled as she brushed her hair back and rinsed her mouth out. She then took the time to brush her teeth and rinse with mouthwash.

"Better?" Bristol asked when she returned.

On the table, he laid out a glass of ginger ale and a few salted crackers he found in the cabinet.

"Yeah, just embarrassed." She took a cracker and nibbled on it. "I didn't think I drank that much."

"What'd you have?" Bristol asked, curiously.

"An Alabama Slammer," she thought a moment. "And then someone gave me a gin and tonic."

"Someone?" Bristol raised an eyebrow.

"Yeah, just some guy who was trying to get a few of us drunk, I guess."

"I'd say he was doing more than that," Bristol shook his head. "Listen, sweetheart, and I say this with respect. Never, *and I mean never*, accept a drink from a stranger, unless it goes directly from the bartender into your pretty little hands."

Rue nodded.

"And furthermore," he continued. Apparently, the lesson wasn't over yet. "Never leave your drink unattended, capisce?"

"Understood. Thanks for rescuing me, Bristol. Though I'm really uncomfortable with the fact that you were tracking me. Was that Darwin's doing?"

Bristol held his hands up. "Look, you didn't hear it from me, but I happen to know he's very concerned about you being in the center of a murder and all. Plus, with your boyfriend's new product launch..."

"Do you think they're connected?" This was the first Rue was hearing of this. Up until this moment, she assumed they were two separate events.

"Look, I've already said too much." Bristol put his forefinger and thumb to his lips as if turning a key to lock his lips.

"Tell you what..." Rue took a sip of the ginger ale. After all, she reasoned, Bristol wasn't a stranger, and he proved to be trustworthy so far.

"What's that?" Bristol folded his arms.

"You don't tell Darwin about my awful state tonight and I won't mention that you spilled the beans about SpencerTech's connection."

"Alleged connection," he corrected.

"Alleged connection," she confirmed, "between Clarissa's death and SpencerTech's launch. My lips are sealed unless Darwin brings it up himself. Deal?"

"Deal," he smiled.

"And thanks again," Rue whispered, quietly.

"Aw, tonight was nothing," Bristol laughed, walking toward the door. "If you saw how many times I had to all but carry Darwin home after he got shit-faced when we used to live..." He caught himself again. "Eh, never mind."

"Thanks again, Bristol," she acknowledged.

"No problem. You just get some rest." Bristol quietly closed the door behind him and made his way back to his cab. A few bystanders eyed him, annoyed. Realizing why, he adopted a limp. "Had to get my mother up three flights of stairs and neither one of us walk none too good," he explained.

They nodded, sympathetically, and kept walking.

Once inside the cab, Bristol made a phone call. "Yeah, not sure if they're still there, but you may want to check out two mugs in the back alley of the Merriam. They seem to be preying on those without their wits about 'em. Not too sure what's going on inside, neither. I suspect there's some funny business with the drinks." He paused to listen to the person on the other end. "Yeah, no problem, Dennis. Happy ta help."

With that, Bristol removed the handicapped sign and made his way toward his garage.

# Chapter 16
# Hangover

Saturday Morning at Rue's Apartment

A tiny beam of sunlight sliced its way through the curtained window, hitting Rue in the eye. She rolled over and shielded her eyes. She had a splitting headache, and she had a taste in her mouth that made her sure something crawled in and died there while she was sleeping.

Rue pulled back the sheets of her bed and dragged herself to her feet, shuffling her way to the bathroom to rinse her mouth out for what became the fourth time since she was sick last night. She still felt queasy, so Rue went back to the kitchen for more of the ginger ale and a few crackers. There were a few gaps in last night's events, but she seemed very clear on Midge ditching her for a boy named Tommy, men chasing her down the alley and Bristol bringing her home where she was finally sick. Rue also remembered what he'd said about Clarissa's possible connection to SpencerTech, but she couldn't let Darwin know. But why wouldn't he have told her? Was he worried she'd talk too much to Spencer? Or that whatever it was would put her in danger? Was Spencer in danger?

She rubbed her head and stopped thinking. Every time she did, the throbbing became worse. How much did she have to drink last night?

Rue left the ale and crackers on the kitchen table and went to cover the window in her bedroom completely and climb back into bed.

Before she did, however, she saw the sliver of a flash of red through the edge of the cloth cover. This was followed by a tap on the window...Midge.

"Good, you're up," she leaned over, peering in the window. "C'mon out on the ledge, I've got Bloody Marys to help recover from last night. Or, I can come in...either way."

It was then that the rest of the evening came flooding back... the grabby dance partner who smelled of cigarettes and whiskey, a well-spoken muscular man who handed her a drink that she now knew had likely been laced with something, and Bristol telling her that she was on "his watch," that night—presumably another thing that she wasn't supposed to know.

Midge finally paused to take stock of her friend. "Wow, you look like crap. What happened?"

"Someone drugged me at the club, two men almost raped me and were it not for one of Darwin's friends intervening, I'd probably be lying dead in a gutter by now."

"Huh," was all Midge could say before finally adding, "Sounds about right for one of my Saturday nights. Glad you're okay, though."

Rue eyed her friend with a mix of bewilderment and anger. This was the same woman who insisted on accompanying her to meet Darwin about a job in broad daylight. Yet somehow Midge was apathetic about today's news. Why? She was beginning to question Midge's mental health.

"So, can I come in?" Midge was wearing jeans and a sweater and already had one leg over the ledge, her clunky leather shoe dangling in mid-air.

"No, Midge, you can't," Rue stopped her.

"Well, why the hell not?" Midge protested, eyeing her curiously after realizing that Rue hadn't called her by her affectionate friend term "Mensa." She pulled her leg back and then squatted down on both feet, waiting for an explanation.

"Why?" Rue rubbed her bloodshot eyes, the pounding in her head matching the pounding of her heart. "Because every time I'm near you, bad things have a way of happening. You try and set me up with Darwin and now I'm a suspect in a murder trial. You drag me to a club and abandon me for a fling with that pimply-faced kid."

"Tommy Marcuzzo," Midge finished. "And he was sweet," she reminisced.

"Men groped me, and I was attacked."

"How was that my fault?" Midge was offended.

Rue let out a long sigh. "It's not your fault, Midge. It's just that these are just two of a long history of catastrophes that all seem to have one common denominator—you."

"Well, gee, if you feel that way about it," Midge pouted.

"I just think I need a little space from you. No knocking on my window any time you feel like it. No messing with my love life, and certainly no rifling through my lingerie drawer."

"Fine," Midge's eyes grew dark. "Go back to your boring life with your boring Spencer. I won't interfere." Midge began her ascent back to her apartment, somehow expecting that Rue would feel bad and stop her. When she didn't, she doubled back. "Oh, and by the way, Tommy used to be an intern at B. A. Ellis

Industries a while back. That lady who took a tumble off the balcony? Clarissa Sauer?"

Rue's ears perked up. "What about her?"

"Astor Ellis was having a not-so-secret affair with her while dating his now fiancé, Portia LaMonte. Tommy constantly had to cover for Astor. Turns out, he dumped her once the papers got wind of it. Didn't you say his family was in the next booth over at the theater? Sounds pretty fishy to me. But, whatever."

Rue felt like a heel, even more so given that she was already well aware of Clarissa's involvement with Astor, but that was information garnered at work and she couldn't share it with Midge.

"Look, Midge, I'm..."

"No, no," Midge waved her hand. "I get it, no more interfering from me. Except you should also know that he somehow convinced his former lover to hooch up to someone at Spencer-Tech and do a little snooping."

Rue thought about this. As far as she knew, Zain was still married to his high school sweetheart, so that left young Max. He might just be gullible enough to be swayed by a pretty, older woman with a lilting voice.

"Why would she help him after he broke her heart?"

"Apparently, he was having second thoughts about Portia who didn't understand him as well as Clarissa. The usual bullshit when a man wants to make sure he's got a plan B lined up in case things don't work out with the current one."

"Or he was just using her."

"Either way, I'm encroaching on your personal space, so I'll just be going." She turned to go. "Oh," Midge circled back, "and just one more thing."

"Yes?"

"Your boyfriend Spencer supposedly signed an intellectual property agreement with B. A. Ellis Industries when he worked for them ten years ago. Astor and Byron Ellis pitched a fit when Spencer launched his company. From their perspective, all of his current ideas came while he worked for them. So..."

"They think he stole from them on a technicality."

"Don't know. Sorry, I'm still invading your personal space." Midge sniffed the air indignantly. "You're just like my *former* friend Louisa. Fixed her up with a perfectly good man. But did she appreciate it, no...insisted on staying with her deadbeat husband. Neither you, nor she, have any appreciation for the lengths I go to help my friends."

"C'mon, Midge. Try to understand."

"Oh, I understand all right. You're forgetting...146 IQ and all. But you know where I am when you realize that life is way more exciting with me in it, than without." With that, Midge climbed the emergency fire escape, stomping as hard as possible along the way, making the metal rails vibrate. Upstairs, she could be heard closing her window—loudly.

# Chapter 17
# Not a Girl



Monday Morning at Darwin's Condo

"How was your weekend, Ms. Brennan?" Darwin asked when Rue arrived for work on Monday morning. Three days later and her head still hurt.

"Fine," she answered. "Pretty quiet," she lied. "And you?"

"About the same," he answered. There was a thickness in the air, the kind you feel where you suspect that neither person is telling the truth, but you don't want to call them out on it.

It had been nearly two weeks since Clarissa's death and reporters had since gotten bored with them. Unfortunately, their stalking had not been without incident, as vandals not only made a mess of Darwin's downtown agency, but they managed to bust a plumbing pipe on the premises, causing considerable water damage. He was still sorting out the mess with his landlord. So, they continued to meet at Darwin's condo, for now.

Rue walked into the kitchen to store a tuna sandwich in the

refrigerator for lunch, setting it on the shelf below one of Darwin's dark-green beverage containers and store-bought Mediterranean salad.

"Do you eat anything for lunch that isn't green?" Rue asked.

"Do you eat anything that isn't sandwiched between processed white bread?" He motioned toward the tuna sandwich she just put in the frig and then turned to point at the bagel she had sitting on her desk along with a cup of tea. "I picked up breakfast for you, as promised."

"Fair point," she acknowledged. "And...thanks."

"Spirulina is good for the little gray cells," Darwin explained, even though Rue hadn't asked. He pointed to his temple.

"You've lost me," Rue admitted.

"My green drink," he explained. "Made up of blended kale, apple, celery, cucumber and a bit of Spirulina...good for the body and brain."

If she hadn't been hung over just two days prior, she might not have looked as queasy as she did at that moment.

"Mind shutting the refrigerator door?" Darwin pointed to where Rue stood with the door to the frig hanging wide open. "Energy is expensive...and, are you okay?" he asked. "You look a little green around the gills."

Rue nodded and closed it haphazardly. "I'm fine. I must have stood too close to your drink," she joked, returning to her desk. *Probably should get a little food in me, though,* Rue thought. She sat and nibbled a few bites of her breakfast bagel and took a tentative sip of her tea, still too hot. Meanwhile, Darwin took her place in the kitchen to pour himself a cup of coffee. He had his own routine, coffee for breakfast and a green smoothie and salad for lunch.

Moments later, Darwin's front door burst open. "I knew you'd come calling when that plain little assistant of yours didn't work out. Second time in less than a week." Monica (who goes by

Monique now) sashayed her way across the threshold of Darwin's home office wearing a tight black dress that only reached mid-thigh with 4" red-spiked heels and a matching scarf wrapped around her neck. The scarf was longer than her dress and nearly reached her knees.

It was then that Monique saw Rue and wrinkled her nose a little.

"Oh," she offered flatly. "You're still here. Hadn't seen you since that day at the Seaport and assumed..." Monique didn't feel the need to finish the sentence. It was only then that Rue recognized her. She was one of the two women cooing over Darwin at her interview.

Darwin ignored the exchange, returning from the kitchen with two cups of coffee. "Good, you're here," he said to Monique as he handed her one of the cups. "Tall, no cream or sugar, right?"

"That's right, baby," Monique accepted the cup. "Just the same as I like my men—tall, dark, and bitter."

"Monique, may I introduce you to Rue. You met Rue at the pier two weeks ago, remember?"

"Oh, I remember," Monique shot Rue a fake smile before taking a sip of her coffee, leaving a bright red lipstick stain on the rim.

"I have an assignment for you both. Monique, I'm afraid you're going to need a different outfit for today, of the jeans and t-shirt variety."

"Boring," Monique set her coffee cup on the table next to Rue and began unwrapping the scarf that was around her neck.

"Candy secured press passes for you both." Darwin walked over to his desk, procuring two clip-on passes. He handed one to each of the women.

"Passes for what?" Rue was curious.

"B. A. Ellis Industries is having a small press event with a behind-the-scenes tour of the company. It's part of their 'transparency' initiative to embrace the media. This works out perfectly for us." Darwin leaned against the back of the couch. "Rue, I need you to play journalist for..." he motioned for her to hand the pass back so he could look at it, "*The Tech Boom Times?*" He shook his head. Candice was having a little too much fun being creative. "Monique, they are expecting a male photographer so..."

"Why can't she be the man?" Monique whined. "It's much easier for a woman to play a man versus the other way around. I can fix her up in no time."

"I like her better as a woman, thank you."

"Oh, I'll bet you do," Monique winked.

Rue was perplexed. Monique smiled and finished unwrapping her scarf, revealing a very large Adam's apple. She proceeded to tug at her hair and a well-fitted wig came off in her hands. Monique then dug into her purse for a cloth makeup wipe, expertly removing her eye, cheek and lip makeup in one swift motion. Rue watched, mesmerized.

"Darwin, honey, help me with the back." Darwin obliged, unzipping the back of Monique's dress part-way, just enough so that she could reach behind her back to unzip it the rest of the way.

"You can change in there," Darwin pointed to the spare bathroom on the other side of the room, next to a closet.

But Monique couldn't resist pulling the top of her dress down and tugging at the heavily padded bra. She turned her back toward both of them, dropping the bra on the floor as she made her way to the bathroom, pausing at the closet with her dress hanging around her waist, to fish out a pair of jeans and a t-shirt that Darwin had left for her.

Once she'd closed the door, Rue asked, "So, I guess Monique stays here a lot, seeing as you have a spare wardrobe for her....er, or him?"

Darwin cleared his throat and walked over to the now-open closet. He pulled out several hangers to show them to her—a dress, a pair of pants, a long-sleeved men's shirt. "Much like an array of costumes you might find at the theater, I have several on hand for a few contractors who do work for me."

Rue paused, taking the information in.

"So, no," Darwin clarified, "I can assure you that Monique does *not* stay here a lot or at all, for that matter."

"Your loss," Monique answered as she re-emerged from the bathroom wearing a black t-shirt and blue jeans, barefoot. Only this time, she was a *he* and the timbre and pitch of his voice were noticeably deeper.

"By the way, it's Monte," he offered Rue his hand as if meeting for the first time. "My given name is Montgomery, but no one but my mother ever called me that. Call me Montgomery, and I'll have to scratch your eyes out."

"Nice to meet you." Rue shook his hand, cautiously, watching as the Adam's apple bobbed up and down.

"What, haven't you ever seen a man this stunning before?" He winked. Frankly, Rue thought Monte looked better as a man with wavy, black hair that reached about an inch below his earlobes. Without the fake eyelashes and presumably, green contact lenses, she could see that his eyes were a deep brown. Honestly, she didn't know why he would want to cover them up. He had a square jaw that seemed more pronounced without the scarf.

"Just surprised is all," Rue choked out. To Darwin, she asked, "So, what's my disguise? Anything in that wardrobe for me?"

"Why would you need a wardrobe?" Darwin asked. "What you're wearing is fine. And you have experience as a journalist. You'll blend right in."

"But I'm Spencer Hargrove's girlfriend," she explained. "Won't someone at B. A. Ellis Industries recognize me and find it odd that the competitor's girlfriend would be taking a behind-the-scenes tour?"

"Funny," Darwin explained. "I guess I hadn't thought of that given that I've never actually seen you and Spencer out in public together."

Come to think of it, neither had Rue. At least not at public events, usually just dark movie theaters and restaurants.

"We could give her a goth-look black wig, white makeup and lipstick. I can fix her up in a jiffy," Monte offered.

"No, then she'll stand out *too* much."

"Then leave her as she is. I promise you; no one will notice that little scrap of a thing in whatever this is," he made a sweeping motion over Rue's plain black knee-length flair skirt and tan sweater. Spencer always criticized her colorful wardrobe, and she was doing her best to dress more demurely for work.

"You realize I'm standing right in front of you, *Montgomery*," Rue hissed.

"Trollop." Monte stuck his tongue out.

"Ladies, please," Darwin chastised. He paused to look at Rue's face, making a little too much eye contact. She felt her cheeks getting warm. "Hmmm," he said.

"What, hmmm?"

Monte stood beside Darwin and began eyeing Rue in the same way.

"Maybe we make a few subtle adjustments, so she looks different enough not to raise any eyebrows."

"Like actually filling out her eyebrows a bit more," Monte suggested.

"Exactly. We can line her lips a little more, so they don't look so thin." Darwin pointed.

"It's rude to point," Rue complained. *And what was so bad about having thin lips? No one had ever complained about them before.*

"A few hair extensions," Monte added.

"Do we have time for that?" Darwin asked.

"Probably not. Perhaps just a beret or hat to tuck her hair in?"

"Excellent idea."

Over the next fifteen minutes, Rue sat miserably as the two men fixed her hair and makeup and added a few pieces of silver and beaded jewelry that a journalist on a budget would wear. Then, she caught a glimpse of herself in the mirror, and realized that maybe she should let other people dress her up from now on. She looked pretty darn cute if she said so herself.

"Now for the important part," Darwin told them. "The assignment is two-fold. One, we need to keep an eye out for Astor Ellis. As head of Research & Development and next in line for the Ellis Industries throne, he will certainly make an appearance. His office is on the third floor overlooking the research lab below. You're going to need to see if you can access his office, either during the tour or when he steps out to lunch, which is almost always at noon sharp."

"What are we looking for?" Rue asked.

"On behalf of our contract with Spencer, we need to survey what his computer setup is, and any clues as to who might be sending him intel and how. And at Gretchen Ellis's request, see if there's a little black book or some evidence as to who else he might be seeing. Personally, I think he's going to behave himself for a while, at least until he takes over the company and he and Portia LaMonte marry."

"But that's still three months away," Monte pointed out. "Men like that can't keep it in their pants for that long, even with a hottie like Portia LaMonte on their arm."

"Perhaps," Darwin acknowledged. "Just be careful. Keep an eye out for surveillance cameras and if it seems too risky, bow out and we'll find another way."

# Chapter 18
# B. A. Ellis Industries

Monday Afternoon at a Press Gathering

Monte and Rue blended with relative ease on the tour. To their surprise, no one actually asked for any form of ID. They merely flashed their press badges and that was enough for the guard at the front desk to motion them to join the rest of the group which consisted of about a dozen other reporters and photographers from local newspapers and TV groups.

A tour guide wearing a sharp blue and white suit jacket and skirt greeted them. She had a small red cravat around her neck and looked more like a stewardess then a host at a tech company.

"We're so excited you've decided to join us today," she beamed a row of perfectly straight and obviously whitened teeth at them. "A few housekeeping rules before we begin our tour," she began. "Photography is permitted everywhere except within the lab itself," she cautioned. "Due to proprietary concerns, the lab is off limits. But our publicist will happily provide you with pre-approved photos should you wish to write an article about your experience today, and," she winked, "we hope you do."

Rue reached into the small hip purse Darwin's wardrobe provided her and pulled out a wintergreen Lifesaver, popping it into her mouth. She offered Monte one just as the tour guide looked at her.

"No food or beverages are permitted in the lab," she smiled sweetly.

Rue tucked the offending mint between her cheek and teeth instead of sucking on it. The woman continued to tick off a list of other rules that Rue was only half paying attention to as she put her mints away, something about touching things in the lab that were hands off, smoking, and well, that's about all Rue heard.

Rue, however, perked up once they'd gotten past the blah, blah, blah history of the company and entered the lab. To Rue, it seemed endless, beginning with the area dedicated toward the future of cell phone technology, then moving on to the next wave of high-speed Internet and something called a "blue tooth" which made no sense to her. There was one section she paid extra attention to, and that was the computer graphics development area where the guide bragged about how they were revolutionizing the way movie animation was created, leading to better graphics and special effects. She remembered hearing Spencer say something like, "One day, entire movies will be played out using the computer animation technology that SpencerTech built." Funny, as this woman was saying about the same thing—almost word for word, except she was crediting Ellis Industries for such inventions.

Just then, they passed Astor Ellis's office, the Astor Ellis who is the current head of Research & Development and next in line as CEO of B. A. Ellis Industries once his father retired and he had secured the hand of the pet supply heiress and influencer Portia LaMonte.

"Will Mr. Ellis be making an appearance today?" Rue asked, casually pointing toward Astor's door so there was no confusion as to which Ellis she was referring.

The guide smiled at her. "Unfortunately, the Ellis family it out of town on business today and won't be joining us. But with any luck, one of our developers will pop by to greet us before our tour has concluded."

That didn't interest Rue, but she tried not to appear visibly disappointed.

It was then that the group was directed to the most awe-inspiring area of all. It was the future of something they called "virtual reality." Rue, feeling as if she had enough trouble with "real reality" followed Monte's lead when he tugged at her arm so they could quietly peel away from the group.

Once the tour had moved on, Monte wasted no time in breaking into Astor Ellis's office. She expected him to use a nail file and a credit card like what she'd seen so often on TV. Instead, he pulled out some small, square device that seemed to magneti-cally connect to the front of the door, just next to the door's handle. He leaned in and listened, for what, Rue couldn't be certain. Then, at just the right moment, Monte smiled and turned the knob. And just like that, the door to Astor's office was unlocked. They quickly crept inside, closing and re-locking the door behind them.

Monte surveyed the room, murmuring senseless words like, "Intel processing unit, HP tower, DSL line and multiline connec-tors," as if committing all of it to memory.

"I'll handle the tech if you dig through the desk and see if you can find anything interesting."

Rue merely nodded. After all, she was an events writer. Investigative journalism was new to her, and therefore, she wasn't entirely sure what she was looking for. But somehow, she wanted to prove herself a worthy assistant to a boss who she really didn't want to work for anyways...did she?

Just then, they heard someone breathing heavily, followed by the jiggling of a door handle.

"Who's in here?" a security guard demanded, fumbling with the lock before bursting into Astor Ellis's office. Monte was sitting at the desk, taking inventory of the computer monitor, computer tower, printer, and related equipment including floppy disks, CDs and external hard drives. His prop camera sat precariously on the edge of the desk. Just as the man entered, Monte spotted a sticky note with a few numbers and letter on it.

Rue looked up. She had been about to rifle through one of the desk drawers when the guard almost caught her red-handed. Monte looked at her, eyes widening as if to ask, *what do we do?* After all, when it came to quick thinking, he typically relied on Candice. Too bad she wasn't there.

In a moment of desperation, Rue did the only thing she could think of. She plopped herself into Monte's lap, wrapped her hand around the back of his head and pulled him in for a kiss. She expected to meet resistance. Instead, he kissed her back, a little more forcefully than was necessary, wrapping an arm around her waist and hugging her to him. She could feel his chest and abs. *Strong,* she thought briefly, allowing her other arm to wrap around his shoulder as she melted into the kiss.

With his free hand, Monte reached forward and palmed the sticky note, slipping it into in his shirt pocket, never losing his lip-lock with Rue.

"Knock it off, lovebirds," the security guard demanded. His eyes started to fall toward the drawer that Rue had opened. Desperate times called for desperate measures. With her toe, she nudged Monte's camera to the ground and heard it shatter. As the guard's gaze fell toward the floor, she shut the drawer.

Monte stifled back a few expletives as they broke from their embrace. As a final act, Rue unclipped her press pass, jamming it into her small purse. Monte followed suit, stuffing his into his back pocket.

"I'm so sorry," Rue sniffed. "We're in the middle of a messy divorce." She crumpled her face. "And working with my husband again," she eyed Monte, lovingly, "was the first real connection we've had in a long time."

"And what does that have to do with your being in Mr. Ellis's office?"

Monte eyed Rue for a moment before answering in the manliest way possible. "We haven't had sex in a year and the broom closet was locked."

"And this room wasn't?" The guard peered at the door handle.

"No," Monte answered.

"No matter. Take your business elsewhere. I'm not going to report seeing you as I don't want to come between a couple trying to work on their relationship, but you most certainly can't stay here, and you're no longer welcome at B. A. Ellis Industries. That clear?"

"Crystal," Monte squatted down to pick up the camera. The front lens had shattered.

"Leave it," the guard motioned to the pieces on the floor. "I'll have maintenance clean this up. Just take what's left of your camera and get out of here."

Just as Monte began standing from his kneeling position on the floor, he spotted something on the underside of the desk—the same police-issue bug taped to it, just like the one Darwin had found recently in his office.

"C'mon honey," he wrapped his arm around Rue's waist and pulled her toward him, once again, a bit closer than necessary. "Let's go home."

"Sorry, again," Rue murmured as she passed the guard. "I promise to write something nice about today's tech tour at B.A. Ellis industries."

"Never mind," the guard gruffly answered, pointing toward the elevator. Once they'd disappeared behind the doors, he placed a call to the front desk. "There's a female writer wearing a beret and a photographer with a broken camera on their way out. Make sure they actually leave the premises. Nah, not necessary. Thanks."

With that, the guard let out a sigh and called maintenance.

"Broken camera aside," Monte acknowledged, "I have to give credit where it is due. That was some fast thinking back there."

"Thanks," Rue beamed proudly. "You know," she laughed, "you sure are a good kisser for someone who isn't attracted to women."

Monte was offended. "Who says I don't like women?"

"Well, I mean...the wardrobe, the 'I like my coffee like I like my men' comment."

"So, because I like to dress as a woman, it automatically means I'm not attracted to them?"

"I guess not?" Rue fumbled. "Forget I said anything. You're a cross-dresser who likes women, not men, got it."

"And who says I don't like men?"

"You're very confusing," Rue admitted.

"Actually, honey," Monte shifted his shoulders. "I'm not confused in the slightest." They took a few back roads toward Darwin's condo, just in case they were being followed. "Exactly how long have you lived in Manhattan?"

"Just over a year," she answered, "why?"

"That explains it."

"What does it explain?" Rue demanded.

"I'm guessing Spencer Hargrove has been your only boyfriend upon arrival?"

"So, what of it?"

Monte stifled back a laugh. "That explains the kiss." He smiled, proud of himself.

"What's that supposed to mean?" The pitch in Rue's voice was creeping up.

"It means you have a lot to learn about living in Manhattan. Honey, you need to get out more."

"I think you're out enough for the both of us," Rue teased.

"Trollop," Monte wrinkled a nose at her. "But I tell you what? If things don't work out with you and Spencer, give me a call. I'll show you what it's like to date a real man."

"No thanks, Montgomery. My ego can't take the idea of dating anyone prettier than me."

"I am pretty gorgeous, aren't I?" Monte acknowledged.

"Exquisite."

Darwin had not yet returned from...well, wherever he was, when Monte and Rue got back from their adventure. Rue felt terrified, and yet exhilarated, at the same time. Her first assignment undercover and it went far better than expected, even when getting caught.

Rue and Monte were laughing about today's turn of events when Darwin finally arrived, carrying a leather satchel and an underarm full of mail, most of it junk.

"You two seem awfully happy," Darwin observed. "Did you kiss and make up?"

Rue's face turned red as she fought back an awkward laugh. Monte merely looked at his bare, buffed fingernails as if he found his cuticles spectacularly interesting. Given that it was Monte, that may have been the case.

Finally, Monte chimed in. "We got interrupted mid-search," he explained.

"Oh?" Darwin was concerned.

"Don't worry, we talked our way around it okay. However..." Monte reached into his pocket and pulled out a small yellow post-it note. "The dumb-ass boss's son at a high-security tech company actually had his username and password stuck to the side of his computer monitor."

Monte then went on to explain, in detail, the computer setup in Astor's office, information which was still largely over Rue's head. She nodded with pretend interest.

"Great work," Darwin snagged the note.

"Oh," Monte continued, "and the place is bugged a la Detective Ortega style. Guess he's still a person of interest in the Clarissa Sauer case."

"Indeed," Darwin answered before turning to Rue and asking, hopefully, "and what was your experience like, today? Discover anything interesting?"

Rue suddenly felt deflated. After all, Monte now knew the soup-to-nuts of Astor Ellis's computer network, his login info, and that he was being hounded by the police. Rue had a whole lot of nothing to contribute.

"Sadly, no," she dropped her gaze. "I'm afraid I wasn't much use at all."

Monte chimed in, "Are you kidding?" He looked first at Rue and then Darwin. "She was...magnifique...truly," he praised. "I couldn't have gotten the intel I did if she hadn't provided a good cover and been quick on her feet."

Rue smiled to herself. She couldn't recall ever being called *magnifique* before. It was kind of nice.

Darwin glanced oddly between Monte and Rue. After all,

aside from Candice, Monte was never particularly keen on praising anyone but himself which told Darwin that in one short afternoon, Rue had managed to earn something that Monte didn't give away freely...his respect.

Moments later, Candice arrived, looking as if she'd had a rough night.

"Look at what the cat dragged in," Monte commented.

"Screw you, Montgomery," Candice chastised, eyed Rue for support and winked. "Just a tough time getting to sleep last night, is all," she explained.

"Oh, I'll bet," Monte spoke in his Monique voice.

Candice was dressed in a pink tank top that was so tight, Rue was certain her breasts were going to pop out at any moment. She also had on a very short, very tight, red leather miniskirt that made it impossible for her to bend over without revealing her thong. And given that Rue knew the woman had a thong on, meant that Candice wasn't even trying to be delicate. Her eye makeup was smeared, giving her a raccoon look, and her concealer appeared to have been applied with a trowel. In short, she was a train wreck that Rue couldn't help but be fascinated and horrified with at the same time.

"What are you lookin' at?" Candice demanded.

"I think she's trying to tell if your boobs are real or not, or if you're even a girl."

"Why would she—" Candice glanced at Monte, still buffing his nails. "Oh," she smiled. "I get it." She walked over to Rue, pulling her shoulders back and thrusting her chest out. "You can feel 'em if you want. I can assure you; I am all woman."

"I'm good, thanks." Rue backed away.

"Ahem," Darwin interrupted. "Candy, would you mind changing out of your...uh...work clothes into...well, your *other* work clothes?" He motioned toward the bathroom.

"Sure thing, boss," she answered, winking at Rue before

leaving the room. She turned the bathroom light and fan on and closed the door behind her.

"Hey, Candy!" Monte called in after her, moments later.

"What? I'm on the toilet! Can't it wait?"

"Uh, yeah. It can wait."

After what seemed like an eternity later, Candice emerged from the bathroom, wearing a pair of blue jeans and a casual blouse. The makeup had been removed and her hair had been combed.

"Much better," Monte commented.

By this point, Rue was already updating notes from today's events into the computer while Monte filled Darwin in on their adventures. He was gentleman enough to soften the part about the kiss, reducing it to a mere peck on the lips. And yet, Darwin still raised an eyebrow and glanced at Rue.

"I can feel your eyes burning into the side of my head, Mr. Fennec," Rue typed. "It was necessary to maintain our cover...no big deal."

"So, what was so urgent that you had to yell at me while I was on the toilet?" Candice asked Monte.

"I was reminding you that Bristol has a gig at the coffeehouse tonight. Are you gonna be up for it?"

"Sure," she answered. "I doubt my assignment will take more than a few hours and I'll have a chance to get a nap in before tonight."

"Well, you missed me telling Darwin how brilliant Rue was today on the investigation."

"Really?" Candice pinched her lips together.

"I think we should bring her along to celebrate her first undercover work."

"You always remember your first," Candice winked.

"A small reminder that you're technically in the office," Darwin cautioned.

"Sorry, boss," Candice answered. To Rue, she said, "Monte is not easily impressed. So, if you got by his overly critical judgment, then you're okay in my book. You should definitely hang with us tonight."

"Okay," Rue agreed. The queasiness from the morning was now replaced with a bundle of nerves and energy. "Are you going, too?" she asked Darwin.

"No," Monte answered for him. "He doesn't fraternize with the help," he laughed. "To be honest, I wouldn't want to be seen with us, either. Our collective hotness is a little too much for most people to handle."

"About today's assignment," Darwin turned back to Candice, ignoring Monte's comments. "I need you to do a little digging into Astor Ellis's personal life. His mother is concerned that his dalliances might interfere with his upcoming nuptials."

"Nuptials," Candice snorted. "You and your big words."

Darwin eyed her, curiously.

"Okay, you got it boss. I'm on it."

# Chapter 19
# Kaffeehaus

Monday Evening at a Coffee House

Rue had been in the city for over a year now and still hadn't scratched the surface of all that was Manhattan. Of course, part of that was because Midge and Spencer were the few people she socialized with on a regular basis. And while Midge was the adventurous one, always taking Rue to questionable places just for the fun of it, Spencer was pretty...*status quo.*

Were it not for a journalism gig that required she interview entertainers and review special events, there was a good chance that Rue wouldn't have made it much past her block, save for Midge's odd outings. Still, Monte had a point. She was pretty green when it came to understanding the Big Apple. And, if she were being honest with herself, she was flattered that he and Candice invited her to the coffee house to hear Bristol's set. She suspected they didn't typically invite people into their little circle, a fact that she didn't take lightly.

She arrived at 8 p.m. wearing a long-sleeved, brown knit dress, faux-leather ankle boots, along with ridiculously large gold-plated hoop earrings that Midge had given her. Somehow, she was distinctly aware of them, making her feel as if her ears were twice as large as her head.

Rue felt a moment of anxiety walking into the crowded coffee house alone, seeing groups and couples all swarming together while the house music played over the loudspeakers. The smell of freshly ground coffee and sweet caramel filled the air. She felt oddly conspicuous despite the fact that no one seemed to actually be looking at her.

In fact, she was about to turn around and walk out when... "Hey, Rue, honey!" Candice waved her arm frantically. "Over here!"

Rue inched her way over to them, turning sideways and slipping between people until she'd made it to the deep-seated, espresso-colored leatherette couch where Candice and Monte sat. Monte's long arms were spread across the back of the couch, legs sprawled out in front of him, ensuring that he and Candice had claimed the entire space including the small coffee table in front of them.

"Cute earrings!" Candice gushed when Rue sat down. "Take a load off. Bristol should be on any minute."

Moments later, a server stopped by the lounge area, placing a small Turkish coffee pot and cup in front of Monte and a raspberry danish and cappuccino before Candice.

"Get you something, hun?" the server asked Rue.

"Uh, yeah. How about a double espresso macchiato...if you have that," Rue ordered, hesitantly.

"And a raspberry danish," Candice called. "Get her a danish, on me!" The server nodded as other patrons quickly began vying for her attention, no one wanting to abandon their comfy couches or pub tables lest someone take it while they were at the coffee counter.

"You sure know your coffee," Candice complimented. "Hope you like raspberry, but if not, I'll eat it. Their pastries here are to die for."

Monte laughed. "She says the same thing about the red bean sticky buns from Chinatown. The girl likes her pastries."

"And it's startin' ta show," she pinched a roll of flab across her midsection. "I can already pinch more than an inch," she complained before settling back into the couch.

Moments later, Bristol took to the stage, pulling up a chair and setting a music stand low in front of him while a man dressed all in black brought him a microphone with a stand. He relieved Bristol of his guitar case after Bristol pulled a Martin acoustic from it. Two other band mates took to the stage, one bearing a fiddle, the other a hand drum. After a few minutes, they each had microphones in front of them. Bristol didn't wait for anyone to introduce them. Instead, he started playing quietly. A wave came over the coffeehouse as the noise flowed into hushed voices and then applause, coupled with a few cheers, as they recognized him. Then, for the first time since Rue arrived, the place grew quiet.

The server placed her hyper-caffeinated beverage in front of Rue along with a sugar bowl, cream, and one raspberry pastry. She didn't talk, merely nodded and darted away.

Bristol began singing a slow and hauntingly sad ballad about lost love. Rue had never heard it before, but like everyone else, sat mesmerized. His voice was melodic and sounded much softer than his day-to-day speech. Just as everyone had settled into that warm glow, there was a long pause and suddenly the fiddler and drummer jumped in as the music transitioned into a Celtic jig. "We're the Clifdens. Thanks for being here," Bristol called. "Be sure to tip your servers. They're workin' hard for you tonight. And be sure to tip your musicians...we can really use the cash." The crowd laughed as several people dropped bills into the tip jar at the edge of the stage.

It was only then that Rue noticed something...his voice sounded Irish. But she didn't remember him sounding that way before. Maybe it was part of his stage persona?

"Seems to be a man with many talents," Rue commented to her new friends. "Great with the get-away cars and—" she paused to avoid mentioning her rescue from Merriam Hall. "And a talented singer, too."

"Not to mention a great songwriter, musician, and—" Candice motioned toward a little girl standing at the corner of the stage clapping her hands together gleefully, wearing a pink dress with bright aqua stockings, her blonde hair in curls, "a great dad," she finished.

The song ended and during the applause, the little girl who couldn't have been more than about five-years-old, bounded up the stage steps, her curls bouncing along with her. Without asking permission, she climbed into Bristol's lap. He set his guitar on the stand that had been set beside him. She settled in, facing the audience, her hands on each of her dad's knees, smiling as if the applause had been for her.

Bristol tousled his daughter's hair before leaning forward, placing his hand on the mic and saying, "No boundaries. Does whatever she likes...just like her mother." The crowd laughed.

The little girl turned her torso, holding her hand up to cup it around her dad's ear as if whispering him a secret.

"That one?" he clarified, still talking into the mic. The little girl nodded.

"And then you'll go sit quietly with your Aunt Candice until your mum arrives to pick you up?"

She nodded, enthusiastically.

"Well," Bristol addressed the crowd. "Seems Evie refuses to go to bed unless we sing her a lullaby. Do you mind?"

The crowd's applause indicated that Evie had them all wrapped around her adorable little finger.

With that, Bristol scooted his daughter off his lap. She stood, wrapping her arms around his neck and leaning into his side as he fetched his guitar. He launched into Edelweiss, his bandmates offering backup vocals. He rocked back and forth as little Evie, who couldn't possibly have understood the meaning behind the song's lyrics at such a young age, sang with him.

*"Blossom of snow may you bloom and grow,"* they sang.

Pretty soon, the entire coffeehouse was singing. For all the people who claimed to have never seen the Sound of Music, Rue thought it an amazing coincidence that so many people seemed to know the words.

Toward the end of the song, one of the Clifden members unhooked his microphone and brought it over to Evie who released the grip on her dad's neck long enough to pull her hair out of the way and lean into the mic to finish the song. "Bless my homeland forever."

The crowd erupted. Evie waited for the noise to die down before she very purposefully grabbed the mic and said in a very rehearsed manner, "And don't forget to tip the band. It keeps me in curls and my dad really needs the cash."

The crowd laughed emphatically as more people dropped money into the tip jar.

"Little hoodlum," Monte shook his head. "Can't believe he's exploiting his daughter like that."

"Oh, c'mon," Candice waved her hand. "It's all in good fun."

"Says you. Just you wait until she grows up swindling men out of their money at the pool hall conning 'em with false tales of suffering so they pay her way to meet her family in Europe."

"I had no idea you were so cynical, Montgomery," Rue teased.

Monte leaned in and whispered, "Yeah, you just keep calling me Montgomery, would you? See how fast I let Darwin in on our little tête-à-tête at Ellis Industries the other day."

"I think you mean Spencer," she clarified, "my boyfriend."

"Do I?" He tilted his head toward her, a churlish grin on his face.

"Why would I care what Mr. Fennec thinks?"

"Why, indeed?" Monte crossed one arm across his chest, resting his other elbow on it and framing his face with his hand.

Rue felt her face grow hot. "Jerk," she scolded.

"Trollop," he countered.

"Hey, I resent that!" Candice chimed in, even though no one was talking to her.

The argument was interrupted when Bristol told Evie, "Why don't you go sit with Aunt Candice."

Candice's eyes lit up as Evie climbed down from the stage and ran over to her.

"Are you really her aunt?" Rue asked, finally remembering to take a bite of her gifted raspberry pastry.

"Honorary title," Candice answered as Evie climbed onto the sofa, planting herself beside Candice and leaning into her chest. Candice wrapped her arm around Evie and gave Bristol a thumbs up. He nodded as his band continued their set.

Just then, Rue caught sight of someone peering in her direction, but when she turned to look, he cast his eyes downward and turned his back on her. The man who sat next to him tucked his head as the two exchanged a few words.

Rue set her danish down, wiping her hands on her dress before standing up. Monte gave her a questioning look.

"Be right back," she said.

The two men remained huddled until she addressed them.

"Max, how nice to see you," she smiled widely as the SpencerTech employee feigned surprise. She turned to the other pimply-faced man. "Tommy? Is that right? I believe my friend Midge and I met you the other night."

Tommy's eyes brightened for just a moment. "How is Midge? She hasn't been returning my calls."

"Couldn't say," Rue answered, feeling somewhat sorry for the man. "Haven't spoken to her much since then."

Tommy looked crestfallen.

"So interesting," Rue commented. "Tommy, didn't you use to work at B. A. Ellis Industries?" Tommy tried to sink into his bar stool. She turned to Max. "And I'm assuming you are still working with my Spencer, else I'm sure I would have heard differently. Is this like a meeting between the Montagues and Capulets?"

"Listen, Rue," Max explained. "Tommy and I have been friends since Kindergarten, long before Spencer ever worked with the Ellis family. His feud with them has nothing to do with me."

"Understood," Rue answered bluntly, the double shot of espresso coursing through her veins. "Just wanted to come over and say hi, so hi!" Her voice pitched upward as a nervous energy overtook her. Her hands began to tremble a little.

Max put his arm out and stopped her as she turned to leave. "Hey, Rue," he spoke softly. "Would you mind not telling Spencer you saw us here? He'd pitch a fit given the current legal battles."

"What legal battles?" Rue asked.

Max's expression revealed that he thought she already knew.

"Perhaps I've said too much."

Rue thought about this a moment. She could walk away and pretend she didn't see Max and Tommy here and mind her own business. But would that make her deceitful to Spencer? She could betray Max, but how would that affect SpencerTech's production so close to product launch (not to mention making her feel like a heel)? On top of that, what good would it do? If Max was, in fact, leaking info to Tommy, he'd certainly be shoring up his accounts and deleting any paper trail following this encounter. Or she could tell Darwin, so they could collect as much info as possible before presenting evidence to Spencer."

Suddenly, Midge's hot-headed voice echoed through Rue's mind, *"Somehow convinced his former lover to hooch up to someone at SpencerTech and do a little snooping."*

Rue made a bold move as both Max and Tommy waited for her response.

"Tell you what, Max," she smiled. "Tell me more about these lawsuits and maybe I won't let Spencer know about your liaisons with Clarissa Sauer, where there's a good chance you spilled the beans about some of SpencerTech's upcoming technology."

Max exchanged confused looks with Tommy. Rue could see the wheels in Tommy's head turning as he calculated a response and figured out *she didn't know.*

"I think you should just tell her," Tommy finally said.

"About?" Max shot Tommy a curious look, eyes growing wide.

"About the lawsuits, of course," Tommy replied, cryptically. "She's working with a well-known investigator, after all. They'd figure it out eventually."

"Right," Max answered. "I guess I'm just surprised Spencer didn't tell you all this himself."

Rue had been wondering that very thing.

"It seems that Astor and Byron Ellis have been challenging a series of copyrights and patents that SpencerTech has on about a dozen different inventions. They claim that he drew up those blueprints while still working for B. A. Ellis Industries, even using their manpower and equipment to develop his ideas on company time."

*That can't be*, Rue thought. *Spencer was too noble to do something like that.*

Tommy chimed in. "I get where he was coming from," he defended Spencer. "If I were an intern working for minimum wage while helping make the company millions, I'd at least want to profit in some small way. After all, B. A. Ellis Industries showed an increased profit of 15% just six months after Spencer Hargrove began interning for them. Did they offer him a bonus for his efforts?" he asked. "No," he answered his own question. "Instead, they gave him a $100 restaurant gift card."

Rue thought about their recent dinner at The View. *Was Spencer living beyond his means, and not as well-off as he let on. If so, by how much?* she wondered.

"It was a bad rap," Max agreed. "But that's all gonna change in a few months. With SpencerTech becoming such a huge success, maybe the two companies will let bygones be bygones."

"I wish I could be as optimistic as you," Tommy shook his head, taking a sip of the coffee he'd let get cold before biting into a chocolate brownie.

"Which products are they suing him over?" Rue asked.

"A bunch," Max answered. "You might want to grab a notebook to write them down."

"Perhaps you could just tell me," Rue answered. "Slowly. Just one at a time."

Max was surprised by this but began rambling off the nature of each lawsuit. In Rue's mind, she started composing patterns not unlike the ones Darwin had taught her for unlocking accounts. She visualized each event as if it were a cartoon in front of her, giving each piece of data colors, shapes, numbers and images in her personal mind map. When he was finished, she answered. "Thank you, Max, you've been most helpful."

He grabbed her arm. "You're not going to tell Spencer, are you?"

*I'm not,* she thought. *But once this case is solved, Darwin might.*

"No," she answered as honestly as possible. "My lips are sealed."

Max smiled nervously, relieved. As she turned to leave, Tommy called over her shoulder. "Tell Midge I said hi?"

"Will do, when I see her," Rue answered, not that she had any intention of talking to Midge again anytime soon. Still, she felt a little sorry that Tommy ended up being another of Midge's casualties.

Once back at the couch, Candice announced. "There she is!" To Rue, she said, "We were wondering what happened to you."

"Candice, thanks for the danish and the invite, but I gotta go," Rue proclaimed.

Monte sat up, bending his knees and pulling his long legs in. "Where are you going?"

"To the office," she explained. "I've got to input some information on a case."

"To the office," Candice was surprised. "You mean Darwin's condo?"

"Exactly," she answered. "I can't access our files from my home computer."

"But it's after 9 p.m.," Monte protested. "Don't you think you should wait until normal business hours?"

"No, Mr. Fennec will understand."

Monte exchanged glances with Candice.

"Just get home safe, honey," Candice called after her.

"Guess I better phone Darwin and let him know that a whirling dervish is heading his way," Monte reasoned.

"Wonder what all that was about?" Candice asked, curiously.

"Aunt Candice?" Evie looked up, sleepily. "When's my mom going to get here? I'm really tired."

Candice kissed the top of the girl's head. "Any moment now, sweetie. You just rest your head in my lap until then."

Evie nodded, laying her head on Candice's lap. Candice rubbed the girl's back for a moment. Evie smiled and drifted off to sleep, despite the music, loud voices, and the whir of milk being frothed for lattes with the aroma of fresh roasted coffee filling her nostrils.

Since it was outside of business hours, Rue didn't use the key code to get in. In fact, she couldn't even get past the night security guard.

"Can I help you?" She stopped Rue at the elevator.

"Yes, I'm just popping up to see my boss, Mr. Darwin Fennec, on the seventh floor."

"You often visit your boss at this hour?"

"Well," Rue put a hand on her hip, "you know how it is." The rather plump security guard did not, in fact, seem to know. "He's actually my boyfriend," she lied.

"I thought you just said he was your boss."

"Just my nickname for him," Rue tried again. "Like Elvis is the King and Springsteen is the Boss?"

"Are you saying that Springsteen is your boyfriend?"

"Well, gee. Wouldn't that be nice?" Rue joked.

The guard was not amused. She picked up the phone and dialed. "Yeah, Mr. Fennec. I've got a lady here who claims to be your girlfriend."

She heard a muffled voice on the other end of the line, but Rue couldn't make out what he was saying.

The guard looked Rue over and pursed her lips. "Looks like

the girl you described, but wouldn't it be easier if you tell me her name?" She listened for a minute. "Uh huh." She turned to Rue, "Your name Hildy? Hildy Johnson?"

Rue paused for a moment before it sank in. She bit her lip. "Yup, that's me."

"Go on," she motioned toward the elevator. "Crazy people and their weird role-playing. It's just sick," the guard mumbled to herself before returning to the romance novel she was reading.

Darwin met Rue at the door wearing white pajamas with blue pinstripes and fuzzy tan slippers.

"Hi, Walter," Rue answered, putting a hand on her hip in her best Rosalind Russell impersonation. "Didn't picture you as a fan of old movies." She brushed past him. "I can't talk now. I've got to record the notes in my head before they leak out!" Rue headed straight for her computer and powered it to life.

Darwin closed the door, standing there in his pin-striped pajamas, eyeing her curiously. He could see that she was pulling up Spencer's files and info on SpencerTech. What he couldn't understand was why she was creating a new file on someone named Tommy.

He wandered into the kitchen and retrieved a bottle of scotch from under the counter, added one ice cube to a small glass and poured. "You want..." he started to ask. He realized that she was too absorbed in her project, so he simply sipped and waited for her to finish her furious typing. He came back into the living room and leaned against the back end of the sofa.

"There!" she finally said, looking up. It was only then that she noticed the night clothes, slippers, and scotch. "Oh," she looked at him. "I'm sorry. Guess I should have called first, but you've got me so trained not to write anything down on paper that I had to get my thoughts archived and protected before I forgot anything!"

"That's okay," he grinned. "I think Monte tried to call and

warn me you were coming but the cell reception was terrible, and the call was dropped."

Rue looked at him blankly. While Spencer had gotten her a cell phone, she still wasn't entirely comfortable using it and she had no idea what it meant to drop a call. "I discovered something," she proclaimed, eyeing the scotch.

"Would you like some?" he offered.

"Ew, no," she wrinkled her nose. "Besides, I'm still coming down after a caffeine high."

"I can see that," he answered.

"I'll let you read my notes in the morning," Rue explained. "But here's the Reader's Digest version. B. A. Ellis Industries has at least five lawsuits out against SpencerTech for 'stealing' proprietary information and selling it. Meanwhile, someone sent Clarissa Sauer to hooch up to Spencer's business partner, Max. Seems she was still loyal to Astor Ellis, even though he dumped her. Looks as if she and Max were having a fling."

"Really?" There was something gnawing in Darwin's chest about that one, but he wasn't sure yet what it was—a premonition of sorts.

"He as good as admitted it."

"What? When did you see him?" Darwin asked.

"Tonight, at the coffee shop with Monte and Candice. I saw Max hanging out with Tommy Marcuzzo."

"The Tommy who used to intern at Ellis Industries?"

"The same. And he even dated Midge for a short time. Small world, isn't it?"

"It would seem so," Darwin appeared unconvinced.

"Anyways, Max begged me not to tell Spencer, saying he and Tommy had been friends long before Spencer had a falling out with Astor Ellis over tech rights."

"So, Spencer doesn't know any of this?" Darwin asked.

"Of course not!" Rue was getting frustrated. "We can't let

Spencer in on this until we have all the facts, otherwise, he can blow our investigation wide open if he lands into Max without... you know...having all the facts."

Darwin bit back a laugh. "If I understand you correctly," he clarified. "I'm the first person you're sharing this information with."

"Yes," Rue answered. "Why is that funny?"

"It's not," he smiled, shaking his head. "I must say, you're on fire tonight. We must remember to keep you overly caffeinated. Seems to help your sleuthing skills."

Rue let out a sigh. "I should probably leave," she said finally.

"Let me call you a cab, Ms. Brennan."

# Chapter 20
# Elektra

Tuesday Afternoon at the Artist Atelier

Rue found the whole idea morbid, but when the model coordinator called her out of the blue to take part in a draped modeling series being called "The Art of Death," Darwin encouraged Rue to participate.

"Why?" Rue demanded of Darwin at his home office that morning. "Is this revenge for my stopping by so late last night? That now you're visualizing me dead?"

"Now who's being morbid?" Darwin protested. "I just thought that it might get you in closer contact with Ursula Gorky, perhaps turn her into a character witness instead of just, well, just a witness."

"Given her friendship with Clarissa and how much she seemed to dislike me when we met up at the club last week, I doubt I'm likely to become her friend anytime soon."

"Club?"

Rue realized her mistake. She had neglected to tell him about Merriam Hall and Bristol, true to his word, kept his mouth shut.

"Let's just say, Midge dragged me to a dance hall and it didn't go so well. Ursula Gorky, and Emma Post were there. That was where Midge met Tommy Marcuzzo."

"Why are you just telling me this now?" Darwin asked, raising his voice in annoyance.

"Don't get your panties in a bunch," Rue defended. "It was a night I was hoping to forget, and Midge and I had a falling out, of sorts. Didn't think I had to share my whereabouts on my off hours," Rue pouted.

"But, just like last night, when you came barreling into my home with news, this is pertinent stuff surrounding our cases. What was different about that night?" Darwin eyed her suspiciously.

Rue cast her eyes to the floor, and Darwin realized...it might be something she didn't want to talk about lest he judge her. Darwin was very skilled at reading people. He softened his voice a little. "Why don't you get me up to speed about Ursula, Emma and this Tommy fellow? Leave out any personal details."

Rue relented, giving the bare-bones facts about Ursula telling the police she saw Rue push Clarissa over the balcony, Emma Post not really being pregnant, and that Midge and Tommy were over, but he still might be connected to the security leak Spencer-Tech was experiencing.

"So, Ursula and Emma are friends?" Darwin confirmed.

"Yes, and both figure models at the Artist Atelier like I am from time to time."

"That makes me even more convinced that you should take the modeling gig. Think of it as undercover work," Darwin reasoned.

"The Art of Death" series was the brainchild of Jaks Liebling, a dilettante who fashioned himself a great artist and instructor despite having no formal training. True, he had a natural talent, but it was his very large contributions to the Artist Atelier in the Lower East Side that garnered him admiration.

He was a legend in his own mind and the worst sort of narcissist. Jaks was the kind that did a fair job of feigning humility. He once held a wildly popular art exhibit featuring a series of "masterpieces" he supposedly painted during his time living in the Caribbean and invited freshman students to submit their tropical-themed works as part of a scholarship program. The student that won would have their tuition paid for one full year. But many claimed it was all for show and he did it to demonstrate how much better of an artist he was than they were and how his fame as a painter had garnered him the funds to support the less fortunate.

His most recent series involved models posing in the tragic death scenes from the world's most popular operas, including Tosca, Carmen, La Bohème, Elektra, and the Flying Dutchman. The opera has never been kind to women.

"Which scene did the model coordinator ask you to be a part of?"

"If I agree to do it, I get to be Elektra."

Darwin suddenly felt a lump in his throat as he unconsciously surveyed Rue from head to toe and then averted his gaze. "So, as a figure model, you have to dance around...naked?" Darwin banished the thought from his mind...eventually.

"No," Rue barked at him. "It's draped."

"What does that mean?"

"It means I get to keep my clothes on. I'll be in costume."

"Oh," was all Darwin said, trying not to sound disappointed.

"And I won't be dancing. I'll probably just be asked to hold a dance-like pose for an unbearably long time. Or worse, Jaks Liebling will have me lying in a dead heap on the floor for six hours a day for three days."

"Six hours? That sounds like a lot."

"It is a lot, Darwin. Being an art model is a lot harder than it looks."

"I'll bet. Well, then, never mind. It was just a thought." Darwin paused for a moment. "If you don't like modeling, then why do you do it?"

"That's just it," Rue explained. "I love it. I may not be an artist myself, but I love being around all that creativity and knowing that I get to be a part of it in some small way."

"But you seem averse to this project. Why?"

"I can't explain it," Rue answered. "There's just something creepy about posing for a death scene for an equally creepy Jaks Liebling."

"I see," Darwin acknowledged. "Well, don't do anything that makes you uncomfortable. We'll figure something else out."

Rue felt her stomach drop. There was nothing in Darwin's voice that sounded disapproving, and yet, just like with Spencer, she felt the need to not disappoint. It was bad enough that she was often disappointed with herself.

*And, on the other hand,* Rue thought to herself, *18 extra hours of contract work modeling, coupled with what Darwin would be paying me as his assistant on top of that and...all that added up to* the realization that Rue was going to be playing a dead Elektra.

# Chapter 21
# Box 11



Late Tuesday Evening at Darwin's Condo

Darwin was having a fitful night's sleep. His head hurt like it always did when he was missing something and an idea was trying pop out of it. He tossed and turned, rolling on his back, then his side, then his other side like a rotisserie chicken. Finally, he drifted back to sleep at 2 a.m.

It was one of those dreams where he was somehow inhabiting a foreign body without knowing who he was or why he was there.

He pulled back a black curtain and there she was…Clarissa Sauer, standing at the balcony in the same flowing red dress she wore the night she died, her fingers lightly stroking the top of the railing as she looked wistfully out toward the stage and the theater seats below her.

"You forgot your gloves," Darwin said to her, handing her the long black gloves she had been wearing the night she died.

She turned to him and smiled softly, her eyes falling toward the floor, tears streaming down her face. She sniffed them back. "He was using me, you know."

Darwin said nothing in return as she accepted the gloves.

She continued, "He thought dating me would make you jealous, and then..."

"He sent you in to spy on me," Darwin finished. Somewhere in the back of Darwin's dream state, he was asking himself, *who am I? Where did that come from?*

"Yes," Clarissa answered. "For a short while, I thought maybe he actually cared about me and that maybe I could come to care for him."

"And how did that work out?" Darwin asked, only this time, it wasn't his voice. It was that of someone else. *Who?*

She rubbed her belly, "You know how that worked out, Astor."

"You know I wish things could be different," he moved toward her.

Clarissa turned her back to him once again. "You don't know how many nights before the show, I'd come up here to your family's box and stand right here, wondering what life would be like if you'd chosen me over Portia."

"I didn't have a choice," Astor defended.

"Of course, you had a choice," she growled. "You're just using Portia for her money and influence, just as Spencer used me. Everyone is busy using everyone else." She paused. "I can't believe I actually started trying to feed you information, as if that would magically bring you back to me."

"You know I didn't ask you to do that," Astor told her, gently.

"Don't you realize," Clarissa sniffed, "that I would have done anything for you?"

"And you come up here, every night to Box 12, imagining a life that can never be?"

Clarissa's eyes furrowed, confused. "Box 12? No." She

reached toward her chest to retrieve the note she'd had secured beneath a bra strap. "You mean box 11, don't you?"

With that, Darwin felt himself being pulled backward and out of Astor's body. As he was floating away, Clarissa turned to him, her voice muffled. It was then that he saw it, a bloodstain on the right side of her body—off center. "Did you ever think that maybe you're missing the obvious, Darwin Fennec? Just like me, you're letting your emotions cloud your judgment."

The next morning, while Rue was on her way to the Artist Atelier for several days of modeling that Darwin managed to convince her was part of her "undercover work" (not to mention the promise of extra cash), he put a call in to Detective Ortega. Surprisingly, Ortega was on the phone almost immediately.

"I know this is going to sound strange," Darwin told the detective, not bothering to exchange pleasantries, "but I need to ask you a question." Darwin didn't wait for permission. "Was Clarissa Sauer's stab wound fatal?"

Darwin could hear Ortega sucking in his breath on the other end of the line. Finally, he cleared his throat and asked, "Please tell me, Mr. Fennec, that you are not trying to investigate the very crime in which you are actually a suspect?"

"I'm not," Darwin defended. "It just so happens that your case seems to have some overlaps with one I'm working on for a client."

"Is that so," Ortega was interested. "And who might that client be?"

"I can't say," Darwin answered. "But—"

"Listen very carefully, Mr. Fennec," Detective Ortega interrupted him. "If you're withholding evidence..."

"I'm not," Darwin repeated. "But what I can tell you is that I think Spencer Hargrove was the father of Clarissa's unborn baby."

There was a pause at the other end of the line. "And how is it that, number one, you knew she was pregnant, and number two, that she was dating...Spencer Hargrove, is it?"

"Come now, detective," Darwin answered. "I'm sure you've already uncovered that Spencer Hargrove used to work for the Ellises and that Rue Brennan is his girlfriend."

"And the pregnancy?"

"Part of my investigation."

"And," Ortega lowered his voice in a whisper as if keeping information to himself. Darwin could hear him shut the door to what he assumed was Detective Ortega's office. "Was your being with Rue Brennan at the theater, the night of the murder, also a part of your investigation?"

"In a way," Darwin confessed. "Yes, except it didn't exactly go according to plan."

"Clearly," Ortega answered flatly.

"Listen, Detective Ortega," Darwin tried again, "what I propose is this—while I can't share specific information about my clients, I am happy to let you in on anything that might assist with your case."

"Well, gee, Mr. Fennec," Ortega mocked, adopting the voice of a young child. "That would be swell!" He coughed before growling into the phone, "You'll let me in on any information you have because you and your 'lady friend' are suspects in a murder investigation. And, for the record, it is highly uncustomary for a police detective to be working with an outsider...what did you say you were again, a cyber-something-or-other?"

"A cyber forensic consultant and private investigator."

"Right," Ortega answered, in a way that suggested he wasn't overly impressed with Darwin's credentials.

"The point is," Darwin sighed. "Should you wish to work together and exchange information, you know where to find me."

"I'll keep that in mind, Mr. Fennec. Is that all?"

"It is, except you haven't confirmed whether the non-fatal wound found on Clarissa's body was on the right or left side."

"Doesn't matter which side, does it?" Ortega raised his voice. "Since you're not on the case!"

"Thank you, Detective Ortega, for confirming my suspicions."

Ortega realized his mistake. "Crafty, Mr. Fennec. Very crafty. Well played." He paused a moment longer. "Okay, since you were good enough to put me on to Spencer and Clarissa's relationship, I can confirm that it wasn't Clarissa's wound that killed her. It was the tumble over the balcony. She broke her neck in the fall."

"And the baby?" Darwin pressed his luck.

"Too young and not far enough along...couldn't be saved, I'm afraid." Ortega could be heard breathing heavily into the phone. "Really strange when you think about it," Ortega finally said. "Penelope...er, Dr. Washburn, thought so, too."

"What was?" Darwin asked quietly.

"Everything about the murder was so well-planned, so calculated. And yet, it was as if they were purposefully trying *not* to harm Clarissa Sauer, nor her baby. Why would a murderer go out of their way *not* to kill their victim?"

# Chapter 22
# The Gala

Four Months Ago, Before Clarissa Was Murdered - At the Artist Atelier

For artists, entrepreneurs, and philanthropists who needed to donate a percentage of their wealth quickly into charitable causes just before tax season, The Gala fundraiser at the Artist Atelier was the event of the season.

The grand entrance and the three surrounding galleries on the main floor were decorated with thousands of white, glittering string lights artfully placed across the ceiling and down the walls. One wall displayed an indoor cascading fountain with a basin covered in ivy vines and a white cherub statue sitting at the edge. The lights were strung in a way that framed the resin, wall-mounted fountain. On the opposite end of the room, a living wall covered in greenery flowed from ceiling to floor, accented with twinkling, handcrafted porcelain fairy figurines and pixies appearing to be tending to a few strategically placed ornamental flowers. At the center of the room was a tall, metal sculpture made of hundreds of silver balls all melded together to look like a woman who was dancing. The artist standing in front of the sculpture posing for pictures and answering questions was presumably the creator of said work who was touting something about it "being on loan from the Guggenheim."

People dressed in evening gowns and tuxes meandered in and out of the galleries, often holding a program in one hand and a beverage in the other. Servers dressed in either all black or all white pants with matching jackets floated around the room, edging their way between patrons, offering up platters filled with hors d'oeuvres such as bacon-wrapped scallops, filet mignon bites, and shrimp on crackers.

The most popular area, of course, were the open bars situated by the living wall and fountain, respectively. The poor cherub sculpture had been accidentally stepped on or leaned upon so many times, it was unlikely to make it through the evening without a few scratches.

Spencer and his date arrived in a taxi. He asked the driver to drop them off a block away from the Artist Atelier, "to avoid getting stuck behind the loading and unloading of limos," he informed his date for the evening.

It's important to note here that Rue was *not* the woman who he helped out of the taxi that evening. Instead of making an appearance with his girlfriend of over a year, he had invited... Clarissa Sauer, who was at this time still very much alive.

Clarissa was wearing a floor-length, black evening gown with a low v-cut front delivering just enough cleavage for anyone who cared to look. Her spiked heels were a shimmering red. She would have been taller than Spencer who dressed in a rental tux and bow tie were it not for the fact that he thought ahead and wore platform shoes.

He opened the car door for her, and she took the hand he offered in a practiced way. After paying the driver, Spencer stood upright, adjusted his jacket and offered his arm to the long-haired beauty.

Clarissa's feet were killing her in those shoes, and she certainly didn't relish the thought of walking another minute in them, let alone a block, but she smiled back at Spencer and didn't complain. Unlike Rue, she never complained about anything and was always agreeable, two traits that Spencer liked best.

"Remember, darling," he reminded her, "only one glass of champagne unless you see me take a second or if we're separated and all of the ladies in the group are drinking. Drink slowly, and if your glass is empty, ask the bartender to refill it with ginger ale."

"Don't worry," she smiled, "I remember. And waive off the hors d'oeuvres unless you accept one first or if I'm in a group where I'm encouraged to eat."

"Exactly, and..."

"Stick with simple foods like watermelon bites and coconut shrimp and avoid potentially messy ones like short ribs or a braised...anything."

"That's right," he kissed her hand. "I promise to make it up to you later with a pepperoni pizza and as much beer to wash it down as you like."

Clarissa Sauer was college-educated. In fact, she was at the top of her class in the dramatic arts program and was on the music world's short list of up-and-coming opera singers of 1997. She preferred the finer things in life like good champagne and messy hors d'oeuvres topped with fancy truffle oils and garlic aioli. And unlike most people, she actually had a palate for it. But she let Spencer "educate" her because she learned early on, you got further in life if you smiled and didn't make a fuss.

What she wasn't counting on was Astor Ellis.

When they arrived, the very first thing Spencer did was survey the room and garner each of them a glass of champagne, presumably so their hands had something to hold while looking sophisticated instead of standing there awkwardly with their arms dangling in the air.

"This way," he guided his date.

For the first time, she balked.

"What is it?" he asked, uncomfortably.

Clarissa spotted Astor Ellis standing next to his reportedly, soon-to-be fiancé, Portia LaMonte. Portia LaMonte's family was the main sponsor for the gala, held to raise money for the elite art school—providing scholarships, renovations, and above all, a "knowledge and appreciation of the fine arts."

Clarissa sucked in a breath. "Nothing," she whispered. "I thought I caught my heel on my dress, but it's fine now." She smiled cautiously.

Spencer nodded as he continued his journey toward his nemesis. At one time, he and Astor had been friends, both working for Astor Ellis's tech mogul father, Byron Ellis. But after three occasions where his ideas were taken without giving him credit and a contract stating that anything he created at any time during his tenure at B. A. Ellis Industries was the intellectual property of the company, Spencer grew bitter. When he quit last year, Astor felt betrayed and so did Spencer. After all, it was Astor who leaked info to his father about some of Spencer's current creations which had been imagined off hours and while still under B. A. Ellis Industries' employ.

They threatened lawsuits, but in the end, the only thing that appeared at this time was cyber warfare. Spencer was certain Astor and his family were hacking into his system and stealing his tech as they had a bad habit of announcing new inventions always just ahead of his own launch. And then there were those inconvenient times when blueprints seemed to go missing as if someone were purposefully corrupting his data.

Initially, he wanted to hire Darwin Fennec and his team to hack into the Ellis family fortress and tech empire and garner a little intel of their own, but Darwin was adamant about ethics. The best he could offer was locking down Spencer Hargrove's computer network and servers, looking for vulnerabilities and sniffing out who might be pilfering information and why.

"Spencer Hargrove, how delightfully surprising it is to see you here this evening," Astor Ellis lied in his annoyingly nasal voice before laying eyes on Clarissa. "And who is your charming date for this evening?"

Astor knew who Clarissa Sauer was. After all, he had been sleeping with her for several months before finally ending it as the time of his stepping into his father's shoes as CEO of B. A. Ellis Industries grew closer, along with his engagement to his girl-friend of two years, heiress Portia LaMonte.

Spencer knew this, too, and so did Clarissa, obviously. The only one who presumably didn't, was Astor's bride-to-be, Portia.

"Ah," Spencer answered eagerly. "May I present, Miss Clarissa Sauer."

"How lovely," Astor acknowledged, taking her hand and holding it for about three-seconds too long. Portia didn't seem to notice. Clarissa, on the other hand, *did* notice. It was sweaty, like it always was when he felt guilty about something.

"Er," Astor fumbled a little, dropping Clarissa's hand. "This is my lovely date for the evening and reason we're all here tonight, Ms. Portia LaMonte."

"How nice to meet you," she greeted Spencer and then set her gaze on Clarissa.

Clarissa's face felt hot. *She couldn't know, could she?* And even more to the point, *did Astor regret his decision?* After all, what they had was special, wasn't it?

Spencer could barely contain his glee nor his contempt for his former friend. Arriving at tonight's most memorable event with the woman he knew for damn sure Astor preferred? Priceless.

Astor boasted, "Thanks to Ms. LaMonte's unwavering dedication, tonight's fundraiser is expected to bring in close to a half a million dollars to support the school."

Clarissa's face dropped slightly. But then, she thought a moment.

"Ms. LaMonte," Clarissa finally smiled, making eye contact with a nemesis of her own. "It's wonderful that you are such a patron of the arts and understand its value in our culture and society."

"Indeed, I do," Portia answered, warmly. "While not an artist myself, I appreciate the talent I see from the young men and women who graduate from this school."

"With that in mind...if I may be so bold?" Clarissa continued.

Spencer's face dropped and his skin went clammy. *What was she doing? This wasn't at all scripted.*

"Yes?" Portia asked. "What is it?"

"I would very much like to audition for the lead role in the off-Broadway production of *If I didn't Care.* Its scheduled opening night is in four months, but it seems I don't have the necessary memberships to allow me to audition."

"And," Portia asked graciously, smiling, "what does this have to do with me?"

"Well," Clarissa, a good 15-years-or-more-younger than Portia answered. "Given your dedication to the arts, young artists, and actresses and your influence, I thought you might...put in a good word for me with the director?"

Portia paused for a moment as Astor and Spencer both sucked in their breaths.

"What makes you think I have any influence over this partic-ular production?" Portia asked.

"Well, it's at the Plymouth," Clarissa tread carefully. "I happen to know that's one of the theaters your family supports. I read that it's one of your favorites." Clarissa fell silent, awaiting Portia's answer.

Finally, Ms. LaMonte smiled. "Well, obviously, I have to hear you sing first," Portia answered. "Astor, my bag," she motioned to Astor Ellis who had been holding her pearl-beaded clutch purse on her behalf. He dutifully handed it to her. "Here," she dug out a business card and handed it to Clarissa. "Call my office in the morning and my assistant will schedule a time for you to sing for me. It's the most I can promise, but..." she paused, looking Clarissa over, judgmentally. "If you're as good as you seem to think you are, then you will have my full support."

"Thank you, Ms. LaMonte," Clarissa spilled, graciously. "I happened to have read in the papers...forgive me for mentioning the tabloids...but..."

Portia nodded in understanding.

"But I heard that you and Mr. Ellis are to be engaged very soon. I would be honored if you might attend the show one evening as a way of celebrating? Assuming it all works out and I'm cast, of course."

Astor's face turned a beet red. *What is she doing?* he wondered. *Is this a sick form of revenge?*

Spencer was confused as well and appalled at her arrogance. *Did she really think that she was as good as all that—she'd natu-rally be chosen if she got the audition?*

Portia, standing there in a creme-colored dress with black sequins that shouldn't have worked together, but did, along with gold-colored shoes complete with chunky heels, didn't miss a beat. She flashed her fake eyelashes and answered in a sultry tone of voice, "We would be delighted." She paused for a moment. "It's at the Plymouth theater, you say?"

"Yes, that's right," Clarissa acknowledged, nodding.

"Well, my family has box seats at many of the theaters in town. Rest assured, if you can impress me enough to get you an audition and top billing in *If I Didn't Care*, we will be there."

It didn't matter that Portia LaMonte was not an actress, singer, dancer, artist, or musician herself, nor that she possessed any skill as an art critic other than knowing simply what she liked and what she didn't. All that mattered is that she had a lot of money...and that meant that her opinion *did* matter...to everyone...and for more than it should.

Clarissa felt something settling at the center of her chest. *What was it? Grief? Jealousy? Sadness?* No, it was something much worse...*worthlessness*. No matter her education, her skills, or who she was as a person, the one she wanted was soon to be engaged to a woman she could never be. She wasn't a well-put-together blonde-haired debutante with razor-thin features and a bank account worthy of kings. She didn't have the confidence, either, at least not in anything other than one thing, her voice.

She clutched Spencer's arm a little tighter. Spencer merely looked over and smiled back. He observed Astor's expression as he clenched his jaw. By Spencer's estimation, despite this odd detour, things were going...perfectly.

It was unclear what Spencer hoped to gain by showing up with Astor's recent ex-lover that evening, not even to Spencer. Somewhere in the back of his mind, he thought perhaps it could serve as blackmail should Astor reveal another one of Spencer-Tech's creations as his own. But even more so, it was leverage if B. A. Ellis Industries followed through on their threats to sue him. He could take the story to the papers and they loved a good scandal, particularly when it involved prominent socialites in the business world.

"That would be wonderful," Clarissa bit her lip. "I'm honored."

"What have I missed?" Gretchen Ellis blew in like a breeze, touching Astor's elbow. "Sorry I'm late, but I had a dreadful time in traffic this evening."

"Mother," Astor greeted, "you remember Spencer Hargrove, don't you? He worked with Dad and I at the office?"

Gretchen gave Spencer a long once over...and again, smiled. "I'm sure if we'd met, I'd have remembered," she presented a hand to Spencer. "Nice to meet you, Mr. Hargrove."

Astor shuddered slightly. "Anyway, he's here with his lady friend, Clarise, is it?"

"Clarissa." Clarissa stewed under her breath.

"My apologies," Astor corrected himself. "Clarissa. Anyway, they have been discussing an upcoming show that she might be auditioning for, thanks to Portia's generous support. Eh, what was it called?"

"*If I Didn't Care,*" Clarissa answered, loudly, accentuating each word. Ironic, as at that moment, she was confident that Astor Ellis didn't care about anything but himself.

"That's right," he smiled slightly. "Anyway, Portia has box seats at that theater, so perhaps the family could make a night of it when the show runs? Might be a nice way to celebrate a certain engagement?" He nodded his head toward Portia as if his mother were daft and unaware of the arrangement.

The only woman in the room more practiced in her demeanor was Gretchen Ellis who immediately responded with, "I'm familiar with your reputation, Ms. Sauer..." She paused while Clarissa sucked in her breath. "As an opera singer," she finished...eventually.

"Oh," Clarissa let out a sigh. "Yes, of course."

"It will be our great fortune to get to hear you sing."

"Assuming she gets the part," Spencer added, helpfully.

Clarissa nodded slightly and forced the tiniest of smiles on her face. But it was all too much. She took a sip of her champagne, handed the rest to Spencer and said, "I need to powder my nose for a moment. Will you excuse me?"

"Of course, my darling," Spencer gallantly offered. "Hurry back, though, won't you? The world is much emptier without you."

Clarissa shot back a practiced smile with loving eyes, willing herself not to look at Astor to catch his expression. She darted into the nearest ladies' room where she cried her eyes out in one of the stalls for the next ten minutes.

Astor and Portia were called away to prep for a presentation that including announcing raffle contests and the sponsors of the evening.

Meanwhile, Gretchen Ellis sidled next to Spencer. "She is lovely," Gretchen commented.

"Nice to see you again, Mrs. Ellis."

"Come now, Spencer. We're alone, no need to be so formal."

"Why did you pretend not to remember me? Or did you forget?"

Gretchen made certain no one was near them when she reached around and pinched Spencer on the bottom. "Of course, I didn't forget," she grinned, her eyes circulating the room and not meeting his gaze.

"What is it that you want, Gretchen?" Spencer eyed the ladies' room door across the floor, wondering when Clarissa was going to return.

"I'm curious," Gretchen ignored the question. "Since your girlfriend—Rue Brennan—your real girlfriend, not this imposter designed to make my son jealous, is actually one of the models of the Atelier, tell me," she leaned in and whispered in his ear, "why is she not here with you? All of the models were invited, free of charge."

"Well," Spencer backed away, sticking a finger in his ear to scratch the itch caused by Gretchen's breath. "She doesn't exactly present well, now, does she?"

"Really?" Gretchen was surprised. "Certainly better than a gold-digger like Clarissa Sauer, don't you think?"

Spencer grew defensive. "Clarissa's not a—" He caught a glimpse of Gretchen's snicker and realized he fallen right into her trap.

"Don't get testy, my dear." Gretchen touched his arm. "But when you've decided you've had enough of this running around with pretty little things that can't possibly help advance your career, look me up. We had a good thing together...once." She winked at him and waltzed away, quickly swarmed by a host of admirers and at least one photographer.

Gretchen was more than 25 years his senior—forceful, confident...and rich.

"Sorry about that," Clarissa apologized when she'd returned, taking Spencer's arm.

"That's okay, my darling," he patted her hand. "What say we get out of this place?"

"Without seeing any of the exhibits?" Clarissa questioned, trying in vain to stretch her toes in her uncomfortable pointed shoes.

"Are you in any of them?" he smirked.

"Of course not," she answered, "I'm a singer, not an art model." Clarissa seemed almost offended at the accusation. She momentarily thought of her friend, Ursula, who *was* in fact, a figure model. But there was a part of her that didn't want Spencer to know that, given his admissions about his own girlfriend's choice in occupation.

"Well then," he replied. "There is nothing here worthy of my attention." He leaned in, pressing his forehead to hers and smiling, as if sharing a secret. "Let's get out of here."

Suddenly, Clarissa felt something in her heart flutter, just a little. *Maybe...*she thought.

# Chapter 23
# The Art of Death

Rue arrived early for the second shift and decided to sit in on the early-morning set. It was the final day of Ursula Gorky posing as Tosca. The model was wearing a bright orange and white gown that trailed behind her on the floor. She was draped across a series of stools covered in gray drop cloths arranged to give the illusion of a castle's parapet. Rue's best guess was that this was the actual act of dying versus the death, with Tosca attempting to throw herself from the parapet. Ursula's arm was wrapped around her face with her opposite arm and leg dangling from the ledge. She was surrounded by a blue hue of dim lighting designed to imitate a moonlit night. On each side of the stage, space heaters whirred loudly, blowing toward the stand to keep the model warm given her limited attire.

Rue found an unoccupied folding chair at the back of the studio and quietly melted into it, trying not to disturb the students who were surrounding the model stand, diligently adding and blending paints to canvas on their individual easels.

At the center of the group stood Jaks Liebling. He was a small and thin man with shoulder-length brown hair that he kept pulled back in a mullet, a pale complexion, and a pointed chin. He wore a murky, chocolate-colored turtleneck and corduroy jeans that went out of style years ago.

While he was commissioning the project, he invited students to participate as well, with the idea that the final exhibit would showcase his work alongside students—which of course, was really to demonstrate how his painting far outstretched everyone else's. And yet, a very appreciative, hand-picked group of the Atelier's best art students were chosen to showcase their final projects.

Jaks glanced over at Rue momentarily and grinned from ear to ear, as if he knew a secret that he wasn't sharing, before returning to his canvas. Rue attempted to crane her neck to see his work and what she saw was somewhat disturbing. He didn't paint the scene with the gray, white, orange, and pale blue colors on the model stand. All of his colors were an ugly mix of black and red that swirled together, making Tosca appear more like a demon in the abstract than an unfortunate heroine who lost the love of her life.

Conversely, several of the students surrounding him had work that was promising, some focusing on the light that was hitting Ursula's back and shoulder, others capturing the fine details of her gown and the way her hair hung haphazardly forward with several unruly strands refusing to lay comfortably. Instead, they sprang upright in frazzled rebellion.

"She sure fidgets less than the last one," a female student commented on Ursula's rigid pose. From her experience, most models were 'squirmy,' making them hard to paint accurately.

The room was quiet, except for the occasional cough or the

sound of someone cleaning off their brush by swirling it in a plastic cup of paint thinner. The room smelled of fresh paint and a combination of linseed oil and Liquin.

Finally, the great Jaks Liebling called the time and ordered a few students to help strike the set. The room came alive with bustling as students began to clear their spaces of canvas, brushes, pencils, and oil paints.

Rue stood, heading over to the unoccupied model changing area to see what costume Jaks had left for her. She passed the first station where Ursula had draped her day clothes over the top of it and headed to the second station where the door was wide open. There was nothing in the small enclosed, open-air room except for a mirror, a chair, and a long gown on a hanger, hooked to the side wall of the station. Rue touched the fabric. It was coarse with noticeably less material than Ursula's costume.

Rue changed quickly as she waited for a fresh crop of students to arrive and for Jaks to decide how to stage the next set. When finished, she plopped her jeans and t-shirt on the chair, along with her phone and coin purse where she kept her apartment key tucked away. As she left the room, she paused by the model stand, waiting patiently alongside other students attempting to strike the set, for Ursula to break from her pose.

There was just one problem.

Ursula Gorky wasn't moving.

Someone thought to turn on the overhead lights above the model stand, while another student touched Ursula's arm and then quickly recoiled. "She's cold," the woman announced, horrified. The young man standing next to the woman moved toward Ursula, carefully rolling the model over and letting out a gasp.

Ursula's lips were blue and her body was stiff. Her throat appeared swollen with a frothy saliva forming around her mouth. Her fingertips were also cold and blue—something that escaped the artists given that there was a blue filtered light above the model stand. The long and short of it? Ursula Gorky was dead.

Detective Ortega rubbed his tired eyes from beneath his glasses. "You mean to tell me that the entire class, including the instructor, spent the last hour painting a dead girl and didn't know it?"

Penelope cleared her throat. "It would seem so," she answered calmly, the forensic scientist taking a few more close-up photos of the body.

"Normally, the models break after 20 or 30 minutes," Officer Dennis offered, "but we were told that Ursula always insisted on one-hour stretches of time so as not to break the 'mood' of the piece. Her last break was at noon."

"So, she died thanks to her work ethic?" Ortega scratched his head.

"Not necessarily," Penelope explained. "We found an open bottle of red wine in the model changing area. I won't know until further examination, but if my suspicions are correct, she died from manchineel poisoning."

"Manchineel?" Ortega was surprised. "You mean the deadly tree?"

"Exactly," she explained. "The sores around her mouth indicate she may have ingested the berry. You're the detective of course, but I'd bet any amount of money we're going to find that this wine is manchineel-berry infused."

"So," Ortega concluded. "We're looking at murder."

"It would seem so at this point," the forensics expert agreed.

"Anything else of interest?"

"Yes, we found scuff marks in the changing area, which could be Ursula's, but given the tread patterns, I'd be willing to bet they came from the same shoe we found on the seat cushion of the theater two weeks ago."

"The one at the crime scene?" Ortega asked for confirmation.

"The same, only this one has traces of cigarette ash on the bottom, as if they'd stamped a bud out before coming inside."

"But no sign of cigarettes or smoke actually in the room?"

"None," Penelope confirmed.

"Officer Dennis?"

"Yes, Detective?"

"Send in Ms. Brennan for questioning. And have Officer Ernie scout the grounds for nearby smoking lounges, both indoors and out. See if he finds anything of interest."

Students had already been separated in the hallway or placed into smaller classrooms, the remaining classes in the school being cancelled for the rest of the day.

"Certainly, Detective." Officer Dennis left to first fetch Rue who was, unfortunately, still wearing the gaudy Elektra costume she had just changed into. He didn't need to ask which one was Rue Brennan as this was his second encounter with the woman.

Also unfortunate, was that Jaks Liebling had reimagined what his exhibit's Elektra would wear, placing Rue in a dress that looked like shimmering lilac flower petals with long bits of fabric cut in strange places to reveal a little too much leg, torso, and cleavage. The shoes were pale-peach ballet flats that were two sizes too big.

Rue crossed her arms in front of her, uncomfortably.

"Ms. Brennan," Detective Ortega stated calmly, "it seems that you find yourself, once again, at the center of a murder investigation. Am I to assume that this is going to be a regular occurrence?"

"Of course not, Detective," Rue tapped her foot nervously. "I was merely early for my modeling shift." She hugged her arms tightly around her. Despite the heat in the building and the space heaters, she was freezing.

Ortega glanced at her costume with disinterest. He seemed unaware that she was shivering.

"Just seems awfully coincidental that the one woman who spotted you on the balcony the day Clarissa Sauer died is the same one who appeared to have been poisoned not two weeks later. Doesn't that strike you as odd?" He looked her over once more.

"Of course, it does," Rue agreed. "But I had nothing to with it and," she noticed that his eyes fell on her chest, "Detective, do you mind if I change out of this ridiculous costume before we continue this inquiry? It's a little...revealing, don't you think?"

"Aren't you a figure model?" he asked.

"Yes, what does that matter?"

"So, you pose naked?"

Rue felt her face turn red. Penelope looked up from her camera where she was taking shots of the crime scene from all angles, concerned.

"Yes, but I don't see how that's relevant."

"So, why would wearing a revealing outfit bother you?"

"Inspector Ortega..."

"Detective," he corrected.

"Detective," Rue raised her voice. "When, where, and under what circumstances I choose to pose nude is my prerogative. It doesn't get decided for me."

"I'm all done photographing the changing area," Penelope offered, sympathetically. "If we need to enter her clothes into evidence, then perhaps we can send Officer Dennis to fetch her a suitable change of wardrobe." She shot Ortega a warning look. "She looks cold."

Ortega beamed a practiced smile. "All right, Dr. Washburn," he nodded before turning back to Rue. "It seems our forensics expert sees your point. Officer Dennis, can you bring Ms. Brennan her clothes?"

"Er," the detective stammered, peering around the corner from the changing area. "I'm afraid they have already been entered into evidence," he explained, "along with all the other costumes and clothing in storage here."

"Great," Rue mumbled.

"Got your phone and coin purse though," he offered, handing them to Rue who accepted them awkwardly. "We went through your list of contacts and text messages, but there's hardly anything on your phone. Do you even use it?" Officer Dennis asked.

"Are you allowed to invade my privacy like that?" Rue wanted to know.

"Tell you what, Ms. Brennan," Ortega offered, ignoring her question. "You go home and put on suitable clothing. We'll call you to resume this discussion in the morning, if need be. But," he added, wagging a finger at her, "don't plan on leaving town until we do, or I'll have no choice but to drag your ass back here and throw you in jail."

Penelope shot him the second *what the hell* look in a manner of minutes.

Rue swallowed a response. "Thank you, Detective," she acquiesced. He turned his attention back to his notes which Rue presumed meant that she had been dismissed.

Just was she was leaving the Artist Atelier, her cell phone rang...Darwin.

"I was just down the block when I heard the sirens. Seems they were heading your way. Everything okay?"

"No, Darwin, everything is not okay," she darted into the nearest ladies' room on the ground floor of the school. "Could you please bring me a long coat or blanket or...something."

"Sure," he answered, confused. "Will my jacket do?"

"It'll have to," she sighed. "Meet you out front."

Darwin did a double-take when Rue made her way through the revolving door of the school's entrance to the street. He bit back a grin as he removed his jacket and handed it to her.

"Something amusing?" she asked as she accepted it, wrapping it around her. Fortunately, Darwin was tall, so it was rather long on her. Rue pushed the sleeves up to reveal her hands. She began flopping ahead in her oversized ballet flats.

"Nope, not a damn thing," he caught up with her, averting his eyes. "Let's catch the F train...unless you'd rather walk?"

"No, Darwin, I most certainly do not want to walk," she grumbled.

At that moment, the sky darkened as clouds quickly rolled in. There wasn't even time to say, "Looks like rain," before the flood-gates opened, drenching them both in drops so cold they felt like ice pellets. Rue shivered, hugging her arms tightly around herself.

A few men whistled as she shuffled past, eyeing her legs. Darwin shot them his best aggressive look, which did very little as there was nothing about Darwin that screamed anger and aggression. Therefore, he wrapped an arm around her, shielding her from onlookers, the cold, and the rain as they hurried toward the train.

# Chapter 24
# Emma Post

Wednesday Afternoon in Detective Ortega's Office

The hardest thing about working with your ex, Detective Ortega decided, was less about the residual chemistry, or about the intimate knowledge you knew about one-another (that everyone else seemed well aware of, too), but was more about the awkwardness of being involved with the very thing that split you up in the first place. In this case, it wasn't infidelity, not another woman. Ortega was obsessed with his work. And every time he and Penelope worked on a case such as this one, he was cruelly reminded of the fact that the one thing that once drew them together (the thrill of solving crimes) was also the very thing that drove them apart.

Even worse was the sad realization that it was happening all over again in his marriage. He knew it and he was pretty sure Penelope's keen observations had witnessed it too. She was just too classy a lady to point it out to him or lord it over him. *What if?* Ortega allowed his mind to momentarily wonder, *what would have happened if I hadn't screwed it up with Penny?* No, he pushed the thought away. He was happily married to Nancy now. No reason to ruminate on the past.

Except he did ruminate. He also wondered why, every time he thought of his current marriage, he felt this bitter twisting in the pit of his stomach. Ortega couldn't be certain if it was over the guilt of feeling as if he were a terrible husband, if there were unresolved feelings for Penelope, or if it were simply the unfortunate truth that he and Nancy were incompatible. The sad reality was, no matter what the cause, it only added to Ortega's self-loathing.

"You're doing it again," Penelope interrupted Ortega's thoughts.

"Was I?" he answered. He didn't need to ask. He knew that his mind had wandered again, and he also knew that it was obvious.

"It's okay, but you should know that this is really weird," Penelope continued.

"What is?"

"The fact that this is the same scenario as the theater. Instead of 1500 theater goers, we have that many students with little or no way to monitor their comings and goings."

"Any accounts of new people being here who shouldn't?"

"Nope," Penelope answered. "We interviewed the model coordinator and all the men and women modeling have been with the school for at least a year and the students all check out, too."

"So, in the case of the theater, there was an unexpected extra usher who is unaccounted for. But here, there's no odd man out."

"Not that we can see," Penelope acknowledged.

"And the manchineel juice found in the wine? Anyone in the group recently traveled to the Caribbean or the Gulf of Mexico?"

"Literally, all of them," Penelope sighed. Ortega raised an eyebrow. "Okay, slight exaggeration, but who doesn't go to Florida in the winter or just to visit Disney World? And the school prides itself on inclusion and diversity, and has an entire exchange program dedicating to ensuring that students from other countries have the opportunity to attend."

"So, another needle in a haystack?"

"Another needle in a haystack," Penelope confirmed.

"There is one odd thing," Officer Ernest interrupted them, standing just outside of Ortega's office.

"And what's that, Ernie?"

"Well, I reviewed the statements from the students several times and three students had the same observation."

"Yes?" Ortega motioned for him to continue.

"They thought the lighting was off on the model stand. Jaks Liebling was particular about stuff like that, so they were surprised he didn't adjust it. They all chalked it up to his unique artistic vision."

"What was so odd about it?" Ortega asked.

"It's beyond me," Ernie admitted. "But supposedly it left a shadow across her face and arm and cast more light on her torso which seemed an odd focal point."

"That isn't the only oddity," Officer Dennis stood beside Ernie. "I just got back from meeting with the model coordinator. It seems Ursula Gorky wasn't the model scheduled to play Tosca. It was Emma Post. The coordinator asked Ursula why she was signing in for Emma's session and she said that Emma called her and asked her to sub for her last minute because she wasn't feeling well."

"Without running it by the model coordinator first?" Ortega asked. "Is that usually how it's done?"

Officer Dennis's head dropped. "Honestly, I hadn't thought to ask that."

"No matter. I think we should pay a visit to Ms. Post."

"Even though she's sick?"

"She could have been a hell of a lot sicker had she showed up for this gig," Detective Ortega reasoned. Penelope shot him one of those *you're being insensitive* looks again. "Er," he re-thought his next statement. "We won't keep her long. What's her address?"

## Visiting Emma Post

Police Detective Ortega and Officer Dennis stopped by Emma Post's tiny apartment in Greenwich Village, passing through Washington Square Park along the way. A few pedestrians stopped to eye them curiously, trying carefully not to make eye contact. An odd man bundled in a tattered jacket, scarf, and knit hat stood on one of the benches. Upon closer inspection, it was evident that he was wearing an elephant nose. Just after the two men walked by him, he lifted his nose in the air and let out his best impression of an elephant roar.

Officer Dennis stopped. "Should we do something about that?"

Ortega eyed the people around him. No one seemed to notice the man, nor care. "Nah, doesn't seem to be disturbing the peace."

Officer Dennis shrugged his shoulders and the two kept walking. Once they'd reached the street where Emma Post lived, there was a distinct aroma of cheap marijuana and incense, presumably to cover up the weed's pungent aroma.

Officer Dennis looked around but there was no obvious source of the smell.

"Stay focused," Ortega cautioned him. "I'm much more

concerned about catching a killer than I am about arresting someone for their recreational habits."

They'd reached Emma's complex and rang the bell for her apartment on the second floor.

"Yeah," a woman's voice called through the intercom.

"Emma Post?" Ortega asked.

"Depends on who's asking," she retorted.

"Police Inspector Ortega," he replied. "I'd like to ask you some questions about Ursula Gorky."

After a long pause, he heard the intercom click again. "You wanna come up or should I come down?" she offered.

"With your permission, myself and my assistant, Officer Dennis, would like to come up if you're feeling up to it."

"Why wouldn't I be?" she seemed flustered. "Never mind, c'mon up."

The officers took the stairs, finding the petite woman waiting on the landing wearing a gray jogging suit and seeming slightly out of breath and pink in the face.

"So, guess you're feeling better?" Ortega asked, flashing his badge. She ignored the question as she touched the edge of the badge with her fingers. "Yours too," she motioned to Officer Dennis. "I didn't stay alive in this neighborhood for 36 years by being stupid."

"Interesting choice of words," Ortega commented. Emma's flushed faced seemed to turn redder.

After peering closely at Officer Dennis's badge, she was satisfied. "C'mon in," she stepped back into her studio apartment, revealing an old white tile floor about three shades grayer than it stood be with several noticeable cracks in it, along with missing grout. Two fold-out chairs sat on each side of a small round table. To the left was an efficiency kitchen. To the right was the bathroom and an accordion-shaped screen that seemed to section off the sleeping quarters. What was most noticeable, however, was how low the ceiling was. The very tall Officer Dennis felt like Alice in Wonderland after eating the cake that turned her into a giant.

"Well, what did you expect for $750 a month in a rent-controlled apartment building?"

"Ms. Post, we're not here to discuss your living arrangement. We were curious about why you called in sick for your modeling gig, sending Ursula Gorky in your place."

Ortega paused to gauge her reaction before adding, "When it appears that you are not sick and that you may have actually been out jogging?"

She looked back and forth between the two men.

"What are you talking about?" she demanded. "I never called in sick." Emma was visibly annoyed. After a long pause while the two men waited for her to continue, she added, "Bernice, the model coordinator called *me*. She said Ursula had a last-minute opportunity to be the understudy for the show our friend Clarissa had been in and needed to swap days to fit her rehearsal schedule. I was happy to help, so Ursula was supposed to take my shift while I covered over the weekend."

"So, the model coordinator...Bernice...called you. Not the other way around?"

"No," Emma shook her head. "Though, I thought it was odd that Ursula hadn't asked me to cover for her herself, but she was pretty shaken up over Clarissa's death, so I didn't think much of it. I was happy for her, though sad as to why the opportunity was suddenly available." Emma's eyes started tearing up and she fought back a few sniffles. "Seems like they were finally resuming production after her death."

Officer Dennis looked helplessly around the meager apartment, noticed a roll of paper towels by the kitchen sink and grabbed a sheet. Handing it to Emma, he said, "I'm sorry for your loss...well, losses. Seems you were friends with both Clarissa and Ursula."

Officer Dennis, while not known for being the brightest bulb in the pack, was not without feeling. And from what he could tell, Emma was sincerely grieving.

"Thanks," she sniffed, accepting the paper towel. "I heard on the news that someone died at the school, but it wasn't until another model I know phoned that I knew it was Ursula."

"I know it's a difficult time for you," Ortega said in a practiced manner. He really wasn't good at situations where feelings were concerned. "But we were told that when Ursula showed up in place of you, it was because you phoned her telling her that you were sick."

"Did Bernice say that?" Emma was surprised.

"She did," Ortega confirmed.

"But that doesn't make sense," Emma answered. "I don't think she's lying, mind you. It's just that when we need to miss a shift, we call Bernice to arrange it. Even if I had phoned Ursula to replace me... which I didn't, I would have followed up with a phone call to Bernice to let her know that I had to miss the sitting, but had a replacement if she needed it. The whole thing sounds a little fishy to me."

"So, you never called Ursula claiming to be sick?"

"Absolutely not."

"And Bernice called you asking you switch days with Ursula."

"Yes, well, I think it was Bernice."

"What do you mean, 'think?'" Ortega pressed her.

"Her throat sounded all froggy on the call, like she had a sore throat or something. Wouldn't have known it was Bernice if she hadn't told me."

"I see," Ortega answered. "Anything else unusual about that call?"

"Not at all," Emma answered. "She just confirmed the day and time of my next session and offered me time and a half for changing the day on such short notice."

"Is that typical?"

"Yeah," Emma nodded. "They always do that if they have to make changes to the schedule in under 48 hours."

"And was there any communication with Ursula from the time Bernice called you until the time—" Ortega caught himself before adding, "of her death?"

"No," Emma shook her head. "In fact, the last time I saw her was at Merriam Hall."

"Merriam Hall?" Ortega was curious.

"It's a nightclub," Officer Dennis and Emma said in unison.

"Yeah," she answered, eyeing Officer Dennis, curiously. He seemed a little too stiff and proper to hang out at Merriam Hall, she decided. And she would have noticed. He wasn't good looking in the Brad Pitt sort of way. In fact, Officer Dennis was a little pudgy around the middle for someone so young, and had a round, boyish face and sandy brown hair parted in the middle in such a way that she could clearly see exactly how his head would develop a bald patch in about fifteen to twenty years. She smiled to herself, but then pushed that thought aside. *After all,* she decided, *can't really trust cops, can you?* She brought herself back into the moment. "I met up with Ursula and some guy she hooked up with."

"Hooked up with?" Ortega asked.

Officer Dennis and Emma Post let out a sigh. Ortega clearly wasn't from their world.

"She was out with some guy she met on some new dating site."

"Dating site? I'm afraid I don't follow. Is this another place in Manhattan?"

"Well," Emma thought how best to explain it. "You know

how people meet one another through newspaper ads...posting a bit about themselves and hoping someone will call or write back?"

"Yes?" Ortega was intrigued.

"Well, Ursula discovered this new way of dating, except instead of the paper, people find one another on the Internet."

"That seems strange," Ortega answered.

"How is that any stranger than meeting someone you don't know via a newspaper ad?" She put her hands on her hips.

"I see your point," he admitted.

"Anyway, she called me to meet her there, just in case he turned out to be a creep."

"Was he?" Ortega asked.

"I dunno," she confessed. "Seemed a little too slithery to me and quick to pass around drinks. But," she laughed, "don't go by me. I have the worst taste in men." She eyed Officer Dennis for a moment, before blushing and dropping her gaze toward the floor, immediately regretting her comment. He lowered his gaze and tapped the tip of his shoe on the tile. All of this escaped Ortega.

Emma thought a moment, interjecting a comment before Ortega could say anything, "There was one odd thing, though." She looked into the distance as if recalling the image to mind.

"What is it?" Officer Dennis encouraged.

"Well, we ran into Rue Brennan," she answered. "You know, the girl that was thought to have pushed Clarissa off the ledge at the theater?"

"We are aware of her, yes." Ortega sucked in his breath, impatiently.

"Well, Ursula was all upset. She was convinced that Rue had something to do with Clarissa's death."

"Did you think that as well?" Ortega asked.

After a moment, Emma answered, "Nah." She shook her head. "Ursula was one of my best friends, don't get me wrong, but she was also a hot head. Always seeking justice for any cause that happened to get her attention that week. Nah, I think if Clarissa got stabbed, Rue was legit trying to help."

"I see," Ortega answered. "Any idea who might want to kill Clarissa Sauer?"

Emma bit her lip.

"Emma?" Officer Dennis coaxed her, as if he knew her better than he actually did. Yet somehow, it worked.

"If Ursula was the social activist, Clarissa was the instigator," she admitted. "Don't get me wrong, Clarissa was smart, classy and had a heart of gold, but she sure knew how to manipulate men to get them to do what she wanted."

"So, you think a man killed her?" Ortega asked.

"I dunno," Emma shook her head. "I just know that girl had a million schemes. She used to say, 'I may have been born a pauper, but by God, I'll die a princess.'"

"What an odd thing to say," Ortega mused.

"With all due respect," Emma eyed Ortega from head-to-toe. From the looks of it, he was well-dressed, well-manicured and well-fed for man of his position. So, either he came from money, or he married well. "But women have gone from being told to marry someone financially stable and be good wives and mothers, to get a job and not be such gold diggers. Except, jobs are a bit harder to come by for poor women and we're paid significantly less than men."

"That's a shame," Officer Dennis wrinkled his brow in sympathy. Ortega shot him an irritated glance. Officer Dennis snapped back to attention.

"Anyway," Emma continued. "Clarissa was a sweet person, but I can't say for certain that she didn't make any enemies along the way."

"And what was so odd about the evening?" Ortega reminded her.

"Well," Emma bit her lip, "Rue showed up which was surprising enough because she seemed a little too square for the likes of Merriam Hall.

Ortega started to mouth the word "square," when Officer Dennis shook his head. Ortega shut his mouth.

"And what happened after she showed up?" Ortega asked, instead.

"Well, I ordered a Long Island Iced Tea and Rue asked me if I should be drinking in my condition?"

Officer Dennis was crestfallen.

"Nah," she chastised him. "Don't look at me that way. I'm not knocked up or anything. I just don't know where she would have gotten an idea like that. I mean, sure, I gained a couple of pounds over the past year...thank you aging!" She looked to the sky. "But that don't mean I'm pregnant. Hell, at my age, I'm not even sure that's possible."

"That is curious," Ortega admitted, clearing his throat. "So, I have one last question."

"What is it?" Emma wanted to know.

"Any reason someone would want you dead?"

"Well, gee. That was morbid."

"You *were* on the schedule to model at the Atelier," Ortega reasoned.

"Nah," she shook her head. "I recognize that I'm not all that and a bag of chips," she pointed to herself, "but, I try to live on the straight and narrow and don't cause problems for nobody. I'd never once consider that the target was me, never."

# Chapter 25
# Rootkit

Wednesday Afternoon at Darwin's Condo

"The shower's just through there," Darwin motioned. "You'll have to go through my bedroom, I'm afraid."

Rue stood in the doorway of Darwin's condo awkwardly. At this point she was used to working there, but most times she was far less...soggy. Rue looked absolutely miserable, wet, cold, and...scared. He hadn't even gotten an update as to why she left the school so abruptly.

"Uh," he eyed her sympathetically. "Give me a second and I'll see if I have something you can change into." Darwin disappeared into his bedroom while Rue remained stock-still on the doormat, not wanting to drip on the floor.

In the distance, she could hear him opening and closing drawers, the shuffle of papers, a loud thunk followed by some expletives. It was almost as if Darwin were less looking for a dry change of clothes and more trying to cover up the mess that was his bedroom before Rue had to pass through it to the shower.

"Okay," he finally emerged, pulling a dry t-shirt over his chest and tugging it in place. "I left a fresh towel in the bathroom along with a warm bathrobe. It's mine. I hope you don't mind." He paused by the hall closet and pulled out an oversized sweatshirt and a pair of small gym shorts out of the wardrobe, handing them to Rue. "Have no idea if any of it will fit you, but it's temporary and," he added, trying not to grin, "still more comfortable than what you're currently wearing. You can rifle through here later to see if something fits you better."

Rue stuck her nose in the air, accepting the clothing as she darted past him. "Thank you, Mr. Fennec." The truth was, she was freezing, so she scurried through his bedroom, merely glancing with a passing interest at a king-sized bed with books stacked on the nightstands that flanked it.

Given the built-in lights above the headboard on each side, it was evident that Darwin was an avid reader. Across the room was a club chair and footstool which sat beside a small dresser. Above it was a large window, black curtains drawn, surrounded by shelving units with more books, an odd collection of model cars, motorcycles, collectable beer steins, and a smattering of action figures, some still in their original casing.

Rue found this amusing as she shut the bathroom door behind her and turned the shower on. Unlike her apartment, Darwin's condo had water that actually ran hot on demand. She let the water run over her and let out a brief sigh of relief. It was momentary, as her mind quickly shot back to the eyes of Ursula Gorky as she lay dead on the model stand.

Back in the main living room, Darwin's phone rang, but it wasn't his cell phone. It was a burner phone, one of several lying in his desk drawer. He retrieved it from his desk.

"Hi, sunshine," he smiled. "Anything new to report on the baby front?"

"No," Ashley sighed. "I swear, if these two don't pop out soon, I'm going to ask the doc to evict them!"

Darwin laughed. "Then why the call...on this phone?" Somehow, this small detail had only now occurred to him.

"Listen, I'll send an encrypted text with more details. But I discovered something interesting on Frat Boy." Frat Boy was Ashley's code name for Spencer Hargrove. She gave all of his clients and even some of his colleagues secret nicknames, often unflattering, unless she particularly liked them.

"We'll get back to why you're working on maternity leave in just a moment," Darwin chastised. "What can you tell me?"

"There was an odd VPN login to his account not ten minutes ago, not at his office, mind you. This one appeared to be someone trying to connect from an address in Ukraine, but after a bit of threat-hunting, it turned out they only wanted it to *look* that way. It was...get this...someone logging in directly from Frat Boy's home computer. And they installed a Rootkit that attacked data on his company network."

"So, either someone broke into his home, he's self-sabotaging his own work for some reason, or..."

"There's someone else staying in the frat house," Ashley confirmed. "Any chance it's your Gal Friday?"

"No," Darwin glanced toward his bedroom. The sound of water from the shower could be heard. "Not a chance. She's in my shower."

"Oh, really," Ashley's ears perked up. "What aren't you telling me, Darwin?"

"It's all completely innocent, I promise," Darwin answered.

"Disappointing," Ashley let out a sigh.

"Is that my brother?" A male voice from behind Ashley called.

"Yeah," Ashley answered. "He's got a woman in his shower, but it's all completely platonic." To Darwin, she said, "Ryland's off to a baseball game, again. If he misses the birth of our sons, I tell you what I'm gonna do with his autographed Yogi Berra Louisville Slugger. I'm gonna stick it where the sun don't shine."

"One, I didn't need that visual, and two, you married the wrong brother. You should have picked me when you had the chance," he joked.

In truth, Ryland and Darwin met Ashley on the playground in grade school. Ryland and Ashley were eight, Darwin was ten. Ryland pulled Ashley's pigtails. All Darwin ever did was plant a kiss on her cheek and stuff a Valentine's Day card in her Wonder Woman lunch box. Still, Ryland won out as he and Ashley ended up marrying fourteen years later. The ten-year-old Darwin had long-since recovered, but he couldn't pass up a chance to remind her about it every so often. "And why are you working? Aren't you on strict bedrest?"

"Yeah, and I'm going nut-balls here. These kids must be doing gymnastics in there. Had to do something to distract me. Hey, listen, hate to cut this short, but lemme send you what I've got before we run out of time."

"Thanks, Ashley. Have Ryland call me if anything changes on the baby front."

"Oh yeah," she remembered. "Just one more thing... that girl Emma? The one who supposedly emailed Beige?" 'Beige' was Ashley's nickname for Gretchen Ellis.

"What about her?"

"The email was sent from the public library. Seems legit, so it really could have been sent from anyone, unless we could somehow track what computer it came from at the exact day and time the message was sent."

"And find out who might have checked into the library and reserved a computer at that time."

"Exactly," Ashley confirmed.

"Thanks, Ashley. Now go get some rest."

Moments after they ended the call, Ashley sent the encrypted messages. Darwin made a few mental notes before dropping the phone on the floor and smashing it, unceremoniously, beneath his heel.

"What did that phone ever do to you?" Rue joked, emerging from the bedroom in Darwin's burgundy terrycloth robe, towel-drying her hair. It may have been calf-length on Darwin, but on Rue, it skimmed the floor.

Darwin grabbed a dust bin from the hall closet and scooped up the mess. "Sorry, you're not the only one having a rough day," he confessed, tossing the remnants of the phone into a small blue bin next to the trash can, for proper disposal later.

"At least you weren't on the scene for a second murder," Rue finally blurted out.

Darwin's face dropped as if she'd socked him in the jaw. "What are you talking about?"

Without thinking about it, Rue took a seat on the couch and folded one leg under her, sinking into it. *Comfy,* she thought. To Darwin, she answered, "Ursula Gorky, the one who saw us from across the balcony at the theater?" She waited for Darwin to nod in acknowledgment. "Dead," she finished.

Darwin's complexion grew sallow.

"Are you okay? I didn't realize she meant anything to you." Rue leaned forward, concerned.

"*She* doesn't," Darwin rubbed his forehead. "But *you* do." Rue searched his face, surprised, but said nothing. After all, she'd made up her mind about Darwin Fennec straight away, and then double-downed on that opinion, no matter what evidence suggested the contrary. To her, he was a womanizer...a cad. Not faithful like her very predictable Spencer.

Darwin took a seat on the club chair adjacent to where Rue sat. "Tell me everything that happened today in as much detail as you can remember."

# Chapter 26
# Everything That Happened

Wednesday Evening at Darwin's Condo

R ue did a fair job of recapping the day's events, though there were so many pieces she didn't know. She began by describing the room, and then the people, and then the unfolding of events from start to finish. Rue also attempted to interject a bit of what she and Darwin had already discovered in case it was useful.

For example, they suspected from their investigations that Clarissa was blackmailing Gretchen Ellis, and they presumed Ursula Gorky was the one person to come forward as a witness that Rue was, in fact, alone in Box 11 with Clarissa before she tumbled from the balcony. The irony that Ursula, too, died from a staged balcony did not escape Rue nor Darwin.

Darwin was able to fill in about Emma Post's email being sent from the library after having spoken with Ashley but left out the small detail of someone else being in Spencer's condo pilfering information. This weighed heavily on his mind. On the one hand, Rue was his assistant, and should be informed. On the other, since Spencer was a paying client, he assumed Spencer would want him to keep this knowledge to himself. Until Rue was out of earshot, this was a conversation he was unable to have with the man, short of sending an encrypted message. This seemed to be a man-to-man conversation though, not something to be sent through email.

And on that same hand was the fact that getting into their personal life was really none of his business. And back on the other hand was the fact that he was really starting to like Rue. He didn't want to see her get hurt, didn't want to be the one to reveal Spencer's affair, and most importantly, didn't want to let his feelings cause him to make any rash decisions. So, he remained quiet.

"What I don't understand," Rue dragged Darwin back from his thoughts, "is how I got mixed up in both murders. Seems awfully coincidental." Darwin tended to agree. "I mean," Rue joked, "it's not as if someone were jealous of me being seen with you so that they tried to take me out at the theater and then at the college, right?"

Darwin's face grew even more serious, if that were possible. "Actually, that thought has not escaped my attention."

"Huh? Why?" Rue whined, slapping the couch with her hands. "I said that as a joke."

"I know you did," Darwin paused to think. "But the fact that you were so close to both murders leads me to think that you are either guilty, which I know you're not..."

"Tell that to Detective Ortega," Rue snorted.

Darwin continued, "Or, you are the scapegoat and someone is trying to frame you, or..."

"Someone is trying to kill me?" Rue finished, solemnly.

"I'm afraid of that possibility, yes."

"For knowing you? Do you have a jilted lover or something who'd have it out for me?" Rue wanted to know.

"Doubtful," he admitted. "But we can't rule out that it's not tied in some way to Spencer's rivalry with B. A. Ellis Industries."

Rue thought a moment. "Can we convince Ortega to put me under some kind of police protection?" Rue asked.

"While he's convinced you're involved in the murders?" Darwin answered. "We can try, but I'm not sure how that'll fly."

"Then, what should I do?" Rue's unfortunate name was living up its reputation and she was falling victim to its built-in paranoia.

"Well, you can't go back to your apartment, that's for sure," Darwin reasoned. "Besides, the reporters are certain to, once again, be all over this."

"Maybe I can stay with Spencer again for a bit. His condo is like a fortress with an armed security guard at the door and everything."

Darwin tried not to shudder at Spencer's name, but he couldn't help it, given what he knew. But he couldn't tell Rue. No, that was Spencer's responsibility.

"That might be the best idea," he relented. "I'd rather us be overly cautious and have it be nothing. Why don't you give him a call?" Darwin motioned toward a spare burner phone sitting on his desk.

Rue nodded, an odd sense of dread coming over her. *What was that about?* She slowly picked up the phone and glanced in Darwin's direction. He took the hint.

"Oh, right," he pointed absentmindedly toward his bedroom. "It's about time I had a hot shower after being out in the rain, too. I'll just be..." he pointed again, "in my room for a few minutes."

Rue nodded and dialed Spencer's number.

As expected, he picked it up on the third ring...always the third ring, never the first, second or fourth.

"Spencer Hargrove," he answered, not recognizing the number.

"It's me," Rue answered.

Spencer paused for a moment. "Oh, hello, darling," he finally answered in what Rue always called his Cary Grant voice, even though the accent wasn't his. Come to think of it, she wasn't sure if it was Cary Grant's either. There was something insincere about his voice, Rue noted. Why had she not noticed that before? It was as if there was a filter over her mind that was slowly lifting, and she was beginning to see things with more clarity. *Well, that's silly*, she chastised herself. And the filter was firmly back in place.

"Spencer," Rue began. "I have some bad news, I'm afraid."

"What is it?" Spencer sounded concerned. "Are you okay?"

"Yes," she assured him. "I'm fine, but...there's been another murder."

"What? Where?"

"At the Artist Atelier, where I was modeling. One of the models I know was murdered."

"Which model?" Spencer asked quickly.

"Ursu—" Rue caught herself. "Wait a minute, why does it matter which one? Do you know them?"

Spencer coughed, awkwardly. "No, of course not. That was a stupid of me," he countered. "Don't even know why I asked it."

"The point is, Spencer, I have now been on the scene of not one, but two, murders."

"Oh, darling. How terribly frightening for you. Are you home? Perhaps you should draw yourself a nice hot bath with those fancy salts you like, and I'll stop by later to hold you and remind you that everything is going to be okay."

Rue could sense a disconnect but reconnecting was a challenge. In the past, she would have blamed herself for this lack of communication. Now, she wasn't sure. She just knew that she was...tired...tired of trying.

"Well, Mr. Fennec is concerned that perhaps I was the target of those murder attempts."

"What? No, that can't be," Spencer reasoned. "Who would want to hurt you? You're too sweet a gal."

"I dunno, Spencer, but Mr. Fennec is concerned about me staying in my apartment. Could I stay with you for a bit? Sorry to do that to you twice in one month, but...it's just not safe."

There was a long pause on the phone line. "Now that I'm thinking this through, I don't think that would be for the best."

"Why not, Spencer, do you not want me there? Or are you worried that I might put you in danger?"

"Not at all," he proclaimed with bravado. "But given that I hired Darwin Fennec to investigate those trying to steal my multi-million-dollar plans, I can't help but wonder if they are trying to get to me—through you."

"Really? I'm not sure..."

"No," he answered quickly. "I'm quite certain that the safest thing you can do is stay far away from me for a while."

"What?" Rue's voice trembled a little. "But I don't want to stay away from you."

"No," he answered quietly. "I can barely stand the thought of not holding you in my arms tonight and reassuring you that everything is going to be okay. But I'm only thinking of your safety."

"What about *your* safety?"

"Nobody will harm me," he was convinced. "They need my brains to keep stealing ideas from me."

Rue ignored the implication that her brains weren't worth anything. Instead, she answered, "But, where will I go?"

"Hmmm," Spencer thought a moment. "Maybe stay with Midge for a while?"

"No," Rue sighed. "That won't work. For one thing, I'm not talking to Midge right now. For the other, she's only two floors up from me. How will that protect me?"

"I could hire a bodyguard for you?" Spencer's voice stretched in the way it does when he was uttering something that made him uncomfortable. And as a man who's invested everything he owned into his business, he likely didn't have wiggle room to procure a full-time security guard for his girlfriend, no matter how affluent he seemed to like to pretend to be.

"No, I'm not sure that's necessary. Honestly, I have no idea what I need right now," Rue's lips quivered a little.

"Tell you what," Spencer caught the waiver in her voice and had to think quickly. "Put Darwin on."

"Er, Mr. Fennec is..." She stopped herself before saying that he was likely in the shower. That wouldn't sound right. At that moment, he emerged from the bedroom wearing a fresh pair of dry jeans and a thin cardigan over the t-shirt he had been wearing. He was busy drying his wet hair with a towel. "Just a moment," she told Spencer. "Mr. Fennec," she whispered, "can you talk to Spencer for a moment?"

He eyed the phone quizzically before accepting it. "Hello, Mr. Hargrove," he greeted. "Yes, yes. She's doing okay. Understandably, just a little shaken up." He listened for a minute. Rue could hear Spencer's muffled voice on the other end, but not what he was saying. "So, no family close by," Darwin acknowledged looking momentarily at Rue.

Rue was beginning to feel as if she were a lost puppy that people were trying to figure out what to do with.

"No," Darwin agreed. "We can't put anyone else in potential danger, either." He paused to listen. "Well, invariably, it's up to her. Though, I'm not sure this is wise or appropriate." He looked at Rue again as Spencer spoke. "Yes, I understand. I'm concerned about her, too. Why don't the two of you discuss it. If she agrees, then I suppose a few days would be all right." Darwin handed the phone back to Rue. "Perhaps the two of you should chat about this. I'll just be in the kitchen." He didn't really have anything to do in the kitchen, but it was the farthest space away in the condo without going back into his bedroom. *Hmmm, maybe dinner,* he thought to himself.

Rue took the phone. "What's going on?" she asked Spencer.

"I just had a nice talk with Mr. Fennec and he and I agreed that it would be best if you stayed there for a couple of days. After all, there's full-time security and cameras in that complex and he has enough associates already working with him that can help look after you. I really think that is the smartest solution."

"Stay with Mr. Fennec? But there's only one bedroom...and he's my boss...and, Spencer, I really don't think this is a good idea at all."

"Are you worried he might put the moves on you? Because I'm pretty sure..."

"No! That's not it. It's just," Rue tried to find the right words, "for someone who is so big on keeping up appearances, it seems odd that you're okay with your girlfriend working and living with her boss. Kinda strange, don't you think?"

"I'd rather that then have anything happen to you," he reasoned.

Rue relented. "I suppose if he's okay with it," she glanced toward the kitchen, where Darwin was pretending to wipe down the counters and not eavesdrop.

"There's a good girl. Just lay low for a couple of days and I'll check on you in the morning."

Rue thought she heard a strange shuffling in the background. "What's that noise, Spencer?" she asked.

"Oh, nothing," he answered, "just...taking off my shoes and trying to balance the phone at the same time. Talk to you tomorrow, my darling." He rapidly hung up the phone before Rue could say goodnight.

"Everything okay?" Darwin called from the kitchen. By this point, he was pulling a box of pasta from the cupboard.

"I'm not sure," Rue answered. "I think so."

"Any dietary restrictions?" Darwin let out an awkward cough.

"Uh, no," Rue answered.

"You okay with pasta and a salad then? It's a compromise between your love of enriched white flour and mine for things that are green," he tried joking.

"Sure," Rue replied. "Though, I'm not really hungry."

"Well, maybe by the time it's ready. You should try and eat a little something." He put a pot of salted water on the stove and turned the burner on to bring it to a boil.

"Need any help?" Rue offered.

"No, thanks. But uh," he pulled a large jar of crushed tomatoes from the pantry. "Perhaps you'd like to pour yourself a glass of wine and fill me in again on everything that happened at the school today, maybe see if there are details you haven't told me yet? If you need something stronger to settle your nerves, I've got a decent Scotch in the cupboard." He pointed. "Oh," he remembered how Rue wrinkled her nose at the suggestion once before, "never mind."

"Wine is plenty strong enough," she answered. The wine rack was sitting in plain view. "Which one should I open?" She touched a hand to one of the bottles.

"Well, what do you like? There's red, white, sweet, dry."

"What's good with pasta?" Spencer usually made these types of decisions for her since she didn't consider herself particularly well versed in wines. The corkscrew opener was hanging on a hook beside the wine rack.

"Well, if you're not opposed to something dryer, go with a chianti or pinot noir. If you want something a little heavier and bolder, try the cabernet sauvignon."

Rue settled on the chianti. She wasn't feeling particularly bold. She fumbled with the corkscrew for a moment but managed to remove the wine bottle's foil and lever the cork. She reached for two stemmed glasses hanging upside-down above the wine.

"Oh, none for me," Darwin shook his head as he poured dry rotini pasta into the now-boiling water. "Probably best if one of us is clear-headed on the off chance something happens."

"What do you think will happen?" Rue asked.

"Hopefully nothing. But just acting out of an abundance of caution." He reached under the counter to retrieve a small food processor. "The larger glass might be better," he indicated. "Brings out the aroma of the wine better."

Rue hadn't realized there was a distinction between the small and large wine glasses other than one probably held more wine than the other, but she swapped the glass and poured herself a modest serving.

Within a short while, Darwin had a simple salad and pasta on the table, along with two forks and two plates. He'd even taken the time to provide a small dish of freshly grated parmesan cheese.

While Rue sipped her wine, Darwin settled on water, pouring a second glass of water for her, just in case she wanted it.

"This is really good," Rue commented after taking a bite of the rotini.

"Thanks," he smiled. "Nothing fancy, but I figure pasta is easy enough to have on hand for a quick meal during emergencies. I mean, one never knows when one's assistant is going to need a safe house." Rue took a larger sip of wine. "Sorry," he apologized. After a long pause, he added, "I think I should send Candy to your apartment tomorrow morning to retrieve some of your clothes...at least enough for a couple of days."

Rue nodded. "Not sure how she'll get past Midge though. I told her to back off, but she's as nosey and clingy as...well, her name!"

"Don't worry about Candy," Darwin was confident. "She's

pretty good at getting in and out of places undetected. And, if Midge does spot her, we'll have a story ready."

"Well, if you think it's safe."

"It'll be daylight," Darwin reassured her. "And I can get Bristol or Monte to go with her as backup."

"So, uh," Rue looked around the room. "I'm guessing that couch is a fold-out bed?" She motioned to the living room.

"Uh, yeah but," he took a sip of water, "I figured you could take my room, to give you some privacy. I'll take the couch."

"No, I couldn't impose like that," Rue objected.

"Nonsense," Darwin disputed. "Besides, if anyone's gonna get in here, it's likely to be through the front door instead of the windows at this level. Best if I'm in the living room."

"What would you do if someone did break in?" Rue wanted to know. "Do you have a gun or know karate or something?"

"No, but I can booby trap the front door and scream like a toddler that's dropped their ice cream if someone trips it. Don't you worry about me," he sat back in the kitchen chair and smiled.

Rue fumbled with the salad tongs, nervously dropping a few bits of lettuce, coupled with diced cucumber and tomato onto her plate. She turned out to be hungrier than she realized.

"Perhaps if we talked about something other than murder or the cases we're working on, this...situation might be a little more comfortable for us?"

"Okay," Rue agreed hesitantly. "What did you want to talk about?"

"I dunno. Something about you, personally," he offered. "Might help me to get to know you better. And I'm happy to do the same."

Rue bit her lip. She almost preferred to talk about murder again instead of her past. "Well, okay. But here's the thing, Mr. Fennec..."

"I wish you would call me Darwin outside of work. No need to be so formal."

"Well, okay." Rue paused, refraining from saying his name altogether. "I'm not super fabulous at talking about myself or overly private stuff from my past."

"Fair enough," Darwin agreed. "How about if I ask you a question and if it makes you uncomfortable, you just say, 'pass.' Would that work?"

"Sure," Rue agreed.

"Do you have any brothers or sisters?" Darwin asked to get the conversation started.

"Pass," Rue answered, forcefully.

"Oh, okay. I thought that was a soft-ball question but..." He thought a moment. "Are your parents still alive?"

"Pass."

Darwin was visibly confused.

"Okay, clearly we're not talking about your family. How about something simple. Where were you born?"

"Pennsylvania," Rue folded her arms, defensively.

"Oh, okay, great. We're getting somewhere. Where in Pennsylvania?"

"Pass."

"Oh, come on, Rue. How the hell am I supposed to learn anything about you if you keep every detail about your life locked up?"

Rue tucked her chin to her chest like a chastised child who was sulking. She sank into the kitchen chair.

"Fine," she thought a moment. "Yellow is my favorite color."

"Is it? Well, that's something..."

"No!" Rue covered her face with her palms. "That's a lie. It's really aqua, like the ocean."

"Then, why did you say yellow?" Darwin was confused.

"I don't know!" Rue wailed. Her eyes were red as if she were ready to start crying. Instead, she bit her lip and sucked in her breath. No tears emerged. "I guess no one's ever taken enough of an interest in me to ask what my favorite color was."

"I had no idea color was so important to you."

"It's not, it's...never mind."

"No, not never mind," Darwin answered calmly. "Surely Spencer takes an interest in you?"

Rue leaned forward and looked him squarely in the eyes. "If he did, then why am I sitting here with you?"

After what felt like an eternity. "Understood," he nodded. "I have another idea."

"Yeah, what's that?" Rue asked.

"Perhaps tomorrow, we can sneak out of here for a bit and take a day out. I can get Bristol to drop us somewhere and I am pretty good at disguises, if I say so myself."

"Wouldn't it be safer to stay put if there's a murderer on the loose?" Rue reasoned.

Darwin tilted his head slightly. "While I cherish the idea of hibernating in my home with you, particularly with the weather being as cold as it has been, I'm fairly certain that one or both of us might go stir crazy for too lengthy a time. Maybe just a short outing?"

"Where would we go?" Rue wanted to know.

"I dunno. Anything you have an interest in seeing in Manhattan that you haven't seen yet?"

"Well," Rue thought a moment. "Monte and Candy were talking about some bakery in Chinatown that had the best sticky buns on the planet." She used air quotes for emphasis. "Maybe there?"

"Ah, I think I know the place," Darwin nodded, wiping his mouth with a napkin and taking another sip of water. "China-town is a good place to visit that won't likely be on anyone's radar. Let's plan on that in the morning. In fact, since your apartment is on the way, maybe we can have Candy meet us en route to drop off some of your clothes."

"And for the rest of the evening?" Rue looked around nervously.

"Settle in with a good book and more wine?"

"That sounds like the best plan of all," Rue smiled. "Hey," Rue realized, "when do I get to ask you personal questions?"

"What did you want to know?" Darwin asked.

"Did you ever date Monte?"

"Of course not. What made you think that?" Darwin was surprised.

"No reason." She paused a moment. "So...you like...girls?"

Darwin choked back a laugh. "If you're trying to ask if I'm gay or not. The answer is no." He took a sip of water. "And for the record. Yes...I prefer women."

"Hmm. Well, what about Candice? Did you ever date her?" Rue fired away.

"No, are you crazy? She's young enough to be my daughter!" Darwin cringed. "You know, for someone who doesn't like me, you seem awfully interested in my personal life."

"You're right, I don't like you," Rue said in a lighthearted way as she chomped down the last of her salad and went back for more pasta. "But do you like me?"

Darwin eyed her for a moment. "Pass."

# Chapter 27
# Chinatown

Thursday Morning in Chinatown

Candice came through, meeting Darwin and Rue just a few blocks from her apartment with assorted clothing and toiletries.

Frankly, Rue was a little embarrassed at having someone else see her modest living quarters, sparse clothing selection, and even sparser collection of makeup, hair products and other accessories. Unlike Midge, Candice was discreet enough to not mention the need to retrieve bras and panties from Rue's underwear drawer. In fact, of all the people that could have been sent, Candice seemed to have a knack for what's needed in a pinch, having picked out just the right assortment of mix and match clothes, jackets, shoes and the like.

She also managed to fit it all into a tiny bag that would be small enough to store in the overhead of a plane. All this led Rue to the conclusion that Candice was used to having to pack and leave town in a hurry.

"Thank you," Rue whispered as Candice threw the bag in the trunk and hastily made her exit. She wasn't sure about how well she could, as Darwin called it, "get in and out of places undetected" while wearing the oversized, pink feathery jacket and the long dangling earrings she currently had on, but she was grateful, nonetheless. This only reaffirmed her belief that bold was the new beige in Manhattan, and the weirder you seemed, the less you stood out.

"No problem, sweetie. Just stay safe," Candice answered, interrupting her thoughts, before disappearing down the steps of the nearest subway line.

Bristol had arrived in the most boring looking blue sedan she had ever seen, but it worked. They blended in with traffic, and before long, Darwin and Rue emerged in Chinatown, Bristol dropping them off on Mott Street.

Rue, for the first time ever, had her hair tied back and tucked under a wig and hat. Her face was powder white with pink cheeks and bright red lips. She overemphasized her eyebrows with a little brush and makeup kit that was stashed in Darwin's hallway closet. He was wearing padding under his sweater and a deerstalker hat pulled over his ears.

Darwin led the way to a small corner bakery with nothing inside but a modest counter and a handful of baked goods. The place could hold no more than around five people at a time before it seemed too crowded. He motioned toward the sweet buns.

"Can I help you?" the young woman behind the counter asked as if on autopilot, eyeing over Rue's shoulder as several more people lined up behind them, the door now held open to accommodate the foot traffic. "Please close the door," she said loudly. "Heat is expensive." With that, the last unfortunate person in line was forced to wait outside in the cold, standing impatiently as those inside made their selections.

"I'll have two of the red bean buns, please," Rue asked. The woman grabbed two from the shelf.

"Heated?" she asked.

"Yes, please," Rue smiled in anticipation.

The woman was annoyed. Heating required an extra minute in the oven. Meanwhile, a few more people gathered outside. While the sticky pastries were heating, she rang them up.

Darwin went to pull out his wallet.

"No, let me," Rue offered, digging through the small backpack she was carrying. "How much?" she asked the woman.

"$1.75 for two," she answered.

Rue's jaw dropped. "That's it?" Had she known, she might have ordered a few more, but the woman's icy stare warned her against making any additional changes to her order. Rue handed her exact change and a minute later, the woman handed over the goods.

Outside, Rue pulled one of the pastries from a small wax bag, and handed the bag holding the other bun out to Darwin. She broke the small, warm sticky bun in half and took a bite.

"Oh, my God," her eyes grew wide as she spoke between chewing. "This is like the most awesome thing ever!"

"I know, right?" Darwin devoured his food. "You got the water, I think?"

"Yeah, reach in my bag," she turned her back. "There are two small bottles in there." Darwin unzipped the backpack, pulled out two tiny plastic bottles, and zipped it back up.

The two made a small toast with the bottles of water, pretending to clink them together.

"How have I lived this long and not tried Asian pastries like this?" she wanted to know. "What am I saying?" she kept talking before Darwin could speak. "Spencer would thumb his nose at anything this cheap."

"Good food is good food," Darwin reasoned. "Doesn't all have to be expensive. Wanna wander?"

"Sure." Rue finished her pastry and licked her fingers, wiping them on her jacket. (Spencer would have hated that, too.)

Unfortunately, Rue discovered that the divine smell of pastries wafting from the bakery did not last once they made their way down the street, where the smell of the fish market smacked them in the face. Rue wrinkled her nose. On display with ice and hanging in windows were every variety of sea life: snapper, bass, raw prawns, crabs, dried silver fish and more. As an omnivore, she'd eaten fish plenty of times, but somehow, seeing so many dead ones in one place made her a little sick to her stomach.

"What kind of fish is that?" Rue pointed to a large hanging gourd with spikes all over it. "A pufferfish?"

Darwin looked up. "No, that's durian. It's a type of fruit. I'd recommend staying away from pufferfish if it's ever served you. Done wrong and it'll kill you." As they walked by the row of fruit hanging in the booth. "Though, in my opinion, durian fruit is not much better," he frowned.

"Not a fan?" she asked.

He shook his head. "Not a fan." Darwin observed Rue's face looking a little sallow.

"Maybe a different part of Chinatown?" he suggested.

"Yes, please," she confirmed, averting her eyes from a worker chopping the head off a large fish.

They darted down the next block and walked until the smell of sea life subsided.

Outside a Chinese grocery sat rows and rows of flowers: delphinium, lilies, roses, carnations, snapdragons, peonies, crocuses and more. Rue leaned in to smell them...definitely better than fish, she decided.

"After the color incident, I hesitate to ask which one is your favorite," Darwin joked...very, very carefully.

Rue laughed, "What, no bird of paradise?"

The woman behind the flower cart merely smiled at them but said nothing.

"Ooh," something in the next shop window caught her attention.

It was a gift shop and in the window sat rows of bonsai trees, a few ceramic cats, multi-colored plastic bowls, tea sets, and a few hanging red ornaments of which Rue was unfamiliar and deeply curious about.

The bell clanged loudly as they entered, but no one bothered to look up. The place was bustling for a weekday.

Rue touched her finger to the top of the tiniest tree she'd ever seen and smiled.

"Serissa Bonsai," Darwin explained. "It gets pretty white blooms."

Rue leaned in for a closer look. "How do you take care of it?"

"Well, instead of traditional watering, you soak the base once a week, add a few drops of nutrient, and trim it when it needs it. They can be a bit temperamental though," he cautioned.

"Hmmm," was all Rue said.

"You like?" A small, older Chinese man asked, pointing to the Bonsai.

"Very much," Rue answered.

"You see," he pointed to the layers on the leaves. "There are three lines—this branch Earth, this one Man and this one Heaven."

Rue nodded. "And how much is this Bonsai tree?"

"This one very special...$35. Plus, you need small shears to trim it and food, yes?"

*Got it.* Rue thought to herself. *I can afford red bean sticky buns, but definitely not Bonsai trees.*

"We'll take it," Darwin answered. "And the food and clippers, too."

"No," Rue protested. "That's too expensive."

"In all the time I've known you," Darwin answered, "which admittedly isn't very long, there are only two things that I've seen make you light up like a kid at Christmas, red bean buns and this Bonsai tree. It's worth the investment."

"Very good," the man smiled, carefully taking the little tree. "Follow me."

At the counter, he cautiously set the Serissa Bonsai in a padded cardboard box along with a small green tube of liquid and tiny metal shears rolled in bubble wrap for safety.

A glimmer of light caught Rue's eyes, just above the shop's doors. She looked up to see an odd-shaped wooden octagon with lines all around it. At its center was a small round mirror. "What kind of mirror is that?" Rue pointed toward the strange, hexagon-shaped mirror.

"A Bagua," he answered. "Very good luck above your door. But must keep heaven on top."

"Heaven?" Rue was curious.

"Yes," he shuffled over to a shelf beside the cash register and pulled out a large box. Inside, he retrieved a small, eight-sided yellow, black, and red mirror with long and broken lines imprinted all around it. He pointed to the three solid lines at the top. "This heaven. It faces up. Hang in your home for protection."

"I'm afraid to ask," Rue pursed her lips, thinking of the Bonsai.

The man read her thoughts. "$2.99."

"We'll take that, too," Darwin chimed in. "$2.99 is a small price to pay for protection."

"Yes," the man smiled, adding it to their spoils.

Rue grabbed the door on their way out. "Well, thank you for that, Mr. Fennec. I didn't expect you to buy me anything today."

"Who says it's for you?" Darwin smirked. "It's for the office. We'll both enjoy it."

"Guess we should head back soon and not press our luck," Rue reasoned. "Plus, you shouldn't have to lug that around the rest of the day."

One thing that Rue discovered about Chinatown were the many scents. They reached the corner where the street smelled of sweet incense. Midway down the block, sandwiched in the middle of other buildings was a Buddhist temple.

"Maybe one more stop?" Rue followed the scent, curiously. She paused in front of the temple where she eyed a large statue through the glass window—a shrine. In front of the Buddha were rows of sand, tea-light candles, and sticks of incense. She noticed someone take one of the sticks, light it, and kneel on a red pad on the floor. After a moment of prayer, they stuck the bottom of the incense into the sand, leaving the top to continue smoking. They pressed their hands together and shook them lightly. Bowing slightly at the Buddha, they then took a seat along one of the rows of chairs running on each side of the statue. Several other people sat there in silence as well as if soaking in the scent during a silent, shared meditation.

The door was propped open so Rue peeked her head inside as if testing the waters. One of the monks, wrapped in an orange and burnt red robe smiled and extended an open palm, welcoming her inside. "Can I?" She pointed to the incense.

"Please," he smiled.

Darwin raised an eyebrow, curiously, but took a seat on one of the chairs, propping the Bonsai tree and other purchases on his lap.

Rue slowly approached the Buddha. She noticed that next to the altar was a bowl full of tiny scrolls marked, "Fortunes, Take one." Behind it was a box with a slit for bills or coins marked, "Donations."

Rue dug through her backpack and pulled out a meager dollar, rolled it up and put it in the donation box. She knelt in front of the altar, took a stick of incense and lit it as she'd seen the previous person do. She held the stick between her palms and looked up at Buddha. His palms were in his lap, a serene look on his face. Rue felt this overwhelming sense of calm, the likes of which she hadn't remembered feeling in a very long time.

*Okay, Buddha,* she thought to herself. *I'm not Buddhist. I'm not even particularly spiritual. But you seem like the understanding sort. I seem to have bad luck follow me wherever I go on account of my name. Maybe you can help? If you or some other helpful spirit is listening, maybe send a little good fortune my way? I guess what I can really use is...clarity."*

With that, Rue placed the incense in the sand, stood and took one of the scrolls from the "Fortunes" bowl. She turned to leave and then remembered. Spinning around, she placed her palms together, sandwiching the tiny scroll in her hands. She shook her hands slightly and tipped her head toward the Buddha. "Thank you," she whispered.

The monk merely smiled at her as she also waved her hands in his direction. He pressed his palms together and bowed in return.

"Well, Ms. Brennan," Darwin commented after they had left the temple. "You are full of surprises. Never pictured you as a Buddhist."

"I'm not," Rue confessed. "Not sure what drew me in there." She unwrapped the scroll.

"What does it say?" Darwin asked.

"It says," Rue read, "'only when the veil has been lifted will you see things clearly.'"

"Odd," Darwin commented.

"No," Rue disagreed, remembering her prayer. "Makes perfect sense."

Just then, Darwin's cell phone rang. He shifted the box to his left arm.

"Here, let me." Rue relieved him of the box. He pulled his phone from his jacket pocket and hit a button.

"Yes?" he answered.

"I have good news and bad news. Which do you want first?" It was Monte.

"How about the good news?"

"They caught the murderer. Some guy named Tommy Marcuzzo confessed to everything. You guys don't need to go around in disguise anymore."

*Really? As in the Tommy who had dated Midge and was friends with Max?* "Wonderful," he finally answered. "And the bad news?"

"Just hacked into junior's computer remotely." *Junior* was their new nickname for Astor, Byron Ellis's son.

"And?" He eyed Rue, pointing a finger that he'd be just a minute more.

"Someone sent him an email with a bit of proprietary information that was suspiciously similar to the tech Frat Boy was going to unveil from his company next month."

"Do you know who sent the email?"

"No, but there's more."

"What is it?"

"Bristol just spotted Frat Boy entering Il Cortile in Little Italy with some woman."

"Who?"

"Dunno, but I don't want to be the one to break it to Gal Friday...er, Rue," Monte corrected himself. "Just letting you know since you're in that neck of the woods."

"Thanks, we'll check it out. Catch you later."

Darwin hit a button and ended the call.

"Everything okay?"

Darwin weighed his decision very carefully. On the one hand, they had just had what could be argued was the perfect day. Why spoil it? On the other, if she discovered Spencer on her own, then he couldn't be accused of revealing it, now could he?

"Actually, yes." Darwin flashed a practice smile, taking the heavy box back from her. "Good news. They caught the killer."

"What? Who?"

"Tommy Marcuzzo, of all people."

"Tommy? Really? Somehow, that young pimple-faced boy didn't seem smart enough to tie his shoelaces let alone execute a murderous plan."

"He confessed," Darwin shrugged his shoulders. "Why would he confess to something he didn't do?"

"Exactly," Rue put her hands on her hips. Something didn't add up, but she couldn't quite figure out what it was.

"Hey, let's discuss it over a meal. It'll be the perfect end to our outing. And—" he nodded toward his belly, "I can lose this ridiculous stomach pillow." He paused at a bench to set the Bonsai tree down. Once he was certain no one was looking, he tugged the pillow from under his sweater, tucking it next to the Bonsai food. He picked the box back up.

"Yeah," Rue smiled back. "What did you have in mind?"

"There's a bistro I heard about in Little Italy. How about a meal that's better than the boxed pasta and canned tomato sauce I subjected you to last night."

"Well, Mr. Fennec, that sounds awesome." Without thinking, she took his arm in her hands. Then, she remembered herself and pulled her hands back, tucking them awkwardly in her jacket pockets. She was hoping he hadn't noticed, but he had. Darwin was just smart enough to pretend he hadn't. "But I would argue that last night's dinner was plenty good."

"But not as good as red bean buns?" he joked.

"Let's not get crazy," she smiled up at him. "Lemmee just check on Midge real quick? She did actually go on a date with this joker. I need to make sure she's okay." She hit the contact list on the cell phone Spencer had gotten her, clicking on Midge's number.

After a moment, Midge answered, pretending to be an answering machine. "I'm not in for traitors posing as friends," she droned. "Please leave your message after the tone. Beep!"

Rue smiled in spite of the fact that Midge was an utter pain in the ass at times. She played along. "Sorry to have missed you, Mensa. But I heard the news about Tommy Marcuzzo. Just checking to make sure you're okay. I guess I'll try back at another time." After a pause with no response, she ended the call. "Okay," she said to Darwin, "I'm ready!"

"It's just this way," he motioned an elbow since his arms were now re-occupied with a small Bonsai tree that seemed to get remarkably heavier the longer you held it.

After a short walk, they reached the restaurant. If Spencer were still there, he was at least discreet enough not to sit by the window. They ventured inside and requested a table.

"Certainly," the host answered. "Right this way."

He was leading them toward a table at the far end of the room when suddenly, Rue heard a chuckle. It was one Spencer used when he was trying to sound interested in something you'd said but really wasn't.

"Hang on," she instructed Darwin. "Be right back."

Rue meandered around tables, finding one in the opposite corner of the restaurant.

There, with his back toward her was Spencer. She could recognize that preppy haircut and neckline anywhere. And he was, quite obviously, holding someone's hand. The woman's head was leaning in as if sharing a secret, so all Rue could see was a suit jacket of beige and a swarm of gold necklaces hanging around her in varied lengths.

The woman, becoming aware of Rue, merely leaned back and smiled, gently releasing Spencer's hand.

"Miss Brennan," she said. "How unexpected to see you... looking like that," she motioned to Rue's wig.

"What?" Spencer pulled his hand back and leapt to his feet. "Rue, I—"

Just across from Spencer was none other than Gretchen Ellis.

Rue's face grew hot. All this talk about being so busy and being so concerned about her safety that she should stay far away from him. Pawning her off as Darwin's responsibility.

"Rue, should you be out in public?" Was all that he could think to say.

She opened her mouth to speak, but no words came out. For the slightest of moments, she thought to yell, but there was a small part of her that didn't want to make a scene, not to preserve Spencer, mind you, but technically, both Spencer and Gretchen were their clients. More importantly, Darwin was waiting anxiously at their table, eyeing the scene but trying not to interfere. She couldn't hurt his business or embarrass him after the nice day they'd just had. She gazed momentarily at a few of the tables surrounding her, mostly couples waiting with baited-breath at what they anticipated happening.

"No," she finally smiled sweetly. "Probably not." Rue left out the part about Tommy's confession. She turned to leave.

Spencer caught her wrist. "Please, let me explain," he whispered.

"Be back at your condo in an hour," she muttered between gritted teeth. "You can explain then." With that, she flicked her wrist to release it from his grasp. She didn't wait for his reply.

At this point, Darwin was already by the front door.

"Let's go," she said curtly.

Darwin merely nodded and followed. Outside, she said, "Sorry to do this to you, Mr. Fennec, but it seems I have some business to attend to. Namely, I have a boyfriend to break up with. Any chance we can have Bristol pick us up and drop me by Spencer's condo?"

"Yes, but are you sure that's wise?" Darwin had a flood of emotions coursing through him at that moment. Joy at Rue's mention of Spencer being an 'ex,' guilt over having her discover Spencer's infidelity in this way, concern over her feelings, and something else which he'd yet to define.

"Yeah," she answered. "I need to have a word with Spencer and then I'll be back at your place, if you don't mind. I know it was supposed to be an off day, but there's more to this than just my relationship at stake. This has to do with our cases. Just not exactly sure how, yet."

Darwin was surprised. He had expected her to be so overcome with emotion that work wouldn't have been a concern. Her focus on their cases was both admirable...and confusing.

As requested, Bristol was there to pick them up and deliver Rue to Spencer's condo in advance of Spencer's arrival. She hadn't a key, mind you. So, she waited on a couch in the lobby. "You gonna be okay?" Bristol asked, sympathetically.

"Yeah." She fought back a tear. "It helps that I'm more angry then heartbroken at the moment."

"Okay, I'm gonna drop Darwin off and be back waiting for you outside in a jiffy."

"Thanks, Bristol," she sniffed. "You're the greatest."

"Aw, we both know that's not true, but you're welcome." He tipped his cabby hat at her and backed into the revolving door, almost falling over in the process. "I'm okay!" he called back, laughing.

Moments later, a very flushed Spencer shot through the same door. The door couldn't move fast enough, despite his speed.

"Rue," he whispered, eyeing the guard who merely shot him a glance and nodded in recognition of Spencer being a tenant. "Could we go upstairs and talk about this?"

"Of course," she smiled sweetly. "Let's do that."

Spencer was surprised at Rue's calmness, something which both disturbed him and impressed him, all at the same time. What was she up to?

# Chapter 28
# The Slut, the Mother, and the Professional

Thursday Evening at Spencer's Condo

Rue's calm demeanor cracked as soon as they reached Spencer's condo. It didn't help that there was an obvious scent of Gretchen's perfume wafting in the air, along with a beige scarf she'd left hanging on the edge of his couch.

"Does she have her own drawer too?" Rue growled, pacing back and forth, eyeing the room for more evidence. "Do you divvy up the space between lovers?"

"Darling, would you please calm down and let me explain?" Spencer attempted to take Rue by the shoulders, but she shrugged him away.

"Don't you 'darling' me you Cary Grant wannabe!" Rue spat.

"So, now we're resorting to childish name-calling?" Spenser chastised.

"Oh, no, you don't," Rue pointed a finger at him. "Don't you *dare* turn this back around on me, you man-whore."

"Again with the name-calling." Spencer's face turned red. "Are you at least going to let me explain my side of things?"

"Oh, forgive me, my sweet," Rue mocked. "By all means, please explain your side of the story, so I can understand how your sleeping with Gretchen Ellis is in any way not cheating on your current girlfriend," Rue pointed to herself, in case Spencer needed reminding.

"What makes you think I'm having an affair with Gretchen Ellis? Did it ever occur to you that it may have been a business meeting?"

"A business meeting in a dark little corner of an Italian bistro where you were holding hands?"

"That wasn't what was happening at all. She was upset. Byron is having another one of his affairs again and I was just comforting her, as a friend."

"Comforting her?" Rue clarified.

"Exactly. So, you see—"

"Then explain this," Rue interrupted, reaching over and lifting a lace bra from the couch and holding it up. "This is at least two sizes too big for me and costs more than half of my entire wardrobe. Is this how you comfort all your friends?"

"Okay," he held up his hands in defeat. "But for your information, Gretchen and I had a minor relationship before you and I ever met."

"So, this was a little stroll down memory lane despite the fact that you're supposedly my boyfriend. Oh, and by the way, she's already married...to your former *boss*! Or did you forget that?"

"Please try to understand. She's just a means to an end. Gretchen has been helping me figure out who at B. A. Ellis Industries has been stealing scripts for the intricate programming that took us years to write and rework and then has been repeatedly trying to infect my system with malware. I suspect his entire business is corrupt."

"Helping...you?" Rue bit her lip. "Let's put infidelity aside for a moment, shall we? Why on Earth would Gretchen Ellis help you damage her husband's business by siding with SpencerTech?"

"Because she believes in me," Spencer whined, just a little. "She knows her husband is a self-absorbed, overweight, misogynist bastard who, I might add, is a chronic philanderer."

"So, that makes whatever the hell this is, okay?" Rue challenged.

"We were going to take down B. A. Ellis Industries together."

"You and I?"

"No, silly. Me and Gretchen."

"She was working with you to sabotage her own husband?" Rue was shocked.

"It was revenge, of sorts."

"For what?"

"For his infidelity, of course."

"And what about your infidelity, Spencer?"

"C'mon Rue," Spencer reasoned. "It's not as if we're married, now, is it?"

Rue's eyes widened. "Forgive me, Spencer," her voice squeaked in a high-pitched tone. "It was silly of me to assume that if you and I were sleeping together, then it meant we weren't sleeping with other people! After a year of being together, I clearly expected too much from you."

"Well, what about you and Darwin?"

"What about me and Mr. Fennec?"

"Mr. Fennec, please," Spencer scoffed. "Don't give me that formal 'Mr. Fennec' shit."

"I assure you, Spencer, my boss has been nothing but professional. And you were the one, after all, who called him 'light in the loafers.' Did you expect there to be some innocent flirtation on the off chance he wasn't enough to pique my interest and distract me from your affair? Is that why you wanted me to work with him? To keep me waiting in the wings for when you were ready for me again?"

Spencer held his hands together in a prayer position and waved his hands in front of his chest as if trying to explain. "You don't understand," he reasoned. "The world doesn't fit into this neat little package that you've created for it. *Relationships* don't follow the Rue Brennan system of how the world is supposed to work."

"Are you trying to suggest that I'm the problem here? That I'm supposed to be okay with all of this?"

"Just think about it for a moment. Look at it from my perspective. I'm trying to create a better life for us."

"You and Gretchen?"

"No, silly. You and I!" he chastised. "But a person in my position needs to keep up certain appearances and have the right connections."

"What is that supposed to mean?"

"Gretchen's influence opened a lot of doors for me. I got to meet with potential investors who otherwise wouldn't have given me the time of day."

"And appearances? It's not as if you could be seen in public with Gretchen, not with her husband's fame and influence."

Spencer coughed and tugged at his tie.

"Oh," Rue answered softly. "But you couldn't be seen with me either, could you?"

Spencer's face dropped. "Listen, darling, I love your free-spirited Bohemian style and that you laugh in the face of societal expectations placed upon us, but when it comes to getting one's foot in the door, it's much easier if I...fit in."

"I see," Rue felt that gnawing in the pit of her stomach.

Suddenly, a lightbulb went off in her brain...clarity! "The day you went to the Gala for the Artist Atelier—the one that I, as a figure model, was invited to by the model coordinator and then unceremoniously uninvited by you..."

"I told you I was sick that day."

"But you didn't want me to go alone." Rue thought on this some more.

"I was worried about your safety without an escort."

"You've never been overly concerned about my safety before, not even now, when I was on the scene of two murders and might have easily been the intended target."

"You're being unfair."

"And you're lying again, aren't you, Spencer?" Rue searched Spencer's eyes. He put up a momentary front, but then slumped his shoulders and dropped his gaze. "You took someone else to the Gala that night, didn't you? Someone more...professional... polished...less *Bohemian*?"

"Yes," he finally answered.

"Who?"

"Does it matter?"

Rue thought on this a moment. "If I'm so embarrassing to you, Spencer, why are you still with me? Excuse me, why *were* you with me?"

"Perhaps our timing was just off," Spencer explained.

"And what does that mean, exactly?"

"Let's be honest, Rue. I'm a hot-blooded male. We're hard-wired that way."

"So, society would have you believe."

"Don't go all Gloria Steinem on me now."

"Screw you, Spencer."

"Classy. Very classy, Rue." Spencer held up a hand. "Would you let me finish?" He waited a moment while Rue crossed her arms and bit her lip. She leaned up against the side of Spencer's living room table for what she knew would be the last time. "There are three types of women in my world, Rue—there's the kind you marry and have children with, the kind you bring to professional events—the colleague who doubles as your pretend wife—and—"

"The slut you sleep with while you're sowing your wild oats."

"Your words, not mine. But in a manner of speaking, yes."

"Which one is Gretchen Ellis...the professional or the slut?"

"I wish you wouldn't talk about her that way."

"Fuck you, Spencer. I don't give a shit about Gretchen and how my words might offend you."

"Again, classy."

"And which one was I, Spencer? The one you take home and introduce to mother? Did I just arrive at the scene a little too soon?"

"Kind of," Spencer admitted. "Though with the mouth on you, I'm starting to wonder."

"Well forgive me, your horniness, for not fitting into the appropriate girl-box you've put me in. I guess I was just supposed to be quiet and sweet, keeping my legs together for everyone but you, while you whored your way through Manhattan. Then, when you were finally ready to settle down, good 'ol Rue will be there, ready and waiting to make a good home for you and pop out a few babies when the time was right."

"I think you're being a little dramatic."

"I think you and I are finished."

"You don't mean that."

"Oh," Rue protested, "but I do. Goodbye, Spencer."

Spencer cleared his throat after Rue had made her powerful march across the floor to the front door. "And your belongings?"

"The one pair of pajamas in the drawer you cleared out for me and my toothbrush? I think I can live without those. You can donate my extra space to Gretchen." Rue opened the door. "Oh, and by the way. Your next quarterly payment is due to retain Mr. Fennec's services. I'll see to it that you have the invoice in the morning."

Spencer stood upright, surprised. "You're not telling me that you plan to stay on as Darwin's assistant after all this, are you?"

"Of course, I am. Unlike you, I'm very adept at keeping my personal life and my private life separate. I'm helping Mr. Fennec with your case and plan to continue doing so until it's resolved."

"What if I were to tell Darwin that I don't want you on the case anymore," Spencer threatened.

"It's not up to you."

"If I'm paying his company, it is."

"That's fine, Spencer. Though, you may want to look at the fine print on your contract with us."

"Us? You and me?"

"No, you idiot. Mr. Fennec and me."

"What fine print?"

"Given our investment in time, materials and resources, and the fact that we're past the halfway mark on our proposal, you're too far into the contract. So, by all means, cancel. But you'll still be required to pay our fee in full."

"That's highway robbery!" Spencer complained.

"No, Spencer," Rue corrected. "That's business. Try reading your contracts before signing once in a while."

With that, Rue slammed the door to Spencer's apartment for the last time, rushing to the elevator before the tears started flowing like a river.

Darwin wasn't there when Rue arrived back at the condo. But Monique and Candice were. Candice had been half-sitting on the edge of one of the desks, flipping through one of Darwin's books on code-breaking when Rue burst through the door. Monique was at Darwin's computer, typing rapidly on the keypad. Bristol, while sympathetic to her situation, had Evie and her younger sister at home fighting off a stomach bug and had to relieve his wife of parent-duty so she could get some rest. Consequently, he dutifully dropped her off at Darwin's place and left in a hurry. His heart sank a little. He knew she was hurting, and was hoping the rest of the team could be there, even if he couldn't.

Rue had done her best to wipe away the tears with the back of her hand and smooth her hair back before returning to what had become both her workspace and her temporary home. Unfortunately, as soon as she saw them both, the tears began flowing.

"Uh oh," Candice stood. "Here come the waterworks." Candice walked over and wrapped her arms around Rue. Rue sniffed back a sneeze. Candice's perfume was a little intense. But at least it overpowered Eau du Gretchen. "Lemme guess, you had it out with that asshole boyfriend of yours. Darwin told us about the incident at the restaurant. Sweetie, I'm so sorry."

Rue nodded, wrapping her arms around Candice and hugging her back, sobbing.

"Men are such a disappointment," Candice offered.

"Hey," Monique protested.

"Present company excluded, of course. Darwin, too."

"That's a little better," Monique hit enter on the keypad and looked up from the screen. "What about Bristol?" he wanted to know.

Candice thought a moment. "Yeah, I'll give him a pass, too, but only cuz that wife of his sorted him out. I also think having two daughters was karma's best revenge."

Rue thought about this a moment. "Do you have a family?" She chastised herself for not having thought to ask sooner.

After a short silence, Candice answered, "These chumps are the only family I got."

Monique nodded. "I was disowned the day my uber-religious father caught me trying on my mom's Sunday dresses. Candy is the closest thing I've got to family. She's like a sister to me."

"The point is," Candice hugged Rue a little tighter. "You didn't deserve what he did to you. But we gotchu. You're part of the Fennec family now," she smiled, leaning back to look at Rue's tear-stained face.

"Fennec family?"

"Yeah, Darwin and Ashley."

"I'm afraid I don't follow."

"Ashley? The gal you probably assumed was Darwin's one-time girlfriend?"

"What about her?"

"Well, that part was true," Monique corrected, laughing. "When he was *five!*" After a few more chuckles, Monique continued. "Ashley's married to Darwin's brother, Ryland. In other words..."

"Sister-in-law?" Rue finished.

"The girl is a quick study," Candice joked. "Well, let's just say, Darwin and Ashley have a knack for picking up orphans and adopting them, in a manner of speaking. And no matter how much time has passed...three months...six...a year, even if we go our separate ways for a while, we always come back to the tribe. And it's like no time has passed at all."

"How did you come to meet him?" Rue asked, immediately regretting it.

"Okay, but don't get all judge-y." Candy pointed a lacquered finger at Rue, closing her book and setting it down on an end table. "Nothing like what you're thinking."

"I thought you were a call girl and Darwin gave you a respectable job."

"Hmm," Candice wrinkled her lips. "Okay, so it is what you're thinking," she confessed. "But not to the *level* that you're thinking."

"Huh?" Rue was confused.

"I was—" she stopped herself. "I *am*...an escort. But I draw the line at funny business."

"Funny business?"

"Use your noggin', Rue," Candice explained. "I still am a part-time escort...a companion, of sorts, to men...er, and some women, if I'm being honest."

"Oh," Rue answered.

"Again, stop with the judge-y!" She wiggled a finger at Rue. "Well, let's just say, one day, things were starting to get desperate in the finance department. So, I thought I'd kick it up a notch. And the first guy I try to hooch up to on the street was—"

"Mr. Darwin Fennec," Monique answered.

"So, he was your first..."

"No!" Candice answered. "I offered him my body. Instead, he offered me a job."

"What would inspire him to do that?" Rue wanted to know.

"I was also really good at picking pockets. Except he caught me trying to steal his wallet. Asked if I wanted to put my skills to better use. He was on a case at the time, and I happened to be in the right place at the right time."

"So, you and Mr. Fennec..."

"Nothin' has ever happened," Candice confirmed as she and Monique exchanged glances. Candice leaned in as if sharing a secret with Rue. "Ya know," she confessed, "you could do worse than Darwin Fennec...as tonight has clearly illustrated."

Rue let out a sigh.

Just then, they heard someone fumble with a keypad and Darwin emerged from the outer hallway carrying what looked like an envelope.

"How are you doing?" he asked Rue. It was only then that she noticed he'd already placed the Serissa Bonsai in the window between their two desks.

"Okay," Rue answered. After a pause, she added, "I told Spencer—" She stopped herself. "I told Mr. Hargrove that we'd have his quarterly invoice to him in the morning." She sniffed a little and then started laughing so hard the tears began rolling down her face.

After a moment's pause, Monique, Candice and Darwin began laughing with her, Monique wrapping his arms around both Candice and Rue in solidarity.

Darwin waited for the trio to break their group hug before he asked, "Er, Candice?" Darwin held up the envelope. "Can I speak with you privately for a moment, in the kitchen?"

Once again, the sad thing about condos in Manhattan, even luxury ones, is that the living room, kitchen, and dining area are often one large, inescapable place. Short of asking her to meet him in the bedroom or bathroom, there weren't many options.

Monique and Rue attempted to occupy themselves at the computer before realizing it was fruitless.

"You didn't actually get to eat a decent meal today, did you?" Monique finally asked.

"No," Rue confessed, her stomach grumbled in confirmation.

"Well, since it's safe for you to go out again, seeing as they caught the killer, why don't you and I pop around the corner for something to eat? I know of a really good Thai place."

"Perfect," Rue answered, gratefully. "I'll grab my coat."

"Heading out for Thai food!" Monique called. "Buzz me if you want us to bring you back something."

Darwin waved an acknowledgment but refocused his attention on the letter he was holding for Candice.

Outside, Rue asked, "What was that about?"

"Darwin trying to reconnect Candy with her family."

"So, she does have a family...outside of the Fennec family, of course."

"Yeah," Monique answered, patting back her windblown hair. "Not my place to say more than that, though. Candy can fill you in when she's ready. Let's eat!" She changed the subject, grabbing Rue's hand and half-dragging her along. Monique was a master at walking in heals, but even the flat-footed Rue had trouble keeping up with her friend's long strides. Fortunately, the restaurant was only two blocks away.

Inside Darwin's kitchen, he and Candice stood, her eyes glued to the floor as she tapped her toe against the tile. Sometimes, everyone forgot that Candice was only in her early twenties. With her makeup, dress and demeanor, people often assumed she was a decade or more older.

"You contacted my parents," she whined. "Without telling me?"

"It wasn't like that, Candice," he answered. "Your dad hired a private investigator who I happened to know. He reached out to me before reporting anything back to your parents."

"Do they know I'm in New York?"

"They know you're safe," Darwin answered. "But they don't know where you are. Here." He handed her the envelope.

"What's this?" Candice sniffed.

"It's a letter from your mom. She sent it to my colleague's post office box, requesting he get it to you."

"Did you read it?" she asked, accepting the letter.

Darwin let out a sigh. "I'm not gonna lie...yeah, I read it."

"But it's a personal letter," she protested.

"And I didn't want to deliver anything potentially harmful to you without at least being prepared...or preparing you."

"What does it say?" she asked, crossing her arms.

"It says they love you and want you to come home."

"And school?"

"They're open to discussing a trade school instead of a business degree if that's what you want."

"Why did it take running away for them to listen?" Candice furrowed her eyebrows.

"Not having kids," Darwin admitted, "I have no idea. Point is, there's a ticket back home with your name on if you decide to use it."

"What if I get back there and it turns out to be a mistake?" Candice sobbed.

"Well, then, you know you've always got a second home in Manhattan. Pretty sure Monte isn't planning on replacing you with a new roommate anytime soon."

"Heh," Candice laughed. "There's no one else but me who'd put up with him leaving his makeup, cologne, and undershorts all over the place. No boundaries, that guy."

Candice took the letter and opened it. After a few minutes, she set it down on the counter.

"Well?" Darwin asked.

Candice didn't say another word. Instead, she ran toward Darwin and wrapped her arms around him in a bear hug. He awkwardly hugged her back. Having little experience in the mentoring department, he didn't really feel equipped for this sort of thing.

"I love you, Darwin," she sniffed. "In a strictly familial and not hitting on you sort of way," she clarified.

Darwin chuckled. "Likewise."

# Chapter 29
# The Truth

Monday Morning at Darwin's Condo

"Good morning, Mr. Fennec," Rue called out cheerfully after tapping the entry code to Darwin's condo and barreling inside. With the murderer caught, Rue felt safe returning to her apartment after she and Monique returned from their Thai food adventure. She tried knocking on Midge's door, but her friend was obviously still avoiding her. But, having heard her voice on the phone being as sarcastic as usual, she felt good knowing that at least Midge hadn't been one of Tommy's victims.

Rue had taken Friday off and had the long weekend to recover and take some time to process her emotions. Since she was not far from Chinatown, she even made a special visit back to the Buddhist temple just to sit for a few minutes, taking in the warm aroma of incense and clearing her head. The following day, she walked along the pier at the Seaport, smiling to herself as she passed the park bench where she had originally met Darwin... which somehow seemed like a lifetime ago.

She pulled herself out of her thoughts and back to the present.

Darwin wasn't home when she arrived. Rue looked around the room, curiously. But given the open container of trail mix and a half-filled glass of one of his green smoothies at his workstation, she figured he'd be back soon. It also appeared that he left his personal cell phone behind, too.

She slung her backpack on the seat of her chair. The chair creaked a little as she settled into it. Rue glanced out the window. The city looked pretty from this height, she decided, particularly since today was the first day they had a light snowfall.

It was only then that she noticed something. Darwin's desk and computer was on the opposite side, facing the faux brick wall. He had given her the view. *Curious*, she thought. *Why would he have done that?*

She paused for a moment to admire the Bonsai tree on the windowsill and the Bagua mirror that Darwin dutifully hung above his door, heaven-side up.

Just then, something beeped on Darwin's computer. Rue was all prepared to ignore it, but it began beeping again, rather persistently. She walked over to his desk. There, on the screen, was an email alert, blinking rapidly. Something was wrong with the server he was using to back up their data. "That can't be good," she said to herself. Her first instinct was to phone Darwin, until she once again noticed his phone staring back at her.

*Well,* she reasoned, *isn't this what she was being trained for? What's the worst that can happen?* If she did nothing, there was a good chance the data would be lost either way.

Rue typed in a few bits of command lines that Darwin had taught her and waited.

Something was wrong.

"Wait a minute," she realized. Someone was trying to hack into their system. Hence the rapid alert. First, she took steps to secure their computers and remote server. Then, she set up a ghost account from what appeared to be Guam (it was the first place she'd thought off, for whatever reason) to pursue whoever was poking around their accounts. *Wait a second,* she recognized that IP address—Spencer!

"Oh no, you don't, you cheating bastard!" Rue did the virtual equivalent of a drop and kick, tossing him offline. She then blocked him. Rue had momentary thoughts of sending some malware to his address but stopped herself. Unlike Midge, Rue stopped at having the devilish thought before ever acting on it. And, of course, Midge was sometimes bat-shit crazy. Rue wasn't.

"What the heck are you looking for, Spencer?" she asked aloud. She systematically began plugging in the code combinations, following Darwin's instructions to memorize the patterns of the codes versus the actual passwords. She logged into the profiles they had set up for Byron, Astor, Gretchen and Portia, but all the notes were current. She moved on to Ursula, Emma and Clarissa, still nothing new and interesting. She went through every profile she had access to, beginning to actually enjoy herself. What used to be a source of frustration had now become easy for her, logging in and out and putting the cryptic codes together so quickly.

"Wonder what my code would look like?" she laughed to herself. Rue typed in the sequence that, to the best or her understanding of Darwin's made-up algorithm, would match a profile for one Rue Brennan. She hit "enter" and that's when she saw it. Her face dropped.

There, in front of her, were detailed logs about her life, including photos of Rue and Midge standing outside of Merriam Hall, Rue and Monte heading to B. A. Ellis Industries, and one image of her stopping for tea at a cart outside of Spencer's condo.

On this one, the caption read, "prefers Earl Grey with light sugar."

There were lists of where she went after she left work, including stops at the bodega around the corner from her apartment and visits to the laundromat across the street. It even noted that she most frequently did her laundry on Sunday mornings at around 8 a.m.

In a separate document was a list of "likes:" theater, art museums, being on the water, writing," and more recently, "Chianti, bird of paradise flowers, Bonsai trees, Buddhist temples, and red bean buns." There was even an extra note that read, "seems to be highly sensitive to caffeine."

The hairs on the back of her neck stood up as she quickly scrolled through pages and pages of her life over the past month, horrified. Somehow, it was fine to keep tabs on who she deemed were the "bad people." They were the greedy, disreputable Ellises and LaMontes of the world. But why had Darwin been keeping such tabs on her?

Then, she saw it, a zoomed in photo of Spencer through the window of an obscure little Japanese steakhouse on the opposite side of town where he lived. Even at a distance, she could make out Gretchen Ellis's pointed nose and smile, as if the photographer had caught her mid-laugh. The timestamp read 6:24 p.m., two weeks prior to her discovery of them.

And then there were two other folders, one marked "Invoices," the other "Receipts." She clicked on "Invoices," and discovered that Darwin had been charging Spencer weekly for services marked as "Monitoring support." It identified the hours when Rue was at work, and the couple of times, off hours, such as their excursion to the theater and Chinatown. Her stomach sank deeper.

She clicked on "Receipts." There, she saw an ongoing log that included a number that distinctly matched her weekly paycheck.

"You're early," Darwin's voice startled Rue. She jumped from her chair. He walked all the way to the kitchen countertop without her even noticing. He dropped a pile of office supplies he'd just procured from a local shop. "I didn't expect you for another hour."

"What is this?" Rue choked.

Darwin gazed at the computer, opened his mouth and then closed it again. "I could ask what you're doing at my computer," he challenged.

"Security breach, and don't change the subject!"

Darwin's eyebrows shot up, curiously as he attempted to peer over her shoulder at the screen.

"Don't bother," she spat. "I fixed it. The larger question is, why do you have a file on me, Mr. Fennec?"

"Oh, crap," he answered, running a hand through his hair. Rue rotated in the chair, wrapping her arms behind her as if hugging the back of it, waiting for an answer. "Look," he put his hands out to his sides as his head swayed back and forth as he formed his words. "I wanted to tell you. In fact, I had every intention of telling you."

"When?"

Darwin sighed. He sat on the arm of the living room couch, crossing his long legs in front of him. He crossed and uncrossed his arms, as if not sure what to do with them but not wanting to come across as defensive. Finally, he jabbed his fingers uncomfortably into his front jean pockets.

"First of all, I had to make sure you weren't involved in either of the two murders," he explained.

"Bullshit, Darwin," Rue answered, angrily. "These records began before you and I officially met. Why were you keeping tabs on me?"

"I can't—"

"Why can't you?" Rue stood, her eyes beginning to well up.

"Client privilege. It would be unethical," he all but whispered, his voice cracking a little at the end. His eyes dropped to the floor.

"Who was the client? Spencer? What does helping him uncover who's stealing tech secrets from his company have to do with spying on me?" She whirled around on the chair and punched in a few codes. Darwin resisted the urge to stop her, secretly worried she was going to delete the files out of spite or discover something new she had missed.

Instead, she began typing. "It was Gretchen, this whole time, wasn't it?" she asked. "She pretended to be on his side, but she's been feeding their inventions to her son and husband, hasn't she?"

"I suspect so, yes," Darwin confirmed.

"And Spencer's affair with Clarissa?"

There was a long silence.

"How did you—" Darwin began.

"I'm an investigator's assistant," Rue retorted. "It's my job to know." She looked down at the computer and began sobbing. "He tried sending her in to seduce Astor, didn't he? To make Astor jealous that Clarissa was with him after Astor left her for Portia LaMonte? She was supposed to steal intel, wasn't she? But instead, she was trying to get back together with Astor."

"I suspect that you're right about that, too." Darwin walked over and rested his arms on her shoulders. She shrugged them off. "Don't try to comfort me, Mr. Fennec. You knew he was cheating on me. Why didn't you tell me? And furthermore, I still don't understand why you were watching me."

Darwin let out a sigh and remained silent during another one of his ruminations. "He paid me to watch you."

"What?" Rue tilted her head back to stare up at Darwin. "So, those receipts for my paycheck? Spencer actually paid you to hire me?"

"Please," Darwin stepped aside and motioned toward the couch. "Perhaps we can sit and talk for a moment."

Rue relented and relocated to the couch, never taking her eyes from Darwin, as if trying to read his thoughts. She wanted to make him say something that would magically make it all right, but she couldn't think of any scenario where that would be possible.

He sat next to her, leaving a good four feet between them, lest she start replaying false scenarios of him being a playboy again, despite all evidence to the contrary. "Spencer did hire me to find out who was stealing information and releasing similar product lines just ahead of SpencerTech. That part was true. What you didn't know was—"

"Yes."

"He wanted me to keep you out of the way until he did."

"Why?"

"I assume it was so he could pursue Gretchen Ellis without fear of your discovering it."

Rue stood. "You helped him cover up his infidelity!"

"I didn't know that at the time, I swear." This time, both hands went to pull back his hair—a sign that he really was stressed. "He told me he was concerned for your safety, a ruse that was conveniently reinforced when Clarissa Sauer and Ursula Gorky died in your presence."

"So, he paid you to babysit me?!"

"Well, it sounds awful when you put it like that."

"Because it is awful, Darwin! And if he truly was concerned, did it not occur to you that he could have told me and hired a bodyguard for me? Why would he send me to work for someone poking their nose into the world of people he deemed dangerous?"

"Well, when you put it like that—"

"Some investigator you are!" She eyed him over, distastefully.

"Hey," he whined. "That was unnecessary."

"And yet completely justified," Rue stood and went to grab her backpack.

Her back was toward Darwin when he said quietly, "It's because I liked you."

"What?" She turned her chin in his direction.

"I thought it was odd too, but the truth is, I liked you...right away, even before I'd met you at the pier that day."

She turned to look at him. "How is that possible?"

"The way Spencer described you. All the things he thought were annoying about you, the way you dress, how you say whatever is on your mind, when you eat with your fingers instead of using a fork—"

"I use a fork, when necessary," Rue retorted. Somehow, that seemed the least relevant thing to say in this moment and she immediately regretted it.

"The point is, all those little things that bothered him, I thought were completely endearing. And when I saw you and Midge out on the balcony during on your birthday—"

"You were spying then, too!"

"For the record, I didn't know it was your birthday or I would have reminded Spencer. The point is, I liked you, and I kinda wanted an excuse to have you around." After an unnervingly long pause, he added, dropping his gaze to the floor once again. "I still like you," he whispered.

Rue was boiling over on the inside, and the words formed before she could stop them. "Well," she answered quietly, "I don't like you."

He threw a hand in the air. "So you keep reminding me."

Rue headed for the door, pausing before unlocking it. "Just tell me one thing,"

"Anything."

"Did you purposefully take me to that Italian restaurant to discover the two of them?"

"I had to do something," he explained. "Ethically, I had to keep my client's information confidential. But personally..."

Rue let out a sigh.

"Where are you going, anyway?" Darwin was concerned. "I know they arrested Clarissa and Ursula's killer, but that doesn't mean I don't worry about you. Besides, you yourself said that something didn't seem right about it. Perhaps going out alone, for the time being, is a bad idea?"

The realization that he was probably right sank in.

"I'm going for a walk. Probably Central Park. They'll be lots of other people out at this time of day. Maybe I'll ask Midge to go with me, even though I vowed never to speak to her again and she has yet to answer my phone calls when I *did* try and speak with her again."

"Just be careful," he cautioned. "I'll keep my cell phone on me should you need me. And, when you come back perhaps you can tell me about the security breach you encountered? Kinda important for me to know, don't you think?"

Rue nodded. "It was Spencer. I backed up the logs. You can access them on the shared drive." She paused for a moment before leaving, looking over her shoulder. "Tell me something, Mr. Fennec. Did you think I would dump him and come running into your arms after I found out?"

"Only in my fantasies," he confessed. "In reality, I just wanted more than anything for you to know the truth."

"Well, thank you for that, at least. It seems I can't trust anyone anymore, not Spencer, not Midge...and not you."

# Chapter 30
# Central Park

Monday Morning in Central Park

Rue walked at a brisk pace, and it had nothing to do with the cold and everything to do with the hopes that she could somehow out walk her anxiety. It wasn't working.

She walked around the turtle pond, eyeing a few small, remote-controlled model sailboats on the water. It was cool enough for her to see her breath as she exhaled and somehow the cold air was a pleasant shock to her face. After all, she needed to cool down.

Rue didn't know what to think. If she were being honest with herself, she and Spencer had been drifting apart for some time, but every time she'd brought it up in the past, he dismissed it, citing work and reassuring her that "everything would be different once his new computer animation software hit the market." They would have more time together, instead of the long nights he'd spent working. It was only now that she understood how he was really spending those long nights.

And what about him pawning her off on Darwin Fennec, as if she were a small child needing a babysitter, filling her with all this crap about finding a suitable career "at her age?" What about any of this seemed like a good idea to Darwin? While it may have been flattering that he paid more attention to her than Spencer ever had, and that she was actually enjoying what she was learning on the job, how dysfunctional would it have been if she'd entertained the idea of dating him? He was only a few years older than her, but he was still her boss and furthermore...he had lengthy records about her, her likes and dislikes, her routine.

Sure, she thought to herself, she could make the argument that it was part of what Spencer asked him to do. She could further deduce that he had at least some reason to think she might be a murder. *But no.* She shook her head. Rue couldn't get past the fact that Spencer was actually paying her salary. That hurt, considering that she thought she was being useful on the job. *Wonder if he expensed the Bonsai tree,* she thought, miserably.

*No,* she decided. Everything that Darwin did was stalker-ish and unacceptable. He had clearly crossed a line.

She approached the large Alice in Wonderland statue, still deep in thought. *And speaking of boundaries, there was Midge...* who she only just now realized was leaning against a magic mushroom kissing a man not much taller than she was... *Jaks Liebling? The art teacher?*

"Oh, Rue," Midge broke away, wiping her mouth. "Fancy meeting you here," she said, nonchalantly.

"I left you a message and *told* you I would be here. I just didn't say *exactly* where in Central Park I'd be."

"Well, still a coinkydink if you ask me," she smiled. "I think you know Jaks from the Atelier, don't you?"

Jaks grinned at Rue in a way that gave her the chills—and not in a good way. "Ah, yes. Almost didn't recognize you without your dancing Elektra dress on."

It seemed odd that he'd choose that reference, considering that the last time she saw him was the day Ursula Gorky died via what they now publicized as an allergic reaction due to drinking manchineel juice-spiked wine that caused her throat to swell up so badly that she suffocated to death. Rue pushed the horrible thought away.

"You two are...dating?" Rue was surprised.

"You caught me," Midge laughed, and twirled a lock of her red hair. "Let's walk. I'm chilly," she commented. Rue fell in step beside Midge with Jaks keeping pace on Midge's opposite side. "Got your message," Midge confessed. "Don't worry, I accept your apology."

Rue hadn't apologized for anything. She just called to check on her friend. She decided to just nod and say nothing.

"Thanks for worrying about me," Midge continued, "but Tommy and I were done a long time ago."

*It was only two weeks ago,* Rue thought to herself. Again, she remained silent.

"And, as you can see, I'm with someone way better."

"And, uh," Rue stammered. "How did you two meet, exactly?"

"Well, after you so rudely left me, I took my sorrows to Atlantic City, where I met Jaks on a beach walk outside the casinos."

"Interesting," Rue answered, "that you both live in Manhattan and yet happened to meet on a beach in Atlantic City...New Jersey."

"I thought so, too," Jaks grinned, kissing the side of Midge's neck. Rue made a sour face, but quickly recovered before he'd noticed. "Kismet, I guess."

"I just wish you'd told me about this guy sooner," Midge grabbed Jaks' face, giving it a playful squeeze. "How long have you worked with Jaks at the school?"

"Actually, I believe I've only modeled for you," she referenced Jaks, "on a handful of occasions. Honestly," she paused, "it hadn't crossed my mind."

"Just look at that face," Midge smiled at Jaks who grinned back at her, eyeing her like a hawk who just spotted a rabbit.

Rue *was* looking...and she didn't get it.

"So, what did you want to talk to me about?" Midge asked. She paused to rifle through the small-beaded purse that was strapped across her chest and hanging at her side. She pulled out a packet of menthol cigarettes and a lighter. "Come to think of it, you seem a little off today. You okay?" She lit it and took a deep inhale.

"I'm fine," she answered. "And when did you take up smoking?"

"What? I've always been a social smoker."

"I've never seen you smoke and we're social."

"Well," Midge explained. "I've cut back a lot. But Jaks reminded me that there are no guarantees in life, so we should just enjoy ourselves as much as possible.

"By giving yourself cancer and polluting the environment?"

"Ladies, please," Jaks interjected. "Don't let me be the cause of your fuss. Call me a hedonist, but I would rather live for today, rather than get old and be full of regrets."

Rue didn't quite get the logic as you have less of a chance of growing old if you're unhealthy. And, if you do manage to live that long, but feel like shit all the time, then you likely would be full of many regrets.

"Hey, Earth to Rue," Midge waved a hand in front of her face. Rue's nose tickled from the smell of smoke and she let out a sneeze. "Bless you. You were about to tell us why you're acting so weird today?"

There was no way she was going to share any personal information with Midge, not with her creepy new boyfriend around. "Just recovering from a stressful couple of weeks...being on the scene of two murders and all. It was a little...jarring."

"Oh, I'll bet," Midge paused a moment, furrowing her lips. "But, at least, they caught the guy who did it. Our guy Tommy. Who knew? Maybe now the police will stop bugging you."

Rue stopped in her tracks. "Who said the police were bugging me?" She eyed Midge, suspiciously.

"Nobody needed to tell me nothin'," she answered. "Reporters and cops were swarming our apartment complex last week asking all kinds of questions about you before the news report about Tommy's confession. Where were you, anyway?" She eyed Rue, curiously. "Staying with Spencer?"

"Exactly," Rue lied.

"Well, probably for the best. Anyhoo, you'll get a kick outta this, Jaks and I pelted them with cherry tomatoes from the fire escape. Freaked one cameraman out who didn't know what was happening. I think he thought he had blood on him from an attack."

While she sympathized with the cameraman, Rue had to admit, that was a little funny. "Well," she laughed, "few people expect assault by cherry tomato."

Jaks let out a hearty laugh, too. Apparently, he approved of this sentiment as it backed up his hedonist logic.

"Wanna join us?" Midge offered. "We're gonna hit a new martini bar for lunch."

Rue eyed her watch. It was only 11 a.m.

"No thanks," she answered. "I gotta get back to work. Told Mr. Fennec I'd be a little late this morning—taking personal time, but that I'd be in before noon."

"Listen to you," Midge laughed. "And how are things going with you and Mr. Fennec?" Midge wiggled her eyebrows.

"We have a great working relationship," Rue lied for the second time. "Jaks, nice to see you again." That was her third lie. "You two enjoy yourselves."

"Oh, we will," Jaks said, placing his hands on Midge's thighs and pulling her in for a kiss.

"Down boy!" Midge joked, flicking the cigarette ash in the snow behind her. She kissed him in a way that suggested he was not at all adverse to a tongue that tasted like tobacco. She then held up the lipstick-stained cigarette for him to take a drag.

Rue wrinkled her nose again. "Okay, well, bye!" She waved a hand, moving away from the couple as quickly as possible.

At least most of Midge's relationships were short term. She was relieved by the fact that this one would likely fizzle in two weeks. She could wait it out.

# If I Didn't Care

## 15 Minutes Prior at Darwin's Condo

One of Darwin's spare track phones rang from his desk—Ashley.

"Tell me you're calling with good news and you just forgot my cell number."

"Just shut up and listen, Darwin," Ashley yelled into the phone, taking several labored breaths in and out.

"What's going on?" Darwin answered. "Are you okay?"

"What's going on is that I'm in labor, but I've got info you need to know before we reach the hospital!"

The sound of ambulance sirens could be heard.

"Are you in an ambulance?"

"Shut it, Darwin, or so help me I'll punch Ryland right in the gut. That's about how I'm feeling right now!"

"I'm pretty sure she means it," Ryland called over her shoulder, laughing. Somehow, Ryland was so overjoyed about becoming a father, that he was willing to overlook his wife's verbal assault.

"Talk," Darwin finally answered, simply.

"Tommy Marcuzzo is innocent. I know he confessed, but something wasn't sitting right with me about it. I did some digging." She paused to suck in a deep breath. "The guy was in debt up to his eyeballs and made a lot of enemies delivering intel on B. A. Ellis Industries to people he shouldn't have." Ashley paused again to rapidly blow in and out a few times before continuing. "Right after he turns himself in and confesses to two murders, $500,000 mysteriously shows up in his bank account and all his credit cards are paid off. Best I can tell is that the money was wired from an offshore account in the Cayman Islands. The point is, a killer is still on the loose, and I got a bad kick-in-the-gut feeling that has nothing to do with babies. You need to look out for Gal Friday."

With that, Ashley hung up the phone. Darwin immediately phoned Rue. Not having used it much, it took her a moment to remember how to answer her cell phone. "What do you want, Mr. Fennec?" she asked, annoyed. She was standing at the front of a food truck and had just retrieved a hot chocolate after waiting endlessly for the man in front of her to make up his mind when there were only four beverage choices on the menu. She nodded to the attendant, plunked her change on the counter and walked away.

"Rue," Darwin sounded anxious. "Are you still in Central Park? Where are you?"

"Just leaving, why?" Rue asked suspiciously, holding the beverage to her lips.

"I need you back here as quickly as you can. Or I can come and get you."

"I don't know..."

"You're not safe," Darwin all but yelled into the phone.

"What are you talking about?" Rue looked around, nervously, lowering the drink before having taken a sip.

"Tommy Marcuzzo's confession was bogus. There's still a killer on the loose."

The hairs on the back of Rue's neck stood up as she remembered Ursula Gorky's blue face and swollen lips.

"I'll be there shortly. No need to come get me," she answered. After she hung up the phone, she glanced back at the food truck, where a loud commotion could be heard. There, on the snow-covered ground, lay the older man, the one who had just been standing in front of her. Two people began CPR as a police officer and medic arrived. On the ground next to him, was a spilled cup of a hot liquid. She didn't know what kind as she hadn't bothered to pay attention to that detail.

Her heart began racing. She dropped her untouched cup into a trash can and all but ran back to the main street, where she made it back to Darwin's condo in record time. This time, however, she opted to go back to their old protocol and retreated to the employee entrance in the back, taking the service elevator up to the seventh floor.

Darwin saw Rue's frazzled expression as she arrived. "Did something else happen?"

Rue huffed and puffed for a minute, struggling to catch her breath after her rapid sprint to the office. Meanwhile, Darwin popped his head out the door, instinctively, looking down the hall on each side before bolting it. Unlike Rue's pillowcase curtains, Darwin's setup was more sophisticated. He flipped a lever and a tan shade dropped from the ceiling, stopping at the bottom of the windowsill, effectively shielding them from view, while still allowing light into the room.

Despite her nerves, seeing something so simple and yet so sophisticated versus what she had in her little studio apartment, made her feel distinctly less than...adequate.

"I'm not sure if it's related or not," she glanced at the window shades, swaying side-to-side nervously, "but after I got my hot chocolate at a food truck, you called. Just then, I saw a man on the ground with people around him. Looked as if he had a heart attack. He had been in line in front of me. Could have been a coincidence, but it spooked me enough to run home...er, I mean, here." Rue caught herself. After all, this was Mr. Fennec's home, not hers.

"Where's the hot chocolate?" Darwin asked.

"What? I threw it away. Why does that matter?"

"Because we could have analyzed it for traces of poison. You didn't drink any of it, did you?"

"Not after what I saw."

"Where was the truck? I'll see if Monte has time to go down there undercover and find out what happened."

He picked up his phone to make the call while Rue removed

her gloves, stuffing them into the pockets of her coat before hanging the coat on a clothing hook by the door. She wrapped her scarf around it and sat her knit hat on top. Rue rubbed her hands together, still feeling the chill from being outside, and eventually sat down at her desk and powered up her computer.

"What are you doing?" Darwin asked after hanging up the phone with Monte.

"Did you ever think," Rue created a new account in her logs, "that instead of following Spencer's idiotic attempts at finding the person or people responsible for stealing his intellectual property..." She turned to Darwin. "Kinda funny, when you think about it."

"What is?" Darwin was confused at her pleasantry, particularly given how angry she had been at him not three hours earlier.

"The irony of it all. He's worried about intellectual property when it's become largely apparent that the doofus gave it away himself when he hooked up with Gretchen Ellis and Clarissa Sauer." She turned and continued typing. Darwin waited for her to continue. "Well, instead of researching him, or finding out the chain of women Astor Ellis has bedded recently, which," she glanced up at Darwin's perplexed face before turning back to the keyboard, "from the looks of Portia LaMonte's tight leash and prenup agreement, hasn't been anyone since Clarissa."

"Prenup?" Darwin was suspicious.

"Yeah, that day Monte snagged Astor's login credentials, we logged in remotely and found an electronic version of a rock-solid prenuptial agreement. They get divorced and she's taking him to the cleaners."

"And where are you going with all of this, exactly?" Darwin crossed his arms, scowling like a disapproving parent.

"That we should be trying to figure out who actually murdered Clarissa and Ursula ourselves, since I seem to be oddly mixed up in it without knowing why. Therefore, Mr. Fennec, I'd like to retain your services."

"I'm sorry, what?" Darwin folded his arms. He was sure he misheard her.

"You pay me well enough, or should I say, Spencer pays me well enough that I've got money in reserve to cover my rent for a couple of months. I'd like to return a portion of that back to you in exchange for your help investigating murder suspects, provided you keep paying me, of course. I think it's only fair Spencer foots the bill since there's probably a connection between B. A. Ellis Industries and SpencerTech behind all this. We just can't see it yet."

"I'm not sure I follow your logic," Darwin admitted. "And I doubt that Detective Ortega would appreciate us meddling in his case." Darwin peered over her shoulder. "Jaks Liebling," he read the bio. A photo of a younger Jaks with a full beard and mustache flashed on the screen. "The instructor who was there the day Ursula was murdered?" He put his hand on the back of her chair. Rue could feel the warmth of his stomach near her back, even though he kept a proper distance from her. She was unsettled by the fact that his presence was both comforting and distracting, at the same time. She tried to focus.

"Yeah," she finally answered. "He was at the park today with Midge."

"What was Midge doing there? Did you call her?"

"I did. But I didn't expect her to show up with *him*," she shuddered at the thought. "Apparently, they met on her last casino run. But something about it is fishy."

The wheels in Darwin's head were turning, but he was having trouble getting all the gears in sync. "Tell you what," Darwin offered, "you start pulling together final reports that we can present to Gretchen Ellis and your boy—," Darwin stopped himself, "and Spencer Hargrove, and I'll see what I can dig up on this Jaks Liebling. It might also be worth my trying to reach out to Ortega one more time. I still think we can help one another out."

"Okay," Rue agreed. She stretched her fingers over the keyboard. They were finally starting to warm up after having been outside in the cold.

Darwin retreated to his own desk computer and started pulling the public records for Jaks Liebling. With Ashley on maternity leave, he would have to rely on his limited hacking skills and Monte's. Monte was decidedly better at ethical info-gathering than he was.

As if on cue, one of Darwin's burner phones rang. It was Monte.

"Whatcha got?" Darwin asked.

"False alarm," Monte answered. "Seems the guy legit had a heart attack. No foul play suspected, but..." he continued.

"But what?"

"But I gathered up a bit of the snow where he spilled his beverage in a container so we can have it analyzed, just to be sure."

"Good thinking," Darwin praised. "I've got another assignment for you if you're up for it."

"You know I am. Lingerie isn't cheap and you're helping keep this gal living in the style to which she would like to become accustomed." It sounded strange when Monte wasn't exactly Monte nor Monique, like now, when he was speaking as Monte with words that Monique would use. Darwin wasn't sure whether he just forgot to add the inflection, or it was his way of messing with people.

"Excellent." Darwin decided to ignore it. "I'll send you an encrypted email with more details." He hung up the phone. "Good news," Darwin told Rue who was now pulling together their reports to begin compiling final evidence packets for their clients. It was a tedious process, but she found it helped turn the focus away from herself, her anger, and her fear. "Looks like the man at the food truck was most likely unrelated, but we should have confirmation soon."

Rue nodded while she kept typing feverishly on the computer. Darwin noticed that, unlike when she first started, she had already doubled her typing speed. He'd also noticed how quickly she became skilled at navigating the client portals, catching and correcting security breaches, and doing boots-on-the-ground detective work. In fact, she was turning into quite the generalist. He'd have to figure out a way to keep her on after Spencer was no longer a client. Darwin turned back to his computer.

"Hey, Darwin?" Rue finally spoke.

"Yes?"

"I'm still mad as hell at you. But if it's all the same to you, I'll stay here tonight for safety reasons. But to be clear, I think it might be best if you didn't speak to me for a while, unless it's about a case. Understood?"

Darwin would take what he could get as long as Rue remained safe. "Understood," he answered quietly.

After Rue left the room, he picked up the phone. He got Detective Ortega's answering machine where he began to leave a detailed message. Halfway through explaining how Tommy Marcuzzo was a scapegoat, someone abruptly lifted the receiver.

"Just what kind of game are you playing, Darwin Fennec?" a very tired Detective Ortega spit into the phone.

"Just thought you should know, Marcuzzo wasn't the murderer. And given that you're in the office late makes me suspect that you know it, too."

"Offshore accounts," Ortega said simply.

"Exactly," Darwin answered.

"Don't suppose you happen to know who the real killer is, do you, Mr. Fennec?"

"No," Darwin admitted. "But despite your protests, I think it's high time that you and I had a talk."

# Chapter 31
# Darwin and Ortega

Tuesday Morning at Darwin's Condo

"I must confess..." Darwin told Ortega. Ortega's eyebrows shot up, curiously. "Not *that* kind of confession," Darwin clarified. Detective Ortega's shoulders slumped, just slightly, disappointed but not surprised. "I didn't expect you to agree to meet with me regarding Clarissa Sauer's and Ursula Gorky's deaths."

Detective Ortega eyed Darwin's condo with interest. He had intended on meeting Darwin in his office in Battery Park until he'd learned about the unanticipated publicity surrounding the case, not to mention the vandalism. The fall-out had died down for a short time, only to be reignited by Ursula's murder.

The police precinct, Ortega decided, would be too intimidating and might put Darwin ill at ease, as if he were being accused of the crimes. Not to mention the conflict of interest their meeting might cause. And finally, Ortega no longer trusted their ability to meet at a local coffee house or some public outdoor location without security concerns. Since cybersecurity was Darwin's forte, he assumed that meeting at his home would be the safest bet.

"Coffee?" Darwin offered. Ortega shook his head, unwrapping the long scarf he'd had around his neck. The weather that day was bone-chilling with wind tunnels between the buildings making it feel a good ten degrees colder than it would normally.

"Nah, I'm good," Ortega answered, hanging his scarf on the back of a chair. He turned toward Darwin, rubbing his hands together, trying to warm them.

Darwin poured himself a cup of coffee and joined Ortega in the living room. "Please, have a seat," he motioned toward his office chair. Somehow the living room couch seemed a little too informal, though he didn't think much of it every time Rue decided to sit there when she was reviewing paper files.

"Nah, I'll stand if you don't mind," Ortega stood akimbo, looking around the place. "Nice setup," he complimented.

"Thanks," Darwin answered, opting to lean on the back edge of the couch as if half standing and half sitting. "But I'm pretty sure you didn't come here to compliment my taste in furniture or my office design."

"You are correct, Mr. Fennec." Ortega paused to brush at his itchy chin. For the third day in a row, he'd forgotten to shave, and the stubble was starting to irritate him. "It's highly uncustomary for a police detective to meet with a person of interest. Truth be told," Ortega continued, "it can be the end of my career if anyone finds out, so if you're recording this, I will politely ask now that you stop."

"I will if you will," Darwin smiled, pausing first to remove the small wire he had attached to his arm before walking over to the footrest set in front of the couch and lifting the top open to reveal the recorder. He switched it off. "Oh, and—" he made his way over to his desk, where Ortega was now standing, "let's not forget this one, too." He pulled the small 'termite' Ortega had just planted there.

"Busted," Ortega laughed. "Anything else I should be worried about?"

"That's it," Darwin answered. "I may be many things, but a liar isn't one of them. Gentleman's agreement that whatever we discuss today stays between us?"

"Agreed," Ortega answered roughly. "It just so happens that I was about to phone you and take you up on your offer to exchange information when your call fortuitously came in. Would you like to start, or shall I?"

"You go ahead, Detective," Darwin encouraged. "Since these are your cases."

Ortega let out a long sigh before continuing. "There are just too many gaps between them, and I hate to admit it, but I'm stumped. When Clarissa was murdered, my first thought was that either you or Ms. Brennan was the killer, and you were covering up for one-another. You were one another's alibi, of sorts." He paused to gauge Darwin's reaction, but his face was neutral. "Then I thought Ms. Brennan might actually be setting you up," Ortega paused again as Darwin's left brow lifted in surprise, just a little. "Given the shoes and the knife angle."

"What shoes? And, what about the knife angle?" This was news to Darwin.

"I'll get to that in a minute, Mr. Fennec. What I'm trying to determine is what Ms. Brennan would have had to gain from killing Clarissa Sauer. And then when Ursula Gorky was murdered, the only person in that entire theater to claim to have seen Ms. Brennan push Clarissa Sauer over the ledge—"

"Allegedly," Darwin corrected.

"Allegedly," Ortega agreed. "Well, since the one person to witness the event, Ursula Gorky, ended up dead, too, and Ms.

Brennan was among the last person to see both women alive, stands to reason—"

"What does?" Darwin played ignorant.

"That Rue Brennan might be a murderer and you're covering up for her."

"I thought this was an exchange of information, Detective Ortega," Darwin challenged, turning a little red in the face. "This feels a little more like an inquiry."

Ortega paused to choose his next words very carefully. "I'm sorry, Mr. Fennec. But please listen to what I'm about to say, very carefully." He leaned in as if there were other people in on the conversation. "Based on the evidence at the scene, the shoes the murderer wore were at least two sizes too big for them and they likely stood on a chair to commit the crime. It's looking more and more that your lady friend Ms. Brennan might have murdered Clarissa Sauer and was trying to set you up. You could be protecting someone who has it in for you."

"Well, that's just not possible, Detective Ortega," Darwin answered simply.

"Why's that?"

"Well, for one thing, when I returned from the men's room, Rue...er, Ms. Brennan, was trying to prevent Clarissa Sauer from falling off the balcony. How the hell would she have had time to stab Ms. Sauer, and then get changed back into an evening dress in time to 'push' her over the ledge?"

"I'm aware of the logistics," Ortega agreed, then crinkled his forehead. "Though you neglected to mention that you were returning from the bathroom in your original statement." He waited for Darwin to explain, but he remained silent.

"Never mind," Ortega continued. "Originally, I thought you did the stabbing, but I'm still convinced someone was trying to make it look as if it were you. Maybe Ms. Brennan didn't know the perpetrator and was just trying to make the most of a situation that presented itself. Or maybe they were in it together. I don't know." Darwin's expression appeared to Ortega as a tortured man caught up in his own thoughts. He eyed Darwin from head to toe as if sizing him up. "What else aren't you telling me?"

Darwin thought long and hard before answering, a lump gathering in his throat. "From what I could see, it appeared as if when Ms. Brennan tried to assist Ms. Sauer, she reached out to grab the woman, but only succeeded in grabbing the knife."

"Did you witness Clarissa Sauer getting stabbed?" Ortega asked candidly.

"No," Darwin answered, "I did not."

"See anyone leaving Box 11?"

"No."

"And how is it that the knife was free of fingerprints, Mr. Fennec?"

"Gentleman's agreement?" Darwin reminded him.

"Gentleman's agreement."

"I wiped them off to protect Ms. Brennan because I knew how it would look."

"And Ursula Gorky's statement?" Ortega seemed unaffected by the confession.

"She was correct that Rue Brennan was, technically, the only one in the booth when Clarissa Sauer fell over the balcony, except that I arrived just at that moment. It makes sense that I wouldn't have been visible to her in Ms. Sauer's last moments. She would have been distracted by her friend's death and wouldn't have seen me."

"Let's overlook the fact that you tampered with evidence for the moment, Mr. Fennec. What makes you so certain that Rue Brennan is not a murderer?"

"What could she possibly have to gain from killing two women who she didn't know personally?"

"As you said, because her boyfriend got Clarissa pregnant.

Thanks for the tip, by the way. We confronted him and he confessed that he was the father. Surprised he didn't mention it to either of you."

"Must have slipped his mind," Darwin answered, considerably irritated. "But Rue wasn't aware of this. I'm certain of it. And Ursula?"

"Well," Ortega scratched his head. "Other than being a friend of Clarissa's, the only motive that makes sense is that your lady friend didn't like having her as an eyewitness to the crime."

"Or," Darwin couched his words carefully, after all, Gretchen Ellis was a client, "perhaps someone in the Ellis family wanted Clarissa and Ursula out of the way since we know Astor had a wandering eye. Ursula was Clarissa's best friend and knew too much."

"As did Spencer—the wandering eye bit," Ortega added. "Two peas in a pod. No wonder they used to be best friends before the tech feud. And which family member might this be?"

Darwin was silent. "I really shouldn't—"

"Gretchen Ellis?" Ortega guessed.

"But I suppose if you figured it out on your own. Well, that would be all right then." Darwin confessed, rolling his eyes.

"Paying for the women's silence would make more sense than murder, don't you think? Affairs in that family aren't exactly uncommon," Ortega reasoned.

"Unless there was more that we've yet to discover," Darwin added.

"Well, there's more to the crime scene, that's for sure," Ortega added.

"More?"

"Yeah. It seems Penelope, er, Dr. Washburn, my forensic scientist, confirmed that the same shoe prints were found at the scene of the second murder at the art school, along with dirt and ash presumably tracked in from outside. And I'm sure you already know about the manchineel poisoning?"

"From leaks to the papers, yes," Darwin confirmed.

"So, there were the same footprints at each location, but in the first murder, it was as if the killer were trying not to cause fatal harm Clarissa or her baby; but in the second location, they were dead set on offing Ursula."

"Interesting choice of words," Darwin commented. "But first things first. You would think that if jealousy were a motive, it would also be less pre-meditated and more spur-of-the-moment. And, as you said, it was as if the killer really wasn't trying to kill Clarissa...perhaps just threaten her? But I agree that Rue seems to be the lynch pin here. How do we know she wasn't the target all along, and maybe the killer messed up...twice?"

"Why? Because I happen to know that Ursula Gorky wasn't supposed to be modeling that day. A lady named Emma Post was. Pretty sure Ursula was the target though, and not Emma."

"Emma Post?" Darwin was surprised.

"You know the name?" Ortega questioned.

"Yes, supposedly she sent a letter to Gretchen Ellis claiming to be pregnant with Astor's baby."

"Another one?" Ortega scratched his head.

"But one of my colleagues traced the email as having come from the local library. But Gretchen also had a blackmail letter that was handwritten, allegedly from Clarissa."

"Think Emma was trying to piggy-back off of Clarissa's blackmail attempt?" Ortega asked.

"No, because she told Rue point blank that she wasn't pregnant."

"She said as much when we interviewed her," Ortega confirmed. "So, who sent the email? And furthermore, who sent the other handwritten note to Clarissa and the letter to Gretchen and why? Because I'll be willing to bet, they weren't the names signed on those letters. In fact, I suspect they were written by the same person. But who?"

"No idea."

"Can I get a copy of that email, along with a copy of the hand-written letter?"

"Certainly." Darwin set his coffee cup on his desk.

"Speaking of which," Ortega continued, "I was hoping you had a sample of Rue's writing, perhaps? Since you work together. Just to rule her out if she is, as you believe, innocent."

Darwin thought a moment. He reached into Rue's desk, pulling out one of her notepads. He settled on a page that had nothing more than her grocery list on it. He then retrieved a flip phone from his desk, snapped what appeared to be a photo of it, and emailed it to himself.

"What did you just do there?" Detective Ortega was surprised. "Is that a camera or a phone? Did you just take a photo on that little thing?"

"It's a prototype of both," Darwin explained. "Not on the market yet, but it's a flip phone that takes photos that people can text to one another."

"Text?" Ortega may have been upper in years, but he liked to pride himself on remaining current on technology trends.

"Uh, yeah," Darwin explained. "A message that you type, or take a photo of, and send without needing to hand-write a physical note or take a picture of it with a professional camera and have it printed at a studio. It's all digital."

"Fascinating," Ortega admitted. "How can I get one? It would help a lot with my investigations."

"As I said, it's not on the market yet." Darwin saw Ortega's face looking somewhat crestfallen. "But perhaps I can see about getting you one in advance of public release after this case is over."

"I'd appreciate that, Mr. Fennec."

Darwin already had copies of Emma's email and Clarissa's note photographed and uploaded to his server. Now, it was just a matter of printing the samples up.

He walked over to his computer and waited as the energy-savor mode switched off and the computer whirred back to life. He dialed into his email account and the two listened to the annoying whir of the server connecting. Moments later, he retrieved the email with the photo of Rue's writing and clicked for it to send the image to a printer located on Darwin's desk. He then clicked to print the other samples he had already uploaded.

Ortega was impressed. "My computer at the precinct takes three times as long to log in."

"DSL line," Darwin explained. This meant nothing to Ortega.

Instead, Ortega smiled. "If it turned out that Ms. Brennan is innocent...well, that would make you very happy, wouldn't it Mr. Fennec?"

"Well, of course, it would, Detective Ortega. She's my assistant and—"

"Nah, that ain't it," Ortega's grin grew wider. "I'm not the most observant of fellows where emotions are concerned. And yet, I can see that your face lights up every time I mention her name. Just how is it that she came to work for you, Mr. Fennec?"

"Her former boyfriend, Spencer Hargrove, recommended her to me."

"Really? Does she have cybersecurity and investigative skills?" Ortega was interested.

"She's learning," Darwin answered.

Ortega paused, staring out the window at the city below. Darwin recognized that deep state of inner brainstorming as one tried to connect the dots and politely remained silent for an unbearably long time. Eventually, Detective Ortega spoke, "I never did find out how you came to be at the theater with Ms.

Brennan that night. Frankly, you seem to be too upstanding a guy to take another man's woman out, particularly one who works for you."

Darwin cleared his throat. "Actually, I was asked on a date by one of Ms. Brennan's friends."

"Really?" Ortega's eyes shot up. "And why is this the first time I'm hearing of this?"

"Because I didn't think it was relevant."

Ortega's face turned beet red. "Not really your place to decide what is or is not relevant to my investigation now, is it?"

"Please, Detective. This was before I had gotten to know you. But now that you bring it up, there is something odd about the whole thing."

"Tell me," Ortega ordered.

"Midge Pasternak, Ms. Brennan's friend, cancelled on me at the last minute and sent Ms. Brennan in her place. I think it was an innocent game of matchmaker."

"But Rue Brennan already had a…match."

"Maybe Ms. Pasternak didn't know that. Or maybe she didn't care," Darwin reasoned. "The odd thing is, Ms. Pasternak appears to now be dating Jaks Liebling."

"The instructor at the Artist Atelier who was there when Ursula was murdered," Detective Ortega confirmed.

"The same. I don't know that it's a coincidence. Perhaps it's worth questioning Mr. Liebling again and doing a bit more digging?"

"Indeed," Ortega nodded his head in agreement before looking down at his watch. "I'll tell you what, Mr. Fennec. I need to get back to the precinct before it seems odd that I'm not there. I'm going to overlook the fact that you lied to me and tampered with evidence. I'm further going to overlook the fact that you had within your possession potential evidence that you kept from the police. Only because I need your help and I believe you and Ms.

Brennan may be innocent after all. But you need to be straight with me from now on, or I can't help you. Understand?"

"Perfectly," Darwin acknowledged.

"I know you sent Ms. Brennan and another guy to sneak into Astor Ellis's office. I'm going to pretend I don't know that, provided you keep me posted about what you find."

Darwin began to protest.

"I know, I know!" Ortega answered. "Client confidentiality and all, but we're talking about the murder of two women. I will do my best not to soil your precious reputation. But in the future, you should choose your clients more carefully, Mr. Fennec."

"What do you mean, Detective Ortega?"

"Since you've been so helpful today, I'm going to offer you a little tip."

"Yes?" Darwin leaned in, eagerly.

"I advise you to spend some time looking up the names listed on SpencerTech's patents and copyrights. Or should I say, one name in particular?"

"What name?"

Ortega lifted his scarf from the back of the office chair before leaving. "You just do your homework, is all I'm saying." Ortega touched his two fingers to his forehead as if to tip an invisible hat. With that, he made his way down the hall. He opted for the staircase instead of the elevator, since Nancy had been complaining that he'd put on a couple of pounds and needed to exercise more. He reasoned that going down seven flights would at least be easier than walking up them.

Once out in the street, Ortega pulled out a tiny tape recorder, no larger than a slim TV remote and clicked play. The micro cassette inside whirred and the conversation with he and Darwin could be heard. He smiled to himself. He may not have Darwin Fennec's fancy phone-camera combo or a DSL line (whatever the hell that was), but he made do with what he had available to him.

He tucked the recorder back in his pocket and headed back toward the precinct.

"I think it's safe to come out now," Darwin called into the bedroom where Rue had been holed up during Ortega's visit.

She opened the door. Behind her, he could spot the recorder and headphones Rue had set up on the end table next to his bed. She stared at him, momentarily.

"What?" he asked.

"Rue Brennan," she repeated her own name.

"What are you doing?"

"Just trying to see if your eyes really light up every time you hear my name," she teased.

"Well, now you're just being mean," Darwin complained, turning his back on her. "Did you get all that?"

"I did," she answered. "Are you sure it was wise to confess to wiping off the knife though?"

"I had to confess something big or else he wouldn't have trusted me," Darwin reasoned.

"Well, let's just hope all of this doesn't come back to bite us in the ass." Rue sat at her computer. "Alright, I need some help getting the audio from your meeting uploaded to Ortega's file. Give me a hand?"

"Sure," Darwin answered. "You drive." He went into the bedroom to grab the recorder, before pulling up a chair next to her and placing the recorder on the table. Rue logged into the new file they created for Detective Ortega, linking relevant information to the Ellis and Hargrove files. "And for the record," Darwin paused, "they do."

"Do what?" Rue was busy typing. "What are you talking about?"

"My eyes light up every time you enter a room and every time someone mentions your name. You just never notice."

Rue felt her face get flushed, her fingers held over the keyboard, trembling slightly. "Well, Mr. Fennec." She hit the wrong keys, cursed under her breath, hit delete, and tried again. "It's a shame because I don't like stalkers and hate men who lie to me."

"Hate?" Darwin was surprised. Rue's eyes remained glued to the computer screen. He smiled and put one hand on his hips. "Dislike, to intense dislike, to hate? Frankly, when you say you hate me, I can't help but think that maybe you really like me an awful lot."

"That's cuz you're delusional." Rue finished typing. "There, it's set up. How do I get the audio from this," she pointed to the cassette tape, "to here?" She pointed to the online file.

"Might be easier if I demonstrate." He took a moment to hook up a cable to the side of the recorder and then to the back of the computer tower. "This is not publicly used technology yet...eat your heart out, Spencer Hargrove."

Rue found this interesting. In all the time that Spencer bragged about his tech savvy, he never actually expounded on any of it—never bothered to teach her anything.

"May I drive?" Darwin asked.

Rue backed up while he took the mouse and dragged and dropped a file that had miraculously shown up on the desktop like a ghost. She saw a twirly image, as if the computer was thinking about it. "Wanna try for yourself? We can delete the duplicate later."

"Sure," she answered.

Darwin unplugged the cable from the computer and recorder and closed out all files. "Okay, from start to finish. You try."

Rue admitted that she had to fiddle a bit to find the right input on the side of the computer, along with the one to the recorder. "What happens if I accidentally choose the wrong port?"

"You'll blow up the entire computer?"

"Really?" Rue was horrified.

"No," he laughed. "But you might bust the cable connector or damage the port. So, let's try not to do that."

Rue went through the motions and within minutes, she had successfully transferred the audio files and managed to encrypt them to prevent a security breach.

"Thank you, Mr. Fennec." She smiled proudly. "I still hate you, but I'm grateful for the training.

"Hmmm," Darwin stood, making his way to the kitchen to grab a salad for lunch. He rifled through the refrigerator, calling into the living room. "Frankly, if you ever claim to detest me, then I'll start to suspect that you're actually falling in love with me."

"Not gonna happen, Mr. Fennec," Rue protested, putting her computer in sleep mode. "I stand by my sentiment."

# Chapter 32
# Jaks Liebling

Thursday Morning at Jaks Liebling's House

When Jaks Liebling failed to show up at the precinct after Detective Ortega's polite request for a follow-up interview, he and Officer Ernest decided to make a special trip to Liebling's house in Newark to pay him a visit.

They sat in the cul-de-sac of his New Jersey neighborhood for a good fifteen minutes before a black-striped, red Dodge Viper drove slowly down the street, pulling into Jaks' place of residence. They watched as his garage door opened and he parked his car inside. It was only when they had confirmed he was there, that they drove their police vehicle into the drive, blocking the garage.

They made their way up a paved path to the front door and rang the bell.

Moments later, Jaks threw the door open vigorously and

gushed, "Did you miss me already?" His smile quickly dropped, however, when he saw Ortega and Officer Ernest standing there.

"Golly, we sure did, Mr. Liebling," Detective Ortega mocked in a childlike voice. "Especially since you neglected to show up for questioning yesterday, despite our request."

"Did I?" Jaks feigned ignorance. "I'm sorry, I didn't receive any such message. Please, come in," he stepped aside, allowing them to enter.

Once inside, he shut the door and escorted them to his living room. It was clear from his decor that Jaks Liebling thought very highly of his own work. The sofa, chairs, console table with built-in wine rack, and even the carpet were a stark white. By contrast, every painting on the wall was black and red, or bright orange. The one exception was a rather large self-portrait which seemed to capture his macabre smile. In short, all of the paintings were ones of his creation.

"Please, have a seat," he offered. Officer Ernest removed his hat and sat on the plush couch.

"I prefer to stand," Ortega answered, eyeing Ernest, who immediately popped back up.

Jaks positioned himself in front of a long white window seat, shielding his face from the sun as he peered outside.

"You were hoping for someone else?" Ortega asked.

"Well," he turned and smiled. "If you must know, I just dropped my girlfriend off at the train station. Hence, why I must have missed your call."

"Midge Pasternak?" Ortega confirmed.

"How did you—" Jaks began, while frowning, before catching himself. "Yes, that's right."

"I see," Officer Ernest chimed in. "You were entertaining."

"Yes," Jaks' eyes widened mischievously. "You could say that."

"If you dropped her off, then who are you expecting to show up here?"

Jaks let out a sigh. "She's a feisty one, that girl," he confessed, "I half-expected Midge to catch a cab near the station and turn right back around and come back to me."

"Why not just call you and ask you to pick her up?" Officer Ernest was confused.

Jaks let out a sigh. "Not well-versed in the art of romantic gestures, are you, son?"

Ortega cleared his throat. "We have a few questions for you, if you don't mind, about Ursula Gorky's murder."

"Certainly, detective," Jaks answered. "Whatever you need."

"Did you know Ursula Gorky or Emma Post?"

"I know they were models at the school. I've worked with them both on many occasions, if that's what you mean."

"And yet you seem oddly unaffected by Ursula's death."

"That doesn't make me a murderer, detective, if that's what you're implying." Jaks sat in a lounge chair by the window, trying not to make it obvious that he was still keeping watch, obsessively sneaking a glance out the window every few moments. "Besides, I read in the papers that they caught the killer. So, why are you here?"

"Not implying anything, Mr. Liebling," Ortega answered. "Just trying to tie up loose ends. Can't just assume the guy we've got in jail was working alone. Not even sure how he slipped onto campus unnoticed. Officer Ernie, if you would be so kind—"

"Of course," Ernest stood, pulling out his notepad and pen. "According to statements, at least three students noted that the lighting on the model stand was off, and they were surprised you didn't adjust it. We're curious as to what they might be talking about?"

Jaks burst out laughing. "Seriously? That's your evidence? The lighting? Was anyone ever killed by *bad* lighting?"

"Someone would have been more likely to notice a poisoned woman on the stand a bit sooner had the light been on her face, don't you think?" Ernest was somber.

Jaks stopped laughing. "I see. Forgive my impertinence, officer. The truth is, I was hoping one of the students would point that out before we began the session."

"So, it was a test, of sorts?" Ortega confirmed.

"Exactly," Jaks nodded. "A test. But since no one did, I thought it might be a fun experiment to see what the students would do with the existing setup." After a long pause, Jaks asked, "Is there anything else?"

"Actually, yes, just a couple more questions." Ernest referred to his notes. "Were you aware of the victim having any particular habits?"

"Habits, officer? You mean like, addictions?"

"Exactly," Officer Ernest nodded. "Like drinking or smoking."

"Can't say that I was. I didn't know any of those girls outside of class. To me, they were just subjects."

"So, you don't know why there would have been a half-empty bottle of wine or cigarette ash in her dressing area?" Ortega asked.

"I'm sorry, I do not. A model's changing station is private. No idea what might have been in there."

"It's so interesting to me," Ortega motioned for Officer Ernest to follow him to the front door.

"What is?" Jaks asked as he followed them.

"Well, I'm not known for being particularly..." Ortega struggled to find the right words, shifting his shoulders from side-to-side.

"Compassionate? Empathetic? Emotionally available?" Officer Ernest offered, helpfully.

Ortega pointed toward Ernie. "Exactly, Ernie," he answered.

"Emotionally available. But I can't help but notice that you seem awfully hung up on your lady friend returning, but not the slightest concerned over...what did you call them...your subjects?"

"Once again," Jaks ticked his head slightly as if a bug had landed on his nose. "That doesn't make me a killer."

"True," Ernest answered. "But it does kinda make you sound like a jerk."

Ortega fought back a laugh but quickly recovered. "Officer Ernie, your manners."

"Sorry, Detective Ortega," Ernest lowered his eyes.

"Thank you for your time, Mr. Liebling," Ortega said.

Officer Ernest and Detective Ortega were outside when Jaks went to shut the door behind them. Ortega caught the door mid-swing. Jaks looked up, surprised. "Just one more thing, Mr. Liebling."

"What is it?" Jaks tried in vain to cover up his annoyance, his calm exterior now being replaced with some other emotion bubbling under the surface.

"What size shoes do you wear?"

# Chapter 33
# Golf Game

Friday Afternoon in Florida

"What's the temperature in New York?" Byron asked as he set up his golf ball on the tee and took a few practice swings.

"Last I checked, it was 38 degrees and cloudy," Gretchen answered, climbing out of the golf cart. This time, she actually wore something other than beige. Today, she was sporting a pleated white golf skirt and matching polo top. On her head was a bleached white visor to protect her face from the sun.

"Maybe we should consider staying in Florida for a few more days?" Astor suggested, taking a swig of water from a bottle he pulled from a cooler attached to the back of the cart. He pinched his thumb and forefinger to his chest, tugging his golf shirt back and forth as if trying to air it out. He was sweating more than the Florida heat warranted that day.

"Not possible, I'm afraid," Portia chimed in as she selected her club for the next shot.

Everyone fell silent as Byron swung. After the ball went sailing, they continued the conversation.

"You were saying, my darling?" Astor's syrupy voice dripped.

Portia hid her distaste. He was a fine enough catch to marry, but his romantic overtures, she thought, were irritating. Perhaps, over time, she could teach him how to sound more genuine, at least when dealing with the public.

"Apparently," Portia continued. "We have a meeting with Darwin Fennec on Sunday."

"You mean that flat foot that has been poking his nose around B. A. Ellis industries?" Byron asked.

"The same," Gretchen finished, stepping in front of Portia in a way that suggested that she'd just been upstaged. Portia retreated, opting instead to reach into the cooler and pull out a single-serve chardonnay bottle and a plastic stemmed wine glass. She poured herself a drink while Gretchen explained.

"And he's not a flat foot. He's a cyber something-or-other investigator. Seems he's asked us if we'd be willing to meet along with Spencer Hargrove for a discussion."

"Discussion?" Astor was aghast. "Why would we want to meet with that traitor?"

Gretchen held up her hands. "Don't ask me, but I think we should take the meeting." She winked at her husband Byron, who winked back before giving room for Portia to take her turn.

They waited as she placed her wine glass on the roof of the golf cart and then moved to set up her shot, club in hand. Portia drew her arms back and rotated her torso as she took her swing.

"Maybe he wants to negotiate a settlement," Astor blurted out as Portia dug her iron into the grass, pulling up bits of soil with it.

"Mulligan!" she yelled, glaring at Astor. He looked back at

her, baffled by her reaction. She quickly softened her face and added sweetly, "Astor, honey, you know I love you. But please shut up while I retake my shot."

Astor played along, putting his thumb and finger to the side of his lips and sliding to the right as if to zip them up.

Everyone was silent as she took her do-over shot. They proceeded to the next hole.

"Did they ever find out what happened to that theater gal and the model they questioned us about?" Byron asked.

"Did you not hear?" Astor was surprised. "Tommy Marcuzzo confessed to both."

"Little Tommy," Byron furrowed his brow. "Well, that can't be. He was always such a nice kid." This seemed to bother Byron so much so, that his reaction annoyed his son.

"Either way, it gets the detective and those reporters out of our hair," Astor said.

"Agreed," Byron nodded. "Still seems out of character for Tommy." He shook his head, muttering for the second time, "Such a nice boy..."

# Chapter 34
# Infidelity

Sunday Morning at the Ellis Estate

"Sure you're ready for this?" Darwin asked as he escorted Rue to the front door of a rather large mansion.

"Yes," Rue smiled, appreciatively. "Thank you for this," she whispered, leaning in, "but I still hate you."

"Noted," Darwin answered, ringing the bell.

Everyone arrived at the Ellis estate almost on schedule, like something from a Whodunit Thin Man or Hercule Poirot Mystery. Rue always thought of those movies as silly and unrealistic. *I mean, really,* she thought. *In what world would a bunch of suspects actually sit around a table just waiting to be accused?*

And yet, here they were.

When Rue and Darwin were ushered into the main library, Gretchen, Byron and Astor Ellis were already seated on a large red, wrap-around couch surrounding a low-lying table with nothing on it, but an oversized vase filled with fake gardenias.

Portia LaMonte was also present, sitting at the edge of a large, dijon-colored high-backed chair next to the couch. Her legs were crossed at the ankles and while Astor leaned his body towards her from his end of the couch, she was purposefully positioned so that she threw a cold shoulder in his direction. It was obvious that she had no intention of giving him the attention he wanted.

Darwin and Rue were offered chairs across from the table, two leather-backed ones that were surprisingly stiff and uncomfortable. Perhaps Gretchen had planned it that way.

The one person still missing? Spencer Hargrove.

When he finally arrived, he looked both perplexed and nervous as his eyes darted around the room between Gretchen, Rue, and then everyone else. "May I ask what this is about?" Spencer furrowed his brow, instinctively leaning over to give Rue a kiss on the cheek before she recoiled, instead directing him to the couch, where Astor reluctantly moved away from his position closest to his fiancé in order for Spencer to have a seat. It was that or have Spencer sit next to his father, Byron Ellis, and he feared that might lead to fisticuffs. Spencer sat on the edge of the couch, resting his hands on his knees, leaning forward awkwardly, making the couch appear about two sizes too small for his tall frame.

Finally, Gretchen nodded to Darwin who stood uncomfortably and cleared his throat. Despite everything, Rue felt sorry for Darwin. He may have been dishonest with her, she reasoned, but as far as deceitfulness went, he was the least deceptive of the bunch. It's sad that in her mind, this was a high compliment.

"I suppose you're all wondering why I've asked you here today," Darwin began (straight out of a whodunit).

"You think?" Spencer held his body tight as if trying not to make any physical contact with the Ellises to the right and left of him as if whatever they had was contagious. Spencer eyed Rue, questioningly. She offered him the briefest of smirks that let him know, in no uncertain terms that one, they were over, and two, this was payback...sort of.

"Spencer," Darwin addressed Rue's now ex-boyfriend. "You hired me because you believed the Ellis family was stealing secrets from you and planning to pass off SpencerTech inventions as their own before yours had a chance to make it to market."

"What's this about?" Spencer stood, angrily. "That was confidential. What kind of an investigator are you, anyway?"

"A tired one," Darwin replied calmly.

"Sit down, Mr. Hargrove," Gretchen ordered.

Spencer sat.

"But you were wrong," Darwin acknowledged. "They weren't stealing anything." He eyed Portia LaMonte, who merely shrugged her shoulders. "There was no way that an heiress was going to marry into this family without some guarantees of continued success and influence, so it was she—a devoted patron of the arts—who thought to send Clarissa Sauer to strategically intercept you, Spencer, on one of your nightly coffee trips to the cafe just across the street from your office."

Spencer's eyes lit up in surprise. He turned his gaze to Portia, who merely averted her gaze.

"You see, Spencer," Darwin explained. "They didn't need to steal secrets to take a product to market before you did. You gave it to them."

"See here!" Spencer protested.

"Shut up, Spencer," Gretchen ordered. Spencer fell silent. To Portia, she said, "I underestimated you, Ms. LaMonte." Gretchen eyed her future daughter-in-law approvingly. "It seems you're going to fit in with this family after all."

Portia turned the corner of her mouth up in a slight smile and the two women shared the oddest familial moment that Rue had ever witnessed.

"Ahem," Darwin cleared his throat in order to regain their

attention. "It wasn't Astor Ellis who got Clarissa Sauer pregnant," Darwin paused for emphasis, "it was you, Spencer."

Rue bit her lip and fought the quivering feeling in her stomach. Darwin had prepped her for this. She knew what was coming, but it still hurt.

Spencer looked first at Rue, shaking his head, then systematically at everyone around the room. There was no denying it. It was true and with today's modern science, very easy to prove. An autopsy could still match the DNA from Clarissa's unborn baby to him. Refusing a paternity test would only further reinforce his guilt.

"But—" was all he could think to say.

"Save it, Spencer," Rue chastised. "You already confessed as much to the police."

"The police? But how…" he continued, helplessly.

Darwin cleared his throat. "May I continue?" The group gave a mournful nod, wishing the family had stayed in Florida after all. "Clarissa fed all of your ideas, the ones you bragged about all those late nights while Rue was waiting for you, to Astor—who, in turn, shared it with his father."

"I could sue you," was all Spencer had to say. "What happened to client confidentiality?"

"I'll get to that," Darwin brushed him aside. "Let's move on, shall we? But Clarissa was a smart woman. You, a young man with a start-up, didn't have nearly as much money and influence as you pretended to have, so she did what she thought she had to…she went to Gretchen Ellis, demanding money to keep the pregnancy—which she claimed was Astor's fault—a secret. But Gretchen knew that this was impossible, given that Astor is sterile."

"Hey, now!" Astor chimed in, standing. For the briefest of moments, his pants stuck to the couch, and then peeled away as he rose. Sweat began to pour off his brow. Portia looked up, surprised. This was news to her. "It's not true," he protested.

"Yes, it is, and sit down," Gretchen ordered.

"Mr. Fennec," Portia finally interjected. "Is there a reason why you feel the need to drag the Ellis family name through the mud and my name in the process?"

"I'm getting to that, Ms. LaMonte," Darwin answered. He paused to take a deep breath, resting a hand on the back of Rue's chair. Without thinking, she touched it, looking up at him supportively—a look that did not go unnoticed by Spencer.

"Clarissa Sauer was murdered before she could collect on her bet, but not before she told her plan to her best friend, Ursula Gorky, who in turn mentioned it to another art model, Emma Post. Several weeks ago, I would have hypothesized that Emma worked independently, trying to ride Clarissa's coattails to success by sending an extortion letter to Mrs. Ellis."

"Vermin," was all Gretchen had to say.

"Financial desperation does funny things to a person," Darwin offered.

Gretchen was offended. "What? Am I supposed to feel sorry for someone because they had the misfortune of being born poor? Or that they didn't have the where-with-all to drag themselves out of squalor as some of us have?" Everyone turned to look at Gretchen, who suddenly felt very conspicuous. She pulled the edges of her cardigan sweater together as if trying to hide behind it.

"The point is," Darwin continued, "Emma Post was not pregnant and most likely did not send the email."

"Then who did?" Gretchen asked.

"We still don't know," Darwin answered.

It was only then that they noticed that Spencer had turned an odd shade of pale. His face giving off a sallow, sickly hue. He seemed, for once, almost remorseful. "I heard on the news that

Tommy Marcuzzo confessed to Clarissa and Ursula's murders. Is that true?"

"I don't think it is," Darwin answered honestly. "I think Tommy was just a scapegoat for someone else." He glanced around the room.

"Are you implying that it was one of us who killed her?" Byron Ellis asked, taking a sip of Scotch that had just been delivered to him by the housekeeper. Everyone started for a moment, having forgotten that he was actually there.

"I am not," Darwin answered simply. "I'm just filling everyone in on the pieces of the puzzle that I know about."

"Why the sudden unveiling, Mr. Fennec?" Gretchen Ellis asked, amused. "What happened to your code of ethics?"

"More of a 'who'," Darwin glanced at Rue whose cheeks turned a little pink. Spencer eyed Rue and Darwin. It was then that he realized that when he hired Darwin to also keep tabs on his girlfriend, that he might be handing over the heart of the one woman who he could have actually counted on to support him. His heart sank a little at the realization. "And sadly," he continued, "I ceased to be ethical the moment I took on Mr. Hargrove as a client...and you, Mrs. Ellis."

Spencer was surprised. This seemed to be happening a lot lately. "What is he talking about, Gretchen?"

*Gretchen?* Both Astor and Portia were visibly surprised. *Since when did Spencer Hargrove address their mother and future mother-in-law as...Gretchen?* Somehow, it seemed perfectly acceptable for her, a considerably older women, to refer to Spencer by his first name, but not the other way around.

Suddenly, Byron Ellis began laughing uncontrollably, so much so that a deep, phlegmy cough erupted from his lungs.

"May I ask what you find so amusing?" Spencer demanded.

Gretchen began laughing as well, standing and walking over to her husband, ruffling what was left of his thinning hair and giving him a peck on the side of his temple. She shook her head as she and Byron exchanged knowing glances.

"Spencer, my boy," Byron Ellis choked, "you made stealing your ideas so much easier when you began sleeping with my wife!"

"What?" Astor and Portia sat up. Spencer eyed Gretchen questioningly before remembering Rue and shooting her an apologetic look. She met his gaze with eyes like daggers.

"Oh, don't look so surprised, Spencer," Gretchen chuckled. "You didn't honestly think I was going to leave my husband for you, did you? You certainly are a young and supple thing, but I can assure you that young and hungry men with big dreams are a dime a dozen in this town." Spencer looked hurt. He opened his mouth to speak, but then closed it again.

"Come now, Spencer," Byron Ellis tried to soften the blow. "I know you had no intention of running off with my wife. You were just using her to get intel on me. It was just business. I get that."

"But, I..." Spencer protested, "liked you," he said to Gretchen, a look of betrayal on his face.

"Oh," Gretchen pouted her lips and leaned over to grab Spencer's face in her hands. "I know you did, you sweet boy." She planted a faint kiss on his lips. "I could just eat you up."

Spencer pulled away, looking to Rue as if for support. Rue, who he had cheated on with not one, but two women...that she knew about. He tried to explain. "I never meant to hurt you. In fact, I hired Darwin to protect you from all this."

"Protect me?" Rue was incredulous. "Did you think we'd end up a happy little couple after you'd introduced SpencerTech's new software to the world? We'd ride off into the sunset as the tech world's newest power couple?"

"Well, kinda," he admitted. "After you'd given up modeling and taken on a respectable job—which I lined up for you, thank you very much."

"So Darwin could babysit me!" Rue yelled. Spencer looked at Darwin, betrayed. Rue caught his gaze. "I figured it out for myself," she explained. "When it comes to investigative work and cyber forensics, Mr. Fennec is a very good teacher."

Darwin smiled in spite of the circumstance. From his best recollection, that was the only time Rue had actually something nice to say about him.

"That doesn't change the fact that you failed to keep my business a secret, client privileges and all," Spencer, of all people, spat angrily at Darwin at the betrayal. "I will sue you for damages and make sure you never work in the investigative industry again."

"I'm still working out the bit about you sleeping with my mother!" Astor's face crumpled as if he ate something sour. He sniffed a few times, as if he'd suddenly come down with postnasal drip.

"Not to mention the fact that you and Spencer were both sleeping with Clarissa Sauer," Portia added, helpfully.

"That's not the point," Spencer sulked. "I trusted him!"

Rue sucked in her breath. She knew what was coming.

"That's all right," Darwin answered. "I'll see to it that you and Ms. Ellis are refunded for everything I charged you...to include the money you gave me to keep Rue in my employ." Spencer's mouth dropped. Every time he thought everything he'd done had been exposed, there was one more nail in the proverbial coffin. Darwin put a hand on Rue's shoulder. She merely smiled. Spencer looked back and forth between the two of them.

"Wait a minute," he darted a finger back and forth. "You two aren't..."

"No, Spencer," Rue finished. "We are not sleeping together, nor are we a couple. Believe it or not, some men and women can work together without sex becoming an issue."

Darwin coughed a little and removed his hand from her shoulder. Instead, he began pacing. "As I was saying," he continued, "I'm refunding all of your money. No use making a good income if you can't go to sleep at night with a clear conscience."

"Oh, don't play all victim with me," Spencer's voice dripped venom. He had a lot of indignation for being a chronic philanderer.

"Shut up, Spencer," Gretchen interjected. She said it so often that Rue thought to have it made into a t-shirt. To Darwin, she answered, "You'll do nothing of the kind. Byron and I will pay your fee in full, so will Spencer."

"What fee?" Astor sat up, rubbing his head. He was very confused.

Gretchen and Byron shared a smile. "My crafty wife," Byron beamed, giving a playful pinch on the bottom, "knew you couldn't keep it in your pants, son," he offered, indelicately. Astor shrank into the couch. "She wanted to make sure there were no other lingering skeletons before you and Portia tied the knot. Had to make sure you were B. A. Ellis Industries material."

Astor eyed Portia, pleadingly.

She took his hand, affectionately. "Don't worry, Astor," she reassured. "I don't give a shit what you do on your free time as long as the press doesn't find out about it. Your mother and I had a long talk about it yesterday and worked everything out." She kissed his hand briefly and forced a smile, as if kissing him were the very last thing she wanted to do at that moment.

He smiled back, weakly. "But what does my mother—"

"You did us a huge service, Mr. Fennec," Gretchen praised, interrupting her son.

This time, Darwin was caught off guard. After all, he was ready to return all the money and expenses he incurred over the past few months for their cases, just to walk away with peace of mind. He fully expected to leave the meeting far poorer than going into it.

"How so?" Darwin asked.

"You've made it easier for Spencer and me to talk, businessman to businessman!" Byron stood, answering for his wife. He walked over to Spencer who shrank a little as if expecting an attack. Instead, Byron grabbed him by the back of the shoulders and shook him with pride. "Spencer, quit fighting the inevitable. You've got a great invention there...several, really. Why make me take it back from you when we can work together? Particularly, since I owned it from its inception? On your own, you'll only garner a small percentage of what we can accomplish with my backing. Together," he made a fist, "we can move mountains!"

"Just a moment...how did you own it first, exactly?" Spencer asked, indignantly.

"Spencer, my boy," Byron asked. "Don't be coy. Where did you do your college internship all those years ago?"

Spencer's face turned gray. "Ellis Media Group," he finally answered.

"And what technology clause did you sign in your work agreement?" Spencer shrank into the couch. "I can tell from the look on your face that you remember. Anything you created while working for any of my companies is the intellectual property of B. A. Ellis Industries."

"But these are my ideas," Spencer whined. "I spent endless nights working for minimum wage, developing plans, only for you to sue me for them later. When all you needed to do was offer me proper compensation and credit!"

Byron's face grew sour. Spencer was not nearly as appreciative as he thought he should be, particularly given that he had been sleeping with his wife and all. And he, from his perspective, tried to run off with his intellectual property, too. "I don't think you realize the length of the olive branch I'm offering you, my boy." He gripped Spencer's shoulder tightly in one hand, pinching it like a vice.

Spencer winced. "So, am I to understand that you're offering to back my inventions and share in the profits?"

"Exactly! It'll be under B.A. Ellis Industries, of course, but what does that matter if it makes you one of the wealthiest men in the country?"

"Perhaps Father would consider starting an offshoot 'doing business as' company?" Astor offered. "The headline would read, 'B. A. Ellis Industries Merges with Up-and-Coming SpencerTech for a Revolutionary New Invention.'"

"Ooh," Portia praised, flirtatiously. "I like it, honey."

"Thank you, darling," Astor leaned in and kissed her cheek. Portia didn't praise him often, and so he relished these moments. She didn't even seem to bristle at his lips, or that his breath was hot on the side of her face.

"Take the offer, Spencer," Gretchen advised. "I promise you, it's the best you're going to do in our world."

Spencer mulled on this for a moment. The thought did have merit.

Byron hemmed and hawed for a moment. "You know, perhaps I'd been selfish. Should have acknowledged you more. But let's resolve this silly dispute and find a way to work together!" He held his arm up like Rosie the Riveter in an overly dramatic display.

"Excuse me," Rue interjected. Everyone looked up, surprised. Aside from Spencer and Darwin, everyone else seemed to have forgotten that she was there. "There's just one small matter we still need to resolve."

"And what's that, my dear?" Gretchen pursed her lips, eyeing Rue distastefully.

"The software that you all are talking about is copyrighted under my name." She paused as everyone let that sink in. "And so are all the patented inventions."

Spencer sucked in his breath and rubbed his forehead. Beads

of sweat began to form, almost immediately. Without thinking about it, Darwin rested a supportive hand on Rue's shoulder once again as he stood behind her as if he was her personal security guard. To Spencer, she added, "C'mon Spencer. Did you really expect me to believe that you were having Darwin look after me so that we could actually be together when all this was said and done? Don't—" she cautioned as he opened his mouth to protest, "lie to me."

He closed his mouth.

"You wanted to keep an eye on me because I was your work-around," Rue continued. "You knew that Byron would lay claims to your inventions because you thought of everything while still working for Ellis Media Group. Rather than avoid a legal tangle, it was easier to put the copyright and related patents, under my name."

"How did you...but I changed them!" Spencer suddenly protested.

"And how did you do that?" Rue asked quietly.

"Not another word, Spencer!" Gretchen warned. "Not until we speak with our lawyers."

But Spencer was fit to be tied. He stood, pointing an angry finger at Darwin. "You did this!"

Darwin held his hands in the air. "I did nothing of the sort. I didn't even know about any of this. It was Ms. Brennan who figured it out."

Spencer's eyes fell to Rue. "You?" He was visibly shocked.

"Turns out you were right, Spencer," Rue smiled. "Administrative assistant to a cyber forensics expert really was the career boost I needed." She leaned in and motioned for him to come closer. He bent over so she could whisper a secret in his ear.

"I changed them back..." she offered softly, adding before standing back up, "star stuff."

It was clear who was now running the show. Rue stood. "Mr. Fennec," she addressed Darwin.

"Yes, Ms. Brennan?"

"I think we should go now."

"I think you're right."

They stood to leave.

"You'll hear from our lawyers," Byron reiterated his wife's earlier sentiment. "You won't get away with any of this!" To Spencer, he spat out, "Stupid boy."

"Don't worry, Mr. Ellis," Rue answered. "I can assure you that I have no interest in being entangled in this mess any longer than necessary and I have no intention of raking you all through the coals, although you probably deserve it. Just see that Mr. Fennec and my fees and expenses are paid, along with a small inconvenience fee for putting me and my name in potential legal jeopardy, and we can make this all go away."

"Are you blackmailing us?" Gretchen asked, horrified. "What about your code of ethics?"

By then, they had reached the front door, which a servant opened for them.

"His code," Rue motioned to Darwin. "Not mine. And besides, this isn't blackmail. Legally, my name was added to everything. I own it...all of it."

"But you know it's not yours," Spencer protested.

"Do I?" Rue asked. To Gretchen, she countered, "This legal battle would present quite a black eye on your family name. All I'm asking for is a small fee in damages. Then, I'll see to it that everything goes back in Spencer's name and you all can duke it out from there."

"I suppose something can be arranged," Byron growled.

"Of course, this still doesn't solve the very obvious problem still looming over this family's head," Portia LaMonte piped up.

Astor looked at his fiancé, bewildered. "We still don't know who murdered Clarissa Sauer and Ursula Gorky, or why."

Both Astor and Spencer shared one last moment of sorrow... the small, human parts of them that actually felt bad that the two women were dead.

And then, the group merely looked at one another and shrugged before returning to business as usual and how Spencer's company would be absorbed into B. A. Ellis Industries.

Darwin and Rue exchanged glances and took their leave. Aside from the two of them, no one else really seemed to care.

"Detective Ortega, you need to see this," Officer Dennis descended on Ortega's office with a level of ambition the likes of which the detective had never seen.

"What is it, Officer Dennis?"

"I had a hunch about that email and the notes you asked me to trace." Officer Dennis was bobbing up and down as if he'd downed thirty cups of coffee. "Turns out, we were able to confirm the person who reserved the computer at the library to send that fake email to Gretchen Ellis, the one that supposedly came from Emma Post?"

"Really?" Ortega was impressed.

"Yes," Officer Dennis nodded, seemingly about out of breath. "But there's more. The handwriting on the note that was found on Clarissa Sauer, supposedly from Astor Ellis, was suspiciously similar to the handwritten name of the very same person...it was the signature on the library card that gave it away."

"Who's signature was it?" Ortega enquired.

"Detective," Penelope Washburn burst into the room. Ortega and Officer Dennis looked up, surprised.

"We think we got a lead on who left the bottle of wine in Ursula's changing room," she nodded to Officer Dennis.

"Same person?" Office Dennis asked.

"Same person," Penelope confirmed. "And as you would say, Detective. My spidey sense is telling me we've gotta get to their apartment complex now before they strike again."

# Chapter 35
# Wine

Sunday Afternoon at Rue's Apartment

Darwin dropped Rue off at her apartment complex after their meeting with the Ellis family.

"Sure you don't want me to come up?" he asked.

"I'm sure," Rue smiled, oddly touched that he was still so concerned about her safety. "Besides, there's no place to park around here. You'll be driving in circles for hours. Thanks, though. Just circle back in ten minutes. I should be ready by then."

Rue was still staying at Darwin's home but needed to stop back to check her mail and gather a few necessities. Honestly, while she felt bad about Darwin taking the fold-out couch, his place was far more comfortable then her own. She denied admitting that it had to do with the fact that he was there and not here.

"Just be careful," he cautioned. "We solved one mystery today, but there's still a murderer on the loose."

"I will. Besides, we just left the Ellis house. If it was one of them, they couldn't get here in time." Rue slammed the car door shut a little harder than was necessary. She just wasn't used to riding in cars that often. Subways, after all, didn't have doors that you could slam.

Darwin watched until she reached the front entrance of her building. A series of angry car horns blew behind him, indicating that he was holding up traffic. Reluctantly, he began driving.

Rue stopped at the post office boxes on the ground floor to retrieve her mail. Aside from a few random grocery store flyers and clothing catalogs, there wasn't much else. She tucked her mail under her arm, pausing to throw her backpack over her shoulder and trudge up the three flights of steps that led to her apartment. Once there, she fumbled in her bag for the key, finally retrieving it from the farthest corner at the bottom.

Inside, she absentmindedly dropped the mail and her backpack on the kitchen table. That was when she saw it...a bottle of wine, the same twist-top one Midge brought her for her birthday. Next to it, sat three long-stemmed wine glasses. They weren't there when she last left her apartment a week ago for the safety of Darwin's condo.

"Surprise!" Midge called, as Rue jumped and then spun around, all but walking into her friend who was now only a few inches from her face.

"Midge," Rue grabbed her heart. "You scared the shit out of me! How did you..." Then she glanced at the open window by the fire escape. "I keep that locked. Did you break into my apartment?"

"I had to! How else was I going to surprise you with exciting news!"

"What news?"

With that, Midge revealed the newspaper she'd been holding behind her back.

"SpencerTech was listed as the top up-and-coming startup, voted most likely to unseat the current high-tech mogul, Byron Ellis of B. A. Ellis Industries."

"Why would you be happy for Spencer. I thought you hated him." Rue was suspicious.

"Kinda do," Midge admitted. "But if he's your boyfriend and stands to make a shit ton of money, then I'm for it, just so he takes good care of my bestie." She slapped Rue on the arm. "In another coinkydink, the tabloids are all the buzz after someone leaked that Astor Ellis fathered two kids while engaged to Ms. LaMonte."

"But that can't be," Rue took the paper, perplexed.

Midge opened the bottle and poured two glasses of wine, leaving the third. She walked back over to Rue and handed her a glass which Rue accepted, absentmindedly.

"Why can't that be?" Midge eyed her curiously.

Midge didn't know about Astor's inability to have children, nor that she'd just had a conversation with the Ellis family, and that Portia LaMonte didn't seem to give a rat's ass about Astor's infidelity so long as it didn't affect the family business and he did a better job keeping it out of the press.

Like watching a video on fast-forward, scenes from the past month started flashing through Rue's mind, starting with the wine glass she was holding. She glanced at it, as the connections started forming. The wine bottle found in the changing area was from the same vineyard as the one now sitting on her kitchen table, a common brand that no one could track to one particular buyer. The scuff-marked chair at the theater from shoes that were obviously too big for the wearer. The strategic setup for Darwin to be there at the theater that night instead of Midge. The falsified letter from Emma Post, the ease at which the killer managed to get onto the Artist Atelier campus. The cigarette ashes...

Midge's eyes lit up, waiting patiently for her less-smart friend to make the connections.

"Have a sip of wine, Rue," Midge encouraged, smiling.

"I don't think I will, Midge," Rue set the glass down, calmly, the hairs on the back of her neck bristled.

"I'll drink mine first, if you like." Midge put her glass to her lips and took a sip. "See, no poison."

"Why, Midge?"

Midge let out a laugh. "Isn't it obvious?" She waited for Rue to figure it out, but she didn't. Finally, she continued, "I saw how disappointed you were when Spencer forgot your birthday and I had my suspicions that he wasn't entirely on the up and up—call it intuition. So, when I saw the chemistry between you and Mr. Darwin Fennec, I devised a plan to get the two of you together."

"Your plan was to murder two women?!"

"Of course not," Midge defended. "My plan was to create a traumatic scene that was emotionally charged enough to throw you two together. Given his detective work, I thought I was being poetic. It was a non-lethal stab wound."

"So, the note that told Clarissa Sauer to meet Astor Ellis was from you—only you directed her to our private booth instead of the Ellis's booth next door."

"Now you're catching on," Midge smiled, gulping down the rest of her glass.

"The usher who went on a smoke break? That was your doing, too?"

"Precisely. I had just enough time to take her place. I stood on the chair to make it look like a taller person had stabbed her. I just didn't have time to wipe off the chair, really didn't see Detective Ortega figuring that one out."

"And you pushed her through the curtain at me."

"Yeah, except Darwin shoulda been there, too. I didn't

account for him having a weak bladder. But once she fell over the balcony, he did the debonair thing of trying to cover for you."

"And Ursula Gorky? She was the one eyewitness that recognized both Darwin and I, and she was set to testify that we were not together when Clarissa fell to her death."

"Another unanticipated glitch," Midge went to pour herself another glass of wine. "Would you feel better if I drank from your glass next? I assure you, nothing here is poisoned."

"No, thank you, Midge." Rue knew she had to call the police and Darwin, but she had no idea how to do that with a murderer in her apartment. She eyed the door.

"Going somewhere?" Midge asked.

Rue tried diverting Midge's attention back to the conversation. "How did you get into the school? Did you apply as a model, or..." Rue's eyes fell to the third wine glass on the table, "did you have help?"

Suddenly, she felt the heat of someone standing directly behind her. She turned to face Jaks Liebling. He was leering at her. "You're right, Midge," he smiled, never taking his eyes off of Rue. "She's not very bright, but she eventually catches on."

"What purpose could the famous Jaks Liebling have for wanting Ursula Gorky dead?"

Jaks smiled. "For the art, of course."

"A little different for me," Midge explained. "I didn't like hearing how she publicly accused you of killing Clarissa Sauer. And given that she was the only eyewitness to the event, she had to go."

"You killed her...because of me?" Rue was horrified. Yet, Midge somehow took this as appreciation.

"It was easy since Ursula was an alcoholic," Midge explained, ironically sucking down a second glass of wine before pouring a glass for Jaks. "I left a half-opened bottle in the dressing room with a love note directed at Emma Post from her 'boyfriend.'

Really, I just made up a name as Emma's legs are closed tighter than Fort Knox, at least according to what I've heard. Anyways, Ursula assumed Emma left it behind and thought nothing of drinking her friend's gift before her set. Honestly, I thought she'd be a goner long before you arrived, but she must have held off until the final sitting...no pun intended." She and Jaks smiled at the joke. Jaks leaning in to plant a kiss on Midge's lips.

"All in the name of romance," Midge sighed. "You and Darwin were meant to be together."

"To romance," Jaks held his glass and clinked it with Midge's now-empty one. She went back for a final refill, but then decided against it.

"Look," Midge pointed to her feet. "I'm even wearing the shoes I did on both nights, a size nine when I'm only a six-and-a-half. Even had them on the morning after Merriam Hall, but you were too hung over to even notice," she laughed. "I'll leave the last glass for you, Rue." They paused for an eternity. Finally, Midge asked, eyeing Rue's horrified expression. "What's wrong?"

Jaks' eyes grew dark. "I told you she wouldn't understand."

"What?" Midge defended. "Of course, she understands. I did it for her." She searched Rue's face for confirmation.

"I don't think she does," Jaks moved closer to Midge. "I told you we should have cut our losses in Central Park and taken her out then."

"I'm not comfortable killing my best friend, Jaks," Midge held her hand up in protest. "Not after I went through such lengths to get her and Darwin together."

Suddenly, the cell phone from Rue's purse began ringing.

"Speak of the devil," Rue joked. "He's supposed to be picking me up in a few minutes for a...work event." Her breathing was labored. She had to remind herself to take long, steady breaths, but they were still coming out choppy.

"Then, by all means, take it," Midge motioned. "But don't,"

Midge held up a small .22 Beretta Tomcat and positioned it at Rue's forehead, "make me have to kill you," she finished. Jaks' face lit up in a creepy way as if watching his favorite porn video.

Rue fumbled through her purse, almost dropping the phone. She caught it on the last ring.

"Hello, Darwin," she forced a smile.

"I've circled the block a few times. Everything okay?" he asked.

"Yes, Darwin, I am almost ready. Just have to grab my business suit and I'll meet you out front," Rue continued, "Midge is here." Midge shuffled from side-to-side, pushing the gun against Rue's forehead as a warning. "She brought me wine to celebrate."

"Celebrate?" Darwin asked, carefully.

"Yes, it seems SpencerTech is getting rave reviews in the tech world." Rue forced as much enthusiasm as she could muster. "I can fill you in on it in a moment."

"That is wonderful," Darwin answered cautiously, speaking a little louder than necessary. "Good for him. Perhaps I can take the two of you out to dinner to celebrate."

"That sounds lovely, Darwin." The mark from the barrel of the gun was beginning to leave an imprint on her forehead. "Just finishing a celebratory glass of wine with Midge. Can you wait for me out front? I won't be but a moment more." She hung up the phone before he could answer.

"Well done," Midge lowered the gun. "Though, I was really hoping you were going to tell me you ditched that lowlife for Darwin Fennec. He's a much better catch if you ask me. Still, that's what best friends do, don't they?" She shook her head before peering closely into Rue's eyes. "Look out for each other?"

"My darling," Jaks chimed in. "How can we let her live now that she knows everything?"

"Relax, Jaks," Midge smiled. "I have a plan." To Rue she announced, "Give Jaks and me a 48-hour lead time to get out of town before you contact the cops. It's the least you can do as a show of gratitude for your closest friend. Deal? After all, I was doing all of this for you."

Rue knew she had to sell it. She also knew that Midge could smell bullshit a mile away. "Okay, Midge," she answered finally, cautiously moving toward the wine bottle and pouring a few ounces into the one untouched glass. "While I disapprove of what you've done, in a show of trust and friendship, I promise not to contact the police...not now, not ever." Rue took a sip of wine and waited expectantly...nothing.

Midge smiled. "I told you it was just wine!" But that settled it. If Rue was willing to trust the wine, then she was willing to trust that Rue would keep her word.

"Let's go, Jaks," Midge motioned toward the window.

"Wouldn't the hallway stairs be easier?"

Midge let out a sigh. "Call me sentimental, but since this is my last time climbing out of Rue's window, let's go this way. It's sort of...ceremonial."

Jaks wasn't happy with this solution, but Midge seemed to be his weakness. He wrapped an arm around her and kissed her neck hungrily. They climbed through the window and began their descent. It was only when they'd reached the second floor that Midge realized her mistake.

She looked up to see a team of police officers swarming Rue's fire escape above them. On the ground level, several sirens rang out as the police also covered the street.

Officer Dennis and Detective Ortega had burst into Rue's apartment moments earlier, just as Darwin arrived. Darwin ran over and wrapped his arms around her. "Are you okay? Are you hurt?"

Rue eyed the wine. "Out of an abundance of caution, I believe we should call an ambulance and take that bottle of wine on the off chance I've just been poisoned."

Hours later, Rue learned that while Midge had been taken into custody, Jaks Liebling got away.

"How is that possible?" she wanted to know, as the nurse wheeled her to the entrance of the hospital, "you had them surrounded."

Darwin put his hand out to help Rue to her feet.

"Apparently, Midge pulled her gun and started firing. She's lucky they didn't open fire on her. It just so happened that she tripped on the last rung of the fire escape ladder and landed face-first on the gravel which was enough to save her. They tackled her and took her in. Guess those shoes ended up being her undoing."

"And Jaks?"

Darwin shook his head. "Somehow, in the commotion, that weaselly little man managed to escape."

Rue signed the papers releasing her from the hospital. As it turned out, the wine was just wine and she hadn't, in fact, been poisoned. Guess Midge really did value their friendship, in her own twisted way. Fortunately, her lack of symptoms meant that she also avoided having her stomach pumped.

"Just one more question, Mr. Fennec," Rue asked as they made their way on foot toward his condo. "How did you know I was in trouble?"

"That was easy, Ms. Brennan," Darwin replied as the doorman opened the door for them at the entrance. "Despite multiple requests, I've never been able to get you go call me by my first name. When you called me 'Darwin' three times in a single phone call, I figured you must have been in trouble."

"Good catch, Mr. Fennec," she punched number seven on the elevator. Moments later, they were standing outside of Darwin's condo. Darwin typed in the key code to his home.

"But just so we're clear," she smiled. "I still hate you."

"Duly noted, Ms. Brennan." He followed after her as she made her way inside. "I'm perfectly comfortable on the fold-out couch and you're welcome to stay as long as you need to until Detective Ortega clears you to return to your apartment."

"That's very thoughtful of you, Mr. Fennec," Rue acknowledged. She set her purse on her workstation, instinctively. *Funny,* she thought. *Under normal circumstances, Midge and Spencer would have been the first people she would have turned to for a place to stay and for support when she needed it. Darwin Fennec would have been the absolute last.* Funny how life turns out.

# Chapter 36
# Incarceration

Wednesday Afternoon in a NYC Correctional Facility

Midge arrived wearing a hunter-green uniform, something that only she could pull off with her bright red hair and freckles. She was actually attractive in the most unattractive suit possible. In fact, had she instead been out on the streets of New York, onlookers might have described her as...adorable. An adorable murderer.

Her eyes lit up when she saw Rue.

"I knew my bestie wouldn't let me down," she beamed after picking up the phone and peering through the bullet-resistant glass that separated inmates from visitors.

Rue was less than enthusiastic as she held the phone to her ear, wondering if she should have used a disinfecting wipe on it first and if psychopathic behaviors were in any way contagious.

"How are you doing, Midge?" was about all that Rue could bring herself to say.

Midge's face dropped. "It's Mensa," she reminded her, "and, hey, I'm the one stuck in here. Why are you so glum?"

"It's because of *why*, Midge. You murdered two women."

"Allegedly," Midge corrected. Rue shot her a look. "Okay, fine. But you would have done the same thing for me."

"No, Midge!" Rue corrected. "No, I would *not* have."

"Really?" Midge tilted her head sideways. "But I was just trying to bring you and Darwin together."

"Well, we're not together," Rue answered. Though, something about this statement felt wrong to her, but she couldn't quite figure out why.

"After everything you've been through?" Midge was incredulous. "How the hell not?! I went through a lot of trouble causing that accounting glitch at Garnet Media so you'd lose your job and have to go work for Darwin."

"That was you?!" Rue stood, eyed the guard on high alert, and sat back down.

"Of course. Darwin's not the only security expert, remember? Why are you so hung up on that man-whore, Spencer, anyway?"

"Spencer and I broke up," Rue confessed, clenching her teeth. She didn't have the energy to ask how Midge knew about the infidelity. "You're missing the point, Midge," Rue explained. "While I appreciate that you were trying, in your weird sort of way, to help me out, murder is not an acceptable way to meet that goal. Do you not understand that?" Rue was on the verge of tears. Midge had been her best friend for over a year now. How did she not know about her homicidal tendencies? What did that say about her assessment of people? Hell, what did that say about *her*?

"Not really," Midge confessed. "Maybe if they were good people to begin with—" she reasoned.

"Who gets to be the judge of that?" Rue wanted to know.

"Obviously, me," Midge smirked. "Though, to be fair, I

hadn't intended on Clarissa dying. I was so careful about leaving her a non-lethal wound that wouldn't significantly harm her or the baby. But she freaked out and then you pulled out the knife when she went over the ledge. Mighta worked out differently if everyone had remained calm."

"Calm? Would you be calm if you were pregnant and someone stabbed you in the stomach?"

"Yes, I believe I would be," Midge was confident.

"And Ursula? You're going to tell me that she was an accident, too?"

"No," Midge smiled to herself. "When Jaks dreamed up 'The Art of Death,' I thought it was absolutely brilliant. He has a 152 IQ, you know, and is smarter than me."

Rue noticed the guard looking at her watch. They didn't have a whole lot of time to left to chat.

"But you killed her, in as horrific a way as possible."

"Oh, don't be so melodramatic," Midge waved her hands. "There are lots worse ways to die."

"Her mouth, esophagus and stomach burned as her throat swelled up and suffocated her to death," Rue reminded her former friend.

"I didn't say it was pleasant," Midge defended. "Just that I can think of worse ways."

"I'll bet you can," Rue sighed, standing up.

"Wait," Midge looked around frantically, as if buying time. "She was ruining everything," Midge explained. "She recognized you and Darwin, and her testimony could have blown the whole plan up. She had to go."

"You didn't need to murder her. I was innocent."

"Look, no one was supposed to die, but then Jaks convinced me that it's way more interesting when someone actually *does* die. We even planned it so that she was on a balcony, too. So poetic!" She smiled as if this explained everything. "It certainly spiced up our romantic life, if you know what I mean." Midge wriggled her eyes, suggestively.

Bile began to rise in Rue's throat. She didn't want to imagine how murdering someone could be construed as an aphrodisiac. She tried a different tack. "And you're not the least bit angry that Jaks Liebling betrayed you? You're taking the heat while he's run off to who knows where?"

Midge smiled to herself and let out a contented sigh. "You can't understand genius." She sat back in her chair, wrapped her arms around herself. "I'm sure he'll come back for me when he's ready."

"Just a couple other questions, Midge," Rue was curious.

"For you, I am an open book," she spread her hands wide to illustrate.

"Am I right in assuming that you sent all the letters? The one to Clarissa Sauer for her to meet Astor Ellis in Box 11, the one to Gretchen Ellis announcing the baby, and the follow-up email to Gretchen supposedly from Emma Post."

"Guilty, on *two* counts," Midge beamed with pride. "Pretty sure Clarissa sent that handwritten note herself. She was a bit of a schemer." She paused a moment. "I know Darwin did a fair bit to train you...not that I was spying or nothin'." Rue was unconvinced. "But I like to think I helped a little. Nice investigative work, overall. For your first attempt, I'll give you a B+." Midge sat backed and hugged herself, beaming about a job well done.

"Managed to even make it look like that email actually came from the library. Great misdirection on my part, if I say so myself...except for the part where they tracked it to my library card. That was unfortunate," Midge mused.

"Take care of yourself, Midge." Rue started to hang up the phone.

"Wait," Midge stood, all but yelling into the phone. The

guard looked up, concerned. "You will come back and visit me again, won't you, Rue?"

"I'm not sure, Midge," Rue confessed.

"It's Mensa!" Midge stamped her foot. "You have to come back." Midge thought a moment. "Did you have the wine I brought you tested?"

"Of course, I did."

"And what did you discover?"

"That it was just wine."

"Exactly," Midge was proud of herself. "I'd never harm my best friend. Friends look out for each other, don't they Rue?" Midge searched Rue's face for some spark of connection but found none.

Rue sucked in her breath. "Goodbye, Midge." She hung up the phone, turning her back on her former best friend, her heart sinking.

"You have to come back!" Midge screamed angrily into the phone and pounded the window before the guard stopped her. "You're my best friend!"

But Rue couldn't hear her. She exited the jail for the first, and hopefully, last time.

# Chapter 37
# "I Know What You're Thinking"

Sunday Morning at Rue's Apartment - One Week After
Everything

A knock at the window drew Rue away from the last chapter of *The Alchemist*. She was at the part where the boy realized that the treasure he was looking for was right where he started and in front of him the entire time. "Well, he was pretty short-sighted," Rue had murmured to herself before looking up to see Darwin crouched outside her window. She was startled for a moment, as in a moment of déjà vu, she had expected Midge.

Rue went over to the window, struggling to lift the heavy glass up just high enough where her voice could clearly be heard, leaving about a three-inch gap between the windowsill and the glass. "What are you doing here, Mr. Fennec?" she demanded. "More specifically, what are you doing crouched outside my bedroom window? It's creepy."

Darwin folded himself up as much as possible in order to get his face low enough to talk through the open air so that she could hear him above the traffic outside. "I know," he acknowledged. "Sorry about that, but I had to tie up loose ends with the remaining evidence in Midge's apartment. It was easier to climb down the escape than knock on your door, given that she had pretty much taken over the fourth floor with multiple computers, servers, filing cabinets and all manner of electronic equipment. No disrespect, but maybe I hired the wrong Gal Friday."

"I knew she did something with IT, but really, the entire fourth floor?"

"It would seem so. By the way, we found records upstairs of Jaks Liebling wiring money to Tommy Marcuzzo's bank account. Another piece of the puzzle solved...Er, so, can I come in?"

"Huh," Rue pondered the news. "Uh, yeah...Not sure a peeping Tom outside my bedroom window is any better than Midge's intrusions, though."

"Perhaps not. But have you ever thought of blinds?"

"These are perfectly good window covers. Know what? Never mind." Rue lifted the window the remainder of the way. Even still, Darwin had to crumple his tall frame like a contortionist to fit through it. Graciously, Rue put out her hands as Darwin gripped her forearms to climb the rest of the way inside, his pure white polo shirt getting tinged with dust as it brushed the window frame. Once inside, Rue directed him. "C'mon into the kitchen. I don't need Darwin Fennec, world's greatest cyber-investigator, snooping through my underwear drawer."

He dusted off his shirt and jeans as much as possible, closed the window and followed her. About four steps later and they were in the kitchen. Darwin peered around the room with interest. It was only the second time that he'd been here.

"Yeah, I know what you're thinking," Rue commented. "It's not at all like your digs, but it's all I can afford at the moment.

And yes, I realize that at my age, I should have accomplished more with my life. You don't need to tell me."

Darwin leaned against the wall separating the bedroom from the kitchen, crossing arms and legs as he looked at Rue with interest.

"What is it?" Rue tugged at her crocheted cardigan, wrapping one side over the other, and hugging herself, nervously.

Darwin tilted his head, giving her one of those devilish smiles that Rue was, obviously, immune to. "It has come to my attention," he answered quietly, "that you rarely, if ever, know what I'm thinking, even when I think I've been pretty forthright about it."

"Really? Because right now, I suspect you must be thinking I'm pretty stupid, letting Spencer use me like that." Rue wrinkled her brow, leaning back against the adjacent wall, just to the left of the refrigerator. Rue fought the urge to actually put her forehead against the side of it to cool her face, which was feeling warmer by the minute.

Darwin took a step toward her, sidestepping the kitchen table. "Quite the contrary," he offered quietly. "You're one of the smartest people I know, even more so than your psychopathic friend Midge who thinks she's wiser than the rest of the world."

"Why are you here, Mr. Fennec?" Rue sucked in her breath, nervously. Everything about him suddenly made her nervous and she didn't know why. It had only been a week since they last saw each other. It was when Midge was arrested. And yet, it seemed like an eternity. Her heart did this little buzzing thing. She took a deep breath.

"I wanted to apologize."

"For what?" Rue barely choked out the question. She felt her face getting flushed and her eyes beginning to water, ever so slightly. "The fact that you spied on me as if I were a common criminal, keeping detailed notes about my daily habits, my likes and dislikes. I didn't bother to read everything, I couldn't. I was too angry." Rue thought she had forgiven him for all that, but clearly it was still bothering her. And now, it just came pouring out, despite the fact that her heart was in her throat just at his being in the same room with her. "For all I know," she continued, "you followed every bit of my life like a stalker, down to what salad dressing I like, to my time of the month."

"I have no idea what type of dressing you like," Darwin recounted quickly. "And, if I'm being honest, you're cranky a lot of times, so it's really hard to tell when you're being hormonal."

"Screw you," Rue grumbled.

"See what I mean?" He grinned. Rue let out a snort, smiling in spite of the fact that she was still angry.

Darwin reached into the pocket of his jeans and pulled out a flash drive. "I should have just shown it to you from the get-go," he admitted, holding it up. "Here's everything I have on you."

"What the hell is that?"

"A flash drive," Darwin explained.

"My question remains." Rue wrinkled her nose.

"Okay," Darwin tried again. "It contains all the data I've collected on you. You can review it whenever. In the meantime, I've deleted and purged any records I have on you."

"Purged? That sounds..." Rue gagged a little at the thought of the incident after Merriam Hall, "permanent."

"It is," Darwin admitted. "So, if you decide to destroy this, then I no longer have any records about you."

Rue thought about this a moment, "So, you won't remember what kind of tea I like?"

"Earl Grey," Darwin answered, without hesitation.

"Or what flowers I prefer?"

"Bird of paradise, for starters. But you also seem to be drawn to blue delphiniums."

"Or my favorite color?" she challenged.

"When under stress, it's yellow, probably because it's such an optimistic color. But other times, it's more like a sea green."

"So, you pretty much remember everything," Rue noticed, quietly. There was that buzzing again. It seemed to start around her heart and then vibrate up around her neck and ears.

"Yes," Darwin admitted, whispering back. His eyes drifted closed for a moment. "Everything."

He let out a sigh as he walked over to the pub table in the corner and set the flash drive down. "Perhaps I should just leave this with you," he offered.

"Any questionable photos of me in my underwear or in the bathroom?"

"Please," Darwin held his hands up. "Nothing remotely like that. You already saw most of it."

"Okay, well, thank you for this, Mr. Fennec."

Darwin paused before asking, "Do you really dislike me as much as you pretend to?" He took a step toward her.

"You're changing the subject again, Mr. Fennec. Of course, I do." Rue scanned the room uncomfortably, as if looking for an escape. "Pretending? Really? Why would you think otherwise?" She touched the fingers of her left hand on the cool refrigerator while her right hand rested gently on the kitchen table as if she wasn't quite sure what to do with these extra limbs. Somehow, the coolness on her fingertips was relaxing, or at least enough of a distraction as to not leave her completely unnerved.

Darwin took another step closer, now just two feet away from Rue who appeared to have noticed this simple fact but said nothing.

"It's the little things, really," he spoke quietly, forcing her to almost lean in to hear him. "For example, you had no trouble confronting Spencer the other day at the Ellis estate and I'm pretty sure you're not terribly fond of him, and yet..."

"And yet, what?" Rue whispered, sucking in her breath.

"And yet, here I am, a man you intensely dislike, hate even, standing in your kitchen. You haven't told me to get lost, and..." he tilted his head in an attempt to lock in on her averted eyes, "you can't even seem to look me straight in the eyes, why is that?"

"Clearly, it's because I am offended by your very presence," Rue blurted out. She didn't mean it. She didn't even know why she'd said it. And yet, she couldn't stop it. Something in her heart did something weird again. She'd have to remember to talk to a cardiologist about that.

"I see," Darwin took another step. "You sure have a funny way of showing it. The truth is, I can't help but think that maybe you really like me an awful lot." He paused, directly in front of Rue, resting his fist and forearm against the wall above her, leaning in for support.

"And what evidence do you have to support such claims, Mr. Fennec?" He was now close enough where she could feel a slight warmth kicking off of his body and an annoyingly pleasant smell of a lavender aftershave.

"In addition to the aforementioned lack of eye contact and a command to leave, I've noticed that you catch your breath every time I take a step closer to you, and..."

"And what?" Rue whispered.

"You don't have your arms crossed in a defensive position. One hand is on the refrigerator and the other on the table, with your torso exposed. And," he added, "the closer I get, the more you seem to lean ever so slightly toward me."

Slowly, Rue lifted her eyes to meet Darwin's. "I'll ask you one more time. Why are you here, Darwin?"

"I told you. To apologize and leave your file with you." It had not escaped him that she, once again, addressed him by his first name, usually that only happened in the midst of what she perceived as danger.

"Is that all?" she challenged.

"No," he finally answered, wrapping one hand around her waist and the other cupping the side of her face. "I wanted to see if there was the slightest chance that..." With that, Darwin leaned in to kiss her, except Rue seemed a bit preemptive, capturing his advance mid-kiss with one of her own. He opened his eyes with surprise as she finally rested her mouth on his. He kissed her back, fervently, following up with a light kiss on the side of her neck. She rolled her head back and looked at the ceiling.

"Darwin?"

"Yes, Rue."

"We should probably just flush that flash drive down the toilet. I don't need to see it."

"It's probably for the best."

"And Darwin?" Rue whined at the sudden realization. By then, Darwin was giving equal time to the other side of Rue's neck, as she leaned in, instinctively.

"Yes, Rue?"

"There's a good chance that I might detest you."

"Well, that's just fine," Darwin smiled, kissing Rue again.

# Epilogue

One Friday Morning in Prison

I t was the most unlikely of escapes. It happened at precisely 5:33 a.m. on a Friday in Brooklyn. The women at a nearby correctional facility were supposed to be heading to a worksite for an assignment, but only one of them would actually make it.

Instead of a random prison break, which would normally send dozens of inmates scrambling to see how far they could get, this one was strategically planned to include built-in safeguards to ensure that no one returned.

One team of female escapees found themselves on an old Volkswagen bus headed toward the Jersey Shore. It caught fire while passing through a toll lane, only to explode moments later, sending shards of debris and female remains everywhere.

Another group sailed past the turnstiles of the R subway line toward Penn Station, only to have several members of the group